TALK OF THE DEVIL

TALK OF
THE DEVIL

IAN FLEMING

IAN FLEMING PUBLICATIONS

Talk of the Devil was first published by
Queen Anne Press in 2008
This edition published by Ian Fleming Publications in 2025
Registered offices: 73–74 Berwick Street, London, W1F 8TE

www.ianfleming.com

001

Print ISBN: 978-1-915797-52-0
eBook ISBN: 978-1-915797-53-7

Typeset in 11.25/16.25pt Minion Pro by Six Red Marbles UK, Thetford, Norfolk

Printed and bound in the UK England using 100% renewable
electricity by CPI Group (UK) Ltd.

EU Authorised Representative: Easy Access System Europe,
Mustamäe tee 50, 10621 Tallinn, Estonia, gpsr.requests@easproject.com

CONTENTS

INTRODUCTION

Ian Fleming is a unique literary figure, inasmuch as he is known for a single creation that has by now escaped any of the normal orbits of writer-to-subject relations. Of course, all authors' reputations eventually become condensed into a phrase or even an adjective – we call something "Dickensian" or reference a "Graham Greene hero" – so the formula "Ian Fleming's James Bond" or even just "Ian Fleming's 007" is in its way an unsurprising epitaph. His name and reputation shine brightest these days in the title sequences of movies that have sometimes a close (*Casino Royale*) and sometimes a very remote (all the other recent Bond films) connection to his writing.

It's an odd fate for an avid and ambitious author – one perhaps shared only by Arthur Conan Doyle, another good writer whose destiny was to be singly sublimated into his own invention. (Singly, at least, if one overlooks the truth that the Jurassic Park series is essentially derived from Conan Doyle's Challenger series, and his *The Lost World*.) And so, the pleasure of this collection of miscellaneous prose that Fleming produced as a working journalist – chiefly over his prime creative years, the nineteen fifties – is to be reminded again of what a fine, evocative, sentence-by-sentence writer he was. Along with Conan Doyle and his close friend Raymond Chandler, Fleming is the best instance of the writer who, without literary pretension of any kind, wrote so well that his adventure stories, whatever their distorting thinness might be as mirrors of reality, keep their claim on our imaginations even when they lose their claim upon our surprise. He talked of himself as a writer of 'suspense', but his books still shine long after whatever suspense they contained is overwhelmed by time and familiarity. We know exactly how the stories will turn out and re-read them anyway. (In truth, we knew exactly how the stories would turn out when they were written – Bond is no anti-hero, he'll *always* prevail – and still we re-read them.)

For Fleming was, one realises turning these pages, above all an observational writer, one who could condense sights and sounds and tastes into a hand-ful of memorable descriptive sentences. It is the *atmospherics* of his Bond books that give credibility to their adventures, and his non-fiction, collected here, is pretty much a continuous distillation onto the page of those atmos-pheres, from London to Turkey to Jamaica and beyond. He makes moods not from self-consciously 'poetic' evocation but from an inventory of essential elements – from objects, things seen and sensed. He does it so well that every writer, in any genre, can still study his sentences and learn from them.

Fleming's life, now recounted several times in successive biographies, was one of significant adventure in the Second World War, and a vivid life as a journalist, chiefly for the *Sunday Times* of London afterwards. Whatever work the winds and weather of the world did on his character, he was born into a daunting family; there's a surprising glimpse of him in the art historian Ken-neth Clark's autobiography, who, talking about Fleming's pretty mother who lived near a Clark family retreat in a remote part of Scotland, admits that he was scared away by "her formidably well-equipped sons, who terrified me then as much as they did when I encountered them in later life."

It is always pleasing to have a pet theory about a writer confirmed by the writer, and not the least of the pleasures of this collection is that Fleming confirms a pet theory of my own. That is, that the writing and example of Peter Fleming, Ian's older brother, was, so to speak, the missing planet X that explains the deviations and odd orbit of Ian's own. Peter Fleming, as too few readers perhaps now know, was the author of several superior travel books in the nineteen thirties – *Brazilian Adventure* and *Travels in Tartary* are the most famous – memorable for their almost Wodehousian humour and their deliberate note of self-deprecating irony. (Afterwards, he went on to write the "Fourth Leader" for *The Times*, the light-hearted 'extra' editorial that dis-tinguished the paper then. Out of solidarity in anonymity – I used to do the same for *The New Yorker* in what was called "light Comment" – I for a long time collected "Fourth Leader" anthologies from the Peter Fleming era when one could find them in London bookstores. They rewarded the reader with high-hearted and charming sentences.)

This reader long imagined that the older brother's adventures – and his tone of light-hearted and unboastful derring-do – must have affected the younger brother's imagination of what a hero was, and indeed here is Ian, writing that,

"In this era of the anti-hero, when anyone on a pedestal is assaulted (how has Nelson survived?), unfashionably and obstinately I have my heroes. Being a second son, I dare say this all started from hero-worshipping my elder brother Peter." Photographs of the young Peter, for what it's worth, look *exactly* like Ian's description of James Bond – with his otherwise puzzling and oft-insisted-on resemblance to the American songwriter and sometime character actor Hoagy Carmichael – more so than photographs of the younger Ian.

What is significantly different between brothers is the tone. Peter's is self-consciously ironic and self-deprecating, in the manner of the Waugh and Wodehouse twenties; Ian's is from early on, taut and essentially earnest, in the thirties and forties manner of Greene and Orwell. In all of these pieces he takes his subjects lightly, but he takes them seriously. The development of Interpol, the art of Raymond Chandler, even the Seven Deadly Sins – for all that he treats these subjects with dapper elegance, and sometimes dapper disdain, they seem to *matter* to him, and he wants to make them matter to the reader. Where Peter, for all that he had a 'good war' in the forties, was still very much a child of the Noël Coward moment, Ian seems to have been made by the War in ways that gave him a tougher inner iron than his brother. His memoir here of the raid on Dieppe, a legendary foul-up that may – or more likely, may not – have taught essential things for the later amphibian invasion of the coast of France, is tight-lipped and taciturn, pained in a manner that suggests a more searing experience than its unemotional tone allows – or, rather, one that its unemotional tone implicitly enforces.

Ian is modern. Though one had a sense from the Bond books that Fleming had many attitudes about foreign peoples typical, unsurprisingly, of a man of his time rather than ours, it is still cheering and unexpected to see how resolutely cosmopolitan he was. He was a fan of the nascent Commonwealth and, here, as in his *Thrilling Cities*, published in his lifetime, he urged his British readers to "Go East, young man" – emigrating or at least living for a time in an emerging new world he saw as more healthily energetic than a sometimes-exhausted Europe. In his list of political desires, he makes paramount the "enthusiastic encouragement of emigration, but more particularly of a constant flow of peoples within the Commonwealth." He had the inevitable prejudices of a British man of the end of the Imperial era, but any charge of significant racism is one that these pages seem to acquit him of.

But above all we read his non-fiction for echoes of his fiction, and for clues as to its hardy excellence. Ian is very much a writer of the post-war boom that, for all the rationing and the stringency of the currency export conditions, still allowed 'luxury' goods and practices into Europe sufficiently to inform his prose. He always seems to be having a good time. Fleming is known, quite wrongly, as a 'placement' writer, someone who used proper nouns of products to give credibility to his work. But this is misleading. As he explains himself, deftly, it was his concentration on all of the specific objects of sight and sound and smell, that, for him, as for any real writer, gave his work its density and its credibility; the 'product placement' was purely accidental. He writes tellingly that:

". . . the real names of things come in useful. A Ronson lighter, a 41/2 litre Bentley with an Amherst-Villiers super-charger (please note the solid exactitude), the Ritz Hotel in London, the 21 Club in New York, the exact names of flora and fauna, even James Bond's sea island cotton shirts with short sleeves. All these small details are 'points de repère' to comfort and reassure the reader on his journey into fantastic adventure. I am interested in things and in their exact description. The technique crept into my first book, *Casino Royale*. I realised that the plot was fantastic, and I wondered how I could anchor it to the ground so that it wouldn't take off completely. I did so by piling on the verisimilitude of the background and of the incidental situations, and the combination seemed to work."

These straightforward words are not the words of a hack, à la Judith Krantz, trying to stuff the pages with chichi references; they are the words of a working writer, determined to lend credibility to fantasy – inventorying the things of this world in order to make credible a plausible alternative one that sits within it. Conan Doyle did the same, in his Victorian world, with his elaborately detailed train schedules and descriptions of bric-a-brac stuffed interiors and his general assertion of the *thingness* of Holmes and Watson's world. Each object credibly registered opens a path for fantasy to enter into.

Elsewhere in these pages, Fleming states with admirable succinctness that "I am excited by the poetry of things and places," adding that "it is surely more stimulating to the reader's senses if, instead of writing 'He made a hurried meal of the Plat du Jour – excellent cottage pie and vegetables, followed by home-made trifle' you write 'Being instinctively mistrustful of all Plats du

Jour, he ordered four fried eggs cooked on both sides, hot buttered toast and a large cup of black coffee.' . . . four fried eggs has the sound of a real man's meal, and, in our imagination, a large cup of black coffee sits well on our taste buds after the rich, buttery sound of the fried eggs and the hot buttered toast." He concludes the self-analysis with another memorable aphorism: "What I endeavour to aim at is a certain disciplined exoticism."

A disciplined exoticism! This is surely what every writer of thrillers of Fleming's kind aims at, and too rarely achieves – and not just writers of thrillers. When we take pleasure again in re-reading *On Her Majesty's Secret Service* or *Thunderball* it is less for the fantasy or 'action' sequences, well-rendered though they are, but for the way that Fleming's knowledge of 'things and places' gives his work, exactly as he wanted, its peculiar poetry. Fleming crisply offering all that he knows about the place and social history of the Boulevard Haussmann in Paris is what makes that locale work, however improbably, as the headquarters of SPECTRE, complete with secret meeting room and Blofeld's electric-executioner's chair.

W.H. Auden once wrote of the centrality of the 'mythopoeic' imagination to literature, meaning the ability of words to conjure up people or places, à la Tolkien, that seem to exist independent of their creators and of the tales their creators tell. He offers Sherlock Holmes as a prime instance – we can always imagine more mysteries for Holmes to solve and we do – and Bond surely takes his place alongside him. But the secret of the mythopoeic imagination, this book reminds us, is not imaginative extravagance but atmospheric specificity: we know Holmes by his fogs, and Bond by his island. Or rather, by the dramatic contrast of white and grey, placid, peaceful London, with its Chelsea squares, with the green and yellow tropics – exactly what he meant, perhaps, by 'disciplined exoticism.' Of all the places that Fleming evokes in these pages, none is evoked with such pleasure and specificity as his beloved Jamaica. Though one senses a certain disappointment on the author's part at being in such bondage as to never become quite as significant a literary artist as he thought he might be – his efforts at a more 'literary" Bond book, in the original *The Spy Who Loved Me* and *Quantum of Solace* never quite worked – that the Bond books allowed him to work and write on his island seems some recompense. His evocation of the island is quite as stirring, in its lulling way, as Hemingway's of Cuba: "Coral rocks and cliffs alternate 'South

Sea island' coves and bays and beaches. The sand varies too, from pure white to golden to brown to grey. The sea is blue and green and rarely calm and still. A coral reef runs round the island with very deep water beyond and over the reef hang frigate birds, white or black, with beautifully forked tails, and dark blue kingfishers. Clumsy pelicans and white or slate grey egrets fish at the river mouths." Lovely and loving sentences! That they formed the background for the most resonant of modern adventure stories is, one feels reading them, almost a lucky by-product of watching a writer at a writer's real work, which is, simply, watching.

Adam Gopnik
October 2024

TWO STORIES

A POOR MAN ESCAPES

*This is one of the earliest known stories by Ian Fleming. It is thought
that he wrote it in 1927 at the age of nineteen while under the tutelage
of Ernan Forbes-Dennis and Phyllis Bottome in Kitzbühel, Austria.
The manuscript resides in the Michael L. VanBlaricum Collection
of Ian Fleming and Bondiana in The Rare Book and Manuscript
Library at the University of Illinois Urbana-Champaign.*

It was Christmas day. Snow paved the streets of Vienna and tiled the roofs
of the houses with white. It wasn't a kind Christmas day, for every now and
then a sharp wind reached down into the slim streets and whipped the surface snow into a blizzard. There was little traffic and few people abroad. Those
who were out of doors hurried along with pinched blue and red faces clutching their fur collars up round their ears and sometimes breaking into sharp
little runs as the wind snapped round their legs. Heavy flakes of snow were
falling sparsely, muffling the air and the ground so that there was little to be
heard but the tread and scuffle of hurrying feet, and the occasional ssh-flop as
a heap of snow slid off a tall roof on to the pavement.

In the Himmel Strasse, a small cul-de-sac blocked by a thin crouching
church, even these soft noises were absent. Heaven Street was undoubtedly an optimistic name for such a disreputable and retiring little lane.
Even the snow, clinging to the roofs of the stooping little houses and
the 50 yards of cobbled way, could only accentuate the disgraces and
poverties of this little street. Even the church, the only excuse for such a
glowing title, had half crumbled into ruin as if ashamed of the part it had
played in causing such an error. The people who overcrowded the half-a-
dozen little houses were in most cases as disreputable as their quarters.
Thieves, tinkers, hawkers, street cleaners and the like, with their wives

and families, made this street their stronghold and formed a small but self-sufficient community.

Amongst the leading lights of this community was a certain Henrik Akst. Some said he was a Pole, others a Norwegian (what was he then?), but he had lived in Vienna 30 out of the 40 years of his life and was generally accepted as a Viennese. He was a news vendor; but on Christmas Day he had no papers to sell and instead he sat watching his wife die. The process was brief, but painful, and when he rose to cover the now tranquil face his own eyes, besides tears, held a wild drawn expression of pain, while his features already thin with hunger assumed a new gauntness.

Leaving the bed, he crossed in two strides to the window which he opened to the drifting snow flakes, and at once the small heat of the room was drained out into the street mercifully taking with it the heavy smell of disinfectants which hung round the bed.

Henrik tidied up the room methodically for the first time in his life. All his meagre belongings he stuffed into his pockets. A razor, a knife, two spoons, a fork, a photograph of his wife in a gilt frame, and other objects as worthless. He made a parcel of some plates and cups, and with this in one hand and an old pair of boots in the other he left the room shutting the door carefully, but without another look for the still figure on the bed. But in a minute he was back to take, with still averted eyes, the bottle of disinfectant from beside the bed, then the door closed finally.

Out in the street, however, he did so far forget himself as to look up at their window, as he always did when he went out, to see his wife waving and smiling at him, but he at once looked away again, and soon he had left the narrow cul-de-sac for the trampled whiteness of a larger street.

The pawnbrokers was open even on Christmas day. He attempted to be genial but with reserve for little of value but stolen goods could come from such a man as the news vendor.

'Selling presents already, eh, my man?' he said, rubbing his hands and eyeing with disfavour the poverty and dejection of his customer.

But Henrik merely greeted him with the customary 'God bless you', and piled his treasures on the wooden board which served for a counter.

At first the pawnbroker was indignant. 'When I'm a rag and bone man, then you can bring that sort of stuff to my shop,' he said, but soon, for he was a kind-hearted man in his way and it was Christmas, he offered two Austrian shillings for the lot. Henrik accepted at once and after blessing the pawnbroker and leaving the shop, he set out towards the distant spires of the cathedral in Stephansplatz and the centre of the town. He hadn't gone far before he felt the thud of something against his hip as he walked. He remembered at once, of course, the medicine. What a pity, he might have got an extra few groschen for the bottle – well, well, it would do for another time! But then he suddenly remembered – but there would be no other time, at least not for about six months, that would be about what he would get. He was about to throw it away – it was a dark red colour – what a lovely pink smudge it would make if he threw it hard into the snow and it broke. No, perhaps it might be some good – he stuffed it back into his pocket. A gust of wind licked round his legs and he broke into a weak, stumbling run, clutching his meagre coat about him with one hand and the two shillings in the other. Curse that bottle. It bumped against him as he ran, and it seemed to weigh a lot, but perhaps that was only because he was so weak, he had eaten nothing for two days. All his small earnings had gone to feed his dying wife. But now, the wind had flicked a little warmth into his body, he clutched the 2 shillings tighter and ran faster.

The Café Budapest was full. The breath of the people and the heat of the stoves and of the kitchen had turned to moisture on the window so that the lights shone out into the street like haloed golden stars. An old couple by one of the tall plate glass windows had rubbed away a little square of moisture, so that they could see the figures outside, and so that the less fortunate people outside could see and envy, and perhaps recognise them, and say afterwards to their friends, 'Do you know who we saw at the Budapest today, why it was the Kirnskys', and everybody would be envious and say, 'but I thought they were so poor, and they're so old now and never go out anywhere.' Frau Kirnsky grinned to herself, old people didn't die as easily as that and besides it was Christmas. She looked affectionately at the old man, who sat mumbling over a cup of coffee, nodding his disjointed old head in time to the music. Hullo, who was this, a musty black shape moved across the window, and bent down to the space which she had cleared. Good heavens, they couldn't allow that sort of a person into the Budapest. There, thank heavens he had gone. But next moment the inner door had opened quietly and Henrik was peering through a slit in the heavy curtain which covered the double doors and kept away the cold. All

5

the waiters seemed engrossed. He noticed an empty table over in a corner, and in a moment he had slipped in and across among the tables to the corner, had hidden his lower half under the tables and was industriously reading a paper held close across his chest. The waiter came up and saw only a pale gaunt little face with a mop of unkempt hair peering at him over the paper. Nothing very extraordinary about this. 'Coffee and double Vermouth,' said Henrik. The waiter moved away and the few people who had noticed his entrance with surprise decided he must be all right if the waiter accepted him. Only the Kirnskys had risen and were moving puzzlingly towards the door, looking with disgust at Henrik. But Henrik noticed nothing, but that he had arrived.

He beckoned to a man passing with a tray of cakes and selected three of the richest paying for them with his 2 shillings. 'Keep the change,' he said magnificently and his position was fairly established. Soon his coffee and vermouth arrived and he was stuffing and drinking away as hard as he could, still holding up the paper as if he was tremendously interested in something he had found in it. In reality he sensed nothing but a blank whiteness in front of him and a wonderful feeling of warmth and triumph. The heat of the room was thawing his body, which was tingling all over, and inside was a little nucleus of fire which was the vermouth, but above all his heart was warm with triumph and a splendid feeling of not caring what happened afterwards. He nodded and the paper dropped a few inches exposing a ragged scarf which concealed the fact that he had no shirt; but he was instantly awake again and pretending to read as hard as ever. But soon again his head was falling forward, the music came to him in waves, which alternated with waves of noise and talk and clatter of cups and spoons, like the rattle of the shingle when a wave has fallen and is sucked back down the shore like a boomerang to be thrown again and again.

Everything was rose coloured and gold. He was floating through an infinite sunset, across green hills towards a distant range of mountains. If only he could get there. He strove to reach them, when suddenly the sunset collapsed beneath him and he fell – thump – thump – thump. He gradually woke up. The waiter was shaking him and hitting him on the back to wake him. Luckily it was the cake waiter to whom he had given the tip.

'You know you shouldn't be here at all – and at any rate if you want to sleep go to a hotel – mind don't do it again or the manager will see and turn you out.' He moved away.

People were staring. Henrik was dazed and still half asleep, but he raised the paper again and held it close before his face. He nodded but pulled himself together – 'Now then Henrik – you don't want to be arrested yet do you – quite time enough when the bill comes and you haven't got any money to pay it with – Quite time, quite, quite – .' The paper fell to the floor and Henrik's chin sank on to his chest. Again he saw the distant line of ragged peaks – black against the last range of the sunset – again came the sudden desire to reach the black distant goal, and again as he seemed certain to reach it the dream gave way around him, and this time it was the manager who was knocking him on the shoulder.

'Here, clear out of this', said a voice from the distance, and the shaking became rougher. Henrik got up displaying all his rags to the scandalised manager and the disgusted onlookers, who had been longing for something to happen to the sleeper.

'But I've paid for my food,' said Henrik grasping at his brief luxury as he saw it escaping before him.

The manager didn't heed him. 'Wait there,' he said, and pushed Henrik back into his seat. He didn't want the indignity of having to lead Henrik out himself with the possibility of a vulgar brawl.

A tear crept from the corner of each of Henrik's eyes and crept down his cheeks. How lovely it had all been while it had lasted. He sank his head on his hands in despair, the sound of the manager calling to the policeman at the corner reached him – what could he do to keep this wonderful world of light and wealth. As if to mock him the music began again, a Viennese waltz drifted through the warm air into the coldness of his despair.

Suddenly he noticed that he was uncomfortable – he was half sitting on something hard which was sticking into him – Of course the medicine bottle. He took it out and looked at it – furtively under the table – and suddenly he noticed the label

Poison

For external use only

or according to the doctor's instructions

and the word 'Lysol' printed in red on a large slip of paper across it. Why, of course. He could have cried out in his happiness – here was his world given back to him – no more of the cold and the snow – no more poverty and squalor – instead the lovely dream, and what was it – oh yes, those mountains perhaps he might reach them one day too.

A vague moment of hesitation came to him, but he heard the policeman scraping the snow off his boots on the wire mat outside and stamping. Quickly he raised his newspaper and under cover of it the precious bottle. A terrible spasm clutched at his body – the bottle fell from his fingers and smashed on the floor – His whole frame stiffened and then relaxed – shuddering. His head fell forward on to his breast.

'There he is,' said the manager, entering with a burly policeman – 'There he is, asleep again – he has no money – arrest him – he can't pay his bill.'

But Henrik had paid and was rich for the first time in his life.

THE SHAMEFUL DREAM

*Ian Fleming was advised that the character of Lord Ower
in this story, written in about 1951, resembled too closely his
employer, Lord Kemsley, and it was never published. It appears
to be unfinished though it is not certain that this is the case.*

The fat leather cushions hissed their resentment at the contact with the shiny
seat of his trousers and hissed again as he leant back while the chauffeur
tucked mutation mink round his knees. The door of the Rolls closed with
a rich double click and with a sigh from the engine and a well-mannered
efflatus from the bulb horn the car nosed with battleship grace away from the
station approaches.

Caffery Bone, literary editor of *Our World*, eased himself forward and reached
for the cigarette case in his hip pocket and took out a cigarette – 'selected with
care an ivory tube' he reflected and for a moment pulled down Elinor Glyn,
Ouida and Amanda Ros from the boxroom and sniffed at their dust. Where
were the euphemisms of today? Perhaps only in America: 'Comfort Station',
'Powder Room', but then we talked of Public Conveniences and 'Loos'. Perhaps they had just been stripped from all languages down to the lingering
taboo words, down to sex and lavatory. Yes, there they were: petting, char-
lies, go somewhere, pansies, a veritable mine of them. 'The Last Shy Words'
would make a good title. But not for *Our World*. Good God no. He could
hear the telephone ringing already: 'Mr Bone?' Yes. 'Linklater speaking. The
Chief says would you slip up a moment.' He could feel the soft pile carpet
and see the drooping walrus moustache saying 'Sit down Mr Bone.' Then
the shiny leather of the single chair, known throughout the building as 'The
Hot Squat', then the redoubtable 'Icy Pause', then 'Mr Bone, my attention has
been drawn . . .'

Bone found that his body had tensed and that the ash had grown long on his cigarette as he stared wide-eyed at the television screen which was the chauffeur's back. He fiddled with the gadgets in the fat leather arm of his seat in search of an ash tray. Silently the glass driver's partition slid down and a voice issuing from the walnut panelling near his right ear said, 'Yes Sir?' Bone started and the ash fell on to the mink rug. 'Oh, er, nothing,' he said. He fiddled some more and the partition quietly closed, but in a moment there came a soft crackling of static and the Nutcracker Suite sounded down from the ceiling. Bloody box of tricks thought Bone as he ground out his cigarette on the sole of his shoe and pushed the stub down between the leather cushions. Different kettle of fish to the modest Sheerline saloon which carried Lord Ower to and from his offices in Fleet Street. Must be Lady Ower's car. Everyone said that she was the one who spent the money.

Bone stared moodily ahead at the rain and the dripping hedgerows and at the shaft of the headlights probing the wet tarmac of the secondary road which would bring him in due course to The Towers.

He still had not solved the problem of the invitation. It really was most disturbing. It could not possibly bode well – only ill. But how ill? That was the question which had occupied Bone's mind all Friday night and all Saturday and was still, at about seven o'clock on Saturday evening, involving him in anguished speculation.

He had the note in his pocket now. He had carefully brought it with him just in case there had been some ghastly mistake. In case it had been meant for someone else, or for another Bone or perhaps for someone called Tone or Cone or even Bole. Directly the butler said, 'I don't think his Lordship is expecting you, sir', Bone would nonchalantly pat his pockets. 'I wonder if I kept the invitation. Ah, yes, let me see, here we are.' Then, as the butler stammered his apologies, Bone would be firm. 'There's clearly been some confusion,' he would say smilingly. 'But I shall really be very glad to get back to London. Important supper party. If the car could perhaps take me back to the station. And please give my compliments to Lord Ower and show him the invitation. I'm sure it will all be cleared up on Monday. No. No. I'm afraid I must insist. Very kind, but I really must be getting back.'

But the chauffeur had definitely enquired 'Mr Bone?' at the station and had been quite sufficiently deferential and somehow the wording of the invitation typed by a secretary in that fat type used, so far as Bone was aware, only by Lord Ower and Sir Winston Churchill had been quite explicit.

> Lady Ower and I would be very glad if you would come down to The Towers tomorrow evening and spend the night. There is an excellent train from Waterloo arriving at Maidstone at 6.45 and there will be a car to meet you.
>
> O.

On the heels of the expensive white envelope brought down by one of the commissionaires on the fourth floor had come a telephone call from the social secretary, Miss Buckle. Yes, he would be delighted. No. A written acceptance would not be necessary. Bone had placed his elbows on his desk, had lowered his head carefully between his hands and while his mind raced he stared unblinking out of the office window into the November dusk.

Bone had been at Ower House for five years. Originally he had been taken on to buy serial rights in English and American fiction for the Big Five in the Ower chain, *Our Women* (four million), *Our Families* (over two million), *Our Beauty* (just started and already past the million mark) and *Our Bodies* the sturdy seed from which the whole crop had sprung. This once lively publication, progressively expurgated in step with its founder's advancing wealth and station, had withered from over four million to 750,000 in the three years that it had taken plain Amos to graduate through Sir Amos to Lord Ower of The Towers, Bearsted, Hants.

A year after Bone's arrival, *Our World* had been founded and Bone became its literary editor.

Our World was designed to bring power and social advancement to Lord Ower whose title and riches had made him increasingly sensitive to jokes about his periodicals. In the old days when he was peddling pornography from his little press off the Charing Cross Road he had gladly suffered ribald enquiries for copies of 'Our Old Man' and worse, far worse. In fact he found they helped him to get advertising when he did the rounds of the truss manufacturers, the restorers of falling hair and arches and 'vital forces' every week and he would laugh jovially at each ghastly new jape and even invent and retail others so that he would seem clubbable and one of the gang. But those bad days were shrouded in the mists of time and now the jokes were more painful and for the matter of that more spiteful, particularly in the House of Lords where his rare visits unleashed a barrage of bad puns and ribaldry which only the man with a skin of an armadillo, which fortunately Lord Ower possessed, could have borne.

Then there was Lady Ower to consider – Belle Ower, a fine lower-middle-class woman from Guernsey with something of the presence and splendour of a Mrs Hackenabusch and with social ambitions that could only be described as atomic. Her most kindly soubriquet was 'The Bellyful', but it was almost a tradition at Ower House that anyone who was sacked should write her an anonymous letter in which 'Our' was conjugated with every obscenity in the book.

All this made Lord Ower put all his periodicals into a subsidiary company and transfer their publication to Manchester where they continued to prosper greatly but relatively out of sight of Westminster and Mayfair. Ower House was cleared of its nose-picking inky-fingered scriveners, Wilton carpet was laid in the corridors and the highest salaries in Fleet Street, laced with generous expense allowances, soon filled it with one of the best second-class newspaper staffs.

For three months they worked in great secrecy, or so the proprietor imagined, on dummies until, just four years before Caffery Bone got his invitation to The Towers, *Our World* was born.

Lord Ower was a very shrewd man and he hit on just that gap in readership which no other publisher had perceived or had had the courage to tackle. The formula, the weekend newspaper on sale on Fridays, Saturdays and Sundays, had already been vindicated when the *Daily Mirror* group started *Reveille* and ran it up to over three million circulation in four years. But that was a 3d. paper for the working classes and Lord Ower was after power and prestige rather than profits from mass entertainment. He aimed where Northcliffe would have aimed, at the new educated classes catered for at the weekend by the *Sunday Times* and *Observer*, and by the *New Statesman* and *The Spectator*, and when he examined this field he discovered a significant, a very significant fact.

On weekdays, more educated people read adult newspapers than they did on Sundays. There was a gap, a fat gap to be filled for the asking. The *Telegraph* sold a million a day, *The Times* 250,000, the *Guardian* 150,000 – a total of 1,400,000 educated people. But the combined circulations of the *Sunday Times* and the *Observer* only came to a million and only about 100,000 read the *New Statesman* and *The Spectator*. Even forgetting the high class readership of the *News Chronicle* (1,500,000) and God knows what they read on Sundays, you still had a gift of 300,000 who appeared to dislike all the weekend reading. With *Our World*, aiming somewhere between the *Observer* and the *Sunday Express* and on sale for 6d. from Friday to Sunday, Lord Ower decided to round up that 300,000 like a sheep dog rounds up sheep and, he chuckled grimly, then start cutting into the quality Sundays as well.

And how right he had been, reflected Bone as he stared out of the window of his office just four years later. 400,000 in the bag, advertising rates up every six months or so, all the best writers stolen or bought from the Sundays and thanks to the Labour policy of the paper, a certain Viscountcy for Lord Ower when this government was out.

And Bone had risen with it until he was now the most sought after literary editor in London and certainly the best paid. Why, three thousand a year and five hundred expenses was almost as much as a cabinet minister and when one added on the sale of review copies, perhaps fifty a week, at several shillings a copy, and the innumerable free lunches with publishers and authors and reviewers, and occasional work for the BBC on The Critics' Circle and so forth it all added up to being just as well paid as a cabinet minister, if not better.

And yet, and yet. On that Friday evening Bone had fingered the stiff sheet of Basildon Bond and had read again the invitation which he already knew by heart. And yet how impermanent it all was, how unstable, how fraught with inevitable doom and the certainty of the sack. The mere fact of appointment to Lord Ower's staff was the first step down that steep place into the sea, not with the mad rush of a Gadarene pig, but with slow inching progress slipping down towards the rocks and foam through the samphire and the centaury, the campion and the thrift. For Lord Ower sacked everyone sooner or later, harshly if they belonged to no union or with a fat cheque if they did and were in a position to hit back. If one worked for Lord Ower one was expendable and one just spent oneself until one had gone over the cliff edge and disappeared beneath the waves with a fat splash. There was a moment's hush in the big building, as there is in prisons at the moment of an execution, and then the cleaners would come in and prepare your office, your oubliette for the next man.

And Bone was ripe for it. He knew he must be because for one thing, of all the senior men on *Our World*, of all the possible targets, he had been there the longest, and that alone made him vulnerable enough. But worse still, only that morning had there appeared, threateningly over the horizon, a cloud maybe no larger than a man's hand but in hue as devilishly black as the very pit. He had been discussing his pages with Waterhouse, the editor, when Waterhouse had suddenly looked up from the proof of a review by Angus Wilson and a short exchange of words had taken place which now, on reflection, seemed to Bone infinitely sinister.

'I should take out "anal-eroticism".'

'But, good heavens, why? We've had it in before.'

'Well, I just would, that's all.'

And with a smile of sympathy, which Bone now saw had been a smile of pity, he put his blue pencil through the words.

It was all so exactly like the way Bone had often tried to save a contributor from dismissal, by juggling with his copy, cutting out phrases or opinions which might provide pegs for an ultimatum from Lord Ower ('Mr. Bone, this man Madariaga must go. His last review caused great offence to the Spanish Ambassador') or even by inserting, at the cost of many friendships and much self-respect, slavish reference to Lord Ower or his interests. Bone grimly remembered his successful and ingenious rescue of Frith, his poetry reviewer, who had unfortunately been seen by Lord Ower wearing a black tie at a ball in aid of the National Theatre which had been attended by minor royalty ('Doesn't do the paper any good, Mr. Bone. Not quite our man, perhaps').

This had been on a Thursday evening with the paper just about to go to bed with a review by Frith of a new book on the life of Shelley which seemed to offer no loophole for any reference, laudatory or otherwise, to Lord Ower.

Bone, who liked Frith and knew that Frith's wife had just had a miscarriage, sat at his desk in despair, desperately rummaging his mind for any means, however hideously inappropriate, of linking Lord Ower's name with Shelley. Then he dashed down in triumph to the printing room and just caught the literary page on the stone.

Next morning a bewildered Frith read as the last sentence of his review:

'The author closes his fascinating study with a reference to the great poet's death at the early age of 33. Curiously enough this is just a year short of half the age of that great contemporary patron of literature, Lord Ower, thanks to whose wisdom and generosity so much space on this page is devoted to the consideration of poets and poetry.'

'I hear Mr. Frith's work well spoken of, Mr. Bone,' said Lord Ower some weeks later. 'What money's he getting?'

'Twenty-five, Lord Ower.'

'Don't let us be parsimonious, Mr. Bone. Good men are hard to find. Make it thirty.'

And now, thought Bone, Waterhouse knew something and was doing his best to protect his literary editor. But what did he know? Had it only been a hint from Lord Ower that the literary page was getting a little 'off-colour' (Lord Ower's euphemism for pornographic) or had there been a conversation rather like this: 'Er, Mr. Waterhouse, what is your impression of Mr. Bone's work?'

'It's very good, Lord Ower.'

'Doubtless, Mr. Waterhouse, but is it the best available to us?'

'Well, er . . .'

'It has been suggested to me, Mr. Waterhouse, that Mr. Bone is getting lazy in his choice of reviewers. Confidentially, er, quite between these four walls, you understand, it has come to my ears that Lord Simonstown was very disappointed not to be asked to review Sir Winston Churchill's last volume. Not the sort of man we want to offend, I'm sure you will agree.'

'Certainly not, Lord Ower.'

'He also seems to have been at pains to avoid commissioning work from Sir Ambrose Borrage, a name I would very much like to see in the paper. A very eminent public servant, I'm sure you will agree, Mr. Waterhouse.'

'Yes, Lord Ower.'

'Well, Mr. Waterhouse, perhaps we've had the best work out of Mr. Bone. I'd be glad to have your thoughts on the problem in due course. Let me have one or two names. We can't leave an important part of the paper in bad hands particularly with the Christmas book season so closely upon us. Thank you. That's all for now, Mr. Waterhouse.'

Had it been like that? Bone certainly felt guilty about Lord Simonstown.

He had known that the dreadful man was a close friend of the Chief's and that he had been furious when the Churchill book had been done, and done brilliantly, by Isaiah Berlin. And as for the unspeakable Borrage, that literary dung-beetle, that cringing hyena, he would sooner commission the children's book reviews from the Dusseldorf murderer than allot him an inch of space on the book page. But then, it didn't matter much what the excuse was. If Lord Ower got tired of your name in the paper or wanted to find room for some new protégé, any peg would do to hang the sack on.

And this invitation had certainly looked on Friday night, and still looked this evening, like the summons to the Last Supper, that dread meal to which senior men were always invited just before they were fired. And Bone had always admired the fiendish invention when its working had, early in his career at Ower House, been explained to him. It seemed such a brilliantly effective piece of inquisitorial machinery, so clean, so final and so devastatingly just and proper, like the moment of truth when the matador looks the bull in the eye and the path of the sword through the air is only a formality.

Take the case of John Dance, a former editor of *Our World*. Bone ghoulishly collected every detail he could of these Last Suppers and then polished them up into little case-histories for his private morgue. Dance drank too much, but he was an excellent editor and the only reason Lord Ower wanted to sack him was because Dance would not support the Labour Party right or wrong, and Lord Ower feared for his half-promised barony unless *Our World* followed exactly the political line of the *Daily Herald*. So Dance was invited to dinner and to stay the night at The Towers. Whisky was put in his bedroom and he naturally helped himself while he was dressing for dinner. A galaxy of fashionable and distinguished guests was assembled in the drawing room when he came downstairs, including, he noticed with alarm, two Labour cabinet ministers and a Bishop. He was offered a cocktail and drank it slowly and carefully but directly it was finished Lord Ower jovially pressed him to another. They went in to dinner and there was sherry with the soup. When he refused it, the butler seemed not to hear him, and before the next course, Lord Ower leant towards him.

'Rather special sherry, don't you think, Mr. Dance?'

'Quite excellent, Lord Ower,' said Dance and drank it with reverence.

With the fish came a heavy Beaune. Dance drank a glass and was surprised when the enigmatic butler filled it up again. There came a pause in the conversation.

'And what do you think of my modest white wine, Mr. Dance?' enquired Lord Ower. 'Not too heavy for your taste I hope.'

'Certainly not Lord Ower,' said Dance, and hastily gulped it down.

Burgundy was served with the roast pheasant and again the unwary Dance finished his glass, only to find when he turned back from his neighbour that it had been charged again.

'It's very fortunate that you are here this evening, Mr. Dance,' said Lord Ower a few moments later. 'I'm trying out some new Burgundy. Now you're quite a connoisseur, I believe. Give me your honest opinion of it.'

There was a deferential silence round the table while Dance went through the motions of savouring the wine and sipping it.

'Ah, Mr. Dance, but with a Burgundy you must surely let it reach the back of the palate. Now,' and Lord Ower fairly twinkled with joviality, 'take a man's draught, and let me know what you think.'

Dance obliged, but in his embarrassment, very nearly did the nose-trick. Lord Ower immediately called to the butler, waving aside Dance's expostulations. 'Jelks, a bottle of the '45. This '43 is clearly not to Mr. Dance's taste.'

And so it went on through the sweet ('Now Mr. Dance, which is your preference between these Yquems?') to the coffee and brandy ('They say it's Napoleon, Mr. Dance, but I really can't believe it. Can you?') and all the while general conversation was proceeding round the table and no-one could have said that Lord Ower was being anything but a most solicitous host.

When finally they rose, it was without Dance. Quite plastered and totally oblivious to his surroundings, he just wanted to sleep, and, resting his head on his arms amid the glasses and the nuts, he knew nothing more until he found himself being carried to bed by the butler and one of the footmen.

Nothing remained to be said on either side. There was no need for good-byes, let alone for a farewell cheque. In the morning, Dance quite naturally and humbly took the train for London, went to the office and collected his salary from the cashier, who appeared not to be surprised, and walked out into Fleet Street. The whole operation, he explained to Bone, just before leaving to take up a modest post on the *Nigerian Echo*, had been as clean as a whistle and as just as the execution of a murderer.

Bone had whistled, in sympathy, but also in admiration.

Miss Fairbanks, the editress of *Our Family*, had been handled with equal brutality but greater finesse.

In private life a fervid supporter of Our Dumb Friends' League and the R.S.P.C.A., all her frustrated parental urge and love of children was transferred to dogs, of which she kept as many as she could in the back garden of her suburban bungalow.

Now, on the face of it, there was absolutely no reason why Lord Ower should have know of this secret passion and therefore no reason to accuse him of bad taste or cruelty to Miss Fairbanks when, at a well-attended dinner-party at The Towers, at which she was one of the guests, he took a most decidedly zoophobic line when Lady Ower brought the conversation round to a recently published report on road deaths.

'Nobody,' Lord Ower turned with friendly concern to Miss Fairbanks who sat on his left, 'nobody can be more distressed at the anguish caused to families by the loss of a dear one in this needless fashion than our excellent Miss Fairbanks, who is of course,' he spoke to the table at large, 'editress of *Our Family*.'

Miss Fairbanks blushed in the sudden limelight and murmured her heartfelt agreement. Everyone assumed expressions of concern with the problem and sympathy with Miss Fairbanks' distress at the casualties it caused amongst her readers.

'There is a partial remedy,' continued Lord Ower, 'and,' he beamed benignly, 'I am going to take the unusual step of inviting Miss Fairbanks to propose this remedy, this partial remedy, in the leader columns of *Our World*.' There was a murmur of assent and applause and Miss Fairbanks positively squirmed with pleasure, while making a small bow of flattered acquiescence. 'My attention has been drawn,' Lord Ower gazed sternly down the table, 'to the fact that a sensible proportion, a very sensible proportion of these accidents is caused by loose dogs upon the highway. These dogs must,' he slapped the table gently, 'be put away, put, ah, painlessly away whenever they are found abroad. Only thus,' and now Lord Ower was peaking in rich leaderese, 'can our British families be spared a proportion, a sensible proportion, of these dreadful wounds.'

Amidst the qualified expressions of agreement which followed, the small cry of pain which came from Miss Fairbanks and the dumb weaving of her protesting hands went unnoticed even, apparently, by Lord Ower.

He turned and gazed blandly into her tortured eyes, and with a gesture of parental authority he silenced whatever she might have been about to say.

'No, no. Do not be modest, my dear Miss Fairbanks. I have every confidence that you are quite up to the task which I have set you. What you write will be inspired, I am sure, by the very creditable sympathy you feel for the bereaved readers of *Our Family*. No considerations, least of all bashfulness, will come, I know, before your paramount duty to your readers and to, ahm, to Ower House.' Then, more firmly, 'And let me see your copy first thing on Monday morning, please. Address it to me personally. This is a subject which is very close to my heart.' And he glanced across to Lady Ower who immediately rose and swept the ladies out of the dining room.

That night, Bone reflected, when he heard the grisly tale, must have been sleepless for Miss Fairbanks. On the one hand, she must have argued, pacing her bedroom in her Jaegar dressing-gown, on the one hand certain dismissal ('You have lost my confidence, Miss Fairbanks. The paper must always come first') and on the other betrayal of her loved ones and the loss of her soul. And yet the leader would after all be anonymous. And it would certainly have no effect.

Miss Fairbanks wrote the leader on Sunday evening with a breaking heart but with fire in her pen and still she did not see the catch, the tails-you-lose, until Mr. Boot, the group editor-in-chief, sent for her on Monday afternoon.

'Sit down Miss Fairbanks.' Mr. Boot seemed genuinely, profoundly disturbed. He puffed busily at his pipe and his gaze hunted the wall above Miss Fairbanks' head.

'Miss Fairbanks, are you a supporter of the Dumb Friends' League?'

'Yes indeed, Mr. Boot,' said Miss Fairbanks brightly.

'You have many pets, yourself? Many little dogs?'

'Oh yes, Mr. Boot. I love them.'

Mr. Boot quietly pushed a galley-proof across the table. Miss Fairbanks bent forward and a glance at the opening sentence was sufficient. Someone had added in bold type the heading 'Our Dumb Enemies'. She blushed to the roots of her hair. Her limbs turned to water. She clutched the table. Finally she faced Mr. Boot. He sat looking at her coldly.

'But, Mr. Boot, Lord Ower told me to. I . . . I simply had to. I . . .'

'Lord Ower knew nothing of your private life or your devotion to animals. He learnt of your hobby this morning. He is quite profoundly shocked, scandalised in fact by your extraordinary breach of journalistic ethics. He described it to me as the worst example of spiritual treachery which has ever come his way. I was only just able to prevent him from referring the facts to the executive of the National Union of Journalists. But for his generosity, it would certainly have been impossible for you to find another job in journalism.'

Miss Fairbanks burst into tears.

'But it was he . . .'

'Miss Fairbanks, I understand that it was quite a casual suggestion over dinner. Did you protest at the time? Did you try to avoid writing this leader? Did you put forward your point of view?'

'No, but, but . . .'

'Then I am afraid, Miss Fairbanks, that there is no more to be said. Lord Ower feels that something sacred has been betrayed. He asks me to tell you to try and strive higher in the future, wherever that future may take you. Your resignation is accepted. Good afternoon.'

And Miss Fairbanks had gone sobbing from the room.

Bone, when he heard the tale, was staggered by its simplicity and its neatness, like the snap of a handcuff, short, sharp and final. Compared with it the slaughter of the Reverend Percy Trimble, author of 'From My Full Heart – A Weekly Handclasp' which appeared in several of the Ower periodicals, had been almost clumsy, at the best inartistic. It was as if the simple cleric was thought to rate no better than a casual side-swipe of the mailed fist, but a knockout blow just the same.

On the Monday morning, as Bone understood it, after a particularly genial weekend at The Towers, the Reverend Trimble had entered his office at Owers House with the feeling that his stock was high with the Chief. Humming the opening bars of the Dresden Amen he sat down to his desk, packed his pipe with Barneys and turned to his voluminous mail on top of which lay a neat paper parcel about the size of a book, a review copy he supposed, until he saw that it bore no stamp or postmark but only his name and the superscription 'ABSOLUTELY PRIVATE AND CONFIDENTIAL', heavily underscored.

Inside the top wrapper was a letter, on the heavy paper used by Lord Ower's private secretary, and then another parcel, bearing the words 'To be opened only by the Rev. Percy Trimble'.

The letter was from Linklater, the private secretary. It read:

Dear Mr. Trimble,

Lord Ower instructs me to return to you this book, which was found by one of the maids at The Towers under the pillow in your room after your departure this morning.

Would you kindly acknowledge its safe receipt.

Lord Ower instructs me to say that in the circumstances which he does not wish to discuss with you, your contributions to the group publications will no longer be required.

Yours faithfully,
Albert Linklater

Feverishly the Reverend Trimble tore the wrapping off the inner parcel. It contained a much thumbed copy of *Fanny Hill* with etchings by Felicien Rops. A random glance at the rosy interlaced bodies was sufficient. Trembling, the Reverend Trimble snatched at the telephone.

'Linklater speaking.'

A torrent of words poured into the apparatus. '. . . scandalous mistake . . . never heard of the book . . . who does he think I am . . . won't stand for it . . . blackening my name . . . libel action . . . wrongful dismissal . . .'

Patiently, coldly, Linklater finally broke in.

'Mr. Trimble, at present this unfortunate affair . . . yes, yes, of course there may have been some mistake, most unfortunate . . . as I was saying, this occurrence will be treated as absolutely confidential, but I should tell you that I have only just been able to restrain His Lordship from placing the facts of the case before the Ecclesiastical Commissioners. If you seek a public investigation, you do so at your own risk, but I should remind you that the staff at The Towers are of course beyond suspicion and without any conceivable motive and it would be even more fanciful to involve the name of Lord Ower himself.'

'But, but, I never . . .'

'Mr. Trimble, if I may give you a private word of advice it is that you should not further exacerbate Lord Ower's feelings of deep distress and disgust. It would be most unwise. And now if you will pardon me . . .' The receiver was replaced with a sharp click.

For half an hour the Reverend Trimble sat with his head in his hands. Perhaps he prayed for guidance. Finally he rose and walked heavily out of the door and down to the cashier's desk.

The cleaners found no book or trace of a book, when they came to make the room ready for its next occupant.

These three case histories alone were surely sufficient to make one's skin crawl when one was faced with that fat quarto sheet of Basildon Bond which had looked at Bone, the night before, like the Knave of Spades had looked to Prince Florizel, a ticket to doom.

In fact, come to think of it, Bone had never heard of any visit to The Towers by any member of the staff which had been anything less than fatal. 'The Last Supper' was no idle cognomen.

The editorial side of the building was nearly empty when Bone had finally walked with a heavy heart out into Fleet Street and into the nearest public house. There he sat until closing time, consuming sausage-rolls and whisky and gazing into his private crystal-ball until it became so clouded with alcohol that he took himself off to a sleeping pill and his bed.

And now in a few minutes the curtain would go up and the play begin.

Bone shook himself out of his painful reverie. The wireless was still playing softly from the roof of the Rolls, but the accompanying susurrus of the balloon tyres on wet tarmac had given way to the rich scrunch of gravel on a drive. There were glimpses of great trees and well-tended parkland, then the long high wall of a kitchen-garden, then a bend in the drive which they negotiated with two quick blasts on the horn and at last they debouched into a wide gravel sweep and up to the broad lighted steps of a house as big as, and rather resembling, the Admiralty.

A liveried footman, alerted no doubt by the chauffeur's signal, was already on the bottom step holding a large umbrella. Such was the pinpoint accuracy of the driver that he only had to reach out his hand and let the handle of the car door slip into it. Bone disentangled himself from the rug and stepped out into the shelter of the umbrella and up the broad stone flags to the iron-studded door, both wings of which had been thrown expansively open by a butler (that butler who seemed to have a minor but significant part, reflected Bone, on these dread occasions) in immaculate tails.

This inauspicious figure bid him good evening and helped him out of his overcoat, folded it neatly on to the hall table beside several other more expensive looking coats and placed his hat upon the folded coat and then his gloves on top of the hat, making a pile, thought Bone, as neat and reverent as the riverside relics of a drowned man.

'This way, please sir,' invited the butler, speaking fruitily from his boots. 'His Lordship asks if you would kindly spare him a moment in his study before you dress for dinner.'

'Humpf,' thought Bone with shaky bravado. 'So soon?' He followed stoically as they crossed the broad hall over the thick pile carpet and through a door into some minor drawing room and across this to another taller door at which the butler knocked softly.

'Come in.'

It was indeed His Master's Voice. It sounded some distance away. A long room, guessed Bone. He steeled himself for the Mussolini treatment. The butler opened the door and preceded him.

'Mr. Caffery Bone, my Lord.'

Bone stepped forward and the door was quietly closed behind him.

'Ah, my dear Bone. Take a seat. Take a seat. I will join you in one moment.'

Forty feet away, at a large desk set across a corner of a long room, Lord Ower's sandy thatch turned down again to his papers.

ON WORLD WAR TWO

LETTER TO *THE TIMES*

The following letter appeared in The Times *on 28th September 1938*

Sir, — Since the immediate future of Europe appears to depend largely on Herr Hitler's intentions, it is most important that we should have a clear knowledge of exactly what those intentions are. The present crisis has shown that to be forewarned is not necessarily to be forearmed, but it may be argued that forearming did not appear necessary when the warning was so incredible. Doubts are dispelled, and it may now be of interest to your readers to learn the exact details of the National-Socialist Party Programme as circulated to members of the party and others on February 24, 1920, four years before *Mein Kampf* was written.

The original 25 points were issued from Munich in the form of a circular which is now extremely rare. I know of only one other copy, in the Nazi archives at the Brown House.

This is a literal translation, from an original copy in my possession, of the preamble and the first three points: —

'The Programme of the German Workers' Party is a "Time-Programme" (*Zeit-Program*). The Leaders will abstain from setting up new goals, after the attainment of the goals set out in the Programme, with the sole object of permitting the continued existence of the Party by artificially stimulating the appetite of the Masses.

'(1)   We demand the union of all Germans within a Greater Germany on the grounds of the right of peoples to self-determination.

'(2)   We demand equality of rights for the German people *vis-à-vis* other nations, and repeal of the Peace Treaties of Versailles and St. Germain.

'(3)   We demand land and soil (colonies) for the feeding of our people and the emigration of our surplus population.'

The remaining 22 points deal with racial questions and other internal matters, and, although they do not concern the purpose of this letter, it is remarkable with what minute fidelity each of these 22 points has been adhered to. One might say with justice that only the above three points remain to be carried out to the letter.

If we finally agree, then, that Herr Hitler means what he says, we must also be clear in our minds whether there is anything in the above three points which runs contrary to England's interests, and, if so, whether we are prepared to shed Europe's blood and our own in preventing their attainment. A possible answer would be that we have no great objection to Germany regaining her pre-War strength so long as we can be sure that she will not use that strength as she did in 1914, or, in other words, that those three points represent the absolute limit of Germany's territorial ambition

It would therefore seem that there will be no peace, no return of prosperity, and no happiness in Europe until England and France agree to the fulfilment of Herr Hitler's stated programme in exchange for a binding disarmament pact, and the guarantee of the traditional protective alliances of the signatory Powers.

If and when Herr Hitler refuses a settlement on these lines – if, that is to say, it is made clear that Germany already aims once again at world domination by aggression – then it will be time to organise this country on a wartime basis and announce to Germany that we shall fight at the first act of aggression against our fundamental treaty obligations.

Above all, should it be necessary to make this announcement, we must hope that the basic issues will be made crystal clear to the world in the immediate future. The policy of keeping our hands free in Europe has confused the German nation and bewildered our own. Moral issues must be disentangled from the instinct of self-preservation, and we must state what we would fight for and why.

Many people must hope that Mr. Chamberlain will deal fully with this broader aspect of the present crisis when he addresses Parliament, as it is to be presumed that it has been fully discussed in his talks with Herr Hitler. I personally hope that if he does not obtain the settlement I have outlined above he will, at any rate, put before Herr Hitler the concrete alternative I mention.

When it is certain that he has done neither then it will be time to turn a reluctant ear either to the dangerous counsels of the slaughterhouse brigade or to the bemused vapourings of those who long for the day when England is another Holland and out of the fight for ever.

Yours faithfully,
IAN L. FLEMING
22B Ebury Street, S.W.1.

MEMORANDUM TO COLONEL DONOVAN

This memorandum was written on 27th June 1941.
Colonel Donovan had been asked by President Roosevelt to
set up the Office of Strategic Studies (O.S.S.), predecessor to the C.I.A.
The attack on Pearl Harbor took place on 7th December 1941.

For what they are worth, I have prepared a few notes on some steps which will have to be taken at an early date in order that your organisation can be set up in time to meet war before Christmas.

I mention Christmas, because it seems to me that unless you make an early attack on inertia and opposition which will meet you at every step, there is a serious danger of your plans being stillborn. By setting up a reasonable target date, which should be attainable, you will be able to measure your progress in relation to this date and meet, in full time, the harmonic periods from which your new machinery is bound to suffer.

I believe, also, that you will find it necessary to devote, now, perhaps one month to installing your new organisation and solving the first major problems. I say 'now', because:–

(1) There is opposition to your appointment which must not be allowed to organise itself.

(2) You need good men, and good men will not be going begging for much longer.

(3) There are some sections of your organisation which will have to start planning now if they are to put up any kind of a show, should America come into the war in a month's time.

So I would like you to read the following fragmentary suggestions as to how a start might be made.

I ACCOMMODATION

You will need a good deal of space for your headquarters. It must be central, secure, and have excellent communication facilities.

I therefore suggest you take over a section of the F.B.I. building, which is ideal from almost every point of view.

ACTION

(1) Arrange with Attorney General and Mr. Hoover.
(2) Appoint a high grade office manager with staff, to put the place in order.

II STAFF

You will need for G.H.Q.:

(a) A first-class personal Chief of Staff, and first-class secretary.
(b) Adjutants to run your divisions.
(c) Managing Editor with staff from a news agency foreign desk to receive and disseminate intelligence from a central office at G.H.Q.
(d) Heads of country sections to feed (c).
(e) Liaison officers to keep contact with and serve Government Departments.
(f) Officer in charge of communications.
(g) Officer in charge of materiel and transport.
(h) Field officers.
(i) Officer in charge of personnel and recruits.

ACTION

(a) McCloy is my only suggestion.
(b) (1) Walter Butterworth to head Economic Intelligence. He is a 'natural' in every respect. (Quick action required.)

(2) Perhaps Henry Luce to organise Foreign Propaganda. (Planning on this should start at once.)

(3) A good 'sapper' to run sabotage. (A practical problem which should not be allowed to romanticise itself.)

(4) Mr. X. for S.I.S. (I have no idea.)

(5) Counter-espionage, – a nominee of Mr. Hoover.

(c) Consult and obtain from head of Associated Press. (Staff should come from <u>one</u> news agency to avoid jealousies and internal friction.)

(d) (1) Far East. Lt.Cdr. McCollum (O.N.I.).

(2) Russia and Scandinavia. Eugene Lyons, former U.P. correspondent in Moscow.

(3) Other countries, no ideas.

(e) To be appointed by departments concerned.

(f) A good Fleet Signals Officer. (Consult Admiral Noyes.)

(g) Consult American Express.

(h) Pool the files of the State Department, Navy and Army, and pick the best. Appoint talent scouts to find more if necessary.

(i) A thoroughly critical and sceptical man for this.

III LIAISON WITH C.S.S. LONDON

ACTION

(1) Request appointment of Commander Arnold Foster for general liaison and planning.

(2) Request use of Captain Hastings for organising communications. (D.N.I. will concur.)

(3) Teleprinter with Bill.

(4) Request C.S.S. to allow your men in the field to work closely with ours. (See my previous memo.)

IV DIPLOMATIC

(1) Enlist the full help of the State Department and F.B.I. by cajolery or other means. You will have to be (and stay) friends with both.

(2) Dragoon the War and Navy Departments. See Miles and Kirk (separately) at an early date, explain your plans and request their full personal cooperation. Be prepared to take action quickly if they don't help.

(3) Leave question of intercept material alone for the time being.

(4) Make an example of someone at an early date for indiscretion and continue to act ruthlessly where lack of security is concerned.

Ian Fleming
Commander, R.N.V.R.

copy to D.N.I.
copy to Mr Stephenson

27th June 1941

THE DIEPPE RAID

Ian Fleming observed the raid on Dieppe on 19th August,
1942 from on board H.M.S. Fernie. *This account was written*
in October 1961, but based on a report written at the time.

We passed through the gate about 1815 on 18th August and proceeded to Newhaven. On the way out of harbour the *Hunt* played her battle cry on the loud-speaker, and the brave sound of the fanfare echoed across to the troops embarking in special assault craft at the jetties.

The wardroom had to accommodate a large number of visitors who were taking part for one purpose or another. Among them was an American General and a Colonel of the United States Marine Corps, both with that appearance of weather-beaten scepticism that the best United States Army Officers have. They had come to watch the behaviour of the small detachment of 'Rangers' which had been training in England with the Commandos, and were to take part in the operation. (Among the 'Rangers' there is said to be an authentic Red Indian called 'One Skunk', who is an expert in the art of scalping, but uncommunicative on the subject. He is being held as a special surprise for the Germans on some future raid.) During the early hours of the evening some of us were initiated into the art of rolling our own cigarettes by the American General, who used for this purpose a substance resembling a breakfast food, but which, he assured us, was the finest Maryland tobacco. None of us was able to produce more than a mockery of a smoke.

The night passed uneventfully. The weather was fine. Rumours that a sea force 4 might be encountered in the Channel were confounded in the event, and the 'Swipers' took the big fleet of small craft through the enemy minefields as clean as a whistle.

At about 0300 while dozing in an armchair I heard the thud of gunfire against the ship's side, and going on deck saw tracers and something like 4-inch being fired about twenty miles to the northward. The night was warm and still, and the red, green and white tracer in the distance seemed undangerous and even friendly. The battle must have been going on fairly close inshore as some of the tracer appeared to be hitting the cliff face and then zooming off into the air. The battle, which was a chance encounter by our left flanking force and German patrol craft engaged on convoy duty, continued intermittently until about 0400. As it turned out the encounter was a vital mishap and a grievous blow to the Operation as a whole, for it reduced by a large percentage the Commando force in assault craft which was to silence the strong defences to the northward of Dieppe.

The fact that these defences, although reduced by the remnant of the Commando force, were never completely silenced, and that certain machine-gun posts in the cliffs to the south of Dieppe also survived, allowed the Germans to enfilade the centre beach and promenade with withering fire and also allowed them, when other targets were absent, to make the life of the destroyers and light craft lying offshore, extremely unpleasant. Towards 0500 bombers came in and the Dieppe A/A defences turned on a magnificent firework display including some attractive red tracer, probably 2-pounders, which soared up into the sky in strings of five or six red shells.

By this time it was beginning to get light and there were indications of a red sunrise on the horizon. The identity of the assault craft of various types, which had followed us across the Channel, revealed itself more clearly as they slipped by to go into the attack.

Soon, from the six-gun position on the cliff top on the enemy's left flank, salvoes of shells started to straddle us, but when their unpleasant sound effects ceased we realised that Lord Lovat's Commando had done its job of demolition and there was general relief.

Perhaps two hours later this Commando came alongside to leave its cot cases with us before proceeding back to England with its mission clearly accomplished. As they lay alongside in their assault craft the men offered a grim spectacle with their faces daubed with black and poisonous green paint. The troops were wild with delight at their success and their enthusiasm was so infectious that I felt that the Germans could not possibly be standing up to our waves of attack. Unfortunately these hopes were soon dashed as reports came over from the close-communication W/T that strong opposition was being met throughout the central sector, and from that moment onwards (about 0800) no good news came from the beach.

As the sun came up over the horizon a gaggle of wild geese about thirty strong, came over in V formation and flew unmoved at about a thousand feet through the gun bursts which were following the tail of a F.W.190, and made off towards the Bay of Biscay.

In the meantime another *Hunt* was standing close up to the cliff and whanging away with her 4-inch at a concealed battery (the splashes looked like about 3.5) which was hammering at a T.L.C. lying helpless about forty yards off the beach below the cliffs on the enemy's left flank. These cliffs, nearly as high as the cliffs of Dover, were reddish brown and fell vertically to the twenty yards of golden sand which separated them from the sea. Already on this sand we could see scattered heaps of dead who, we rightly feared, were our own men. The *Hunt* finally silenced the battery, though there remained other enemy guns of a smaller calibre in caves in the cliff face.

During this period we had been moving at some ten knots parallel and about seven hundred yards away from the beach, making smoke to protect the landing craft as they went in, and the pool of those which had made their get-away after disembarking their troops and vehicles. It had turned out a perfect day and the sun was shining from a blue sky. One could pick up every detail of the scene when the smoke allowed it, but there was little sign of movement on the beach, although heavy firing was continuous inside the town.

DOG FIGHTS BEGIN

Spitfires had been overhead in sheaves since daylight and no German aircraft had showed themselves by about 0900, but then F.W.s and Me.s put in their appearance and some magnificent dog fights developed, accompanied by terrific fire from the invasion fleets, not all of which was of assistance to the R.A.F. Our own pom-poms and Oerlikons had been very active, scoring, we imagined, many hits on any German aircraft which came within range. During the heat of one of these bursts of fire I was standing by the port Oerlikon wishing that our steel helmets did not give one such a headache and

36

afforded the same protection as the German, Russian or modern United States types, when I noticed one of the spare gun's crew sitting on a crate of ammunition engrossed in a book. I looked over his shoulder – the title of the book was 'A Fortnight's Folly'. The reader's eyes were popping out of his head with excitement as he greedily turned over the pages.

Very soon the German bombers arrived. Personally I had been rather concerned at their absence, fearing that they might be waiting for our withdrawal to put in a huge concentration, and I pictured flight upon flight of Ju.s and Heinkels smashing the puny, small craft, after hours of firing at shore targets and German fighters had exhausted the A/A ammunition of the escorting vessels.

So it was quite a relief to see the three Ju.88's standing out distinctly from a sky full of fighters, and see their sticks of four 500-lb bombs come sailing slowly towards us. This particular consignment fell right across the acre of small craft round which we were circling, but after the spray and smoke had subsided no damage appeared to have been done unless some craft had been blown to pieces without trace, and I do not think they were. They just had time to drop their bombs before the fighters got to them, guided by the bursts of 4-inch shells, and the chases were on. As the naval gunfire died down we could hear the swift stutter of the Spitfires' cannon and everybody held his breath as the enemy made a despairing spring for distant French airfields. One bomber was shot down while still over the sea and crashed to the north of us in a fountain of flame and spray, and the others disappeared into the distance over the cliffs with the fighters tearing after them.

At the end of the day, before we heard the B.B.C. announce the results of the air fighting, I think most of us would have guessed that perhaps thirty Germans had been destroyed for the loss of twenty of our aircraft, for that was about what we had seen shot down or appearing a certain kill. The majority of losses must have occurred far out of sight in France.

A quarter of an hour or so later we saw that most heartening sight, a single Ju.88 hit fair and square by a 4-inch shell and explode high up in the sky with a great orange flash from which small pieces of black wreckage fluttered down into the sea.

There was an extraordinary medley of sounds during the battle. The volume of the naval 4-inch predominated with their usual whip-lash crack;

then there was the continual undertone of machine gun fire with the heavier punctuation of Oerlikon-type guns, the hasty bark of pom-poms, and the soft stutter of fighter cannon far above. Over all one heard the varying hum of the R.A.F. cover, occasionally overshadowed by the deep whine of a Junkers going into a steep dive to let go his bombs. But the noise which I remember best was the deliberate, wooden, knock, knock, knock of (I think) German anti-tank guns. This noise seemed so unhurried and deliberate that it cut through the permanent welter of sound with a disturbing authority. It was the sort of noise one hoped we were making, rather than the enemy.

At about 0930 our fast bombers came on the scene in waves. Flying at medium height or just above the level of the sea, they poured into the Dieppe area, dropping heavy bombs with a short delay action so that they had turned and were skimming back before we heard the terrific crash of the explosions. We prayed that these bombs had done more than demolish some boarding houses and hotels of the Victorian age and that each one had caught an enemy strong point fair and square, but the enemy firing kept on whatever fear there may have been in the hearts of the defenders at the appalling holocaust let loose, and hopes that resistance might be cowed by the terror and weight of our air attack and naval bombardment, never revived again.

All this time gallant R-boats and landing craft had been putting in to the beaches to take off the wounded under the direction of a determined Surgeon-Commander whose cheerfulness and zeal persisted until the following day and was a tonic to all who saw him.

We took many cot cases and walking wounded on board; I talked to some of them. There was not one man who did not show outstanding cheerfulness and courage after what he had been through on the beaches. The danger in which they still stood on board our ship from air and land bombardment meant nothing to them in comparison with what they had already experienced.

I was shown some letters taken by one of these from a German. He sounded a dull and ordinary fellow from the correspondence he was carrying – a statement of his account with the Darmstaedter Bank in Breslau showing 524 marks and some pfennigs in his favour, a seed catalogue from a firm in Breslau, a receipt from the compulsory State Insurance Office, and two or three of those inane postcards with conventional good wishes which Germans love to receive and send in sheaves.

ORDER FOR WITHDRAWAL

By about 1000 it was clear that the withdrawal due to begin at 1100 must be effected without further delay as the progress necessary to carry out later phases of the original plan could clearly not be achieved. Soon the message came from the Headquarters ship and the pool of empty craft broke up and made slowly for the beaches into the teeth of the enemy's counter fire. At the same time the ban on the use of our 4-inch armament imposed to safeguard the delicate W/T apparatus which we carried, was removed and all escort vessels opened up on land or air targets to give covering fire to the naked little force of landing craft as it approached the beaches. I saw a large gun-boat, whose chief role had had to be abandoned owing to the way things had developed, pumping 4-inch shells with incredible rapidity and spite into the enemy defences and tearing great chunks of rock off the cliff face protecting enemy gun positions.

Incidentally, this vessel contained the detachment which was my own special concern during the operation. I had been instructed to return to England independently directly a certain mission had been accomplished and when it was clear that the gunboat was not going to be able to carry out her original intentions, the Government exhortation, 'Is Your Journey really Necessary?' came to my mind, heavily underlined by the shells from the shore batteries which came zipping through our rigging.

At about this time we were hit at the base of the funnel by something like one of the French 75's which the Germans employed in such profusion on coastal work. The shell killed one man and wounded four or five others and by an unfortunate chance put out of action the 4-inch remote control. Later I was talking to one of the crew of the starboard Oerlikon about the casualties. He pointed at the dead man who was still lying on deck under a blanket with the back of his head blown off – 'It's a funny thing, you know, sir,' he said, 'only this morning that chap was saying he had a pain in his neck, and now he certainly has got a pain, but he can't feel it any more.' The rest of the gun crew laughed as if it was the best joke they had ever heard. The American General who was standing nearby took me aside later in the day – 'You sure are the most fatalistic people in the world,' he said. 'Well. Perhaps we are a bit phlegmatic,' I answered, 'but it's probably only a line we shoot when there are distinguished visitors about, in the hopes of giving them a bit of a shock.' The General shook his head sceptically as if he did not wish this great truth he had discovered to be taken away from him.

By about 1100 the withdrawal was under way and there were already groups of craft in the distance heading towards England protected by M.G.B.s and Free French Chasseurs. As we rounded up a group of craft about a mile from the shore, to follow them, we saw a stick of bombs leave a Ju.88 and crash across the fo'c'sle of the *Berkeley*. Then the smoke came down over the ship and she was obscured from our eyes until two heavy explosions reverberated and a huge mushroom of yellow and black smoke rose into the still air. We thought she must have sunk with all hands, but it turned out later that the casualties were not so tragic as we had feared. As we headed for England I looked back through a break in the smoke at Dieppe. Two or three houses only stood up on the sea front like teeth in a gaping jaw. There was practically no movement, although heavy firing was still going on. It was a scene of utter desolation and destruction which one was glad to leave, though with a heavy heart.

I never saw any civilians on the beaches or who escaped. The French in Dieppe must have had a terrifying time. They were bombed (on an empty stomach) before dawn and subsequently at intervals until mid-day. There must have been bullets flying round each street corner and shells of all sizes whanging into the rickety houses from all points of the compass. I believe some fugitives got down to the beaches, but were mown down before they could embark. One can only hope that they were avenged by a few stout francs-tireurs who made use of all confusion to slip a knife or bullet into some quaking Nazi soldiery.

At all events, there can be few who read this who will know Dieppe again in their lifetime as a pleasure resort with well-kept gardens, tidy hotels and cafes, or who will taste again the delicious 'filets de sole Dieppoise' dispensed by a famous restaurant behind the promenade (I mean behind 'the outer perimeter of anti-invasion defences').

The casino too (a strong point of German defence) will be long in rebuilding. When I last saw it (after the *Berkeley* and others had paid off the gambling scores of generations of English holiday-makers) it was a drunken mockery of a building and I confess to an unholy delight (remembering painful pre-war visits to French tables) at seeing one of these establishments getting the smile wiped off its face.

The headquarters ship and the large gunboat followed us after an interval, and then came the gallant light craft which had remained to pick up survivors and take in tow disabled craft or destroy by gunfire those which could not possibly be brought home.

At that moment it seemed a long way back to Newhaven, steaming at five or six knots so that the landing craft proceeding under their own power could keep up. There were worries about E-boat or U-boat attack and an ever-present anxiety that France might disgorge wave upon wave of heavy bombers. We did not realise what immense damage had been done to the G.A.F. that day by our pilots, nor what an extremely unpromising target our fighter-umbrella made us. This umbrella had been with us faultlessly throughout the day, and also away out in the haze of our flanks, over the German airfields, or up at 20,000 feet where the scribbling of vapour occasionally betrayed the presence of an aircraft.

I had kept studiously off the bridge during the heat of the battle so as not to get in the way, but on our way back I went up and talked to the Captain, a young public school entrant in his early twenties who had handled his ship beautifully throughout. He was really Number One in the ship, but the Captain (renowned for his political opinions and his dash on a motor bicycle) had collided the day before the Operation with some immovable object and been relegated to Haslar to his eternal chagrin.

WINGED WORDS

On the bridge I heard the Wing Commander in charge of Ship-to-Air Communication, talking to his Fighters like a second to his man in the ring. 'There's a Bandit bearing green 75 – he's just above you and you can't see him. Turn right a bit – and a bit more – there, you're on him now!' And off the 'Spit' would go with two or three of his fellows behind him. These quiet 'ringside' talks had been going on since dawn. The Wing Commander had stayed on the job for ten hours without faltering. The moment he handed over his earphones to his Number Two, and came down to the Captain's cabin for a minute's respite at about 1800, a Ju. dropped a couple of bombs in the middle of the convoy. Almost before the sound of the explosions had died away, he was out of his chair and up on the bridge, and he never left his post again until nightfall.

Another star performer among so many others on the bridge was the gunnery officer, a young Canadian, who directed his pom-poms like a coach at an American ball game. 'Come along, after pom-pom, a bit quicker please. Right. You're below him. Now you're on to him. Stay where you are and give him hell. Good shooting!' And then a pause – and then, 'Well done, after pom-pom, but you can open up earlier. Don't forget the Ju.88 can do about 350 when he's dropped his bombs – allow for that when he's turning away.'

It was about this time (1700) when three Ju.s came out of the huge cloud of smoke we had left behind, right on the tail of the convoy. There were Spitfires to right of us and Spitfires to left of us, but none in the vicinity of these three 88's, and our fighters seemed an unconscionable time in heeding the urgent advice of the Wing Commander.

On they came in faultless formation, while the gunnery officer exhorted the after pom-pom. Finally they came within range. The red tracer went up at them in a steep curve and seemed below, but almost immediately it got on to the great black target and the starboard plane broke slowly away just at the moment when we expected twelve 500-lb bombs to fall slowly down on to the tail of the convoy. It was probable that all three planes were hit or at any rate considerably deterred, for the first and most nervous of the three was immediately followed by the other two just as the Spitfires came screaming down on them. We watched the pursuit far to the south and had the satisfaction of seeing one plunge, flaming, into the sea.

It had occurred to me earlier in the day that with such heavy fighter cover as we possessed, it would have been better if the naval gunners had left the destruction of the enemy to our fighters, since I felt sure that our fire must have deterred, if not damaged, many of our own aircraft. But when I put this to the Wing Commander, he said that the bursts of our shells round an enemy plane were a help to the fighters in giving them direction, and certainly in this instance there is no doubt the bombers could have released their bombs before the Spitfires got on to them unless accurate naval fire had deterred them in time.

After this, and with the exception of the attacks by a single bomber which caught the Wing Commander in the Captain's cabin, the convoy was not further molested. It was a cheering sight to see Beachy Head. As we drew nearer to the English coast the sea became glassy calm and the sun started to set on a scene which seemed all the more pleasant after what we had witnessed that day. Later, the rain came down and the wind freshened. The operation had been completed, so far as the weather was concerned, with hardly an hour to spare.

At about 1900 we left the convoy to be shepherded into Newhaven by the light escort vessels, and the destroyers and gunboat made good speed for their home port where we finally berthed at about 0030. Shortly after berthing I left the ship with the American General and the Colonel of the Marines to find a welcome bed in the best hotel, which we stormed regardless of protest. The *Hunt* must have been glad to be shot of her many guests so that she could mend her scars, of which there were not a few, in peace, remove an unexploded shell from her coal bunkers, and return to her unremitting grind with the East Coast convoys. She had good cause to be pleased with the part she had played in this memorable foray.

Ashore there was a long and sad queue of ambulances and Red Cross cars stretching almost to the dockyard gates, while under a single arc light the indefatigable Surgeon-Commander put his last energy into the vital job of getting the seriously wounded quickly to hospital.

It had been a long and nerve-wracking day and it was difficult to add up the pros and cons of what was a bloody gallant affair. But one thing was clear: intelligence, planning and execution had been nearly faultless. The machinery for producing further raids is there, tried and found good. Dieppe was an essential preliminary for operations ahead. But the fortunes of war (vide that damnable mischance on our left flank) must be with us next time.

INTREPID

SILHOUETTE OF A SECRET AGENT

This article accompanied the serialisation of The Quiet Canadian *by Montgomery Hyde in the* Sunday Times, *October 1962. It was later included as a foreword to the American edition of the book,* Room 3603, *published by Farrar, Straus and Co. This is taken from the original typescript.*

In the higher ranges of Secret Service work the actual facts in many cases were in every respect equal to the most fantastic inventions of romance and melodrama. Tangle within tangle, plot and counter-plot, ruse and treachery, cross and double-cross, true agent, false agent, double agent, gold and steel, the bomb, the dagger and the firing party, were interwoven in many a texture so intricate as to be incredible and yet true. The Chief and the High Officers of the Secret Service revelled in these subterranean labyrinths, and pursued their task with cold and silent passion.

Sir Winston Churchill in Thoughts and Adventures

In this era of the anti-hero, when anyone on a pedestal is assaulted (how has Nelson survived?), unfashionably and obstinately I have my heroes. Being a second son, I dare say this all started from hero-worshipping my elder brother Peter, who had to become head of the family, at the age of ten, when our father was killed in 1917. But the habit stayed with me, and I now, naïvely, no doubt, have a miscellaneous cohort of heroes from the Queen and the Duke of Edinburgh through Sir Winston Churchill and on downwards to many Other Ranks, who would be surprised if they knew how much I admired them for such old-fashioned virtues as courage, fortitude, and service to a cause or a country. I suspect – I hope – that 99.9% of the population of these islands have heroes in their family or outside. I am convinced they are necessary companions through life.

High up on my list is one of the great Secret Agents of the last war who, at this moment, allowing for the time factor, will be sitting at a loaded desk in a small study in an expensive apartment block bordering the East River in New York. It is not an inspiring room – ranged bookcases, a copy of the Annigoni portrait of the Queen, the Cecil Beaton photograph of Churchill, autographed, a straightforward print of General Donovan, two Krieghoffs, comfortably placed boxes of stale cigarettes and an automatic telephone recorder that clicks from time to time and shows a light, and into which, exasperated, I used to speak indelicate limericks until asked to desist to spare the secretary, who transcribes the calls, her blushes. The telephone number is unlisted. The cable address, as during the war, is INTREPID. A panelled bar leads off the study, and then a bathroom. My frequent complaints about the exiguous bar of Lux have proved fruitless. The occupant expects one to come to see him with clean hands.

People often ask me how closely the 'hero' of my thrillers, James Bond, resembles a true, live secret agent. To begin with, James Bond is not in fact a hero, but an efficient and not very attractive blunt instrument in the hands of government, and though he is a meld of various qualities I noted amongst secret service men and commandos in the last war, he is, of course, a highly romanticised version of the true spy. The real thing, who may be sitting next to you as you read this, is another kind of beast altogether.

We know, for instance, that Mr. Somerset Maugham and Sir Compton Mackenzie were spies in the '14/'18 war, and we now know, from Mr. Montgomery Hyde's *The Quiet Canadian,* that Major-General Sir Stewart Menzies, K.C.B., K.C.M.G., D.S.O., M.C., a member of White's and the St. James's, formerly of Eton and the Life Guards, was head of the Secret Service in the last war – news which will no doubt cause a delighted shudder to run down the spines of many fellow members of his clubs and of his local hunt.

But this man sitting alone now in his study in New York is so much closer to the spy of fiction, and yet so far removed from James Bond or *Our Man in Havana,* that only the removal of the cloak of anonymity he has worn since 1940 allows us to realise to our astonishment that men of super qualities *can* exist, and that such men can be super spies and, by any standard, heroes.

Such a man is 'The Quiet Canadian', otherwise Sir William Stephenson, M.C., D.F.C., known throughout the war to his subordinates and friends, and to the enemy, as 'Little Bill'.

To strip him to his bare and formidable bones, he was born on January 11th, 1896, at the junction of the Assiniboine and Red Rivers, just outside Winnipeg, where the Scottish Highlanders established the first British settlement in the name of the Hudson's Bay Company towards the end of the Napoleonic Wars. It was from one of these early Scottish settlers that 'Little Bill' was descended. He was good at mathematics and boxing, but, before he could choose a career it was August 1914 and he went straight from school into the Royal Canadian Engineers, and was commissioned before his nineteenth birthday.

In 1915 he was badly gassed and invalided back to England, but during his convalescence he was seized by the flying bug and in due course received his Wings in the Royal Canadian Flying Corps. By the time he was shot down (in error by the French) he was credited with twenty German planes, including that of Lothar von Richthofen, brother of the famous German ace. These exploits earned him the M.C., D.F.C. and the Croix de Guerre with Palm.

Before he was shot down and captured by the Germans (he escaped, of course, from Holzminden) in his spare time, and fighting for the R.F.C., he won the Amateur Lightweight Championship of the World (he retired from the ring, undefeated, in 1923).

After the war, having built up a bit of capital by purloining from Holzminden and subsequently patenting a new type of can-opener, he went into business for himself in various technical companies, for one of which he invented a new system for the transmission of radio pictures, and for another of which, in 1934, he entered the winning aircraft in the King's Cup air race. In the City of London he will be particularly remembered for his connection with Sound City Films, Earl's Court, Alpha Cement and Pressed Steel, and it was through private intelligence work in Germany connected with the latter that he was able to give his old friend Winston Churchill the figure of a German expenditure on armaments amounting to £800 million annually. This figure was used by Churchill in a Parliamentary question to Neville Chamberlain and was not denied by the latter.

'Little Bill' developed his sources of intelligence in Scandinavia and

Germany, and it was quickly arranged that the fruit of these should be passed to the Secret Service with which, from then on, he became ever more closely associated, until he was appointed by the then Colonel Menzies as Head of the British Secret Service for all the Americas. In the end it was Churchill who gave him his marching orders. Churchill told him, 'Your duty lies there. You must go.' He went.

Well, that is the man who became one of the great secret agents of the last war, and it would be a foolish person who would argue his credentials; to which I would add, from my own experience, that he is a man of few words and has a magnetic personality and the quality of making anyone ready to follow him to the ends of the earth. (He also used to make the most powerful Martinis in America and serve them in quart glasses.)

I first met him in 1941 when I was on a plain-clothes mission to Washington with my chief, Rear Admiral J. H. Godfrey, Director of Naval Intelligence, the most inspired appointment to this office since 'Blinker' Hall, because, when the days were dark and the going bleak, he worked so passionately, and made his subordinates do the same, to win the war. Our chief business was with the American Office of Naval Intelligence, but we quickly came within the orbit of 'Little Bill' and of his American team mate, General 'Wild Bill' Donovan (Congressional Medal of Honor), who was subsequently appointed head of the O.S.S., the first true American Secret Service. This splendid American, being almost twice the size of Stephenson, though no match for him, I would guess, in unarmed combat, became known as 'Big Bill', and the two of them, in absolute partnership and with Mr. Edgar Hoover of the F.B.I. as a formidable full-back, became the scourge of the enemy throughout the Americas. As a result of that first meeting with these three men, the D.N.I. reported most favourably on our secret service tie-ups with Washington, and 'Little Bill', from his highly mechanised eyrie in the Rockefeller Centre and his quiet apartment in Dorset House, was able to render innumerable services to the Royal Navy that could not have been asked for, let alone executed, through the normal channels.

Bill Stephenson worked himself almost to death during the war, carrying out undercover operations and often dangerous assignments (they culminated with the Gouzenko case that put Fuchs in the bag) that can only be hinted at in the fascinating book that Mr. Montgomery Hyde has, for some reason, been allowed to write – the first book, so far as I know, about a British secret agent whose publication has received official blessing.

'Little Bill' was awarded the Presidential Medal of Merit, and I think he is the only non-American ever to receive this highest honour for a civilian. But it was surely the 'Quiet Canadian's' supreme reward, as David Bruce, today American Ambassador to the Court of St. James, but in those days one of the most formidable secret agents of the O.S.S., records, that when Sir Winston Churchill recommended Bill Stephenson for a knighthood he should have minuted to King George VI, 'This one is dear to my heart.'

It seems that other and far greater men than I also have their heroes.

ON CRIME AND ESPIONAGE

.

THE SECRETS OF INTERPOL

*A compilation of three pieces that Ian Fleming wrote when covering
the General Assembly of Interpol in Istanbul between 4th and
18th September 1955 as special representative for the* Sunday Times.

The twenty-fourth General Assembly of the International Criminal Police
Commission, generally known as 'Interpol', opens here on Monday. Through
the courtesy of the United Kingdom delegate, Sir Ronald Howe, Deputy
Commissioner of the Metropolitan Police, I shall be able to report on some
of its deliberations.

Interpol is the longest arm of the law: with the major exception of the Iron
Curtain countries, it reaches all round the world. Its object is to counter the
growing internationalism in crime and to abolish national frontiers in pursuit
of the criminal.

From its modest foundation in 1923 in Vienna, Interpol has continued
to expand. Today it is firmly established in fifty-two countries, and the murderer, counterfeiter or smuggler can hardly find safe refuge on the face of the
earth from the deadly hand of the central Interpol radio station near Paris.

Every year the police chiefs of the member States meet to coordinate new
methods of detection so as to keep ahead of the constantly improving science
and ingenuity of the criminal, and every stock 'Commissaire' from the detective fiction of the world is today arriving in this romantic city by air and sea
and, more appropriately, by Orient Express.

On Monday, under the presidency of the formidable Monsieur F. F.
Louwage, O.B.E., Inspector-General of the Belgian Ministry of Justice and
President of the I.C.P.C. since 1946, there will begin a week of conferences on
the major aspects of modern crime. These are some of them:

First, the General Secretariat will present a report on the Illicit Drug

Traffic, notably in opium, cannabis, morphine and cocaine. The Secretariat will report that Lebanon remains one of the principal supply centres for opium; that the Chinese, followed by the French and Italians, are still the chief traffickers in opium and that the amount of opium sized in 1954 increased by nearly 250 per cent over 1953.

As to cocaine it will be no news to the delegates from the American Narcotics Bureau that the United States remains the chief target of traffickers and that Cuba has developed into an important entrepot for the Bolivian suppliers, and it will only confirm their suspicions that Italy, with its channels into American gangland, remains the chief European centre for the cocaine traffic.

The report gives details of certain cases in which the I.C.P.C. played a decisive role. Typical is the capture of about 330 kgs. of opium, hashish and morphine base, and the twelve arrests effected as a result of co-operation through the I.C.P.C., of the American Narcotics Bureau with the police forces of Greece, Lebanon, Turkey and Syria. This is one of the biggest hauls since the war.

The conference will leave this realm of high drama and depravity to listen to some suggestions by Sir Ronald Howe for tightening up the policing of air traffic.

Apart from the flight of criminals, the smuggling of gold bars, diamonds and drugs by air has, in different parts of the world, become a serious problem, as has the security at airports of legitimate air freight such as bullion, precious stones and banknotes.

These problems are complicated by the speed with which a criminal can cross the world – perhaps before his crime has been discovered; by the ease with which privately chartered planes can land in a pretended emergency at unguarded airfields, and by the vast expanse of aerodromes themselves.

Mr. J. W. Kallenborn, the great authority on forgeries and head of the I.C.P.C. office at The Hague, will next raise the whole subject of cheque forgeries which, particularly with the increased use of travellers' cheques, is becoming vastly more important than the counterfeiting of currency. Mr. Kallenborn's recommendation is that a standard form of cheque should be adopted for each country and that an attempt should be made to make cheque forms as inviolable to counterfeiters as most currencies now are. He will even mention cases of cheque forgers printing cheque forms of their own design and drawn on imaginary banks, knowing that these can be passed through bank employees already confused by the present multiplicity of shapes, sizes and designs.

Even before the war, counterfeit cheques yielded far greater returns than counterfeit notes and Mr. Kallenborn will quote some fabulous achievements, including in 1931 the cashing of a forged cheque for the then majestic sum of 3,000,000 French francs, the full story of which I would very much like to know.

Mr. Kallenborn's plea will be supported by Dr. Giuseppe Dosi, head of the National Central Bureau in Rome, who will discuss the general relationship between policing and banking. He will detail the most modern methods of bank robbers (those who have seen the French film *Rififi* will have little to learn from them), including the latest electric drills, oxy-hydrogen blowpipes and the like, and he will make the unqualified statement that there is no such thing as a perfectly secure underground vault, safe or metal container, which can be depended on to protect its contents unless supplemented by a permanent guard or regular inspection. The dictum of Dr. Dosi is: 'The degree of safety of any safe is inversely proportional to the time available to the safe-breakers.'

The nature of delinquency invariably takes up a great deal of the time of each General Assembly. Next week Dr. J. F. de Echalecu Y Canino, Professor of Criminal Psychology and of Neuropsychiatry of the Direccion General de Seguridad, Madrid, will re-affirm the theory that the more serious types of crime have their ultimate origin in the region of the cortical and the sub-cortical layers, and that nearly all crime is a bio-sociological phenomenon.

On the same line of country, Professor Castroverde Y Cabrera of Cuba will urge that health statistics should invariably accompany crime statistics in the dossier of a criminal because of the close connection between disease and crime. The painful stimulus of disease, he will say, provokes the individual to extremes of action and, since all extremes of action are anti-social, to crimes.

The Australian delegation will come back to earth with some hard facts about the migration of criminals, with particular reference to certain groups of 'new Australians' who have settled in Australia since the war. Among them are Europeans whose crimes indicate that the perpetrators were trained in their nefarious activities in their mother countries, and the Australian police will make a plea for timely warning of the arrival of these undesirable migrants.

Since certain of the member States may be very happy to ship such people off to the other side of the world, I am doubtful that they will achieve more than airy promises.

However, the Australian police may make progress with their plan for coding the visual identification of the human being, which is basically an extension of the finger-print system to cover the human face.

There is nothing new in the use of a *Portrait Parlé* such as 'John Brown. 50 years. 5 ft. 9 in. Brown hair. Blue eyes. Low forehead. Straight nose. Wide straight mouth. Round chin and double neck cords', but the Australians would codify this particular description into 'John Brown, A4, D2, E3, R3, G4, H4, H2, 12 L13, M10, U41' which will certainly have attractions for the Radio Communications Branch of the I.C.P.C. Their documentation contains the complete catalogue of *Portrait Parlé* descriptions, from which I am interested to note that there are fourteen official face shapes from 'pyramid' to 'flabby'; seventeen nose peculiarities from 'lump on tip' to 'dilated nostrils' and five splendid eyelids described as: 'hooded bags under eyes, blear-eyed, crying eyelids' and 'reversed lower lids'. I also observe that violet eyes do not exist, but that green eyes do, and that 'soup-strainer moustache' is officialese.

On problems of communication, the General Secretariat will make a plea for better radio discipline, and Inspector Sanjuan of Madrid will demand a secure cypher for all Interpol transmissions. He will preface his request with a short history of the secrecy of communications beginning with a method which was new to me. Apparently the first means of secret communication was to shave the head of a slave and write the message in indelible ink on his bald pate. Once the hair had grown to a reasonable length, the slave would be sent out on his journey and at his destination the hair would be shaved off again and the message read. This strikes me as more ingenious than those bits of paper modern heroes are always swallowing.

Amongst other subjects to be dealt with will be some highly technical proposals by Professor Charles Sannié, head of the Criminal Identity Department of the Paris *Préfecture de Police*, for an extension of the Bertillion finger-print system. His object is to defeat forged finger-prints – an ingenious invention of the modern criminal by which he actually profits from the accuracy of the finger-print system.

As an example, Professor Sannié will mention the case of a prisoner in gaol who impressed his prints on a piece of glass and gave the glass to someone else. This second party left it on the scene of a burglary which was committed while the owner of the prints had the best possible alibi of being himself in prison. He will also mention the moulding of false finger-prints on to rubber fingerstalls and other ingenious gambits.

Perhaps the most important but least technical discourse will be given by the President of the I.C.P.C. himself. Monsieur Louwage will discuss aspects of juvenile delinquency, and it is pleasant to record that in urging police all over the world to avoid becoming 'bogeymen', he will quote as the desirable attitude the firmness but friendliness of the London 'Bobby' and the success with which he gains the confidence and affection of youth.

There will be nothing particularly new in what Monsieur Louwage has to say, but his words will certainly not be amiss in a conference of the chief bogeymen from fifty-two very different countries.

THE GREAT RIOT OF ISTANBUL

This week's great riot of Istanbul – the worst insurrection in the history of modern Turkey – is a reminder that Great Britain is very fortunate in being an island nation. She has never built up those hatreds that fester between neighbours in a suburban street and lead to fisticuffs and end up in court and a shameful half column in the evening paper – the hatreds that gather and come to a head between two families or even two generations in the same house and that sometimes end in murder – the hatreds between Arab and Jew, German and Frenchman, Pole and Russian, Turk and Greek.

This was to have been a great week for Turkey. Obedient to the undying memory of Ataturk, she has continued to mould her destiny away from the East and towards the West, perhaps in defiance of her stars and certainly in defiance of her true personality, which is at least three-quarters oriental.

To begin with, she successfully changed her spots. She abolished the fez, the harem, her Sultans. (Only twelve eunuchs remain in the 'Association of Former Eunuchs' that held its annual reunion here last Sunday. Thirty years ago there were one hundred and ninety. Fifty years ago the Sultan had four thousand.)

She turned her fabulous palaces – and they really are fabulous – into museums. She imported large quantities of French and English culture, German machinery and American taxicabs. She played her cards carefully during the last war. Then she joined N.A.T.O. She bolstered her currency with a tough exchange rate (difficult and dangerous for the operators).

The educated Turk became a carefully dressed provincial Frenchman with a Homburg and a briefcase and a ballpoint pen. Mr. Conrad Hilton, a man who considers even England a bad risk for an hotel, built the Istanbul Hilton, the most fabulous modern hotel in Europe. The international conference delegates flocked, like the quail whose season opens also this week, into the Golden Gates and this was to be the sixty-four dollar week in a record season.

This week would surely have made the recently joined member of the European Club eligible even for the committee, for the prospect of busy, modern Istanbul would surely please even those most sensitive confidential agents of the modern State – the police and the economists.

On Monday in an atmosphere of friendly efficiency began the Twenty-fourth General Assembly of the International Police Commission (Interpol), and the police chiefs of the world went into a conclave on such matters affecting the public safety as I described last Sunday. That is Monday. On Wednesday the 200 delegates to the conference of the International Monetary Fund started coming in to discuss that very delicate matter, the credit of nations – including the credit of Turkey. Between these two days the Turkish Common Man broke out from behind Turkey's smile of welcome and reduced Istanbul to a shambles.

On Wednesday morning martial law was declared and the official Interpol lunch arranged by the Chief of Police of Istanbul had to be cancelled as its venue, a restaurant, had been razed to the ground. That evening the heads of the police of fifty-two countries, after getting off cables to their wives, were confined for their safety to their hotels. There, with the banker economists of the International Monetary Fund, the two congresses lugubriously danced at the centre of the curfew.

The whole damage, a small fraction of which I witnessed, was done in eight hours of darkness by the peaceful light of a three-quarter moon. At six o'clock the fuse of hatred against the Greeks that had been creeping through

56

the years reached the powder with reports that Ataturk's birthplace at Salonika had been bombed by Greek terrorists. (In fact only a window had been broken by a bomb thrown at the Turkish consulate in Salonika. The proprietor of the leading evening paper and his editor are among the 2000 rioters now under arrest.)

Spontaneously on both sides of the Bosphorus in every noisome alley and smart boulevard hatred erupted and ran through the streets like lava.

Several times during that night curiosity sucked me out of the safety of the Hilton Hotel and down into the city, where mobs went howling through the streets, each under its streaming red flag with the white star and sickle moon. Occasional bursts of shouting rose out of the angry murmur of the crowds, then would come the crash of plate-glass and perhaps part of a scream.

A car went out of control and charged the yelling crowd and the yells changed to screams and gesticulating hands showed briefly as the bodies went down before it. And over all there was the trill of the ambulances and the whistling howl of the new police cars imported from America.

When, nauseated, I finally got back to my hotel a muddy, tough-looking squadron of cavalry were guarding the approaches, but they never fired their 1914–18 Mausers, and I think there was no shooting by either side during the riot. It was a night of the long staves and these were quickly put away at dawn when the Sherman tanks came in and the first Turkish Division got a grip of the town. For it is broken, and millions of pounds' worth of damage was done that night. Countless businessmen are wiped out, including several British merchants, and the Consulate and the rest of the British community are rallying to their help.

And now the normal disorder of Istanbul is being re-established, and on a higher level Ankara and Athens are doing their own mopping-up. In a day or two the police chiefs and their cohorts will depart. As for Turkey, her splendid progress in the international game of snakes and ladders has suffered. She has landed on a snake and must now go back and wait patiently until she can throw a six and get back into the game again.

DELINQUENTS AND SMUGGLERS

Despite the respective resignation and dismissal of its joint hosts, the Turkish Minister of the Interior and the Istanbul Chief of Police, the Twenty-fourth General Assembly of the International Police Commission tactfully averted its gaze from the surrounding shame and chaos, completed its labours and on Wednesday, discreetly thankful, took to its heels. Thanks to the heroic efforts of the secretariat much was achieved and many criminal loopholes have been blocked. But the most solid achievement was not in the final minutes of the assembly but in the public and private airing of the problems and cases of the police chiefs from 52 different countries.

Here, without committing Governments, and without the befogging intrusions of national sentiment, embarrassing topics could be discussed on the technical level. Thus the head of the Austrian delegation could talk over piracy from the Pacific pearling grounds with the Police Chief of Tokyo, the head of the Egyptian Sureté could raise with the Inspector-General of Police of Tel Aviv the increased drug traffic from the Arab countries, and Mr. Donald Fish, B.O.A.C. chief security officer, could offer private advice to the director of the new Delhi intelligence bureau on certain ingenious ruses used for concealing gold bars in aircraft.

Unofficial pooling of experience and knowledge is far more important and practical than the adoption of joint resolutions by representatives of 52 different countries with widely varying customs and legal systems. For example, juvenile delinquency sounds an easy topic to discuss. Everyone agrees that there should be less of it. But no resolution will cover even the words 'juvenile' and 'delinquency' as applied to, say, India, Scotland and Norway, yet alone the other 49 States. What about the criminal status of juvenile homosexuality, for instance? When you come to statistics, how do you explain that as against an international norm of 17 per cent, the percentage of crime committed by juveniles is 0.5 per cent in Denmark and 44.5 per cent in Scotland? In fact, the age of puberty – much later in Denmark – comes in as well as the differences in criminal law and the relative stringency of Scottish courts, and perhaps the Irish element in Glasgow. That is an example of the difficulty of codifying crime and therefore of codifying methods of prevention.

On the other hand, on a matter like gold-smuggling Interpol can be of real value, and it is probable that India, which is the chief target for the traffic, as America is for narcotic smugglers, will get real co-operation as a result of the remarkable facts her delegation laid before the assembly. It seems that she is being deluged with illicit gold. During 1954 nearly 40,000 ounces, valued at about £6 million, were seized by customs and police in 229 cases, involving 236 foreign nationals, and the delegation admitted that this haul can represent only a fraction of the illegal imports. Apparently it is coming in from all the gold-producing countries of the world – from Australia by steamship via Macao, Hongkong and Singapore; from Africa by fast lugger via Egypt, Syria and the Persian Gulf; from America by air via London, France, Switzerland and the Middle East. All this represents one of the most fabulous criminal networks in history, and the many Interpol States involved will now co-operate to crush it.

Other smaller points of interest that came up in discussion include the following. The U.S. Customs are particularly troubled by diamond-smuggling from Belgium and by the smuggling of watches and watch-movements from Switzerland. Regarding the latter, Dr. Grassberger, from Vienna, where next year's Interpol conference will take place, observed that it is better to get real smuggled Swiss watches than counterfeit ones. For the past two years an Austrian gang have been running a side-line to the smuggling of watch-movements; they put cheap watch-movements in formerly discarded watch-cases, forge famous names on the dials and smuggle these too.

The United Nations delegate reported an interesting technical process for discovering the geographical origin of smuggled narcotics. The U.N. Narcotics Division has discovered that by alkaloid and spectrographic analysis the nature of the soil in which captured opium was grown, and thus its country of origin, can be determined, greatly facilitating the pursuit back down the pipeline.

Sir Ronald Howe, deputy commissioner at Scotland Yard, presented the common-sense view of the Metropolitan Police and the Home Office on many recommendations where a conservative voice was needed. For instance on the occasion when the delegate from Chile suggested that your finger-prints should be verified before you could cash a cheque! As chairman of the sub-committee on policing the air routes, he fought for the rights and comforts of the passenger, and as a result we may see a simplification of the dreadful embarkation and disembarkation cards and a check to the practice in some countries of depriving the transit passenger of his passport during overnight stops.

(Incidentally I found unanimity among the senior delegates that Sir Ronald should be invited to become President of Interpol when M. Louwage of Belgium in due course resigns. This will be a great tribute to the prestige abroad of Scotland Yard.)

The corridors of the ornate Chalet Palace where the meetings were held were a splendid listening post. Here the Chief of Police of Thailand told me of the two elephants which form his riot squad. 'Very effective against small villages,' he explained. Mr. Charles Siragusa, head of the U.S. Bureau of Narcotics, explained his methods for 'leaning on' Lucky Luciano, the famous American gangster who was deported from America and now lives in Naples. 'He won't explain how he happens to stay so rich,' said Mr. Siragusa; 'so my Italian police friends have interpreted this as withholding information from them and have put him on parole. That means that he may not consort with criminals and has to be indoors by 11 o'clock every night. One day soon he will happen to talk to a waiter with a police record or get home a few minutes late and will find himself in gaol. That is what we call "leaning on" someone.'

The Director of the Paris Sureté talked of the iron-clad conspiracy of silence among the Dominici family. The Australian delegate complained of the expense of the Petrov case, which has not only left Australia with the burden of keeping Petrov alive but has meant the abstention of Russia from Australian wool sales for over a year. The famous Professor Soedermann, from Sweden, told me of a hitherto unpublicised plot to kill Hitler in 1942, and so on.

The one police chief who has been sadly missed this year is the delegate from Burma. Last year at Rome the assembly was discussing sex crimes and one by one delegates from the major Western powers reeled off their formidable and grisly statistics. Finally the Burmese delegate diffidently climbed to the rostrum. 'I must apologise to the assembly,' he said, 'for I have no statistics on this subject. We are a backward nation and have no sex crimes. But as our civilisation catches up with those of the distinguished delegates who have been speaking I hope we may do better. Next year I will try to bring some good statistics on this matter.' Perhaps this year he was ashamed to come back still empty-handed.

AIRLINE DETECTIVE

The foreword to Airline Detective: The Fight Against International
Air Crime *by Donald Fish was written in June 1961. It refers back to
Fleming's reports from the Istanbul Police Conference of 1955.*

One day in the summer of 1955 I was sitting in the innermost sanctum of
Scotland Yard – the private office of the C.I.D. – admiring, with Sir Ronald
Howe, some forged five pound notes and gossiping about crime in general. It
was a chance, purposeless visit. I had had to do with Ronnie Howe during my
wartime years in Naval Intelligence and the friendship had continued.

Ronnie Howe said that he would be flying to Istanbul in a few days' time
for the annual meeting of Interpol, why didn't I come?

I had imagined that these meetings of Interpol would be top secret affairs
held in remote and heavily guarded police headquarters. In fact it transpired
that they were much like the meetings of other international organisations in
smart hotels with banquets and speeches and open sessions during which the
top policemen of the world read learned papers from flower-banked podi-
ums. Their main object was friendly contact and, if secrets were discussed,
they would be confined to private luncheon parties or hotel bedrooms.

Ronnie Howe said that the only other journalist who ever bothered to
attend was Percy Hoskins of the *Daily Express*, and it crossed my mind that if
he, by far the most brilliant crime reporter in England, thought these meetings worthwhile, so should I.

I was at that time Foreign Manager of the *Sunday Times* and, thanks to the
kind heart of Lord Kemsley, more or less able to write my own ticket so far as
foreign assignments were concerned. So I fixed things up and in due course
flew off in the same plane as Ronnie Howe, Percy Hoskins and a man called
Donald Fish who, it turned out, had something to do with airline security.

It was great fun in Istanbul and by scraping together fragments from official papers and speeches and tying them up with informed gossip, I was able to write two long despatches on 'The Secrets of Interpol' whose success was assisted by the Istanbul riots which took place conveniently over that weekend on which I was able to give a scoop to my paper.

The next year I went again to the conference, this time at Vienna, but my revelations of the year before had put the police chiefs on their guard and, on this occasion, I was only able to produce a pretty thin three-quarters of a column. The learned papers read by the police chiefs had been more rigorously censored than before and were more carefully guarded, and the gossip dried up in my presence.

I skipped the next year's meeting in Lisbon, and that was the end of my acquaintanceship with Interpol.

At the two earlier meetings the British quartet saw a lot of each other and I was interested, and rather annoyed, to note that on no occasion was I able to extract a single grain of news or information from Donald Fish. Ronnie Howe was always generous in providing Percy Hoskins and me with snippets of background, though he was always careful to distinguish between what was secret and what might be published. In fact I think he cannily used me on one occasion to warn the British public about forged travellers' cheques. But as least he 'gave', and he realised that Percy Hoskins and I had somehow to justify our existence at these conferences. Donald Fish couldn't have cared less. No amount of wheedling or badgering would persuade him to yield one word of information about the work of his little air security committee, which got on with its business far from the madding throng of the conference hall. He ate and drank and chatted with us, this tall, rangey man with the poker player's eyes, but he revealed nothing, and both Percy Hoskins and I had to admire him for it, knowing what we had been able to extract from national police chiefs temporarily in their cups, or suffering from that suppressed vanity that affects men who know many secrets for which an audience is always forbidden them.

No, Donald Fish was one of the securest security men I have ever met, and now that he has retired and B.O.A.C. has allowed him to tell some of his stories, the reader can be pretty certain he is getting the real stuff. There is nothing wishy-washy in these seventeen chapters, which are some of the best I have ever read in any language on police work.

Security, except when it becomes counter-espionage, is a dreary subject and I have never envied the security men I have met in my life because so much of their work is of the 'policeman on the beat' variety – testing door handles and window frames, and investigating mysterious noises that are always loose shutters. The reward for the work lies in the occasional scoop, and it is the hallmark of the true security officer that when the scoop comes along his mind is not so dulled by previous routine that he fails to recognise it.

Donald Fish and I had dinner together one evening at Sachers in Vienna at the end of the 1956 Interpol meeting, and he did admit that he had had exciting times with B.O.A.C. in between stretches of drudgery. He was due to retire in two or three years' time and I urged him to think of writing his memoirs, but, like so many expert technicians, he admitted that he couldn't really distinguish between the wood and the trees in his job, and that anyway there was something magical about writing and he couldn't master the art. This or that incident had of course been exciting, but he simply couldn't get it down on paper. I told him not to despair, but just to do his best and then find a professional writer to smooth the corners of his prose and prune out the irrelevancies and the libel.

In the event he followed my advice. B.O.A.C., perhaps as part reward for his services, were indulgent in allowing some of their secrets to be laid bare, and Donald Fish teamed up with John Pearson of the *Sunday Times* to produce a book that reads true and yet is attractively written. A highly successful series in the *Sunday Times* resulted, a promising television series is in the offing, and there is this book.

Many people who have led exciting lives have talked to me, as they will with any author, about 'writing something when they retire'. Donald Fish's book with its solid writing, unobtrusive background and local colour, is technically an example of how a man, himself untalented in story telling, can yet contrive a thoroughly expert distillation of some of the exciting things that may have happened to him.

To say anything more about the book would be to write a review of it. This is not my task, and what I have written so far is merely to explain how I came to be asked to write this introduction. I will now leave Donald Fish and his book with my blessing and, quite out of context, tell two stories about 'security' that have always stuck in my mind.

During the war one of the Assistant Directors of the Naval Intelligence Division in which I was employed, was responsible for security – the physical security of ships and dockyards, the prevention of loose talk, the security of communications and so forth – thoroughly dull work that was often allotted to rather dull individuals. In 1942, Noël Coward had obtained Admiralty permission to use one of H.M. destroyers for the film *In Which We Serve* and he was naturally anxious to discover her name and when she would be available for filming.

Noël Coward, who told me this story, knew the Assistant Director of Naval Intelligence of that date and he frequently rang him up to find out when the ship would be available for filming, but since the whereabouts of H.M. ships was a deadly secret he always received a dusty answer, until one day Coward was delighted to get a call from the Admiralty. The Assistant Director of Naval Intelligence himself was on the telephone, and immensely mysterious.

'I say Noël, you know what they do in India, hunting I mean?'

'What the hell are you talking about?'

'Well, you know people go on safari and they shoot things?'

'So I'm told.'

'Well, now, the thing they shoot will be available at Portsmouth next week.'

At last Noël Coward got the message. 'Tigers!' he called excitedly. 'You mean she's called *The Tiger*?'

'For God's sake be careful, dammit! This is an open line.'

Those who were in the war will have their own stories along these lines, but I think the saga of Mohammed Ali, the green tea merchant, was probably unique in its example of security gone mad.

The political warfare experts, picking up the strings from the end of the 1914/18 war, began dropping leaflets over Germany almost as soon as war was declared, and we all remember how asinine many of those leaflets were. For some idiotic security reason the leaflets were known by the code word of 'Nickel', though why they should have a code word at all nobody could understand. Anyway when the time came for the invasion of Africa, it was decided that a 'Nickel' should be prepared to rally the North African Arabs to the allied cause. Something simple was devised with a crude picture of Winston Churchill on one side and Roosevelt on the other, and some such slogan as 'Victory rests with the Allies'. In a 'Top Secret' folder this project was put into the machinery of the Political Warfare Department, finally reaching, by devious routes and under a watertight cover story, the sole Arabic expert in the Political Warfare Department – a certain Mohammed Ali, a green tea merchant from Casablanca who had rallied to the Free French and had come over to England after the collapse of France.

Mohammed Ali was instructed to translate the English slogan into Arabic characters and the finished product was then printed in its millions and trillions and shipped out to Gibraltar in cases marked 'oranges' or 'beer', and carefully stored in some top secret depot in the Rock in preparation for the great day.

The day came, fighters from the Fleet Air Arm were loaded up with consignments of the vital 'Nickel' and took off again and again all through the day of the landings, sprinkling the whole of Morocco and Algiers with the leaflet.

After the invasion had succeeded, an American intelligence officer who had taken part in the landings came over to Gibraltar and found his way to the leader of the Allied Political Warfare group. He had a handful of the leaflets and he said to the propagandist in charge, 'What the hell's this stuff you've been dropping all over the country?'

Stiffly the political warrior replied, 'Those are leaflets to rally the Arabs.'

'Do you know what they say?' asked the American.

'Yes,' said the propagandist, 'of course I do. They say "Victory rests with the allies"'.

'No, they don't,' said the American. 'They say "Buy Mohammed Ali's Green Tea"'.

Well, those are two stories about 'security' – the Evelyn Waugh model, so to speak. The Donald Fish marque is something very different indeed.

THE GREAT POLICEMAN

A review for the Sunday Times *of* The F.B.I. Story
by Don Whitehead. 1956.

'I heard Jack say he had searched the town to find the kind of kit he wanted, and he had gift-wrapped it and placed it in his mother's luggage as a surprise for her when she reached Alaska.'

It was a dynamite bomb that Jack had gift-wrapped and it blew to kingdom-come Jack's heavily insured mother and forty-three other people in United Airlines Flight No. 629 eleven minutes out of Denver.

When the F.B.I. had pinned the crime on Jack Graham he said to his guard, 'You can send my mail to Cannon City Prison until next month. After that you can send it to Hell.'

The book opens with this nerve-shattering case of November 1955, and the author then proceeds to tell the story of the F.B.I. with similar illustrations from the American crime sheet.

The modern F.B.I. *is* Edgar Hoover. Hoover joined the Bureau, at the age of twenty-two, shortly after the greatest sabotage act of all time, when von Rintelen and Boy-Ed brought off the Black Tom explosion of two million pounds of dynamite stored in America's biggest arsenal in New York Harbor. Hoover was put in charge of enemy alien registration until, at the end of the war, the entire personnel of the bureau was swamped with the round-up of American deserters who, by June 1918, had reached the staggering total of 308,489, or roughly 25 divisions.

Then came the scandals of the Harding administration in which the head of the F.B.I., William Burns, and the notorious detective Gaston B. Means were more or less deeply implicated. President Coolidge's first step in house-cleaning was to appoint Harlan Stone as Attorney General and it was in 1924 that Stone summoned 29-year-old J. Edgar Hoover to his office, scowled at him and appointed him head of the F.B.I., a position that Hoover has held to this day.

How has Hoover, in defiance of all history, remained head of a national secret police force for thirty-three years, surviving almost unchallenged five Presidents and eleven Attornies General?

I met Edgar Hoover in 1940. I was in Washington with my chief, Admiral Godfrey, who was on a mission to coordinate the Naval Intelligence effort before America came into the war. In the confusion of fledgling intelligence organisation, there were two solid men in America – the brilliant Canadian, 'Bill' Stephenson, who represented British Intelligence in North America, and Edgar Hoover. Hoover, a chunky, enigmatic man with slow eyes and a trap of a mouth, received us graciously, listened with close attention (and a witness) to our exposé of certain security problems and expressed himself firmly but politely as being uninterested in our mission.

Hoover had his channels with Bill Stephenson and his commonsense, legal-istic mind told him it would be unwise to open separate channels with us. He was, of course, quite right. Our constitutional link with American Intelligence could only lie with the Office of Naval Intelligence of the navy Department and it was, in fact, with this admirable Department that we forged the rela-tionship that lasted throughout the war.

Hoover's negative response was soft as a cat's paw. With the air of doing us an exceptional favour he had us piloted through the F.B.I. Laboratory and Record Departments and down to the basement shooting range where, at that time, his men had their training in the three basic F.B.I. weapons – pistol, automatic shot gun, and the sub-machine gun. Even now I can hear the shattering roar of the Thompsons as, in the big dark cellar, the instructor demonstrated on the trick targets. Then, with a firm, dry handclasp, we were shown the door.

My impression of the F.B.I. then, and my impression of the occasional agents I have since met, is that discipline and thoroughness, rather than intuitive brilliance, is the backbone of the Bureau and that these solid virtues, together with incorruptibility and absolute loyalty to his superiors, are the reasons for Hoover's long survival. Add to these the absence of greed for pol-itical power and, despite his bachelorhood, a life totally untouched by scandal and you have in Edgar Hoover a Civil Servant whom any Government would welcome as guardian of its secrets. (Not quite all its secrets: Hoover knew nothing of the atomic bomb project until his own undercover agents in Communist cells on the West Coast began picking up gossip about the Manhattan Project!)

In England, we are inclined to think the F.B.I. played a dubious role at the time of the McCarthy purges, but it would be wrong to tar Hoover with that brush. The F.B.I. had to obtain and give evidence, but Hoover resolutely refused to open his files to the McCarthy investigators. Hoover's point of view was that a raw file, containing unconfirmed suspicions that inevitably implicated others and that gave away only the black side of a man with nothing of the white, was a weapon which should never be used against an individual except to build up a case that would subsequently stand in law.

He successfully resisted all McCarthy attempts to gain access to his records on any man, while accepting his duty to provide the Senate Enquiry with the normal security check on its suspects.

No doubt the F.B.I. has its grimy secrets and certainly, as all police forces, it has made mistakes, but the impression I have of the F.B.I., now strongly reinforced by reading *The F.B.I. Story*, is that the Bureau is probably the best-run Department of the American Government. In a country where a serious crime is committed every 13.9 seconds it would be bad news if it wasn't!

As for the book itself, I have nothing but praise for Mr. Whitehead. He has written in admirable prose a first-class documentary which can be read with real excitement by the crime addict, but which will also serve as good contemporary history. It is an excellent book.

SOVIET ESPIONAGE INC.

SOME NOTES FOR A BALANCE SHEET

This article, taken here from the original typescript, was published in
Esquire *in November 1960, with the title 'The Russians make Mistakes too'.*

Soviet Russia has the greatest espionage machine in all history. Mr. Herter
said on June 13th that the Communist countries had 300,000 agents operating throughout the world. I assume he was referring to centrally organised
agents each with a code number, a specific task and some kind of pay roll.
But a powerful ideology such as Communism disposes of a vast unseen
army of sympathisers. These may be more or less secretly convinced Communists 'agin' their national government of the day, or they may be those
hosts of faceless ones with a grudge. Today, as at few other times in history, the world is divided into two great enemy camps and the small mean
man seeking revenge can strike his little blow by looking up the nearest
Soviet Consul or Ambassador in the telephone book and writing him a
letter like this:

> Dear Sir, you may be interested to know that in Workshop No. 25,
> department of hydraulics, Aeronautics Division, of the Magnum
> Combine factory at Blankville, we are working on a light weight fuel
> pump with the following specifications . . .
> Since my pals tell me this is probably designed as part of the fuel
> system of an inter Continental missile I think you should know about it.
> Signed: A Well Wisher

This kind of letter in the hands of the central evaluating machine in Moscow or
Leningrad can be worth diamonds, and it costs not a dime. And the interesting

point about free-lance espionage is that it is 99% one way – from the Western bloc to the Eastern bloc.

The sort of Liberal Socialist society in which we all live in the West does not attract the man with a grudge he wants to work off by way of revenge. But Communism is militant. 'They' will know what to do with a letter like this. 'They' will put it to good use and hit back with it, hurting my country, hurting my factory, hurting my foreman, who said yesterday that I was a useless incompetent.

This is only a tiny side-issue in the great espionage battle between the East and the West – a small bonus the revolutionary always picks up from the camp of order and establishment. Where the Soviets have the really big edge over the West is that, particularly in peacetime, you cannot buy good 'informations' for money alone. People will always risk their lives for an ideology however misbegotten, but a spy who spies only for material gain is a far rarer and less reliable bird than the public imagines. Russia has other advantages. She has almost complete control of her frontiers and of her communication and postal systems. She herself has one of the most difficult languages in the world to learn, while the cultivated Russian is probably the best linguist in the world. Apart from the Communist parties and organisations which democracy allows to flourish in her midst, Russia can call upon several nationalities, Poles, Czechs, Balts, Hungarians, for instance, who can disappear quite easily into the communities of these nations living in the West, whereas in a highly stereotyped country such as Russia, to send a White Russian into that country would be tantamount to murder (one reason why the U2 was not only a better penetrator but virtually the only one to hand).

Having all these cards in her hand, what weaknesses are there in the Russian espionage system? Very few. Probably the greatest is that the Russians, like the German Secret Service in the last war, are biased evaluers of intelligence. Preferring the 'pretty picture', they will too often be given too pretty a picture by agents who are in any case overzealous. (One of the chief dangers I see today is that Russia should allow herself to under-estimate the West by incorrect evaluation inspired, for instance, by the much publicised Nuclear Disarmers in England or by the equally publicised failure of individual American missiles. And, above all, by the constant breast-beating in the West.) The other source of weakness is the intoxicating effect that contact with Western freedoms may have on even the most highly trained Soviet agent who was 100% Communist when he was posted as Assistant Military Attaché to Ottawa, Washington, London or Paris, but whose loyalty to the system gradually disintegrates.

It is in this latter realm that the West has had its greatest victories in the espionage war.

The blackest day for the immense Russian spy organisation was probably September 5th, 1945, when a humble cipher clerk in the Soviet Embassy in Ottawa walked out carrying with him over 100 top secret papers revealing the Soviet network in Canada. It was only a few weeks after the dropping of the first atomic bomb on Hiroshima. Two months earlier in Potsdam President Truman had chatted amiably with Stalin and told him about the bomb. On the surface Russia and the West had never been closer.

Igor Gouzenko's defection came like a thunderclap – to the West, and most probably to the Russians too. At first Canadian officials would not even take him seriously. But the Royal Commission which was eventually set up to investigate his revelations led to the conviction of six Canadian traitors, including a Communist M.P., Fred Rose, who was revealed as one of Russia's key men in Canada.

But more than that – the Gouzenko defection not only alerted the U.S.A., Britain and Canada to the existence of a hitherto largely unsuspected Russian spy organisation; it resulted in a remarkable 'chain reaction' which in the end led to the discovery of much more vital spy-traitors. Among those to whom Gouzenko eventually brought disaster were Dr. Klaus Fuchs, Dr. Allan Nunn May, Harry Gold, David Attenglass and Julius and Ethel Rosenberg.

Today, Gouzenko is a Canadian. No picture or official description of him has ever been circulated. He lives with his wife, Pinea, and two children some-where in one of Canada's vast farmlands. Always within reach are the Canadian Mounted Police. He has a job, and an income of £35 monthly for life from a trust fund set up by a grateful Canadian millionaire. His autobiography which was a best-seller and made into a film, brought him some £50,000.

It was the young British Dr. Allan Nunn May who was the first victim of Gouzenko's revelations. It must have been a bitter blow to the Russian net-work. Born on May 2nd, 1911 at King's Norton, near Birmingham, England, May had a brilliant record at Cambridge. In 1942 he joined the Cavendish

Laboratory there, where many early atomic discoveries were made. In 1943 he was moved to Canada, and in due course saw much top secret atomic experimental work in Chicago and various vital U.S. installations.

Colonel Zabotin, officially the Russian Military Attaché in Ottawa, but actually chief spy in Canada, was instructed by Moscow to contact May, who had never made any secret of his left wing sympathies. Zabotin used a subordinate, Lieutenant Pavel Angelow, to make the contact.

From then on May became 'Alek' in the Russian spy file. For months he handed over all the information on atomic research in the U.S.A and Canada he could find.

Then May was told he was to return to London. Elaborate arrangements were made by the Russians to make renewed contact with him there. He got back just after Gouzenko defected, but he never kept the appointments made for him. Did he fear that the net was closing? We shall never know. Five months after his return he was arrested. At the Old Bailey on May 1st, 1946 he pleaded guilty to giving away secrets to a 'foreign power'. He was sentenced to 10 years' penal servitude. The information he gave the Russians has been valued at £1 million in terms of research costs. In return he received 700 dollars and two bottles of whisky.

This was a blow to the Russian, but at the same time they achieved some kind of gain. The U.S. clamped down for the time being on giving further secrets to their allies.

Klaus Fuchs has been described as the most deadly and baffling spy in all history. He was caught four years after May. Born near Frankfurt in 1911 he went to Kiel University.

As a youth he joined the Young Communist League. After Hitler came to power and the Communists went underground he came to Britain where he was befriended, and studied at Bristol and Edinburgh Universities. As an alien he was interned when war broke out, first in the Isle of Man then in Canada. He was later released and was brought back to England for scientific research. Before long he had already made contact with Russian agents, and handed over information. In December 1943 he went to America, and before long he had a comprehensive picture of U.S. atomic projects. It was a wonderful scoop for the Russians.

The Russians merely took him over in New York when he arrived there from England. His contact man was Harry Gold. Fuchs only knew him as 'Raymond'. They met soon after Fuchs arrived at Columbia University. They recognised each other by signs prearranged by Moscow. Gold carried gloves and a book, Fuchs a tennis ball.

Fuchs gave Gold a flow of major intelligence hidden in newspaper wrappings. Gold passed them on to Yakovlev, Russian Vice Consul in New York, and top spy.

By this time Fuchs was living at Los Alamos. He told Gold, and thus Moscow, when the first trial of the atomic bomb was about to be held. No wonder Stalin did not appear very interested when Truman told him about it at Potsdam. He already knew all about it.

In 1946 he returned to Britain. At first he made no attempt to contact the Russians. But early in 1947 he did so. He had eight meetings with their agents in two years.

Only his illness in 1948 appeared to prevent him having more. By this time the F.B.I. were hot on the trail of the leakages which had become so apparent. All clues pointed to Fuchs. The British were told by the Americans of their suspicions in 1949. But there was still no evidence. There followed two strange interviews with top British security officer William Scardon. The first got nowhere. The second, a few months later in January, 1950, was at Fuchs' own request. He talked. He was arrested. The Lord Chief Justice sentenced him to 14 years. The sentence was the maximum possible. In most other countries it would have been death.

Harry Gold, the middleman between master spy Fuchs and the Russians, was the next to go. He joined the Russian network in the days of the great depression, long before Stalin and the atom bomb. He was trained – an old hand – and by 1943 was regarded as a first class operative. That was why he was chosen to deal with Fuchs.

He did his job with his usual cunning and resourcefulness. When Fuchs was caught and sentenced he was working for the Philadelphia General Hospital. Perhaps he had some uneasy moments. But for 20 years he had got away with it. Why not this time?

But now in his prison cell, Fuchs was still willing to talk. For hours F.B.I. men grilled the master spy in prison. Literally hundreds of pictures of suspects were shown to him in the effort to get him to identify his contact man.

A picture of Gold, now under suspicion as a result of information from a woman, Elizabeth Bentley, who had become disillusioned with the Communist Cause, was shown to Fuchs. He failed to recognise him. In a desperate move the F.B.I. took moving pictures of Gold. They were flown to London. Fuchs recognised him from his walk and mannerisms of posture. It was the end for Gold. He was sentenced to 30 years' imprisonment.

The tangled skein first loosened by Gouzenko was to unravel still further.

Among Gold's contacts had been a David Attenglass. He was a sergeant in the U.S. Army – a machinist technician. His sister, Ethel, had married Julian Rosenberg, a communist. In 1944 Attenglass was sent to Oak Ridge, Tennessee on secret atomic work. The red network went into action. The Rosenbergs were asked to persuade Attenglass to 'co-operate'. Attenglass's wife, Ruth Printz, was co-opted by the Rosenbergs to 'persuade' him. From then on it was easy. Although in a subordinate position, Attenglass was smart enough to glean, either directly or by intelligent deduction, many of the most vital details of the atom bomb.

The war ended. Attenglass started an engineering concern with his brothers and Rosenberg.

He must have forgotten most of his spy work when he read in the papers of Fuchs' arrest. Rosenberg realised the danger. First it would be Gold and then Attenglass. He gave him money to decamp to Mexico but Attenglass stayed. He was arrested, pleaded guilty, and was sentenced to 15 years.

Above all he talked, and that meant the end for the Rosenbergs. Unlike Attenglass, they fought to the end, but were sentenced to death on April 5th, 1951, the first American citizens ever to receive the death sentence in peacetime for spying. Through legal delaying devices and appeals they avoided their fate for another two years. They died in June 1953.

It was the end of the Fuchs spy ring. Who knows when it might have been discovered – if at all – but for Ivor Gouzenko.

The bitter spy war went on. The F.B.I. picked up many useful small fry but its next big catch was Colonel Rudolf Ivanovich Abel of the Russian Counter Intelligence Service in August 1957.

It was a nasty setback for the Russians. The F.B.I. triumphantly described him as 'the highest ranking Soviet national ever arrested in the United States as a spy'.

He slipped into the United States illegally from Canada in 1948 and used short wave radio for direct communication with Moscow. He received concurrent sentences of 30, 10 and 5 years, and fines totalling 3000 dollars.

His code name was 'Mark'. He was given away by Lt. Colonel Reino Häyhänen, a self-confessed Russian spy who fed him with information.

In 1954 the Russians had a serious setback in Europe. A Russian secret police agent and two East German secret police surrendered to the Americans. The Russian was Captain Nikolai Khoklov, of the M.V.D. He said he had been sent from Moscow to West Germany to murder an anti-Communist Russian in Frankfurt named Georgi Okolovich.

The three men carried guns disguised as cigarette cases. They had special silencers, were electrically fired, and for good measure their lead bullets held a deadly poison. The plan was named 'Operation Rhine'.

Not only did Khoklov give a full account of his mission, he gave much useful overall information on the workings of the M.V.D. and details of the murder of Leon Trotsky in Mexico. He said he surrendered to the West because his wife, whom he had left behind in Russia, told him she would have nothing to do with an assassin.

The same year, far away in Australia, the Russians had perhaps the worst setback of all. Vladimir Mikhailovitch Petrov, 45-year-old Third Secretary of the Soviet Embassy in Canberra, asked for political asylum. It was the biggest break since the Gouzenko case – bigger in that Gouzenko was a small time cipher clerk. Petrov was head of the Soviet Secret Police in Australia.

Australia might at first sight seem unpromising ground for spying, but in fact it held many vital secrets.

There was the 1600 mile desert rocket testing range at Woomera, the desert establishment at Salisbury near Adelaide, and the great uranium mines at Rum Jungle and Radium Hill.

Petrov asked for asylum at the end of his three-year term in Australia.

Following the Gouzenko precedent in Canada, Mr. Menzies, the Australian Premier, promptly appointed a Royal Commission to investigate Petrov's revelations.

This time the Russians seemed really worried. As with Gouzenko they claimed that Petrov had embezzled money and should be handed over to them as a 'criminal'. They changed the use of 'brutal violations of the generally accepted norms of international law'. And they broke off diplomatic relations with Australia, hastily recalling their entire Canberra staff.

This time something had gone badly wrong.

One of the first results of Petrov's disclosures was the arrest in New Caledonia, France's most distant colony, of a French woman diplomat, Madame Renée Ollier, who was named as having told Russia about arms shipments to Indo-China.

In the event Petrov's disclosures showed that his spy ring had failed to secure any military or strategic information of vital importance. The great value of his evidence was its detailed description of the complicated set-up of the Soviet spy organisation, its efforts to secure informants, and its methods of keeping contact with Australians who had visited the Soviet Union. It resulted in a useful tightening up of Australian security methods.

The Petrov case had unusual human drama appeal. Mrs. Petrova was a cipher clerk in the Russian Embassy. At first she maintained that her husband had been kidnapped and that she wanted to return to Moscow.

Three Russians, two of them typical strong-arm men, were urgently flown out to Australia to take Mrs. Petrova back to Moscow. There were extraordinary scenes at the Kingsford airport at Sydney. Tightly gripped on either side by her escorts she was more or less dragged into the waiting 'plane, dazed, weeping and bedraggled. A huge crowd tried to prevent her leaving. They declared she called out 'I don't want to go, save me'. They roared and booed and attacked the couriers, who eventually struggled with the weeping woman.

Then, dramatically, Mrs. Petrova stayed after all. She was taken off the 'plane at Darwin, northernmost airfield of Australia, having told the pilot that she wanted to stay.

The pistol-carrying strong-arm men, at first aggressive, were disarmed, and sent on their way discomforted.

Now, like the Gouzenkos in Canada, the Petrovs are Australian citizens living under another name.

It was five years before Moscow recovered from this rebuff and resumed diplomatic relations with Australia.

The man who perhaps duped the Russians more successfully than anyone else is Russian born film producer Boris Morros.

For twelve years he posed as a Soviet spy, and was probably America's most successful secret agent. He made some of the Laurel and Hardy films and won fame with his *Carnegie Hall*. He was born in St. Petersburg and first came to the U.S. in 1922 as producer of the Chauve Souris company. He has said that in his counter-spying activities he made 68 trips to Europe, including Moscow and Berlin.

He was closely connected with the arrest in 1957 of Jack Soble, his wife Myra Penskaya Soble and Jacob Albam in New York on charges of handing over information to the Russians.

In 1959 Morros also named Mrs. Alfred Stern, formerly Miss Martha Dodd, daughter of Professor William E. Dodd, a pre-war U.S. Ambassador to Germany, as a Soviet spy. Before they could be arrested they escaped to Mexico, from where they are believed to have made their way to Russia.

Morros has stated that the Russians told him they had 55 business firms in the U.S. as spy covers. They wanted him to expand his Boris Morros Music Company in Los Angeles into another cover firm and also to start a television firm.

Morros first became entangled with the Soviet spy web in 1947 when he accepted an offer by a Russian to bring his father from the Soviet Union to join him in America. But he lost no time in informing the F.B.I. of his entanglement, and from then on played his perilous double game for twelve years.

But what does all this amount to? Mr. Herter has proudly announced that in recent years some 360 persons in eleven free countries have been convicted of espionage for the Soviet Union. 241 were in West Germany, 65 in Finland, 15 in Norway, 13 in U.S.A., 11 in Sweden, 7 in Denmark, 6 in Britain, 2 each in Turkey and Holland, 1 each in France and Japan.

Numerically, it should be noted, this haul, mostly from West Germany, amounts to only about 1% of the Soviet espionage army at home and abroad. Statistics are meaningless in this respect, for Gouzenko was worth a whole division of miscellaneous spies. To get more Gouzenkos, to win the espionage battle, it is no good offering material things. We in the West must build up an ideology, a democratic image, lacking many of its present weaknesses and flaws, and we must shape ourselves incontrovertibly into the winning side. When these two things have been achieved, we shall get all the 'informations' we want, but by that time, of course, we shall no longer want them, nor will the Soviets, because by that time the cold war will have been won, and the espionage war with it. In the meantime, in my book, we are almost certainly losing the latter.

GARY POWERS AND THE BIG LIE

From the Sunday Times, *March 1962.*

I have strong views about the Powers Case. It will go down to history, I think, as one of the classical espionage cases, classical in the sense of its majestic mishandling. I have nothing against Powers himself. He wasn't a spy; he was just an extremely good pilot employed to operate an espionage device, one of the finest ever invented, a high-altitude photographical reconnaissance aircraft called the U2.

In connection with this aircraft, which in fact was nothing but a very good 'Spy in the Sky', I have the impression that Americans can lie more safely in their beds today, and Englishmen, too, because of the intelligence brought back by planes of the U2 class piloted by young daredevils such as Powers. These planes, I believe, brought back target information whose possession by America, more voluminous and more accurate than could have been obtained by a million ground spies – if one could have got them in there and out again, which one couldn't – has made it as possible as any other factor for America to negotiate from strength with Russia – to be able to tell Russia, or perhaps just to leak it discreetly, that in the case of a mass blast-off of I.C.B.M.s by Russia the sources of the attack and other military objectives in the U.S.S.R. could be devastated within minutes, bringing her, however much damage she might do to America and England, militarily to her knees.

So let us take off our hats to the Spy in the Sky and move on to what went wrong in the case of Powers.

Everyone knows that a spy gets paid danger-money for doing a very dangerous job. He knows that if he is caught he is going to get tortured in his most sensitive parts – and, believe me, it is those things the professional spy thinks of far more than of death itself – and then he is going to be killed. It has been so ever since the man from the opposition crept under the tent flap in the desert and listened to the plans of the enemy tribal chiefs and then, with luck, ran all night with the news to where the camp fires of his own side were burning away in the hills. It has gone on like that through all history, and it is one of the most exciting of all human adventure stories – the single man, in the darkness, facing death alone for the sake of the great mass of his own countrymen.

But the essence of the game – for, in a way, it is a tremendous game – is that, if the spy is caught, and whatever truth is tortured out of him, he is totally disavowed by his own side. Spying is a dirty business: why, I have never quite understood. But the convention has always been maintained. If you are in uniform, you are okay. If you're in civilian clothes you're a pariah. Smith? Never heard of him, and Bang! you're dead.

Now every country in the world employs spies and always has done. Nowadays the big corporations employ them also, to spy on the other fellows' plans and designs – but that is another story. And it is total hypocrisy for any country to adopt a holier-than-thou attitude, to get on a high horse if they catch one of the other fellow's spies. They're damned glad they caught him, and the chief of the Red secret service chuckles at the discomfiture of the chief of the Purple secret service, and that's that.

But in the Powers case things went badly wrong. Powers was in fact a skilled pilot and not a spy – though he probably got plenty of security briefing and knew what he was in for, as he confessed straight away to the Russians, in accepting the huge sums of danger money. What went badly wrong was the handling of the case by the American Government. (And here let me say that I am discussing this espionage case purely as a writer of spy thrillers. Let's keep politics out of it. We in England made almighty fools of ourselves sending a middle-aged romantic called Crabb out on a ten-mile underwater swim in Portland Bay to examine a Russian cruiser of the Sverdlov class. The only good thing that came out of that mess was that we kept our mouths shut and stuck to our story that we'd hardly ever heard of a man called Crabb.)

What happened in the Powers case? The Russians broke the story first, though presumably the C.I.A. knew, or guessed, that something bad had happened to Powers (I am told, by the way, that two or perhaps three other U2 planes had been lost before this one, though in these cases the pilot had either been killed or taken his death pill). The next move was with America, and now was the time for the Big Lie.

This is how I, or rather M., the fictional head of the secret service in my James Bond stories, would have handled it. He would have said, through our Foreign Office, as follows: 'Thank you very much indeed. One of our experimental aircraft is indeed missing from our Turkish base and your description of the pilot fits in with a man who escaped yesterday from detention at that base. This man Powers is a most unreliable person who has a girl friend in Paris (to explain the foreign currency Powers carried) and he hijacked our plane with the object, presumably, of flying to her. You are quite correct to hold him in detention, and he must clearly suffer all the rigours of Soviet law in the circumstances. Please return our plane and equipment in due course. Sorry you've been troubled. P.S.: Powers suffers from hallucinations and delusions of grandeur. Pay no attention to them.'

Or something like that – bland, courteous, firm, but throwing Powers cold-bloodedly to the dogs. After all, it was against a contingency like that that he had been paid several thousand dollars a month. That was danger money. He was expendable. Expend him!

Instead, what happened? Endless havering by the State Department, lies, half-truths and finally admissions from on high that led at least in part to the total collapse of the Summit meeting in Paris. If the Big Lie had been spoken, and stuck to, it would have been in the true traditions of espionage. The democratisation of espionage has muddied the ancient stream that dates back to the man crawling under the tent flap to spy on the sheikhs. Just look at the trouble it caused!

And, just by the way, I don't for a moment believe that Powers was shot down at 68,000 feet by Russian rockets. I believe it was sabotage at the Turkish base – delayed action bombs in the tail section. Turkey is a bit too close to Bulgaria for comfort. And the Bulgars are the best bomb technicians in the world.

Finally, as an Englishman, I sincerely hope that a U3 is already flying and that a U4 is on the drawing-board. But may they be backed by the Big Lie as well as by young chauffeurs like Powers. This mess wasn't Powers' fault, or his plane's – least of all that of Allen Dulles. It was the fault of the men who think that espionage is a dirty word. It isn't. It has got to be done well, that's all – from the Powers of this world, all the way up to the President and the Prime Ministers.

ON WRITING

FOREIGN NEWS

Ian Fleming's contribution to the Kemsley Manual of Journalism *published in 1950. He was foreign manager for the Kemsley Newspapers, and as such responsible for foreign correspondents, from 1945–1959.*

Foreign news is no more or less important than any other category of news, but it is more difficult and expensive to obtain, and our insularity makes the digestion of foreign news more of an effort both for the editorial machine and for the public.

These factors make it necessary for foreign news to be obtained and presented by specialists, and they also postulate that the newspaper publisher and his editorial staff should find it desirable to present foreign and Commonwealth news to the public very often at the expense of more 'popular' and more easily digestible material. When it is realised that the Foreign Services of the responsible newspapers and newspaper groups cost in each case considerably more than 100,000 pounds a year, it will be appreciated at what a cost newspaper publishers are prepared to fulfil this duty to their publics.

It is perfectly true that the great news agencies, and in particular Reuters, are capable of providing any paper with an excellent and comprehensive service of foreign news, but agency services are not exclusive and by the nature of things they lack personality. Thus, since individuality is the life-blood of newspapers, proprietors of responsible papers throughout the world are just as insistent on exclusive sources for their foreign news as they are for the other contents of their newspapers.

The Kemsley Imperial and Foreign Service (known for short and in its cable address as 'Mercury') was founded in the autumn of 1945 on the fine team of war correspondents which served the *Sunday Times* and other papers of the Kemsley group throughout the war, and it has developed and expanded in accordance with the combined judgements of our editors.

In London there are two broad categories of Foreign Service – that of the more serious newspapers whose correspondents are permanently resident in the major cities throughout the world, and that of the more 'popular' newspapers, which find their public more interested in the roving star reporter who treats the world as his oyster.

The latter system is attractive. The clear eye and perspective of the special correspondent from London can translate the foreign scene in sharper, simpler colours than the man-on-the-spot who by long residence and experience has become part of that scene. The man from headquarters also has a fresher sense of English news values. His editor will have briefed him personally. If the story is political or economic, he will have informed himself of the Whitehall background.

But the danger of the system is that while he may perhaps produce better journalism he will certainly miss many grains of truth. His emphasis will generally seem misplaced to an expert and sometimes his hurried attempts to 'mug up' on a situation will result in a travesty, undetected perhaps by the British public, but which will do harm to the reputation of his paper. As for the local 'string' or part-time correspondent, at best he will have had his brains sucked dry, his thunder stolen and his chances of handsome space rates dashed to the ground. At worst, valuable private contacts will have been 'blown', he will have plenty of painful explaining to do at the Ministry of Information and the British Embassy, and his local prestige may have suffered irreparably.

Those are the attractions and the disadvantages of the roving correspondent. The Times quietly makes the same differentiation in a recent advertisement for its foreign coverage:

The discoveries of the travelling correspondents who set a girdle round the earth by a world-hop from capital to capital have their own undoubted value. Foreign news, different in kind, more balanced in perspective and more cumulative in effect, is provided by the team of staff correspondents of The Times posted in almost every important world centre.

In a perfect world the foreign editor's crystal-ball would allow him to reinforce this or that centre before the news breaks. As it is, it will be generally found that one must accept being caught unawares and that hasty dashes by staff men from home are too expensive and generally too late. Moreover, having expensively got your ace reporter to the spot, you are apt to run his copy too long in order to justify the expense.

Accordingly, all 'Mercury' correspondents are static, with the exception of a senior representative in Paris who is well placed and admirably qualified for sudden sorties across neighbouring frontiers.

The diagram [not reproduced here] shows the dispositions of our Foreign Service as at the end of 1949. From this it will be seen that considerable strength lies in the Commonwealth, that we are at the moment weak behind the Iron Curtain (Warsaw and Prague appointments are pending. Countless applications for visas for Moscow have been refused or ignored), and that we are comparatively weak in South America. This important territory is the bane of all foreign editors. It is vastly expensive (a staff correspondent would cost some 4000 pounds per annum in any South American capital) and it is singularly unproductive of what is currently known as 'news'.

At this point some comments are offered on 'What is Foreign News'.

This is no place to discuss the ethics of popular journalism or the desirability of plain or coloured wrappers for the news, but there is no doubt that the allergy of our island people to what happens 'abroad' requires that foreign news shall be presented with particular skill. It is useless, for instance, to insist that the tired Sheffield steel-worker should understand all about O.E.E.C., unless the desire to know about it is first implanted in his breast. This can best be done by relating O.E.E.C. to his family's rations and his own output of steel – and that is popularisation, and very often oversimplification of the news.

I am personally not an enemy of simplification, and if I ever was I have been thoroughly converted by Mr. George Schwartz's brilliant simplification of economic problems in the *Sunday Times* every week. To simplify without distortion is a very great art and one at which, in particular, foreign correspondents need to be adept. Critical though one may be of American journalism, and of the verbosity and turgidity of many American correspondents in particular, it will probably be admitted that English journalism has much to learn from the contents of the American magazine *Time*.

But simplification will always seem naive and often misleading to the expert, and it is in fact this art of the good journalist which gives rise to the hackneyed generality: 'When I read in the papers anything I know about, they always get it wrong'.

Traditionally, as I have suggested above, foreign news is considered to be rather 'difficult'. The Englishman's knowledge of geography has always been hazy and he dislikes having to remember the difference between Bucharest and Budapest. He is not interested in even the simplest political facts about those countries which are not at war with him. But apart from its normal duties, 'Mercury' is at pains to obtain foreign news which is not necessarily political or economic, and to present a more human picture of 'abroad' to the readers of the newspapers which it serves.

For guidance in this and other matters, such as deadlines, cable instructions and other administrative affairs, all 'Mercury' correspondents are provided with a small reference book. In addition, all staff correspondents receive a letter from the Foreign Department once a fortnight, and string correspondents once a month. They also are sent a detailed weekly cable and feature report which gives general comments on the service. Cuttings of their own stories, and occasionally of opposition despatches for comparison, reach them weekly.

Occasionally all correspondents receive a memorandum on some aspect of their work, and it may be of interest to reprint here the gist of the latest of these memoranda (issued in September, 1949). This was prepared at my request by my deputy, Mr. Iain Lang, who is also Foreign Editor of the *Sunday Times*, and it deals with the type of foreign news which editors generally would like to receive.

In the 'Mercury' Correspondent's Reference Book, paragraph 17 lays down that 'in the case of the *Sunday Times* the paramount requirement is thoroughly informed straight reporting on major developments in political, economic and cultural affairs'. This directive (which I drafted) may possibly be criticised as an example of the 'pompous, lifeless phrasing' deprecated in paragraph 18 (which I also drafted). The present memorandum is an attempt to clear up any misunderstanding which it may have caused.

With a few exceptions (and here it is assumed that each correspondent will give himself the benefit of the doubt), our Foreign Service is apt to be dull. It does provide a sound and reasonably comprehensive survey of political events and tendencies, and of economic news. So far, so good. But too seldom does the service recognise that there are any interests in life apart from politics or economics, or suggest that the writers are warm-blooded mammals sharing a varied and exciting existence with other human beings.

The reference to 'cultural affairs' may seem forbidding. In his latest book T. S. Eliot describes 'culture' as including such phenomena as 'Derby Day, Henley Regatta, a Cup Final, pin tables, boiled cabbage cut in sections, Wensleydale cheese . . .' If so pontifical an observer can take so wide a view, there is no need for a newspaper correspondent to be less catholic.

Not only is most of our foreign service restricted in subject, it tends (again with exceptions) to be dull in treatment. Correspondents have read the request for 'straight reporting' as a directive to write despatches in the dim, depersonalised prose of a Blue Book or a corporation by-law. We do not want the correspondent's view of the facts to be coloured by prejudice, but we do hope for a little colour and sparkle in presenting those facts.

Most correspondents naturally wish to see themselves on the Leader Page of our newspapers. They send 1000-word features written in a form which they imagine to be suitable for that page, and not adaptable for use on a news page. This leads to disappointment. The Leader Page is carefully planned in advance, and is not a target for unsolicited contributions. If we want foreign pieces for the Leader Page, we will ask for them.

But we do want concise topical messages which will entertain readers as well as instruct them. These readers are not all middle-aged, male political specialists; they include young men *and women* interested in intelligent reporting of the wide range of interests and activities which make up civilized life.

Our editors want *news* of these interests and activities – news, as opposed to essays or critical studies, however erudite or graceful. For example, if Picasso were to turn his attention from pottery to fretwork, if Rossellini were to be converted to the 'ten-minute frame' technique, if the Broadway theatre were to break out in a rash of Gilbert and Sullivan revivals, if a research team in a Buenos Aires clinic develops an effective treatment for the common cold, if an important discovery of neolithic cave painting is made in Tanganyika, we feel that our readers should be the first in this country to know of these developments.

To sum up: please approach our papers less solemnly (there is a distinction between seriousness and solemnity), please extend your range of subject, please forget the Leader Page, please be brisk and brief, and please use your ingenuity to make all your messages read as *news*.

So much for the type of foreign news which 'Mercury' *endeavours* to obtain and purvey to all our editors. It seems clear that the public, or at any rate the public which reads the newspapers of the Kemsley Group, are aware that the world is shrinking and are increasingly interested in foreign and Commonwealth news, and some proof of this can be found in the steady increase in the total 'Mercury' wordage published in our papers. In 1946 the total wordage published was about 2,500,000. Now, four years later, it is just under 4,000,000, and this is apart from the vast agency coverage which is carried by the Group every day.

What sort of people are the ninety-odd correspondents of 'Mercury'? Here is their composite outline: ninety-eight per cent are of British nationality by birth; sixty-three per cent have had a university education. Their average age is thirty-eight. Seven out of the eighty-eight are women (and very good too). Speaking statistically, each correspondent knows 3.01 foreign languages. To 'Mercury', London, each of these skeleton shapes has a vivid personality apart from his journalistic virtues and vices.

As far as possible, staff correspondents are drawn from candidates within the Group, and thirty-three per cent at the end of 1949 were associated with Kemsley Newspapers before they were recruited to 'Mercury'. Candidates both from within Kemsley Newspapers and from outside are not wanting to fill even the most modest positions abroad, but, alas, some journalistic experience plus wartime service overseas do not make a foreign correspondent, and the ideal is, of course, a rarity.

The following are the ingredients for this ideal foreign correspondent: he must be a credit to his country and his newspaper abroad; he should be either a bachelor or a solidly married man who is happy to have his children brought up abroad; his personality must be such that our Ambassador will be pleased to see him when occasion demands. He must know something of protocol and yet enjoy having a drink with the meanest spy or the most wastrelly spiv. He must be completely at home in one foreign language and have another one to fall back on. He must be grounded in the history and culture of the territory in which he is serving; he must be intellectually inquisitive and have some knowledge of most sports. He must be able to keep a secret; he must be physically strong and not addicted to drink. He must have pride in his work and in the papers he serves, and finally he must be a good reporter with a wide vocabulary, fast with his typewriter, with a knowledge of shorthand and able to drive a car.

This is a composite picture of an *ideal* foreign correspondent, but many of these attributes are essential to the profession and, unfortunately, too few candidates possess that basic quota.

Some twenty of our men have the status of staff correspondent, many are on a small retainer – a hundred or two hundred pounds a year – and earn space rates which in lively centres average 30 pounds a month or more, while others are on space rates alone if the centre is an inactive one.

Thus it will be seen that a 'string' correspondent cannot live by 'Mercury' alone. He is usually a free-lance who has emigrated more or less permanently abroad, or else a senior member of the staff of a local newspaper, or possibly a business-man. I have no objection to the string correspondents of 'Mercury' working for any publication which is not in direct competition with ourselves, with the sole proviso that their first allegiance should be to 'Mercury' in the unlikely event of conflicting service requirements reaching them from ourselves and some other authority at the same time.

The Foreign Department in Kemsley House which directs these correspondents contains small sections concerned with administration and travel, foreign features, the Commonwealth, diplomatic news, syndication and research. The latter covers such matters as the purchase of foreign serial rights and intelligence on forthcoming books and feature articles in foreign countries. In addition, there is, of course, the foreign news-room and cable staff with the tasks of editing and onward despatch of incoming cables, producing the daily cable report which contains a critical summing-up of each day's service, and other semi-editorial duties.

Cables and airmailed material come in throughout the day, as does the foreign telephoned news which is handled by the telephone reporters at

Kemsley House. According to the time of day (we have a host of deadlines – only five quiet hours in the twenty-four), this raw material is translated out of cablese and passed to the news desks of the *Daily Graphic* and of the Kemsley Group papers throughout the week, and on Saturdays to the news desks of the *Sunday Chronicle*, the *Sunday Empire News*, the *Sunday Graphic* and the *Sunday Times*, and also to the Kemsley Group desk for transmission to our northern Sunday papers, the *Sunday Mail* in Glasgow and the *Sunday Sun* in Newcastle. The news desk of the Kemsley Group, after a preliminary subbing, puts the material on the teleprinter network which serves Kemsley Newspapers throughout England, Scotland and Wales. In the news-rooms of each paper, it is then dealt with according to each individual editor's decision.

Airmailed or cabled foreign feature material for the provincial papers is sent to individual editors through their London editor at Kemsley House, or direct to the editor if his paper is printed in London. The majority of these foreign and Commonwealth features are ordered from 'Mercury' by the individual papers with a lively awareness of forthcoming foreign topics.

Two or three times a week a background dispatch, prepared in the Foreign Department by the diplomatic correspondent or the Commonwealth representative, is put on the wire. This service, started at the request of our editors, is designed to give readers a brief interpretation of some complicated foreign issue, or to supply a preview of forthcoming foreign occasions, such as an international conference.

Throughout the day a steady flow of service messages controls and directs the stream of incoming despatches. To save those pennies which add up to hundreds of pounds a year (communication costs claim some thirty per cent of the upkeep of a foreign service), cablese is freely and ingeniously used and every device allowed by the cable companies is employed to save words.

Broadly speaking, the cable companies allow portmanteauisms so long as they are not contrary to the general usage of the English language. Thus, OFF-START, ONPRESS, CRITICALLER, INTERESTINGEST, CANT, WONT, TWAS, WEVE, are allowed, while monstrosities such as RATHERN (for 'rather than'), SMORNING where s stands for 'this', TOOM (for 'to whom'), SLATES (for 'as late as'), while not prohibited, will be counted as two or more words.

World-wide syndication of material from all our papers is an important sideline which, since it was initiated some four years ago, has contributed sensibly to reducing the overheads of the Foreign Service. There are now approximately 600 newspapers in twenty-five countries throughout the world carrying one or another of the 'Mercury' Syndication Services.

From what I have said, it can be seen that foreign and Commonwealth news presents its own particular problems to any newspaper organisation. It only remains to commend 'Mercury's' motto to all who aspire to this exciting branch of journalism – 'GET IT FIRST – BUT FIRST GET IT RIGHT'.

MUDSCAPE WITH FIGURES

An article on The Riddle of the Sands *by Erskine Childers*
published in The Spectator *on 5th August 1955*
following a reissue of the book by Rupert Hart-Davis.

Some people are frightened by silence and some by noise. To some people the anonymous bulge at the hip is more frightening than the gun in the hand, and all one can say is that different people thrill to different stimuli, and that those who like *The Turn of the Screw* may not be worried by, for instance, *The Cat and the Canary*.

Only the greatest authors make the pulses of all of us beat faster, and they do this by marrying the atmosphere of suspense into horrible acts. Poe, Stevenson and M.R. James used to frighten me most, and now Maugham, Ambler, Simenon, Chandler and Graham Greene can still raise the fur on my back when they want to. Their heroes are credible and their villains terrify with a real 'blackness'. Their situations are fraught with doom, and the threat of doom, and, above all, they have pace. When one chapter is done, we reach out for the next. Each chapter is a wave to be jumped as we race with exhilaration behind the hero like a water-skier behind a fast motor boat.

Too many writers in this genre (and I think Erskine Childers, on whose *The Riddle of the Sands* these remarks are hinged, was one of them) forget that, although this may sound a contradiction in terms, speed is essential to a novel of suspense, and that while detail is important to create an atmosphere of reality, it can be laid on so thick as to become a Sargasso Sea in which the motor-boat bogs down and the skier founders.

The reader is quite happy to share the pillow-fantasies of the author so long as he is provided with sufficient landmarks to help him relate the author's world more or less to his own, and a straining after verisimilitude with maps and diagrams should be avoided except in detective stories aimed at the off-beta mind.

Even more wearying are 'recaps', and those leaden passages where the hero reviews what he has achieved or ploddingly surveys what remains to be done. These exasperate the reader who, if there is to be any rumination, is quite happy to do it himself. When the author drags his feet with this space-filling device he is sacrificing momentum which it will take him much brisk writing to recapture.

These reflections, stale news though they may be to the mainliner in thrillers, come to me after re-reading *The Riddle of the Sands* after an absence of very many years, and they force me to the conclusion that doom-laden silence and long drawn-out suspense are not enough to confirm the tradition that Erskine Childers, romantic and remarkable man that he must have been, is also one of the father-figures of the thriller.

The opening of the story – the factual documentation in the preface and the splendid Lady Windermere's Fan atmosphere of the chapters – is superb.

At once you are ensconced in bachelor chambers off St. James's at the beginning of the century. All the trappings of the Age of Certainty gather around you as you read. Although the author does not say so, a coal fire seems to roar in the brass grate; there is a glass of whisky beside your chair and, remembering Mr. Cecil Beaton's Edwardian decors, you notice that the soda-water syphon beside it is of blue glass. The smoke from your cheroot curls up towards the ceiling and your button-boots are carefully crossed at the ankles on the red leather-topped fender so as not to disturb the crease of those sponge-bag trousers. On a mahogany bookrest above your lap *The Riddle of the Sands* is held open by a well-manicured finger.

Shall you go with Carruthers to Cowes or accompany him to the grouse-moor? It is fag-end of the London season of 1903. You are bored, and it is all Mayfair to a hock-and-seltzer that the fates have got you in their sights and that you are going to start to pay for your fat sins just over the page.

Thus, in the dressing-room, so to speak, you and Carruthers are all ready to start the hurdle race. You are still ready when you get into the small boat in a God-forsaken corner of the East German coast, and you are even more hungry for the starter's gun when you set sail to meet the villains. Then, to my mind, for the next 95,000 words there is anticlimax.

This is a book of great renown; and it is not from a desire to destroy idols or a tendency to denigration that this review – now that, after the statutory fifty years, *The Riddle of the Sands* has entered the public domain – is becoming almost too much of an autopsy. But those villains! With the best will in the world I could not feel that the lives of the heroes (and therefore of my own) were in the least way endangered by them.

Dollmann, villain No.1, is a 'traitor' from the Royal Navy, whose presence among the clucking channels and glistening mudbanks of the Frisian Islands is never satisfactorily explained. His job was 'spying at Chatham, the blackguard', and the German High Command, even in 1903 when the book was first published, was crazy to employ him on what amounts to operational research. He never does anything villainous. Before the story opens, he foxes hero No.1 into running himself on a mudbank, but at the end, when any good villain with his back to the wall would show his teeth, he collapses like a pricked balloon and finally disappears lamely overboard just after 'we came to the bar of the Schild and had to turn south off that twisty bit of beating between Rottum and Bosch Fat'. His harshest words are, 'You pig-headed young marplots!' and his 'blackness' is further betrayed by the beauty and purity of his daughter, with whom hero No.1 falls in love. (It is always a bad idea for the hero to fall in love with the villain's daughter. We are left wondering what sort of children they will have.)

Von Bruning, villain No.2, is frankly a hero to the author, and is presented as such; and No.3, Boehme, though at first he exudes a delicious scent of Peter Lorre, forfeits respect by running away across the mud and leaving one of his gumboots in the hands of hero No.2.

The plot is that the heroes want to discover what the villains are up to, and, in a small, flat-bottomed boat, they wander amongst the Frisian Islands (and two maps, two charts and a set of tide-tables won't convince me that they don't wander aimlessly) trying to find out.

This kind of plot makes an excellent framework for that classic 'hurdle race' thriller formula, in which the hero (despite his Fleet-Foot Shoes with Tru-Temper Spikes and Kumfi-Krutch Athletic Supporter) comes a series of ghastly croppers before he breasts the tape.

Unfortunately, in *The Riddle of the Sands* there are no hurdles and only two homely mishaps (both of the heroes' own devising) – a second grounding on a mudbank, from which the heroes refloat on the rising tide, and the loss of the anchor chain, which they salvage without difficulty.

The end of the 100,000-word quest through the low-lying October mists is a hasty, rather muddled scramble which leaves two villains, two heroes and the heroine more or less in the air, and the small boat sailing off to England with the answer to the riddle. Before 1914 this prize must have provided a satisfactory fall of the curtain, but since then two German wars have clanged about our heads and today our applause is rather patronising.

The reason why *The Riddle of the Sands* will always be read is due alone to its beautifully sustained atmosphere. This adds poetry, and the real mystery of wide, fog-girt silence and the lost-child crying of seagulls, to a finely written log-book of a small-boat holiday upon which the author has grafted a handful of 'extras' and two 'messages' – the threat of Germany and the need for England to 'be prepared'.

To my mind it is now republished exactly where it belongs – in the Mariners Library. Here, a thriller by atmosphere alone, it stands alongside twenty-eight thrillers of the other school – thrillers where the action on the stage thrills, and the threatening sea-noises are left to the orchestra pit.

BANG BANG, KISS KISS

HOW I CAME TO WRITE *CASINO ROYALE*

Ian Fleming often gave accounts of how he came to write
Casino Royale. This one was written in 1956.

I really cannot remember exactly why I started to write thrillers. I was on my holiday in Jamaica in January 1951 – I built a house there after the war and I go there every year – and I think my mental hands were empty. I had finished organising a Foreign Service for Kemsley Newspapers and that tide of my life was free-wheeling. My daily occupation in Jamaica is spearfishing and underwater exploring, but after five years of it I didn't want to kill any more fish except barracudas and the rare monster fish and I knew my own underwater terrain like the back of my hand. Above all, after being a bachelor for 44 years, I was on the edge of marrying and the prospect was so horrifying that I was in urgent need of some activity to take my mind off it. So, as I say, my mental hands were empty and although I am as lazy as most Englishmen are, I have a Puritanical dislike of idleness and a natural love of action. So I decided to write a book.

The book had to be a thriller because that was all I had time for in my two months' holiday and I knew there would be no room in my London life for writing books. The atmosphere of casinos and gambling fascinates me and I know enough about spies to write about them. I am also interested in things, in gadgetry of all kinds, and it occurred to me that an accurate and factual framework would help the reader to swallow the wildest improbabilities of the plot.

I sat down at my typewriter, and writing about 2000 words in three hours every morning, *Casino Royale* dutifully wrote itself. I rewrote nothing and made no corrections until my book was finished. If I had looked back at what

I had written the day before I might have despaired at the mistakes in grammar and style, the repetitions and the crudities. And I obstinately closed my mind to self-mockery and 'what will my friends say?' I savagely hammered on until the proud day when the last page was done. The last line 'The bitch is dead now' was just what I felt. I had killed the job.

But then I started to read it and I was appalled. How could I have written this bilge? What a fool the hero is. The heroine is the purest cardboard. The villains out of pantomime. The torture scene is disgusting. And the writing! Six 'formidables' on one page. Sentences of screaming banality. I groaned and started correcting.

When I got back to London, I did nothing with the manuscript. I was too ashamed of it. No publisher would want it and if they did I would not have the face to see it in print. Even under a pseudonym, someone would leak the ghastly fact that it was I who had written this adolescent tripe. There would be one of those sly paragraphs in the Londoner's Daily. Shame! Disgrace! Disaster! Resign from my clubs. Divorce. Leave the country.

Then one day I had lunch at the Ivy with an old friend and literary idol of mine, William Plomer of Jonathan Cape, and I asked him how you get cigarette smoke out of a woman once you have got it in. 'All right,' I said, 'This woman inhales, takes a deep lung full of smoke, draws deeply on her cigarette – anything you like. That's easy. But how do you get it out of her again? Exhales is a lifeless word. "Puffs it out" is silly. What can you make her do?'

William looked at me sharply. 'You've written a book,' he said accusingly.

I laughed. I was pleased that he had guessed, but embarrassed. 'It's not really a book,' I said, 'only a *Boys Own Paper* story. But the point is,' I hurried on, 'I got my heroine full of smoke half way through and she's still got it in her. How can I get it out?'

I needed no more pressuring from William. He was a friend and would tell me the horrible truth about the book without condemning me or being scornful or giving away my secret. I sent him the manuscript. He forced Cape to publish it. The reviewers, from the *Times Literary Supplement* down, were almost staggeringly favourable. People were exuberant, excited, amused. I wrote 'Author' instead of journalist in a new passport.

And so it went on. I took Michael Arlen's advice: 'write your second book before you see the reviews of your first. *Casino Royale* is good but the reviewers may damn it and take the heart out of you.' In 1953, in Jamaica, I wrote *Live and Let Die*, in 1954 *Moonraker*, and in 1955, *Diamonds are Forever*, which Cape is publishing just before Easter. When I sent the manuscript of this to William Plomer I said, 'I've put everything into this except the kitchen sink. Can you think of a plot about a kitchen sink for the next one? Otherwise I am lost.' But this time William couldn't help me.

And now I am off to Jamaica again with a spare typewriter ribbon and a load of absolutely blank foolscap through which James Bond must somehow shoot his way during the next eight weeks.

THE HEART OF THE MATA

A review of The Spy's Bedside Book, *an anthology of spy
stories to which Ian Fleming was also a contributor.
It was edited by Graham Greene and Hugh Greene in 1958.*

I cannot understand why the great spy novel has never been written. The
true spy is a fascinating figure – a lonely, nervous, romantic controlled by an
organisation which is hobbled by security, lack of funds, and official scepticism. Tragedy – the tragedy of the futile – is inherent as much as in his success
as in his failures. If, by some brilliant stroke of luck or craft, he discovers a
vital truth, even if it is believed by his Service, it will almost certainly be dis-
believed by his Government, *because* it is a Secret Service report. For Secret
Services are rarely trusted by War Ministries.

I remember the early reports of the V.1s reaching the Admiralty and subsequently being debated by the Joint Intelligence Committee of the Chiefs
of Staff. These reports, from Vienna where many of the components were
being manufactured, from the environs of Peenemunde, and from workers
in the Todt Organisation who were constructing the launching sites on the
Channel coasts, were obtained by Secret Service agents at great risk. How
many lonely men and women ran the gauntlet of how many dangers to get
this vital intelligence through the maze of couriers and cut-outs to the secret
wireless transmitter that, under the ears of the enemy D/F vans, transmitted
it to London?

For weeks, even months, scepticism greeted these priceless messages.
Finally the sheer weight of them demanded a check by the Photographic
Reconnaissance Unit. The results confirmed the Secret Service reports and
the bombing of the V.1 sites and factories began at the eleventh hour.

This is not to criticise Whitehall – we would have lost the war if we had sent out our bombers every time a secret agent reported a secret weapon – but to underline the tragedy of the spy. He gets a poor salary and little, if any, reward for his services. He has no social standing in the community and remains all his life 'something in the Foreign Office' while his wife, watching her friends' husbands climb the ladder, remains just the wife of 'something in the Foreign Office'. And, on top of it all, the fruits of his dangerous labours rarely give satisfaction outside the Department of the Secret Service which controls him.

Here, it seems to me, is the stuff of a great novel which no-one has even attempted and whose fringes have only been touched on by Somerset Maugham, Eric Ambler and Graham Greene.

Seduced from the drab truth by the emotive lushness of espionage, most writers of spy fiction (or spy fact for the matter of that) choose the easier and more profitable thriller approach and, with the exception of the three I mention above, it is only the best of the others – Buchan, George Griffith and O. Henry – who can be re-read except as a joke. They do date so terribly these fairy stories of our 'teens – their language, their steam-age wars, their moustaches, their exclamation marks! Even their gimmicks lack the high seriousness with which the thriller writer should approach his subject. One shivered pleasurably at Khoklov's explosive cigarette lighter, but, surely, even in those days of other smoking habits, William Le Queux's explosive cigar which blew the Privy Counsellor's face off must have made our fathers chuckle rather than shiver. One can use a poisoned nectarine but not a poisoned banana.

In fact, it is these lowlights of spy literature which make *The Spy's Bedside Book* required reading for anyone who likes thrillers or detective stories. It is all here: the hazards, the tricks, the delights, of the profession, wrapped up in an attractive package which includes an authentic old-time advertisement by The Stereographic Camera Company, 'For Accurate Copies of All Documents, A Necessity for Blackmailers, Spies, and Gentlemen of the Press'.

It is probably that note, the note that makes the book such fun, that inspired the rather incongruous reflections at the beginning of this review. They were the reactions of one of the fifty or so contributors to this anthology who is reminded that the art of thrilling ought to consist of rather more than shouting 'Bang!' in an authoritative voice.

TROUBLE IN HAVANA

Ian Fleming's review of Our Man in Havana *by*
Graham Greene, written for the Sunday Times *in 1958.*

Spies are rapidly getting the same old-fashioned look as the rest of the bric-a-brac of pre-Sputnik wars. Somehow there does not seem to be much point in stealing plans of aircraft, tanks and submarines when every year, and almost every month, the distance between the blue-print and the junk heap gets less and less. Already this summer the 'Terriers', rattling down the roads on their summer manoeuvres, have seemed like something out of a rich boy's play box, or the windows of a print shop. Surely nobody could be seriously interested in purloining one of those anti-tank weapons they carry so proudly! After all, couldn't one buy the whole outfit at Hamleys with, of course, a crib to their radio code thrown in? It is rather pathetic that all the glamorous trimmings of war seem as dated as the bustle or the busby. What shall we dangle in front of our grandchildren's eyes instead of a V.C.? Or will they just re-name it and award it for Vigorous Citizenship?

The modern military spy is a ticking instrument in a stark room on a mountain top, measuring gigantic explosions across the roof of the world. The quiet-spoken linguist with a cyanide pill in his coat button has gone out with the rat-catcher and the chimney sweep, and Mr. Graham Greene gives him a last savage kick down the steps of the big, anonymous building near Maida Vale.

Mr. Wormold, 'Our Man in Havana', is a typical Graham Greene reluctant hero – troubled, anxious, sensitive, loving – with a vacuum cleaner agency in Cuba. Abandoned by his wife, he dotes on his daughter, an adorable nymphet in her teens who has caught the eye of the villainous, and admirably drawn, Segura, Chief of the Secret Police.

Wormold is recruited by the British Secret Service without quite knowing what is happening to him. He sets up a cursory and entirely notional network of agents, using names picked at random from the local Country Club members list. He earns good money with his farcical secret reports and spends it on his daughter's whims. Unfortunately, Wormold is, in turn, spied upon and suddenly two of the Country Club members whose names he has been using are assassinated. Caught in this ghastly web, an H-Certificate Charley's Aunt situation develops which I, for one, would prefer to have seen worked out to its logically horrific climax, but the author is kindly and allows us and his reluctant hero to escape to a more or less happy ending.

Mr. Graham Greene has chosen to heighten, rather than lower, the grotesque temperature of his story so that what could have been terrible and true becomes a savage farce. To my mind, the almost Wodehousian treatment of the Secret Service (its Chief wears a black monocle over a glass eye) is a weakness, and the only weakness in the book. For the rest, this is brilliant and utterly compulsive reading and in the highest class of what the author describes as his 'Entertainments'.

As with all Mr. Graham Greene's books, what delights most of all is the sheer intelligence of the writing. To watch an intelligence of this quality at work on every page, in every sentence even, is a freshet in the desert, a blessed island in the Sargasso Sea of post-war letters. In his latest book this high intelligence, never, I think, so evenly sustained by the author, is as easy to recognise as pre-war whisky.

RAYMOND CHANDLER

This account of Ian Fleming's friendship with Raymond Chandler
was published in the London Magazine *in December 1959.*

I knew Raymond Chandler for about four years and these are all my memories
of him, together with some random comments and reflections and most of the
letters we exchanged. Not many people knew Chandler, so I will not apologise
for the triviality of our correspondence. It fitted in with our relationship – the
half-amused, ragging relationship of two writers working the same thin, almost-
extinct literary seam, who like each other's work. But I do apologise for dragging
my own books and what he wrote about them into this biographical note. Unfor-
tunately, there is no alternative. We came together over my books and not over
his, and our friendship would not have existed without them.

I first met Raymond Chandler at a dinner party given by Stephen and Natasha
Spender some time in May 1955. He was just coming out of the long spell of
drinking which followed the death of his wife. She died after a three years' illness in their house at La Jolla, in California. When the police arrived they found
Raymond Chandler in the sitting room firing his revolver through the ceiling.
Chandler never recovered from the tragedy and, whatever the reality of his married life, his wife became a myth which completely obsessed the following years.

He sold his house in California and every scrap of furniture that reminded
him of her and came to England, perhaps in one of those flights back to one's
youth and childhood (he was educated at Dulwich and worked for some time
in London) that badly hurt people sometimes resort to.

He was very nice to me and said he had liked my first book, *Casino Royale,*
but he really didn't want to talk about anything much except the loss of his
wife, about which he expressed himself with a nakedness that embarrassed

me while endearing him to me. He showed me a photograph of her – a good-looking woman sitting in the sun somewhere. The only other snapshot in his note case was of a cat which he had adored. The cat had died within weeks of his wife's death and this had been a final blow.

He must have been a very good-looking man but the good, square face was puffy and unkempt with drink. In talking, he never ceased making ugly, Hapsburg lip grimaces while his head stretched away from you, looking along his right or left shoulder as if you had bad breath. When he did look at you he saw everything and remembered days later to criticise the tie or the shirt you had been wearing. Everything he said had authority and a strongly individual slant based on what one might describe as a Socialistic humanitarian view of the world. We took to each other and I said that I would send him a copy of my latest book and that we must meet again.

Chandler had taken a flat in Eaton Square and he rang me up in a few days to say that he enjoyed my book and asked if I would like him to say so for the benefit of my publishers.

Rather unattractively, I took him up on this suggestion and wrote to him on May 26th:

Your elegant writing paper makes you sound very much at home, and I shall call you up next week and see if you would like to walk round the corner and pay us a visit . . .

Incidentally a good restaurant in your neighbourhood is Overton's, directly opposite Victoria station. Book a table and go upstairs where you will find an enchanting Victorian interior and the best paté maison in London.

I wouldn't think of asking you to write to me about *Moonraker* but if you happen to feel in a mood of quixotic generosity, a word from you which I could pass on to my publishers would make me the fortune which has so far eluded me.

Incidentally, *The Spectator* is almost girlishly thrilled that you will do *The Riddle of the Sands* for them and the things you said to me and I published about Prince's Bookshop have brought Francis a flood of new business. So the impact you are having on London is that of Father Christmas in Springtime.

The first sentence of his reply of June 4th contained some very kind words. He went on:

> I cannot imagine what I can say to you about your books that will excite your publisher. What I do say in all sincerity is that you are probably the most forceful and driving writer, of what I suppose still must be called 'thrillers' in England.
>
> Peter Cheyney wrote one good book, I thought, called *Dark Duet,* and another fairly good one, but his pseudo-American tough-guy stories always bored me. There was also James Hadley Chase, and I think the less said of him the better. Also, in spite of the fact that you have been everywhere and seen everything, I cannot help admiring your courage in tackling the American scene . . . Some of your stuff on Harlem in *Live and Let Die*, and everything on St Petersburg, Florida, seems to be quite amazing for a foreigner to accomplish.
>
> If this is any good to you would you like me to have it engraved on a gold slab?

I answered:

> 6th June, 1955
>
> These are words of such gold that no supporting slab is needed and I am passing the first sentence on to Macmillan's in New York and Cape's here, and will write my appreciation in caviar when the extra royalties come in.
>
> Seriously, it was extraordinarily kind of you to have written as you did and you have managed to make me feel thoroughly ashamed of my next book which is also set in America, but in an America of much more fantasy than I allowed myself in *Live and Let Die*.
>
> There's a moratorium at home at the moment as the Duke of Westminster (whom may God preserve) has ordered us to paint the outside of our house and the whole thing is hung with cradles and sounds of occasional toil.
>
> But they will be gone in a few days' time and I hope you will be one of the first to darken our now gleaming doorway.

I wanted him to come to lunch to meet my wife, who had not been at the Spenders', and at last it was arranged.

The luncheon was not a success. The Spenders were there and Rupert Hart-Davis and Duff Dunbar, a lawyer friend of mine and a great Chandler fan. Our small dining room was over-crowded. Chandler was a man who was shy of houses and 'entertaining' and our conversation was noisy and about people he did not know. His own diffident and rather halting manner of speech made no impact. He was not made a fuss of and I am pretty sure he hated the whole affair.

Almost a year later he was back again in England and Leonard Russell invited him to review my next book, *Diamonds are Forever*, for the *Sunday Times*. It was the first review Chandler had ever written. I quote these extracts to show the sharp, ironical mind:

Later there is a more detailed, more fantastic, more appalling description of Las Vegas and its daily life. To a Californian, Las Vegas is a cliché. You don't make it fantastic because it was designed that way, and it is funny rather than terrifying . . . and of course Mr. Bond finally has his way with the beautiful girl. Sadly enough his beautiful girls have no future because it is the curse of the 'series character' that he always has to go back to where he began . . . The trouble with brutality in writing is that it has to grow out of something. The best hard-boiled writers never try to be tough, they allow toughness to happen when it seems inevitable for its time, place and conditions . . . There are pages in which James Bond thinks. I don't like James Bond thinking. His thoughts are superfluous. I like him when he is in the dangerous card game; I like him when he is exposing himself unarmed to half a dozen thin-lipped killers, and neatly dumping them into a heap of fractured bones; I like him when he finally takes the beautiful girl in his arms, and teaches her about one-tenth of the facts of life she knew already . . . But let me plead with Mr. Fleming not to allow himself to become a stunt writer, or he will end up no better than the rest of us.

I wrote and thanked him for the review and there was this exchange of letters:

Dear Ian,

Thank you so much for your letter of Wednesday and if the payment for my outstanding review had been received a little earlier I should have been able to eat three meals a day.

I thought my review was no more than you deserved and I tried to write in such a way that the good part could be quoted and the bad parts left out. After all, old boy, there had to be some bad parts. I think you will have to make up your mind what kind of a writer you are going to be. You could be almost anything except that I think you are a bit of a sadist!

I am not in any Hampstead hospital. I am at home and if they ever put me in a hospital again I shall walk out leaving corpses strewn behind me, except pretty nurses.

As for having lunch with you, with or without butler, I can't do it yet – because even if I were much better than I am I should be having lunch with ladies.

I replied on the 27th of April:

Dear Ray,

Many thanks for the splendid Chandleresque letter. Personally I loved your review and thought it was excellent as did my publishers, and as I say it was really wonderful of you to have taken the trouble.

Probably the fault about my books is that I don't take them seriously enough and meekly accept having my head ragged off about them in the family circle. If one has a grain of intelligence it is difficult to go on being serious about a character like James Bond. You after all write 'novels of suspense' – if not sociological studies – whereas my books are straight pillow fantasies of the bang-bang, kiss-kiss variety.

But I have taken your advice to heart and will see if I can't order my life so as to put more feeling into my typewriter.

Incidentally, have you read *A Most Contagious Game*, by Samuel Grafton, published by Rupert Hart-Davis?

Sorry about lunch even without a butler. I also know some girls and will dangle one in front of you one of these days.

I had no idea that you were ill. If you are, please get well immediately. I am extremely ill with sciatica.

1st May, 1956

Dear Ian,

I am leaving London on May 11th and should very much like to see you before I go. I suggest that we have lunch together at one of your better Clubs if you can arrange it.

I don't think you do yourself justice about James Bond and I did not think that I did quite do you justice in my review of your book, because anyone who writes as dashingly as you do, ought, I think, to try for a little higher grade. I have just re-read *Casino Royale* and it seems to me that you have disimproved with each book.

I read several books by Samuel Grafton, but the one you mention I don't know; I will order it.

I don't want any girls dangling in front of me, because my girls do their own dangling and they would be extremely bitter to have you interfere.

You know what you can do with your sciatica don't you?

He then went off abroad. Since the death of his wife, he was lost without women and, in the few years I knew him, he was never without some good-looking companion to mother him and try and curb his drinking. These were affectionate and warm-hearted relationships and probably nothing more. Though I do not know this, I suspect that each woman was, in the end, rather glad to get away from the ghost of the other woman who always walked at his side and from the tired man who made sense for so little of the day. In June he wrote to me from New York:

9th June, 1956

I didn't like leaving England without saying good-bye to the few friends I knew well enough to care about, but then I don't like saying good-bye at all, especially when it may be quite a long time before I come back. As you probably know, I long overstayed the six months allowed, but I had a compelling reason, even if I get hooked for British income tax. I am also likely to lose half my European royalties, which isn't funny. It's all a little obscure to me, but there it is. And it doesn't matter whether your stay in England is broken half a dozen times. If the time adds up to over six months within the fiscal year, you are it.

I am looking forward to your next book. I am also looking forward to my next book.

I rather liked New York this time, having heretofore loathed its harshness and rudeness. For one thing the weather has been wonderful, only one hot day so far and that not unbearable. I have friends here, but not many. Come to think of it I haven't many anywhere. Monday night I am flying back to California and this time I hope to stick it out and make some kind of a modest but convenient home there.

I am wondering what happened to all the chic pretty women who are supposed to be typical of New York. Damned if I've seen any of them. Perhaps I've looked in the wrong places, but I do have a feeling that New York is being slowly downgraded.

Please remember me to Mrs. Fleming if you see her and if she remembers me (doubtful). And how is His Grace the Duke of Westminster these days? Painting lots of houses, I hope?

He also sent me an almost illegible letter about an earlier book I had written called *Live and Let Die*.

We exchanged letters:

22nd June, 1956

Dear Ray,

How fine to get not one but two letters from you – and one of them legible at that. I hope you have left a forwarding address with the Grosvenor or otherwise you will think me even more churlish than you already do.

I simply cannot understand your tax position and I certainly do not believe that we will try and squeeze your European royalties out of you for over-staying your time a little. If it looks like something fierce of that kind, please let me know and I will make an impassioned appeal on your behalf.

Eric Ambler has a new thriller coming out next week, which no doubt Prince's Bookshop will send you. If not, I will. It is better than the last two but still not quite the good old stuff we remember. I have done a review for the *Sunday Times* headed 'Forever Ambler' which struck me as a good joke.

My own muse is in a bad way. Despite your doubts, I really rather liked *Diamonds are Forever* . . . It has been very difficult to make Bond go through his tricks in *From Russia, With Love,* which is just going to the publishers.

Shall be in and around New York and Vermont for the first fortnight in August and, in the unlikely event that you should happen to be in reach of the area, please let me or Macmillans, New York, know and we will share a Coke in which the contents of a benzedrine inhaler have been soaked overnight. Which, I understand, is the fashionable drink in your country at the moment.

4th July, 1956

Dear Ian,

I have already ordered Eric Ambler's new thriller since he told me about it some time before it came out. I think the title of your review, 'Forever Ambler' is a pretty good joke in the third class division.

Of course I liked *Diamonds are Forever* and I enjoyed reading it, but I simply don't think it is worthy of your talents.

It is unlikely that I shall be in New York or Vermont in August. It is much more likely that I shall be in Paris. Frankly a Coke in which the contents of a benzedrine inhaler has been soaked overnight hasn't reached La Jolla. What does it do to you? The fashionable drink in this country is still Scotch.

Dear Ray,

I cannot believe that you will end up by having trouble over your tax problems here. Our tax gatherers do not come down hard on the foreign visitor, and I am sure they will accept your medical alibi. I strongly advise you not to worry about the problem until faced with some kind of a demand.

As for my opera, you are clearly living under a grave misapprehension. My talents are extended to their absolute limits in writing books like *Diamonds are Forever.* I am not short-weighting anybody and I have absolutely nothing more up my sleeve. The way you talk, anybody would think I was a lazy Shakespeare or Raymond Chandler. Not so.

My only information to help you on your Paris visit is that on Thursdays, in the night club below the Moulin Rouge, there is amateur strip-tease which might bring a flicker even to your worldly eyes. But I have not sampled it, so this information is not guaranteed.

Now get on with writing your book and stop picking your nose and staring out of the window.

Whenever we were together, I would try and make him write, but the truth of the matter was that it had nearly all gone out of him and that he simply could not be bothered. He had an idea for a play, though I do not know what it was about, and he finally put together his last book *Playback,* which began splendidly and then petered off into a formless jumble of sub-plots, at the end of which Philip Marlowe is obviously going to marry a rich American woman living in Paris. I asked Chandler if this marriage would come off and he said he supposed it would. This would be the end of Marlowe. She would come along and sack his secretary and redecorate his office and make him change his friends. She would be so rich that there would be no point in Marlowe working any more and he would finally drink himself to death. I said that this would make an excellent plot and that perhaps he could save Marlowe by making Mrs. Marlowe drink herself to death first.

I pulled his leg about his plots, which always seem to me to go wildly astray. What holds the books together and makes them so compulsively read-able, even to alpha minds who would not normally think of reading a thriller, is the dialogue. There is a throw-away, down-beat quality about Chandler's dialogue, whether wise-cracking or not, that takes one happily through chapter after chapter in which there is no more action than Philip Marlowe driving his car and talking to his girl, or a rich old woman consulting her lawyer on the sun porch. His aphorisms were always his own. 'Lust ages men but keeps women young' has stuck in my mind.

Mr. Francis, Chandler's bookseller in London and one of his closest English friends, told me that in the old days, before Mrs. Chandler died, Chandler would carry on a non-stop, ironical commentary on people and books and Fate in exactly Philip Marlowe's tone of voice. He corresponded a lot with Francis and I have borrowed the letter in which he talks about his particular craft.

30th October, 1952

As to Maugham's remarks about the decline and fall of the detective story, in spite of his flattering references to me, I do not agree with this thesis. People have been burying the detective story for at least two generations, and it is still very much alive, although I do admit the term 'detective story' hardly covers the field any more, since a great deal of the best stuff written nowadays is only slightly if at all concerned with the elucidation of the mystery. What we have is more in the nature of the novel of suspense. I'm going to write him a long letter one of these days and take up the argument with him. I may even write an article in reply if anybody wants to print it. I should have valued his references to Philip Marlowe even more if he had remembered to spell Marlowe's name correctly. Some of this stuff of Maugham's was published a long time ago. The fascinating and acid little vignette of Edith Wharton for example was published in the *Saturday Evening Post,* and I still have the tear sheets (I think) from the issue. And I seem to recall that Edmund Wilson took rather nasty issue with Maugham about Maugham's claim that the writers of straight novels had largely forgotten how to tell a story. I hate to agree with such an ill-natured and bad-mannered person as Edmund

Wilson, but I think he was right on this point. I don't think the quality in the detective or mystery story which appeals to people has very much to do with the story a particular book has to tell. I think what draws people is a certain emotional tension which takes you out of yourself without draining you too much. They allow you to live dangerously without any real risk. They are something like those elaborate machines which they used to use and probably still do use to accustom student pilots to the sensation of aerial acrobatics. You can do anything from a wing-over to an Immelmann in them without ever leaving the ground and without any danger of going into a flat spin out of control. Well, enough of that for now.

Around Christmas, 1957, I got one of those giant postcards 'From the World-famous Palm Canyon' in the Colorado Desert. This was hastily followed by another one in which he suggested that I had teased O., his companion of the year before, about their journey together abroad. I wrote back on 29th November 1957:

> Why do they think that Palm Canyon is 'world-famous'? What world do these people frequent?
>
> It was fine to see your gusty script again and to know that you are still alive, and I heartily approve your plan to move over here. Perhaps you will get so bored here that you will be forced to get on with that long-overdue book.
>
> Naturally I never rag O. about you. She's been telling tales. She is a wonderful girl and I guess you are very good for each other.
>
> Hurry up and come along.

He came back to London in the Spring and we saw more of each other. He was in a bad way, drinking heavily. Like other heavy drinkers, he had been told to stick to wine instead of spirits and he consumed innumerable bottles of hock which cannot have been good for his liver. We had lunch together at Boulestin's one day with the charming English literary agent with whom he was proposing to go to Tangier to get some sunshine. I told him that I had been in Tangier in April and that it rained the whole time. I persuaded him that he should go to Capri instead. The idea came to me that he should meet Lucky Luciano in Naples and write a piece about him for the *Sunday Times*. I thought this would be a great scoop and I took a lot of pains arranging the meeting. The whole thing was a failure. They duly met in a hotel in Naples which is Luciano's favourite hideout and Chandler completely succumbed to Luciano's hard-luck story. Chandler had an extremely warm and sentimental heart, just as Philip Marlowe attractively has in the books. Luciano admitted that he had laid himself open to prosecution, but said that he had been made a fall-guy by the then District Attorney because he had the right sort of gangsterish name, because the big boys were too hard to tackle, and because plenty of convictions, of which Luciano's was one, would be good for the political careers of some of the Government officials involved.

Chandler wrote a lengthy article on this theme. It did not contain any of the visual reporting I had hoped for and nothing of the drama of the meeting between these two men. Instead, it was a long exculpation of Luciano and a plea for cleaner Government. This was sheer bad writing and, since it would not suit the *Sunday Times* or America, I doubt if it has ever been published.

When Chandler came back a month later he was full of the idea of writing a play about a wronged gangster. This would have been very much in Chandler's later vein and I did all I could to encourage him, but he refused to go forward with the idea until he had obtained Luciano's sanction. It was again typical of him that, although he need not have involved Luciano's name or the details of his case in any way, he felt the man had been kicked around enough and must now be treated gently. Luciano replied that he would rather Chandler did not write this story and that was that.

About this time, Chandler and I were booked to give a 20-minute broadcast for the B.B.C. on The Art of Writing Thrillers. When the day came, it was very difficult to get him to the studio and when I went to pick him up at about eleven in the morning his voice was slurred with whisky.

However, the broadcast went off all right because I kept out of the act and concentrated on leading him along with endless questions. Many of Chandler's replies had to be erased from the tape and, in particular, I remember that, in discussing Mickey Spillane and his retreat to expiate his 'guilt' into the arms of the Seventh Day Adventists, Chandler commented 'in a way, it's a shame. That boy was the greatest aid to solitary sin (he used a blunt word for it) in literature'. Later he apologised to the two pretty girls in the control room and one of them said, 'It's quite all right, Mr. Chandler, we hear much worse things than that'.

At lunch together that day we talked about our writing techniques. While waiting for him, I had jotted down some questions on the back of Boulestin's cocktail price list (from which I now note with surprise that a Sidecar costs 6/6d.). I could not think of anything except the usual stock questions. He said he wrote his books in long-hand, very slowly and going back again and again over what he had written the day before. He often got stuck for weeks and even months. I said I could not do any correcting until the book was finished. If I looked back at what I had written the day before I would be so appalled by its badness that I would give up. He commented that my system probably gave the book pace which he regarded as the most important quality of any thriller. He worked, as one can see, endlessly over his dialogue and most of the wisecracks, as one can also see, were his own. He did not work to a particular routine a day, but in sprints and often sat up all night and kept going. *The Big Sleep,* which first made him famous, had been written quickly in about two months and this had made him the most money because it was written before taxation killed the rich writer. It was also made into a film and he had earned enough to retire on through it. He agreed that Dashiell Hammett was his first love among thriller writers and that he had learnt most from him and from Hemingway. Hammett, he said, had never let his work decline. He had just written himself out like an expended firework and that was that. In the end, said Chandler, as one grew older, one grew out of gangsters and blondes and guns and, since they were the chief ingredients of thrillers, short of space fiction, that was that. He picked his names from the Los Angeles telephone directory and his chief source of inspiration was a particular friend in the Los Angeles Police Department. (He told me his name but I have forgotten it.) Marlowe? Well yes, one put a certain amount of oneself into one's hero because one knew more about oneself than about anybody else, but he also put his own unattractive traits into his gangsters and other subsidiary characters. The women were just women he had seen on the street or met at parties. He would never kill Marlowe because he liked him and other people seemed to like him and it would be unkind to them.

That was the last time I saw him or heard from him. I went abroad and, when I came back, I heard that he had had D.T.s and had gone back to California. Such news as I had of him remained bad and it was only a week before his death that I called on our mutual friend, Mr. Francis, of Prince's Arcade Bookshop, who had a permanent order to supply Chandler blind with any book that caught Francis's fancy. I told him I had sent Chandler a copy of my last book and asked him what else he had sent. Francis told me that he had not sent anything for months. He had not been asked to do so. We agreed that this was the worst news we had heard. 'That's bad,' I said and left the bookshop thinking that it was, in fact, very bad news indeed.

The long and perceptive obituary in *The Times* would have given him real pleasure. I wish I had been the author so that I could have repaid him for the wonderful tribute he had written out of the kindness of his heart for me and my publishers. How pleased he and his publishers would have been with the final sentence in *The Times*: 'His name will certainly go down among the dozen or so mystery writers who were also innovators and stylists; who, working the common vein of crime fiction, mined the gold of literature.'

THE GUNS OF JAMES BOND

This is taken from Ian Fleming's original typescript dated 4th July 1961.
It was published in Sports Illustrated *in March 1962, and then in the*
Sunday Times *in November 1962, with the title 'James Bond's Hardware'.*

Some reviewers of my books about James Bond have been generous in commending the accuracy of the expertise which forms a considerable part of the background furniture of these books. I may say that correspondents from all over the world have been equally enthusiastic in writing to point out errors in this expertise, and the mistakes I have made, approximately one per volume, will no doubt forever continue to haunt my In-basket.

But it is true that I take very great pains over the technical and geographical background to James Bond's adventures, and during and after the writing of each book I consult innumerable authorities in order to give solidity and integrity to his exploits. Without this solid springboard, there would perhaps be justification for the frequent criticisms that James Bond's adventures are fantastic, though I maintain that such criticism comes from people who simply do not read the newspapers or who have not taken note of the revealing peaks of the great underwater iceberg that is secret service warfare. The frogman mystery of Commander Crabb; Khokhlov and the bullet-firing cigarette case with which his Russian masters hoped to have a West German propaganda expert assassinated; the whole of the U-2 affair – what incidents in my serial biography of James Bond are more fantastic than these?

It was in pursuit of verisimilitude that my friendship with Geoffrey Boothroyd was born in May 1956, and I think it may be an interesting sidelight on the work of two enthusiasts, one in thriller writing and the other in gun lore, for me to print, here our correspondence and then to recount the rather bizarre sequel to the long and forceful letter that came to me one day from Glasgow.

Boothroyd to Fleming, 23rd May, 1956:
I have, by now, got rather fond of Mr. James Bond. I like most of the things about him, with the exception of his rather deplorable taste in firearms. In particular I dislike a man who comes into contact with all sorts of formidable people using a .25 Beretta. This sort of gun is really a lady's gun, and not a really nice lady at that. If Mr. Bond has to use a light gun he would be better off with a .22 rim fire and the lead bullet would cause more shocking effect than the jacketed type of the .25.

May I suggest that Mr. Bond is armed with a revolver? This has many advantages for the type of shooting that he is called on to perform and I am certain that Mr. Leiter would agree with this recommendation. The Beretta will weigh, after it has been doctored, somewhere under one pound. If Mr. Bond gets himself an S. & W. .38 Special Centennial Airweight he will have a real man-stopper weighing only 13 ozs. The gun is hammerless so that it can be drawn without catching in the clothing and has an overall length of 6½". Barrel length is 2", note that it is not 'sawn off.' No one who can buy his pistols in the States will go to the trouble of sawing off pistol barrels as they can be purchased with short 2" barrels from the manufacturers. In order to keep down the bulk, the cylinder holds 5 cartridges, and these are standard .38 S&W Special. It is an extremely accurate cartridge and when fired from a 2" barrel has, in standard loading, a muzzle velocity of almost 860 ft./sec. and muzzle energy of around 260 ft./lbs. This is against the .25 with M.V. of 758 ft./sec. but only 67 ft./lbs. muzzle energy. So much for his personal gun. Now he must have a real man stopper to carry in the car. For this purpose the S. & W. .357 Magnum has no equal except the .44 Magnum. However with the .357, Bond can still use his .38 S.W. Special cartridges in the Magnum but not vice versa. This can be obtained in barrel lengths as follows: 3½", 5", 6", 6½" and 8¾" long. With a 6½" barrel and adjustable sights Bond could do some really effective shooting. The .357 Magnum has a M V of 1515 ft/sec and a M E of 807 ft/lbs. Figures like these give an effective range of 300 yards, and it's very accurate, too, 1" groups at 20 yards on a machine rest.

With these two guns our friend would be able to cope with really quick draw work and long range effective shooting.

Now to gun harness, rigs or what have you. First of all, not a shoulder holster for general wear, please. I suggest that the gun is carried in a Berns Martin Triple Draw holster. This type of holster holds the gun in by means of a spring and can be worn on the belt or as a shoulder holster. I have played about with various types of holster for quite a time now and this one is the best. I took some pictures of the holster some time ago and at present can only find the proofs but I send them to you to illustrate how it works. I have numbered the prints and give a description of each print below.

'A' Series. Holster worn on belt at right side. Pistol drawn with right hand.

1. Ready position. Note that the gun is not noticeable.
2. First movement. Weight moves to left foot. Hand draws back coat and sweeps forward to catch butt of pistol. Finger outside holster.
3. Gun coming out of holster through the split front.
4. In business.

This draw can be done in ⅗ths of a second by me. With practice and lots of it you could hit a figure at 20 feet in that time.

'B' Series. Shoulder holster. Gun upside down on left side. Held in by spring. Drawn with right hand.

1. First position.
2. Coat drawn back by left hand, gun butt grasped by right hand, finger outside holster.
3. Gun coming out of holster.
4. Bang! You're dead.

'C' Series. Holster worn as in A, but gun drawn with left hand.

1. Draw commences. Butt held by first two fingers of left hand. Third finger and little finger ready to grasp trigger.

2. Ready to shoot. Trigger being pulled by third and little finger, thumb curled round stock, gun upside down.

This really works but you need a cut away trigger guard.

'D' Series. Holster worn on shoulder, as in 'B' Series, but gun drawn with left hand.

1. Coat swept back with left hand and gun grasped.
2. Gun is pushed to the right to clear holster and is ready for action.

I'm sorry that I couldn't find the better series of photographs but these should illustrate what I mean. The gun used is a .38 S.W. with a sawn off barrel to 2¾". (I know this contradicts what I said over the page but I can't afford the 64 dollars needed so I had to make my own.) It has target sights, ramp front sight, adjustable rear sight, rounded butt, special stocks and a cut away trigger guard.

If you have managed to read this far I hope that you will accept the above in the spirit that it is offered. I have enjoyed your four books immensely and will say right now that I have no criticism of the women in them, except that I've never met any like them and would doubtless get into trouble if I did.

Fleming to Boothroyd, 31st May.
I really am most grateful for your splendid letter of May 23rd.

You have entirely convinced me, and I propose, perhaps not in the next volume of James Bond's memoirs but in the subsequent one, to change his weapons in accordance with your instructions.

Since I am not in the habit of stealing another man's expertise, I shall ask you in due course to accept remuneration for your most valuable technical aid.

Incidentally, can you suggest where I can see a .38 Airweight in London? Who would have one?

As a matter of interest, how do you come to know so much about these things? I was delighted with the photographs and greatly impressed by them. If ever there is talk of making films of some of James Bond's stories in due course, I shall suggest to the company concerned that they might like to consult you on some technical aspects. But they may not take my advice, so please do not set too much store by this suggestion.

From the style of your writing it occurs to me that you may have written books or articles on these subjects. Is that so?

Bond has always admitted to me that the .25 Beretta was not a stopping gun, and he places much more reliance on his accuracy with it than in any particular qualities of the gun itself. As you know, one gets used to a gun and it may take some time for him to settle down with the Smith & Wesson. But I think M. should advise him to make a change; as also in the case of the .357 Magnum.

He also agrees to give a fair trial to the Berns Martin holster, but he is inclined to favour something a little more casual and less bulky. The well-worn chamois leather pouch under his left arm has become almost a part of his clothes, and he will be loath to make a change, though, here again, M. may intervene.

At the present moment Bond is particularly anxious for expertise on the weapons likely to be carried by Russian agents, and I wonder if you have any information on this.

As Bond's biographer I am most anxious to see that he lives as long as possible and I shall be most grateful for any further technical advices you might like me to pass on to him.

Again, with very sincere thanks for your extremely helpful and workman-like letter.

Boothroyd to Fleming, 1st June.

I was truly delighted to receive your charming letter. This is the first time I have had either the inclination or the temerity to write to the author of any books that pass through my hands; quite frankly in many cases the rest of the material is not worth backing up by correct and authentic 'gun dope.' You have, incidentally, enslaved the rest of my household, people staying up to all hours of the night in an endeavour to finish a book before some other inter-ested party swipes it.

If I am to be considered for the post of Bond's ballistic man I should give you my terms of reference. Age 31, English, unmarried. Employed by I.C.I. Ltd. as Technical Rep in Scotland. Member of the following Rifle Clubs: N.R.A., Gt.

Britain, English Twenty Club, National Rifle Association of America, non-resident member. St. Rollox Rifle Club, West of Scotland Rifle Club, Muzzle Loading Association of Gt. Britain. I shoot with shotgun and rifle, target, clay pigeon, deer, but, to my deep regret, no big game. (I cherish a dream that one day a large tiger or lion will escape from the zoo or a travelling circus and I can bag it in Argyle St., or Princes St., Edinburgh.) I do both muzzle loading and breech loading shooting, load my own shotgun and pistol ammunition. Shoot with pistol mainly target and collect arms of various sorts. My present collection numbers about 45, not as many as some collections go but all of mine go off and have been fired by me. Shooting and gun lore is a jolly queer thing, most people stick to their own field, rather like stamp collectors who specialise in British Colonials. Such people shoot only with the rifle and often only .303, or only .22. There are certain rather odd types like myself who have a go at the lot, including Archery. It's a most fascinating study if one has the time, and before long it's either given up and you collect old Bentleys or it becomes an obsession. We all have a pet aspect of our hobby, and mine is this business of 'draw and shoot', or the gun lore of close-combat weapons. On reflection it is pretty stupid as it's most unlikely that I shall ever do this sort of thing in earnest but it has the pleasant advantage of not having very many fish in the pond and however you look at it you are an authority. In Scotland I have the space to do this sort of thing, and have two friends who are not 150 miles away to talk to. I seem to have taken up a lot of space on this, must want to impress you!

I have written one thing on Scottish pistols, but tore it up after reading a really superb effort by an American. He had access to a lot more weapons and anyway, no use kidding myself, he knew how to write or the magazine re-wrote it for him. Since then I've found a new thing for an article which will be written before the end of the year and sent to America. This will be on the firm of Dickson in Edinburgh, who are old established gun makers. Lots of pictures of ye olde craftsmen at the bench, the more pictures the less writing. I have also given one or two lectures on firearms to the T.A., Home Guard and the Police. Occasionally we are able to give demonstrations of some of the things we talk about but as some of the tricks require an expenditure of about 10,000 rounds of ammunition one cannot afford to become an expert trick shot.

Now to the work. I doubt very much if you will be able to see a S. & W. Airweight model in England, at least in a shop. I therefore enclose S. & W. latest catalog, which shows current models. Perhaps you would let me have this back, as I have to send it off to another chap who is going to S. America and he wants to buy a gun when he gets there. The only people in London who may have S. & W. new-model pistols will be Thomas Bland and Sons, William IVth St., Strand. Current demand for pistols in this country is restricted to folks going off to Kenya, Malaya, etc. The few that know anything about pistols for close up work will probably buy modified guns from Cogswell and Harrison. This type is a cut-down S. & W. .38 Military & Police Model generally similar to the photo enclosed. You have seen this gun of mine and were quite interested. You may retain this print if you wish. (I had to learn photography as well, this is an improvement over earlier work.) I'm sorry I can't help regarding an actual inspection of a new-model S. & W. The only people who may have one are Americans in this country or James Bond.

Re holsters. A letter to S. D. Myres Saddle Co., 5030 Alameda Blvd., P.O. Box 1501, El Paso, Texas, will bring you their current holster catalog. The Berns Martin people live in Calhoun City, Mississippi, and a note to Jack Martin, who is a first-class chap and a true gunslinger, will bring you illustrations of his work. Bond's chamois leather pouch will be ideal for *carrying* a gun, but God help him if he has to get it out in a hurry. The soft leather will snag and foul on the projecting parts of the gun and he will still be struggling to get the gun out when the other fellow is counting the holes in Bond's tummy. Bond has a good point when he mentions accuracy. It's no good shooting at a man with the biggest gun one can hold – if you miss him. The thing about the larger calibres is, however, that when you hit someone with a man stopping bullet they are out of the game and won't lie on the floor still popping off at you.

Regarding weapons carried by Russian agents. I have had little experience of using weapons from behind the Iron Curtain or of meeting people who use them. I did once meet a Polish officer who was some sort of undercover man and cloak-and-dagger merchant and he used an American Colt Automatic in .38 cal. I would suggest that a member of SMERSH would in all probability make his choice from the following and use for preference either a Luger with an 8", 10", 12" or 16" barrel with detachable shoulder stock or a Mauser 7.63

Automatic with shoulder stock for assassination work from a medium distance, say across a street. A short-barrel 9 mm. Luger (Model 08), 4" barrel, might be carried for personal protection, although it is rather large to carry about. In the same class as the Luger and having equal availability to someone employed by SMERSH would be the Polish Radom P.35. This takes the standard Luger cartridge and also the more powerful black bulleted machine pistol 9 mm round. It closely resembles the Colt Model 1911, or perhaps more so the Colt 9 mm Commander. Another choice would be the Swedish 9 mm Lahti. This is a strong and very well-made pistol strongly reminiscent of the Luger. It weighs 42 ozs loaded as compared with 32 ozs for the short barrel Luger.

The Russian Tokarev pistol Model 30 appears to be the standard side arm of the Soviets, and once again is a close copy of John Browning's basic pistol, calibre 7.62 Russian or 7.63 Mauser and designed in the 1930s. This pistol looks like the Belgian Browning auto pistol made by Fabrique Nationale, Liège, except that it has an external hammer. There is no manual safety, and if the gun is carried loaded at full cock, obvious safety hazards exist. Carried at half-cock the gun undoubtedly would be safer, but the hammer design is such that cocking the hammer is not an easy job and the first shot would be a slow one from the draw.

In this same general class would be the Walther P.38, which was used by the German army as a replacement for the Luger. Evidence is that the pistol is not quite as good as it might be, this being probably due to production difficulties met with during the war. This also takes the 9mm cartridge. One of the advantages of the Walther is that it can be used double action, i.e., there is no need to cock the hammer for the first shot provided the barrel has a cartridge 'up the spout'. After the first shot the gun operates as does the normal auto pistol.

For carrying on the person the following arms could be chosen: Walther PPK 7.65 mm, Mauser HSc. 7.65 mm or the Walther PP in 7.65 mm cal., Sauer Model 35 in 7.65-mm calibre.

The above represent a class of weapons similar to the Beretta but of rather better quality.

All of the above were tested for accuracy, endurance, etc., by the US Army Ordnance Corps in 1948. Also included were the Jap. Nambu and the

American Colt 1911 AI Auto. In accuracy the Nambu came first, followed by the Russian Tokarev, the Sauer being third. Colonel F. S. Allen, U S A F, who wrote an article on the findings of the O.C. tests, concluded by saying that for an emergency defence weapon he would have a special .38 Special lightweight S.W., a decision which I heartily agree with.

I hope that when the SMERSH operative, armed perhaps with one of the guns mentioned above, meets Bond, your friend will be able to adequately demonstrate the effectiveness of Anglo-American cooperation, a competent English pistol man behind a truly lethal .38 Special.

The above should give some idea of the type of weapon likely to be carried by SMERSH men, the Russians being rather similar to ourselves where fire-arms are concerned, they do not hesitate to use foreign weapons if they are better than those produced by themselves. An instance of this was their use of the Finnish Soumi light machine gun during the last war. In brief, one could be safe in arming an agent of SMERSH with the Tokarev, Radon, or Luger in that order. Pocket weapons would be either German Mauser or Walther.

Please convey warmest regards to Mr. Bond and assure him of my closest interest in his activities and very willing cooperation in his 'gun needs' for as long as he wishes. Instead of remuneration, an introduction to Solitaire [one of Fleming's glamorous heroines] would more than adequately compensate me for the little trouble I have taken. Between you and me, I quite enjoy it.

Fleming to Boothroyd, 22nd June, 1956.
I have been away in Vienna, and seeing a man about a flying saucer in Paris, and I have only just had your letter of June 1st with enclosures.

Thank you again most sincerely for taking all this trouble, and also for sending me the very interesting information on your own career and hobbies. You certainly seem to lead a full life!

I am intrigued by your mention of archery. I have long thought that Bond could do a lot of damage with a short steel bow and appropriate arrows. What do you think of this suggestion, and do you know someone who would instruct me on weapons, ranges and so forth?

I am returning the Smith & Wesson catalogue and, since I am off to New York at the end of July, I propose to purchase a Centennial Airweight.

Would this not, in any case, be the best weapon for Bond? There is no hammer to catch in his clothes.

I am vastly intrigued by your own M. & P. model and by the way you have beautified it. Bond will certainly adopt your two-thirds trigger guard. I don't intend to go too deeply into the holster problem and I intend to accept your expertise in the matter of the Berns Martin holster.

Only one basic problem remains in changing Bond's weapon, and that is in the matter of a silencer. It would have to be an extremely bulky affair to silence a .38 of any make and I simply can't see one fitted to the Centennial. Have you any views?

As a matter of fact, a change of Bond's weapons is very appropriate. In his next adventure, which deals with an intricate plot by SMERSH to kill Bond, he finally gets into really bad trouble through the Beretta, with silencer, sticking in his waistband.

It is too late now to save him from the consequences of ill-equipment, but in the book that follows, if I have the energy and ingenuity to write one, I shall start off with a chapter devoted entirely to his re-equipment along the lines you suggest.

But in this chapter the matter of a silencer will have to be overcome and, in fact, in his latest adventure which I mention above he could hardly have used an unsilenced .38 in the room at the Ritz Hotel in Paris where he wrestles fruitlessly with his snarled gun.

Turning to foreign weapons, have you by any chance got the article by Colonel Allen on the findings of the O.C. tests, or could you tell me where it appeared? It sounds most useful to my purposes.

Once again, please accept my very warm thanks for your kindness in taking Bond's armoury in hand and sorting it out. As a small recompense for your trouble I am sending you a shiny and rather expensive book on Odd Weapons which has just appeared and which perhaps you do not possess. It is not exactly on your beat, but it may entertain.

Boothroyd to Fleming, 29th June.
Silencers. These I do not like. The only excuse for using one is on a .22 rifle using low-velocity ammunition, i.e., below the speed of sound. With apologies, I think you will find that silencers are more often found in fiction than in real life. An

effective silencer on an auto pistol would be very ponderous and would spoil the balance of the gun, and to silence a revolver would be even more difficult due to the gas escape between the cylinder and the barrel. Personally I can't at this stage see how one would fit a silencer to a Beretta unless a special barrel were made for it, as the silencer has to be screwed on to the barrel, and as you know there is very little of the barrel projecting in front of the slide on the Beretta.

This business of using guns in houses or hotels is a very strange one. So few people are familiar with what a gun sounds like that I would have little hesitation in firing one in any well constructed building. This remark is only regarding the noise or nuisance value. I would not fire a pistol in a room without some thoughts on the matter, as bullets have a bad habit of bouncing off things and coming home to roost. I have fired .455 blanks at home on several occasions even in the middle of the night without any enquiries being made, the last time was at Christmas when I blew out the candles on the Christmas cake with a pistol and blanks. To conclude, if possible don't have anything to do with silencers.

Fleming to Boothroyd, 12th July.

I sympathise with you about not liking silencers, but the trouble is that there are often occasions when they are essential to Bond's work. But they are clumsy things and only partially effective, though our Secret Services developed some very good ones during the war, in which the bullet passed through rubber baffles. I have tried a Sten gun silenced with one of these and all one could hear was the click of the machinery.

I rather like the picture of you going through life firing bullets 'in any well-constructed building'! But I agree with you that one could probably get away with a single shot in a hotel bedroom. Your Christmas trick would, of course, be helped by its association in a listener's mind with cracker-pulling.

The late summer is the time of year when, spurred on by Mr. Michael Howard of Jonathan Cape's, I am putting the final corrections to the typescript of the current James Bond adventure, usually written in January and February. Michael Howard wants to get the typescript into page proofs, to which I must give a last polish in September so that he can go to print for publication six months later, around Easter time. Late summer is also the time when he and

I get our heads together about the design of an appropriate jacket for the book. The volume I was then working on was *From Russia with Love,* and, with my correspondence with Geoffrey Boothroyd in mind and remembering the excellent trompe l'oeil jacket for Raymond Chandler's *The Gentle Art of Murder,* published by Hamish Hamilton in 1950, my idea for a jacket was a gun crossed with a rose, so I decided to approach Dickie Chopping, who is probably the finest trompe l'oeil painter in the world and for whose work I have a great admiration.

Dickie Chopping having agreed, in principle, the next requirement was a suitable gun. I at once thought of Geoffrey Boothroyd's favourite – the .38 Smith and Wesson Police Positive whose barrel he had sawn to 2¾", and whose trigger guard he had cut away for quicker shooting, and I wrote asking for the loan of the gun. Geoffrey Boothroyd agreed. His beautiful gun came down to me by registered post and was sent on to Dickie Chopping, who at once set to work, commenting in a letter around the middle of September, 'It has been the very devil to paint, but fascinating.' And then fate stepped in via an urgent trunk call from Geoffrey Boothroyd.

On the night of September 15th, 1956, there took place in Glasgow a multiple crime, later to become famous as the 'Burnside Murders'. Three people were murdered on this bloody night – wife, daughter and sister-in-law – and recovery of the bullets from the corpses revealed that they were of .38 calibre. The police had a record of all owners of .38 weapons in the neighbourhood and Geoffrey Boothroyd, on the list of suspects, received an urgent visit from a police sergeant asking to see his Smith and Wesson. A thoroughly worried Boothroyd had to admit that this was in the hands of a certain Ian Fleming living in London, and he now warned me over the telephone to expect an early visit from Scotland Yard.

With the C.I.D.'s deadly efficiency, the visit resulted in a matter of hours, and it was fortunate that I not only had an alibi for the night in question but also a firearms certificate covering a .25 Browning automatic which I had occasionally carried during the war on Naval Intelligence duties, and a .38 Special Police Colt revolver which was presented to me as a memento of our friendship by General 'Wild Bill' Donovan, head of the American Secret Services known as O.S.S., with whom I had had frequent and close association in wartime.

But of course I did not possess the suspect gun. This was in the hands of Dickie Chopping in his studio in Essex! My imagination boggled at the impact of a police visit on this sensitive person, who would, in any case, obviously be without a firearms certificate. Fortunately the sergeant from the C.I.D., having read through my correspondence with Geoffrey Boothroyd and Dickie Chopping and after making copious notes, accepted my plea not to descend upon poor Chopping so long as the suspect gun could be quickly returned to me and so back to its rightful owner.

Fortunately that same afternoon Dickie Chopping came to see me with his completed painting for the book jacket and with the gun, so a telephone call to Scotland Yard and the hasty despatch to Glasgow of the incriminating weapon closed the incident so far as we were concerned.

As to the Burnside Murders, the husband, a prominent Glasgow man, was arrested, but was later released, and with the aid of his solicitor eventually laid the trap which brought the true culprit to account.

The man responsible was a certain Peter Manuel. He was arrested, and these three and several other murders were laid at his door. Manuel conducted his own defence and was later convicted and executed for his crimes. His gun had, in fact, been a Webley and not a Smith and Wesson. Both are made in .38 calibre but the rifling is different.

The Chopping jacket was a tremendous success, both in England and America, and from that day on he and I and Michael Howard of Cape's have devised all the James Bond jackets, which have now become something of a hallmark with the book trade and have earned prizes for Jonathan Cape.

With the page proofs of *From Russia with Love* finally out of the way, my mind was busy with the next in the series of James Bond's adventures – *Dr. No* – and I retired as usual to my small house in Jamaica to write this in January and February of 1957. It is in this book that 'The Armourer', a certain Major Boothroyd, is called in by M. to give judgement on James Bond's weapons, the inadequacy of which, at the end of *From Russia with Love* so nearly cost him his life.

Major Boothroyd echoes the strictures of Geoffrey Boothroyd, and James Bond, much to his preliminary annoyance, departs on his mission against the redoubtable Dr. No with a Walther PPK. 7.65 mm with a Berns Martin triple draw holster for close work and a Smith and Wesson .38 Centennial Airweight for longer range work.

Unfortunately, even after the careful coaching by the real life Boothroyd, one of the dreadful technical errors that dog each of my books here again crept in.

The Berns Martin holster can, in fact, only be used with revolvers and not me but the real life Boothroyd received a sharp letter which said, 'If he (Bond) carries on using this PPK out of that Berns Martin rig I shall have to break down and write a rude letter to Fleming. I realise that writers have a whole lot of licence but this is going too far!'

However, James Bond has now become accustomed to his new weapons, and in their proper holsters they have been put to good use in subsequent exploits.

I didn't actually meet Geoffrey Boothroyd until March 1961, when I went to Glasgow with Michael Howard to appear on Scottish television, where I had the baffling experience of being interviewed by a young man who had never read any of my books.

At a subsequent party, Geoffrey Boothroyd was one of the guests, and we were enthusiastically photographed shooting at each other with the famous Smith and Wesson with the sawn off barrel and cut away trigger. Boothroyd, the expert, escaped unmarked from this duel. The thriller writer, less tough and rustier on the draw, was doomed, a very few days later, to suffer a heart attack which laid him temporarily as low as a real stopper from the Smith and Wesson.

Mark you, I am not actually nominating Boothroyd as mine own executioner, but it certainly was a curious sequel to an already bizarre relationship!

THE SEVEN DEADLY SINS

In May 1962 Ian Fleming wrote the foreword to The Seven Deadly Sins,
*a collection of essays by distinguished writers such as Evelyn Waugh,
Edith Sitwell and W. H. Auden. The idea for the book had been Fleming's.*

I have various qualifications for writing an introduction to this series of distinguished and highly entertaining essays.

First of all I invented the idea of the series when, a couple of years ago, I was still a member of the Editorial Board of the London *Sunday Times*. This Board meets every Tuesday to comment on the issue of the previous Sunday, discuss the plans for the next issue and put forward longer-term projects.

It is quite a small Board of seven or eight heads of departments – I was Foreign Manager at the time – together with the Editor and the Proprietor, Mr. Roy Thomson, and we are all good friends, though at this weekly meeting, beneath the surface of our friendliness, lurk all the deadly sins with the exception of gluttony and lust. Each one of us has pride in our department of the paper; many of us are covetous of the editorial chair; most are envious of the bright ideas put forward by others, anger comes to the surface at what we regard as unmerited criticism, and sloth, certainly in my case, lurks in the wings.

The same pattern is probably followed at all executive meetings in all branches of business. When someone else puts up a bright idea, however useful or profitable it may be to the business concerned, traces at least of Envy, Anger and Covetousness will be roused in his colleagues. Yet, on the occasion when I put forward this particular 'bright' idea for the future, I seem to remember nothing but approbation and a genial nodding of heads.

The project was outside my own sphere of action on the paper and I heard nothing more of it until I had left the *Sunday Times* to concentrate on writing thrillers centred round a member of the British Secret Service called James

Bond. So I cannot describe what troubles the Literary Editor ran into in his endeavours to marry the Seven Deadly Sins to seven appropriate authors. So far as I can recall, the marriages I myself had suggested were closely followed, except that I had suggested Mr. Malcolm Muggeridge to write on the theme of Anger on the grounds that he is such an extremely angry man. In the event, as you will see, Mr. W. H. Auden was the brilliant choice.

My next claim to introduce these essays was my suggestion to Mr. Lawrence Hughes, a friend of mine and a Director of Morrows, that he should publish them in a book. Usually when one makes brilliant suggestions to a publisher a dull glaze comes over his eyes and nothing happens. But in this case Larry Hughes was enthusiastic and, despite all kinds of copyright problems, energetically pursued my suggestion and gathered these seven famous English authors together between hard covers – no mean feat if you know anything about copyright and literary agents.

So you might think I could justifiably allow myself a modest indulgence in the deadly sin of Pride. You would be mistaken. I have read and re-read these essays with pleasure and profit, but their moral impact upon me has been uncomfortable. To be precise and truthful, the critical examination of these famous sins by some of the keenest brains of today has led me to the dreadful conclusion that in fact, all these ancient sins, compared with the sins of today, are in fact very close to virtues.

To run through the list. I have always admired the Pride of Dame Edith Sitwell, the pride which, with her proudful brothers, has carried this remarkable literary family through battles of opinion and taste reaching back to my youth.

The Covetousness of Cyril Connolly, which he takes off so brilliantly in his piece of fiction, is one of his most endearing qualities and he would be a smaller and less interesting man without it.

The Gluttony for life, food, drink and women of Patrick Leigh-Fermor are the essence of his tremendous zest for everything. Lust? If Christopher Sykes is lustful, may he, and I for the matter of that, long remain so.

Envy has its ugly sides, but if I, as a second son amongst four, had not been envious of my elder brother and his achievements I would not have wished all my life to try and emulate him. As for Anger, surely we all need more rather than less of it to combat the indifference, the 'I'm all right, Jack' attitudes, of today.

Of all the seven, only Sloth in its extreme form of accidie, which is a form of spiritual suicide and a refusal of joy, so brilliantly examined by Evelyn Waugh, has my wholehearted condemnation, perhaps because in moments of despair I have seen its face.

How drab and empty life would be without these sins, and what dull dogs we all would be without a healthy trace of many of them in our make up! And has not the depiction of these sins and their consequences been the yeast in most great fiction and drama? Could Shakespeare, Voltaire, Balzac, Dostoevsky or Tolstoy have written their masterpieces if humanity had been innocent of these sins? It is almost as if Leonardo, Titian, Rembrandt and Van Gogh had been required to paint without using the primary colours.

The truth of course is that generally speaking these Seven Deadly Sins were enumerated by monks for monks, and one can easily see how mischievous and harmful they could be within a monastery.

We do not live in a monastery, but in a great pulsating ant heap, and this brings me back to the moral confusion into which I have been thrown by these essays and which amounts to feeling that there are other and deadlier sins which I would like to see examined by authors of equal calibre in a companion volume to this.

I have made a list of these Seven Deadlier Sins which every reader will no doubt wish to amend, and these are my seven: Avarice, Cruelty, Snobbery, Hypocrisy, Self-righteousness, Moral Cowardice and Malice. If I were to put these modern seven into the scales against the ancient seven I cannot but feel that the weight of the former would bring the brass tray crashing down.

But is this loose thinking? Could it perhaps be argued that if we are free of the ancient seven we shall not fall victim to their modern progeny? I personally do not think so, but it would need better brains than mine and a keener sense of theological morality than I possess to pursue the argument. As a man in the street, I can only express my belief that being possessed of the ancient seven deadly sins one can still go to heaven, whereas to be afflicted by the modern variations can only be a passport to hell.

And by the same token, what about the Seven Deadly Virtues?

What about the anal-eroticism which the psychologists tell us lies at the base of Frugality? How much is Charity worth when it springs from self-interest? Is political acumen a virtue as practised by the Communists? What hell Sociability can be! Where is the line to be drawn between Deference and, not to use a more vulgar, hyphenated word, Sycophancy? Neatness in excess becomes pathological, so does Cleanliness. How often is Chastity a cloak for frigidity?

But I have held you for too long from these wonderful, and each in its different way exciting, essays and I must at all costs avoid that deadliest of all sins, ancient or modern, a sin which is surely more durable than any of those I have enumerated – that of being a Bore.

THE ART, OR CRAFT,
OF WRITING THRILLERS

The transcript of a talk given to an Oxford student body in May 1962.

When I was your age, I was occasionally forced, for I never went willingly, to 'go to a lecture'. Today I don't remember a single word of anything any lecturer lectured me about. I would watch the man's face, rather as one does when one stops the car to ask someone the way. You watch the man's face without listening to his instructions and you then say thank you and drive on.

Apart from watching the lecturer's face, I used to keep a sharp eye on the pile of typescript in front of him and gratefully note the turning of each sheet. Having come to my private conclusions about his face and his clothes and the probable length of his lecture, I would drift off into a pleasant day-dream until the wonderful moment when the doors were opened and one could dash out into real life again.

So I sympathise warmly with all of you who observe this thick pile of paper and I apologise for it. Unfortunately I have not only got a bad memory but I also have nothing to say, and it is only by working very hard that I have got together what is commonly known as a lecture on the subject your President has chosen for me. But I can give you one word of encouragement; my talk is not going to be as long as it looks. The typing on this paper is not only triple-spaced, it is also in jumbo sized type printed by the same make of machine that fired off Sir Winston Churchill's scorching minutes during the war. So the pages will flip over quickly and, since what I am going to say has no relevance to your scholastic duties you can sit back and think of food and games and love until I have finished.

I gather that you would like to know how to write a thriller, and I shall tell you how to do it – exactly. What I shall tell you about writing will be very different from what you would hear from the mandarins of literature with whom I share the honour of addressing you in this Michaelmas term. When I scan the programme, which your amiable and energetic President has assembled, I feel out of place everywhere except in the 'Refreshments, band, females' that you enjoyed last Saturday.

I am not an angry young, or even middle-aged man. I am not 'involved'. My books are not 'engaged'. I have no message for suffering humanity and, though I was bullied at school and lost my virginity like so many of us used to do in the old days, I have never been tempted to foist these and other harrowing personal experiences on to the public. My opuscula do not aim at changing people or making them go out and do something. They are not designed to find favour with the Homintern. They are written for warm-blooded heterosexuals in railway trains, aeroplanes or beds.

I have a charming relative who is an angry young literateur of renown. He is maddened by the fact that more people read my books than his. Not long ago we had semi-friendly words on the subject and I tried to cool his boiling ego by saying that his artistic purpose was far, far higher than mine. He was engaged in The Shakespeare Stakes. The target of his books was the head, and, to some extent at least, the heart. The target of my books, I said, lay somewhere between the solar plexus and, well, the upper thigh. These self-deprecatory remarks did nothing to mollify him and finally, with some impatience and perhaps with something of an ironical glint in my eye, I asked him how he described himself on his passport. 'I bet you call yourself an Author,' I said. He agreed with a shade of reluctance, perhaps because he scented sarcasm on the way. 'Just so,' I said. 'Well, I describe myself as a Writer. There are authors and artists and then again there are writers and painters.'

This rather spiteful jibe, which forced him, most unwillingly, into the ranks of the Establishment, whilst stealing for myself the halo of a simple craftsman from the people, made the angry young man angrier than ever and I don't now see him as often as I used to. But the point I wish to make is that if you decide to become a professional writer you must, broadly speaking, decide whether you wish to write for fame, for pleasure or for money. I write, unashamedly, for pleasure and money. I say unashamedly because writing for money was once a respectable profession. Balzac did it, and so did Dickens. In fact, when Dickens found that reading his works aloud brought in more money than writing, he more or less gave up writing. Walter Scott may have enjoyed writing to begin with, but subsequently he only turned out books to satisfy his creditors. Trollope wrote for money as strenuously and impersonally as if he were working at the coal face. And then of course there was that man, what was his name again? who obviously hadn't the smallest idea he was writing as well as he was. He wrote for his supper in the troubadour fashion. When he became famous and 'got into the money', so to speak, he blew it all on having a coat of arms designed for himself and buying the biggest house in, where was it now? Stratford-on-Avon, and then had to sit down and churn out some more reams of blank verse to pay for it.

All this is heresy, and of course there is a big difference between being respectably married to a rich muse and being a literary prostitute, but I would like to make the point that, where fame is the spur for some, money is for others.

I also feel that, while thrillers may not be Literature with a capital L, it is possible to write what I can best describe as 'Thrillers designed to be read as literature' whose practitioners have included such as Edgar Allan Poe, Dashiell Hammett, Raymond Chandler, Eric Ambler and Graham Greene. I see nothing shameful in aiming as high as these.

All right then, so we have decided to write for money and to aim at certain standards in our writing. These standards will include an unmannered prose style, unexceptional grammar and a certain integrity in our narrative.

But these qualities will not make a best-seller. There is only one recipe for a best-seller and it is a very simple one. You have to get the reader to turn over the page.

If you look back on the best-sellers you have read, you will find that they all have this quality. You simply have to turn over the page.

Nothing must be allowed to interfere with this essential dynamic of the thriller. That is why I said that your prose must be simple and unmannered. You cannot indulge in 'beautiful, beautiful' prose. You cannot linger too long over descriptive passages. There must be no complications in names, relationships, journeys or geographical settings to confuse or irritate the reader. He must never have to ask himself 'Where am I? Who is this person? What the hell are they all doing?' Above all, and this goes for so many thrillers and detective stories, there must never be those maddening recaps where the hero maunders about his unhappy fate, goes over in his mind a list of suspects, or reflects on what he might have done or what he proposes to do next. There must be no wads of space-filling prose. By all means set the scene or enumerate the heroine's measurements as lovingly as you wish but, in doing so, each word must tell, and interest or titillate the reader before the action hurries on.

I confess that I often sin grievously in this respect. I am excited by the poetry of things and places, and the pace of my stories sometimes suffers while I take the reader by the throat and stuff him with great gobbets of what I consider *should* interest him, at the same time shaking him furiously and shouting 'Like this, damn you!' about something that has caught my particular fancy. But this is a sad lapse and I must confess that in one of my books, *Goldfinger*, three whole chapters were devoted to a single game of golf.

Well, having achieved a workmanlike style and the all essential pace of narrative, what are we to put in the book – what are the ingredients of a thriller?

Briefly, the ingredients are anything that will thrill any of the human senses – absolutely anything.

In this department, my contribution to the art of thriller writing has been to attempt the total stimulation of the reader all the way through, even to his taste buds. For instance, I have never understood why people in books have to eat such sketchy and indifferent meals. English heroes seem to live on cups of tea and glasses of beer and when they do get a square meal we never hear what it consists of. Personally I am not a gourmet and abhor wine-and-foodmanship. My own favourite food is scrambled eggs. In the original typescript of *Live and Let Die,* James Bond consumed scrambled eggs so often that a perceptive proof reader at my English publishers Jonathan Cape's, suggested that this rigid pattern of life must be becoming a security risk for James Bond. If he was being followed, his pursuer would only have to go into restaurants and say 'Was there a man here eating scrambled eggs?' to know whether he was on the right track or not. So I had to go through the book changing the menus.

This business of meals may seem a small thing to worry about, but in fact it is a part of all successful writing, which consists of writing interesting words rather than dull ones. Leaving out the economic factor, that is, the actual price of the food, it is surely more stimulating to the reader's senses if, instead of writing 'He made a hurried meal off the Plat du Jour – excellent cottage pie and vegetables, followed by home-made trifle' (I think this is a fair English menu without burlesque), you write 'Being instinctively mistrustful of all Plats du Jour, he ordered four fried eggs cooked on both sides, hot buttered toast and a large cup of black coffee.' No difference in price here, but the following points should be noted: firstly, we all prefer breakfast foods to the sort of food one usually gets at luncheon and dinner; secondly, this is an independent character who knows what he wants and gets it; thirdly, four fried eggs has the sound of a real man's meal and, in our imagination, a large cup of black coffee sits well on our taste buds after the rich, buttery sound of the fried eggs and the hot buttered toast.

You may well say that all this is nonsense, and so it would be if your target was the reader's intellect rather than his senses. However good the cottage pie and the trifle, eating them in one's imagination, as the reader will, is a banal experience and banality is the enemy of the English thriller writer. What I endeavour to aim at is a certain disciplined exoticism.

I have not thought this theme out very carefully, nor have I re-read any of my books to see if it stands up to close examination, but I think you will find that the sun is always shining in my books – a state of affairs which minutely lifts the spirit of the English reader – that most of the settings of my books are in themselves interesting and pleasurable, taking the reader to exciting places round the world, and that, in general, a strong hedonistic streak is always there to offset the grimmer side of James Bond's adventure. This, so to speak, 'pleasures' the reader and takes him out of his dull surroundings into a warmer, more colourful, more luxurious, world. In a fashion, which I suppose nowadays would be described as a 'subliminal', this predisposes him favourably towards the book.

At this stage, let me pause for a moment and assure you that, while all this sounds devilish crafty, it has only been by endeavouring to analyse the success of my books for the purpose of this essay that I have come to these conclusions. In fact, I write about what pleases and stimulates *me*, and if there is a strong streak of hedonism in my books it is there not by guile but because it comes out through the tip of my ball-point pen.

All right, now we have style and pace and plenty of pleasure. What other ingredients must we add?

In my case, though not in the cases of such masters as Ambler, Hammett and Simenon, my plots are fantastic, while often based upon truth. They go wildly beyond the probable but not, I think beyond the possible. Every now and then there will be a story in the newspapers that lifts a corner of the veil from Secret Service work. A tunnel from West to East Berlin so that our Secret Service can tap the Russian telephone system; Crabb's frogman exploit to examine the hull of the Soviet cruiser; the Russian spy Khoklov with his cigarette case that fired dum-dum bullets; the Gouzenko case in Canada that led to the arrest of Fuchs; The Man Who Never Was – the corpse with the false invasion plans that we left for the Gestapo to find on the Spanish coast. These are all true Secret Service history that is yet in the higher realms of fantasy, and James Bond's adventures into these realms are perfectly legitimate. Even so, they would stick in the gullet of the reader and make him throw the book angrily aside – for a reader particularly hates feeling he is being hoaxed – but for two further technical devices, if you like to call them that. First of all, the aforesaid speed of the narrative, which hustles the reader quickly beyond each danger point of mockery and, secondly, the constant use of familiar household names and objects which reassure him that he and the writer have still got their feet on the ground. This is where the real names of things come in useful. A Ronson lighter, a 4½ litre Bentley with an Amherst-Villiers supercharger (please note the solid exactitude), the Ritz Hotel in London, the 21 Club in New York, the exact names of flora and fauna, even James Bond's sea island cotton shirts with short sleeves. All these small details are 'points de repère' to comfort and reassure the reader on his journey into fantastic adventure.

Again I repeat that this technique is not, or certainly was not until I came to write about it, guileful. I *am* interested in things and in their exact description. I see no point in changing the name of the Ritz to The Grand Hotel Majestic, The Dorchester to The Porchester, or a Rolls-Royce to a Hirondelle. The technique crept into my first book, *Casino Royale*. I realised that the plot was fantastic and I wondered how I could anchor it to the ground so that it wouldn't take off completely. I did so by piling on the verisimilitude of the background and of the incidental situations, and the combination seemed to work.

Well, I seem to be getting on very well with picking my books to pieces so we might as well pick still deeper.

People often ask me, 'How do you manage to think of that? What an extra-ordinary (or sometimes extraordinarily dirty) mind you must have.'

I certainly have got vivid powers of imagination, but I don't think there is anything very odd about that. We are all fed fairy stories and adventure stories and ghost stories for the first twenty years of our lives and the only difference between me and perhaps you is that my imagination earns me money. But, to revert to my first book *Casino Royale,* there are three strong incidents in the book which carry it along and they are all based on fact. I extracted them from my war-time memories of the Naval Intelligence Division of the Admiralty, dolled them up, attached a hero and a villain and a heroine and there was the book.

The first was the attempt on Bond's life outside the Hotel Splendide. SMERSH had given two Bulgarian assassins box camera cases to hang over their shoulders. One was of red leather and the other was of blue. SMERSH told the Bulgarians that the red one contained a high explosive bomb and the blue one a powerful smoke screen, under cover of which the two assassins could escape. One was to throw the red bomb and the other was then to press the button on the blue case. But the Bulgars mistrusted the plan and decided to press the button on the blue case and envelop themselves in the smoke screen before throwing the bomb. In fact, of course, the blue case also contained a bomb powerful enough to blow both the Bulgars to fragments and remove all evidence which might point at SMERSH, so, when the Bulgar with the blue case pressed his button, both Bulgars were blown to pieces before the red bomb could be hurled at Bond.

Far-fetched, you might say. In fact, this was the identical method used in the Russian attempt on Von Papen's life in Ankara in the middle of the war. On that occasion the assassins were also Bulgars and they were blown to nothing while Von Papen and Frau Von Papen, walking from their house to the Embassy, were only knocked down and bruised by the blast.

As to the gambling scene, this grew in my mind from the following incident: I and my chief, the Director of Naval Intelligence – Admiral Godfrey – in plain clothes, were flying to Washington in 1941 for secret talks with the American Office of Naval Intelligence before America came into the war. We were taking the Southern Atlantic route and our seaplane touched down at Lisbon for an overnight stop. We had talks there with our Intelligence people and they described how Lisbon and the neighbouring Estoril were crawling with German secret agents. The chief of these and his two assistants, we were told, gambled every night in the casino at Estoril. I immediately suggested to the D.N.I. that he and I should have a good dinner and then go along to the casino and have a look at these people. We went and there were the three men, whose descriptions we had, playing at the high Chemin de Fer table. The D.N.I. didn't know the game. I explained it to him and then the feverish idea came to me that I would sit down and gamble against these men and defeat them, thereby reducing the funds of the German Secret Service. It was a foolhardy plan which would have needed a golden streak of luck. I had some £50 in travel money. The chief German agent had run a bank three times. I bancoed it and lost. I suivied and lost again, and suivied a third time and was cleaned out. A humiliating experience which added to the sinews of war of the German Secret Service and reduced me sharply in my chief's estimation.

It was this true incident which is the kernel of James Bond's great gamble against Le Chiffre.

Finally, the torture scene. There were many tortures used in the war by the Germans, but the worst were devised by the Moroccan-French. What I described in *Casino Royale* was a greatly watered down version of one of these French-Moroccan tortures known as 'Passer à la Mandoline which was practised on several of our agents.

So you see the line between fact and fantasy is a very narrow one and, if I had time, I think I could trace most of the central incidents in my books to some such real happenings as I have described.

We then come to the final and supreme hurdle in the writing of a thriller. You must *know* thrilling things before you can write about them. Imagination alone isn't enough, but stories you hear from friends or read in the papers can be built up by a fertile imagination and a certain amount of research and documentation into incidents that will also ring true in fiction.

A house is being demolished in the suburbs of Oxford, a Victorian villa let us say. In the cellars, the demolition team unearths a tiny theatre with a small stage and a dozen seats. Everything is upholstered in a faded red velvet. There are signs of recent use. What was this little theatre for? What went on there? Immediately our imagination takes off and is sent orbiting like a Sputnik in the sinister realms of black magic, Aleister Crowley, Cinémas Bleus, murdered virgins and the rest. What about that Cambodian student at Balliol? They say he eats live mice dipped in honey. Things with a capital T have been disappearing from the operating theatre of the hospital. What has happened to Prunella McNought, the pretty young physicist 'à la cuisse hospitalière', as the French put it so gracefully, at Lady Margaret Hall? She hasn't been seen for weeks. And so on and so forth. You see! We are almost there. All we need is a caricature of you for the hero, the four fried eggs, the hot buttered toast and the large cup of black coffee and 'The Blonde With A Bomb In Her Bustle' is on the bookstalls.

Having assimilated all this encouraging advice, your heart will nevertheless quail at the physical effort involved in writing even a thriller. I warmly sympathise with you. I, too, am lazy. Probably rather lazier than you. My heart sinks when I contemplate the two or three hundred virgin sheets of foolscap I have to besmirch with more or less well-chosen words in order to produce a 60,000 word book.

The method I have devised is this: I do it all on the typewriter, using six fingers. The act of typing is far less exhausting than the act of writing and you end up with a more or less clean manuscript. The next essential is to keep strictly to a routine – and I mean strictly. I write for about three hours in the morning – from 9.30 till 12.30 – and I do another hour's work between 6 and 7 in the evening. At the end of this I reward myself by numbering the pages and putting them away in a spring-back folder. The whole of this four hours of daily work is devoted to writing narrative. I never correct anything and I never look back at what I have written, except to the foot of the last page to see where I have got to. If you once look back, you are lost. How could you have written this drivel? How could you have used 'terrible' six times on one page? And so forth. If you interrupt the writing of fast narrative with too much introspection and self-criticism you will be lucky if you write 500 words a day and you will be disgusted with them into the bargain.

By following my formula, you write 2000 words a day and you aren't disgusted with them until the book is finished, which will be, and is in my case, in around six weeks.

I don't even pause from writing to choose the right word or to verify spelling or a fact. All this can be done when your book is finished.

When my book is finished I spend about a week going through it and correcting the most glaring errors and rewriting short passages. I then have it properly typed with chapter headings and all the rest of the trimmings. I then go through it again, have the worst pages re-typed and send it off to my publisher.

They are a sharp-eyed bunch at Jonathan Cape's and, apart from commenting on the book as a whole, they make detailed suggestions which I either embody or discard. Then the final typescript goes to the printer and in due course the galley or page proofs are there and you can go over them with a more or less fresh eye. Then the book gets published and you start getting letters from people saying that Vent Vert is made by Balmain and not by Dior, that the Orient Express has vacuum and not hydraulic brakes, and that you have mousseline sauce and not Béarnaise with asparagus.

But what, after all these labours are the rewards of writing, and in my case of writing thrillers?

First of all, they are financial. You don't make a great deal of money from royalties and translation rights and so forth and, unless you are very industrious and successful, you could only just about live on these profits but, if you sell the serial rights and film rights, you do very well. Above all, being a comparatively successful writer is a good life. You don't have to work at it all the time and you carry your office around in your head. And you are far more aware of the world around you. Writing makes you more alive to your surroundings and, since the main ingredient of living, though you might not think so to look at most human beings, is to be alive, this is quite a worthwhile by-product of writing, even if you only write thrillers, whose heroes are white, the villains black, and the heroines a delicate shade of pink.

SOME CAEN, SOME CAIN'T

A tribute to Herb Caen to mark his 25 years as a columnist for the
San Francisco Chronicle, *September 1963. Ian Fleming had written*
the Atticus column for the Sunday Times *from 1955 to 1957.*

No harm in starting off with a really bad joke. Master, or rather Past-master Caen has several times exercised his lamentable sense of humour at my and James Bond's expense and I am glad of this opportunity to strike back.

But a valid truism lies behind the execrable pun. To the uninitiated, it looks easy enough to be a columnist. What could be more simple than to sit down at the typewriter and ramble on about the passing scene – the human comedy?

After all, Boswell was no genius. He just wrote down what he saw and what he thought – commonplace stuff. He was no Shakespeare, no Shelley – a competent reporter with ink in his veins.

Ah, but that's the point! You must have ink in your veins. You really must love writing and communicating in order to sit down and write around 1000 words a day in such a fashion that people will read them. And that is what a daily columnist has to do.

Every day, come hangover, come flu, come lack of inspiration, come ailing wife or bawling children, he must go confidently and with seeming omniscience on stage and show himself to the public in naked black-and-white.

No excuses! you are a columnist, and by God you've got to fill your column to the satisfaction of your readers and, though this may be rare, to your own.

I know these things because I once wrote a column myself. I did it for three years and chucked it about five years ago when James Bond came to my rescue.

I was Foreign Manager of the *Sunday Times* (the real one. Not yours!)

145

and I thought that its gossip column, which went, and still goes, by the pompous name of 'Atticus' was so bad that I would have a bash at it in between coping with the future of the world and the marital tangles of my foreign correspondents.

I renamed the column 'People and Things' by Atticus, because I am interested in Things, and got into business. It went down all right, though I received more kicks than ha'pence from an editor whose sense of humour differed from mine, and from the readers who appeared only interested in writing in when I made a mistake, and to this day I am proud of two paragraphs of undying merit from that long stint.

The first, through a careful study of the psychology of the drinking American, correctly forecast the winning Miss Rheingold for that year (you see how right the editor was. Perhaps .007 per cent of *Sunday Times* readers had even heard of Rheingold beer).

The second, revealing the existence of a Grimsby troglodyte who smoked kippers as they should be smoked, brought in 4700 letters (a record for the paper) and incidentally made a fortune for the old man.

Is there a common denominator between my modest achievement and Herb Caen's majestic record? What's all this about Fleming anyway? We want to hear about Herb. Patience! Pacienza! Geduld!

Yes, there is a common denominator. Every columnist, and Herb Caen is a shining example, must be interested in everything, even in those matters which are outside his readers' ken, and he must communicate his enthusiasms to the reader, and, secondly, he must have some vague social purpose – a desire to help and instruct his readers and if possible right an occasional wrong (rescue the kipper merchant for instance).

But above all, whether exposing a peccant mayor or police chief (a favorite sport in the United States, I believe) or just writing about the smog, he must at all costs avoid being a bore.

For half a generation, and from the evidence of this anniversary accolade, Herb Caen, writing for perhaps the most wideawake community in the United States, somehow has managed, day in, day out, to avoid being a bore. For what it is worth, we have not, in Great Britain, got one journalist with anything like the same record.

And, in conclusion, I will tell you something else which is even more to his credit, and something which may be news to you. Some time ago, amongst my cuttings (clippings) I received a column by Herb Caen which affectionately but devastatingly sent up James Bond, pulling the author's leg almost out of its socket.

A saboteur in the way for SMERSH, I surmised and tucked the author's name away in my 'unfinished business' file.

When next in New York, I asked one of the hamlet's most famous editors about this fellow Caen.

'He's one of America's greatest columnists,' he said. 'We'd all like to get him. Trouble is, nothing on earth will drag him away from San Francisco'.

Well, feed your captive audience well. He's good for another 25 years at the coal face.

ON TRAVEL AND TREASURE

WHERE SHALL JOHN GO?

Ian Fleming's first article on Jamaica was published
in Horizon *in December 1947.*

My Dear John,

You are one of the million or more English citizens who intend to seek fortune and freedom abroad and I would like to encourage you because I don't believe we can go on borrowing money indefinitely to feed forty-eight million people. But I know you are vacillating between various corners of the world which have these essential virtues: English-speaking, sterling area, good weather, food, friends and 'freedom' (whatever you mean by that). I also know from your letters that although you have considered many refuges which have these blessings, you are alarmed by the social ambience of all of them.

On the one hand you are appalled by the tea-and-tennis set atmosphere in many of the most blessed corners of our Empire. You smell boiled shirts, cucumber sandwiches and the L-shaped life of expatriate Kensingtonia. At the other extreme you fear the moral 'dégringolade' of the tropics, the slow disintegration of Simenon's 'Touriste de Bananes'. In your imagination you hear the hypnotic whisper of the palm trees stooping too gracefully over that blue lagoon. You feel the scruffy stubble sprouting on your chin. The cracked mirror behind Red's Bar reflects the bloodhound gloom of those ruined features which contort painfully as you cough into a soiled handkerchief. You know you'll be dead before the next monsoon.

So it is in your mind's eye, and so it might easily be if you plumped for tropic sloth and had not the leather morale of a Scottish missionary.

But a middle way between the lethe of the tropics and a life of fork-lunches with the District Commissioner's wife can be achieved and I believe you will achieve it in Jamaica. In a desultory fashion I have examined a large part of the world – most of Europe, some of Canada and Australia, bits of Africa and a few islands, including Hawaii, Capri, Cyprus, Malta and Ceylon, America, including San Francisco and Florida. Even two short periods of work in Moscow (like the Gorbals but much larger and much, much duller when you've finished sightseeing). After looking at all these, I spent four days in Jamaica in July 1943. July is the beginning of the hot season and it rained in rods at noon, yet I swore that if I survived the contest I would go back to Jamaica, buy a piece of land, build a house and live in it as much as my job would allow. I went back in January '46, chose a site, designed a house, chose an agent and an architect and by last December all was finished. This year I had five weeks' holiday in the new house and I wish it could have been six months.

I live on the North Shore, opposite an invisible Cuba, on the eastern corner of a tiny banana port called Oracabessa (Golden Head). My neighbours, both coloured and white, are charming and varied. I have no regrets.

Jamaica, one of our oldest colonies and the most valuable of our British West Indian islands, is slightly smaller than Northern Ireland. It contains 1,250,000 souls, ten per cent of whom live in Kingston, the capital. At a *very* rough guess, I should say that there are 50,000 white inhabitants or constant visitors, and another 100,000 who would seem white to you or me. But enough of statistics. You can find them all in the *Encyclopaedia*, *Whittaker*, the *Handbook of Jamaica* or the *Handbook of the West Indies*. One of these will be in your public library. From your subscription library you can borrow any amount of travel books and novels about Jamaica (*High Wind in Jamaica* is mostly about Cuba), and you will note extensive literary associations with Monk Lewis, Beckford of Fonthill and Smollett. Cyril Connolly spent part of his 'blue' or post-graduate period here and Augustus John is amongst its many portrayers.

An atlas will show you that the island looks very like a swimming turtle – side view – with a range of mountainous hills stretching along its middle from its tail to its eye. At its tail, where also Kingston the capital lies, is a real mountain, the Blue Mountain, 7000 feet high, which grows the finest coffee in the world (with the same name). You will drink this coffee cold-distilled. That is, the coffee, freshly ground, is percolated over and over again with cold water until a thin black treacle is produced. This is very strong and contains all the aroma which, by roasting, would otherwise be lost on the kitchen air. A third of a cup with hot milk or water added will spoil you for all of the more or less tortured brews you drink in England.

The Blue Mountain, which *is* often blue, precipitates a good deal of rain at the Eastern end of the island and this end is therefore wetter and perhaps even more fruitful than the rest; but the spine of mountainous country which runs the length of the island has the same beneficial effect and gives Jamaican weather a variety which is stimulating and extremely healthy. (I can assure you that sun and calm blue seas and brassy heat can be more wearying and exasperating than the grey but ever-changing porridge in which you live and make sour moan.)

Another pleasant peculiarity of the weather, which has some simple but immaterial cause, is that at nine o'clock on most mornings throughout the year the 'Doctor's Wind' blows lightly in from the sea until, at six in the evening, the 'Undertaker's Wind' comes on regular duty and blows, from the centre of the island, the stale air out again. (Your room, or your house, should face so as to take advantage of this benefice.) On most nights of the year you can sleep with a light blanket if your room is fortunately placed on the island, but it will be clear to you that one cannot generalise about the weather or the temperature on an island with mountains all along its spine. This also applies to the humidity which, in the hot season, can be considerable at some corners and some levels, but unimportant at others. You must just find these things out for yourself and not listen to generalities.

As you can imagine, the landscape varies with the altitude. In parts the uplands, with their stone-walled meadows and Friesian cattle, remind one of Ireland or the Tyrol – except for the orchids and the backdrop of tropical trees and the occasional green lightning of parakeets or Bengal flame of a giant Immortel. Then you drop down often through a cathedral of bamboo or a deep-cut gully of ferns, into a belt of straight tropical vegetation – palms, cotton trees and Jamaican hardwoods such as ebony, mahoe, red bullet and the like. Amongst them grow thick the tribe of logwood and dogwood. Indigo comes from logwood and the bees make particular honey from its yellow blossom. (There is another variety of dogwood called 'Bitchwood', but this is politely referred to as 'Mrs. Dogwood'. I will tell you more of this likeable Jamaican *pudeur* later on.)

You will pass through meadows of sensitive plant (local name 'Shamelady') and pick some of the 2000 different varieties of flowers. There are innumerable butterflies and hummingbirds, and at night, fireflies of many kinds. In the distance, the sea will be breaking in silver on the reef and, because of the phosphorous, you will look like an Oscar if you bathe in some of the bays after dark.

The lowlands and the valleys which comb the flanks of the hills are all sugar cane, citrus, cultivated palms and bananas and various fruit-vegetables like mangoes, breadfruit, guavas, soursop, naseberries and the like. The cattle here will be mostly sleek Indian herds, imported (and now thriving) because of their tick-resistance. Another import you will see every day is the mongoose, brought in to kill the snakes. He has killed them all and has long since started on birds' eggs with disastrous consequences to all who build their nests in banks and near the ground. The only bird you will see too many of is the carrion crow, protected because he scavenges impeccably and with hideous magic the dead dog in the forest and the fish spines in your 'yard'.

The coastline is very varied. Coral rocks and cliffs alternate 'South Sea island' coves and bays and beaches. The sand varies too, from pure white to golden to brown to grey. The sea is blue and green and rarely calm and still. A coral reef runs round the island with very deep water beyond and over the reef hang frigate birds, white or black, with beautifully forked tails, and dark blue kingfishers. Clumsy pelicans and white or slate grey egrets fish at the river mouths. There is every kind of tropical fish from big game to breakfast. The latter are caught in seines or boxnets. All varieties of shellfish, of course, and beautiful sea-shells from conches to cowries (better on the South coast beaches like Negril and Black River). Black crabs are a great delicacy and are eaten highly spiced. Every now and then they march inland in herds (cf. lemmings in reverse) and if your house is in the way they march through it or over it and if your body or bed is in the way, they march over that too, and your face.

On your drives (New Standard, drive-yourself, costs about £10 a week) you will come upon many of the famous Jamaican 'great houses', particularly if you leave the excellent main highways and venture along the quite viable parochial roads. Such are Cardiff Hall, just sold by the Blagrove family after unbroken tenure since Cromwell gave it to an ancestor; Bellevue Plantation belonging to the Bryces; Harmony Hall in its fine palm-grove; Prospect, belonging to Sir Harold Mitchell; the ruins of Rose Hall (read *White Witch of Rose Hall,* by De Lisser, hotblooded sadism and slaves set in the 1850s) and many others.

A curious part of the island is the Cockpit Country known, the map says, 'by the name of Look Behind'. When taxes were introduced (1790) the Maroons, the Spanish Negro inhabitants of this province, would not pay. The Governor sent a company of redcoats up into their hills to enforce payment, but the Maroons repulsed them, set up their own government and refused allegiance to the Crown. They still refuse it, and are the only corner of the British Empire to do so. Their 'colonel' is a coloured man who, with all his 'government', wears a Sam Browne belt as a badge of office. He does very little governing except to maintain the rights of his people vis-à-vis the Governor. His people work and mix with their neighbours, intermarry and go and come as they please. But, since they pay no taxes, no roads have ever been built in the province and there are no public facilities such as post offices and social services. The terrain has never been surveyed and, if you look at the map, you will see a large white patch with the red veins of the roads coming to a full stop at the perimeter. There is nothing more to it than that and the inhabitants are quite uninteresting, but it's pleasant to live in a colony where a touch of zany persists.

A most remarkable feature of Jamaica is the abundance of mineral springs and baths. Some of these are already modestly developed and commercialised but only to the extent of some fifty bedrooms at the two main spas – Bath and Milk River (I wager there will be 500 in twenty years). Milk River has the highest radio-activity of any mineral bath in the world – nine times as active as Bath, England, fifty times as active as Vichy, three times as active as Karlsbad and fifty-four times as active as Baden in Switzerland. While you are curing your rheumatism or sciatica (or just having an aphrodisiac binge) you can fish for tarpon or a crocodile suitcase, all at 14/- (crocodile £1 extra).

As an amateur speleologist you will like the caverns and sinkholes which abound in the limestone hills. Up to a mile long, few of these have been explored and many are doubtless stuffed with pirate treasure including Sir Henry Morgan's hoard and the savings accounts of rich visitors from Columbus onwards.

The local music is Calypso, not as inventive as the original Trinidad varieties, but with the same electric rhythms. You can hire a good trio for upward of ten shillings an evening and they will play happily (happier with some rum) until the small hours. There are cheerfully unprintable versions of most of the songs, but you won't notice the words unless you master the Welsh intonation of the Jamaican voice and the occasional colloquialisms.

Bad or indecent language is almost absent from the native vocabulary. Thief, liar, badman are about the strongest words you will hear and these will mean real hate or rage. 'Will you do me a rudeness?' means 'will you sleep with me?', to which a brazen girl will reply 'you better hang on grass, I goin' move so much'.

Despite your visit to the Milk River, you would be very ill-advised to try any 'rudeness' with the local beauties. It would be unpopular with both coloured people and whites. For other reasons I would advise you to give a miss to the stews of Kingston although they would provide you with every known amorous constellation and permutation. One of the reasons why our Atlantic Squadron is based on Bermuda instead of Kingston (the Americans wanted us to contribute to the defence of Panama) was the veto of our naval health and welfare authorities. Kingston is a tough town – tough and dirty – despite all the exhortations of *The Daily Gleaner* (my favourite newspaper above all others in the world) and the exertions of the quite admirable Jamaican police force.

Apart from the shortcomings of Kingston, the only serious drawbacks to the island are the mosquitoes, sandflies, grass-ticks and politics. None of these are virulent hazards. Mosquitoes will only be met near swamplands and rivers, where they will force you to use netting and DDT. Sandflies are quite damnable on some beaches. They are tiny midges which bite hard and I can only advise you to use Milton on the bites and avoid some beaches. Grass-ticks will fasten on to bare skin if you walk thoughtlessly in cattle country. They will cause intense grief. It is most unlikely that you will try much cross-country walking owing to the nature of the country and the heat. If you do, wear high boots or tuck your trousers into your socks.

Politics? well, it's the usual picture – education bringing a desire for self-government, for riches, for blacker coats and whiter collars, for greater share (or all) of the prizes which England gets from the colony, for motor-cars, race-horses (a Jamaican passion), tennis clubs and tea parties and all other desirable claptrap of the whites. Two men are fighting each other to take over the chaperonage of Jamaica. Bustamante (a gorgeous flamboyant rabble-rouser, idol of the labour unions) and Manley, K.C. (the local Cripps and white hope of the Harlem communists. Brilliant and perhaps wise, he controls the black coats and white collars and has the right wife to help him. Between them they are the intellectual focus of the island). You would like both of these citizens although they would both say that they would want to kick you out. Neither has an able deputy and it is impossible to say who will succeed to and perhaps fuse this forked leadership. Holding wise and successful sway is the Governor, Sir John Huggins, with an admirable Colonial Secretary, H. M. Foot, brother of Michael and the rest of that remarkable brood. Lady Huggins, 'Molly' to the whole population, is a blonde and much-loved bombshell who wins tennis and golf tournaments and wrestles with the Colonial Office about the rights and concerns of all women of Jamaica. Heaven knows what the island will do without her.

I do not believe that you will find Island politics a grave danger in the future or that you will get your throat cut in the night as some Jamaican penkeepers (landlords) will have you believe. I expect that Jamaica should slip fairly quietly into a Caribbean Federation (perhaps with Dominion status) and that the liberality and wisdom of our present policy will take the edge off passions which were high some years ago. There will always be a racial simmering and occasional clashes between coloured and white vanities, but personally I rely on liking my neighbours at Oracabessa, on a dog called Himmler and on a Spanish tomb in my garden which is full of 'duppies' (local ghosts).

Well, those are the hazards of Jamaica and I think you will agree that they compare quite favourably with the more civilised risks – spivs, road-death, flu and vitamin deficiency – which infest your English life. (I have cancelled out Russians and atom bombs against Jamaican hurricanes which may, in the autumn, blow you over and your roof off at about five-yearly intervals.)

Food is delicious and limitless, but the cooking uninspired and 'English' unless you fight against it. Unbounded drink of all sorts (rum at 6/- a bottle up, Dutch liqueurs from Curaçao, French wines from Martinique and Guadeloupe, gins and whiskeys from England) and infinite cigars rolled in Havana on Jamaican thighs. New motor cars from England, America and France, and excellent textiles from Britain. (Good tailors and seamstresses will make you anything in one day to three, but best give a model to copy.) There are no permits or coupons and prices are reasonable (cheap outside Kingston or Montego Bay). Servants are plentiful but varied and are twelve to twenty shillings a week. They require exhortation and a sense of humour, which the majority appreciate. Hired labour will cost you 3/- a day (female) and 4/- (male) and furniture-makers are many and good. All labour requires exact instructions, constant reminders and an absolute veto on making things look 'pretty' (food, furniture, gardens, clothes). There is too much cruelty to animals, which are regarded as strictly expendable. Drivers tip their whips with heavy wire and attack the tender parts of their beasts with malignant and unerring precision. There is, of course, plenty of heavy drinking, particularly on Friday and Saturday nights, after pay-day, and there is some smoking of Indian hemp, or Marihuana or 'ganja' as it is called locally. (If you are caught at this, or at cockfighting, you will get about twelve strokes of the Tamarind switch, which I fancy is more painful than it sounds.)

Local black magic (obea) is scarce and dull but credited by most. It consists largely of brewing love-potions and putting on hoodoos. If you find a white chicken with its head cut off lying on your doorstep you have, or should have, had it. But the Jamaicans are most law-abiding and God-fearing and have a strictness of behaviour and manners which will surprise and charm you. Don't mistake me, these are no angels. The people go to law constantly over trivialities to give their neighbours evidence of their social advancement and often for the simple fun of hiring a white man. They fervently adhere to one of the religious denominations as you or I might join a Club, and when they go to church it is to swing 'Rock of Ages' and go right to town with 'Come all ye Faithful'! (The Salvation Army plays their jazz straight.) Nevertheless and for whatever reasons, law and the church are a great counterweight to the human extravagance which the hot sun breeds. I think you will appreciate the fairly solid civic framework which contains this tropic luxury. It is just enough to raise in you that moral eyebrow which the heat might otherwise have drugged.

I have not talked about the intellectual and artistic life in Jamaica because I am not particularly intellectual or artistic and I might misinform you. Nor have I mentioned the sort of people you may meet and make friends with in the island for there is the whole gamut, from Lord Beaverbrook to a glorified beachcomber with a fixation on swans.

Now, John, while I strongly advise you and your friends to come here for a holiday I cannot urge you to immigrate because I haven't done so myself and I really don't know how you would all stand up to it, what you would do when you got here, or what all your standards of living are. Jamaica is a small world with few industries which can afford learners. If you are all competent in your trades and professions (outside the middleman professions) you should be able to find a niche, but you must have enough money to live on while you look round and enough for your return passage if you don't succeed or don't like it. Remember that unless you are exceptional, you will be competing with coloured people in the lower ranks of all the jobs, and you will find this difficult and perhaps exasperating. If you are thoroughly competent, with really solid references, you may find a short cut through friends, or friends of friends. But, to begin with, work will be very hard and earnings small. Later, I guess you should do well since I am sure many new industries will come to Jamaica and much foreign capital and, if you are on the spot, you may get into one of the new enterprises. But don't forget, nearly all offices are in Kingston and I am not at all sure how you would like living there.

If you have your own resources, both material and spiritual, I think you could live a happy and modest life on £500 to £1000 a year, with a house, servants and all the rest. It will cost you about two to three thousand to build a house. The land will be about ten to a hundred pounds an acre, depending on situation. You MUST have a good water supply and a clear title. Rents vary all over the island. Income Tax is much the same as in England, but I fancy rather easier on the lower brackets.

If you come for a holiday, come between November and June. The other four months are hot and rainy. You can fly direct by British South American Airways in two days (£130, single). If you are very lucky you can travel in a banana boat, which is the cheapest way. The easiest in these days would be to get across the Atlantic by ship or plane and then fly down via Miami (three hours to Jamaica). Order your rooms in advance through a travel agency, but take a chance if they say 'full up'. You can send any amount of money to Jamaica by ringing up your bank and telling them to do it.

Well, that's enough, John. I can't think of anything else and if you want to know any more you must read some books or write to the Jamaica Hotels Association, Kingston, or one of the other addresses you will find in the

Handbook of Jamaica. You could also get in touch, but very politely, because they are not a travel agency, with the West India Committee, Norfolk Street, London.

Come soon and bring Ann and the children. The schools are excellent and the new West Indian University is just going up. I will give you a feast. The menu will be: Booby's Eggs – Black Crab – Roast Stuffed Sucking Pig with Rice and Peas – Guavas in Syrup with Cream – Blue Mountain Coffee, Yellow Chartreuse (pre-war). Pork-Chop's trio will play 'Gimme a shilling with a Lion upon it', 'Linstead Market', 'Iron Bar' and 'Saturday Night' and we will watch the fireflies and listen to the distant surf on the reef.

Tell the others,
Ian.

DIVING THROUGH
TWENTY-TWO CENTURIES

AN UNDERWATER REPORT ON
MEDITERRANEAN TREASURE

An article for the Sunday Times *on Jacques Cousteau's*
exploration of a Greek galley that had sunk in 250 BC off
a small island near Marseilles. April 1953.

Marseilles.

The mistral blew itself out during the night and we sailed at seven in the morning from the Vieux Port. Above the hullabaloo of the fishermen selling their miserable catch to the restaurant keepers (miserable in quality; the basis of bouillabaisse is scorpion fish and conger eel) there was a shout as three 'week-end' divers from the submarine factory at Toulon jumped off the tram and ran for the *Calypso* just as we were casting off. 'They're typical,' said Cousteau, as he took his ship out fast between the ranks of fishing smacks and pleasure craft that line this beautiful and ancient harbour. 'They get no pay. It's dangerous – we lost one of our best divers during the winter – and yet they give up their spare time to the wreck. Very few of my divers are paid hands. Those that are are permanent members of the crew, who dive and man the ship as well. Today we have the proprietor of a vineyard, a building contractor and a garage hand on board, and now these men from Toulon.'

I spoke to one of them – a young man as thick as a chest of drawers, with the curly black hair and fine swarthy features of a Phoenician. He had lost all the fingers of one hand on the detonator of a German mine, yet he was so strong that everyone used him as a sort of human machine tool. When anything had to be bent, broken or unscrewed it was brought to him and, with a great intake of breath, his hands would grapple with the object until it obeyed.

'I like diving,' he said, in answer to my question, 'because each dive is a new adventure. And we will go anywhere with the Commandant'. The truth, I believe, lay chiefly in the second reason. I have seldom seen such a devoted team, nor such iron discipline with so little display of authority. The only orders issued that day were from the bridge to the engine-room.

The golden Notre Dame de la Garde, 300 feet up in the sky, looked down on us from her eminence above the town as we came out of the harbour into a heavy swell from the north-west.

Below the Pharo light the dramatic statue of a dead seaman in the arms of an angel was no encouragement to a fair-weather spear-fisherman who intended to pioneer underwater journalism; and the ghost of the Man in the Iron Mask hanging round the torture chambers of the Chateau d'If, which we passed to starboard, led to thoughts of the possible fate of the 'man in the aluminium aqualung'.

The *Calypso* rolled heavily in the beam sea, and it was a relief to reach the shelter of the first of the barren, uninhabited islands that tail gradually off to the tiny rock of the Grand Congloué.

Commandant Cousteau talked on the radio-telephone to the team on the treasure island. '*Calypso* speaking. Hallo, Port *Calypso*, Hallo, Port *Calypso*. Over.' And the cheerful voice on the island came back, 'Bonjour, Command-ant. J'écoute'. Questions were asked about the state of the sea off the island, and about the results of the previous day's diving. A ring had come up in the suction pump. Great excitement on the bridge. Was it gold? No, copper, but certainly a finger ring.

The archaeologist was dubious, but elated. The galley probably carried a crew of about 16, he told me. 'They must all have had their personal effects on board – perhaps even some presents for girlfriends in Marseilles. But there are months of work ahead before we shall see the whole picture. For the time being we only know that she sank in about 250 BC and that she carried a big cargo of wine and medium-priced pottery of all kinds. All the rest is specu-lation. In July we are going to invite the world's leading archaeologists to a reunion at Marseilles. By then we hope to have most of the wreck on display in the museum, and they will be able to argue it all out for themselves. There will probably be bloodshed. It will be great fun.'

This cheerful young expert from the Musée Borély in Marseilles is the butt and the mascot of the white ship's company. They play endless jokes on him. The favourite one is to smuggle some mysterious object down to the wreck and then to bring it up all covered with mud – a doorknob or the handle of a chamberpot – and watch his excitement and delight change to mock rage. And yet, when there is a real find they hang on his lips and listen with awe as he tells how it fitted into the life of more than 2000 years ago.

Suddenly the island was ahead of us, a white rock sparsely covered with seagrass and flowers and inhabited only by lizards and sea birds, rising straight out of the waves. The house-flag, depicting Calypso, daughter of Atlas and queen of the bottom of the sea on a green background, fluttered up above the yellow cabin that with the rest of the installation cost so much blood, sweat and tears before the winter set in. We could hear the roar of the suction pump, whose thick tube is suspended over the sunken galley from a boom that reaches out from the base of the rock.

On board the *Calypso* the powerful German compressors began to clatter as the air cylinders were filled to 300 lb. pressure for the divers, the first of whom was already climbing into his skin-tight foam-rubber suit. We had hardly tied up a cricket pitch away from the rock, before he was over the side and the day's work had begun.

And so it went on all through the day, web-footed Martians stumping heavily to the ladder and disappearing, suddenly light and graceful, into the gunmetal depths. The reassuring fountain of bubbles that meant all was well 150 feet below, the chronometer ticking away their minutes, and the occasional rifle shot to the surface of the sea to recall some enthusiast who had overstayed his 15 minutes on the wreck.

A steady, well-devised, cautious routine that left no room for mistakes. And every half an hour the thrilling chatter of the winch bringing up the wide net container piled high with the treasures the divers had put into it.

Then we all hurled to the dripping muddy pile of gifts, like children unleashed on a Christmas tree, carrying anything strange or new in triumph to the archaeologists, sorting, cleaning, panting under the weight of the objects that under the sea the divers had lifted so easily, quickly clearing the container so that it could go down again to this wonderful bargain basement whose doors had been thrown open to us by Cousteau.

I can not describe the romance and excitement of the scene better than to say that it contained at the same time elements from *King Solomon's Mines*, *Treasure Island* and *The Swiss Family Robinson*.

The sea had become glassy calm beneath a strong clear sun, swarms of fish played around the ship among the rich food rising from the disturbed sands of the wreck. The seagulls chattered and cawed among their nests in the cliffs, and Commandant Cousteau's two sons, aged 12 and 14, played and swam and climbed, to remind us all that this whole affair of buried treasure really belonged to the children in all of us.

After lunch, and a good deal of argument, I was allowed to go down as far as my physical resistance would allow, so that I could see the reverse of the medal – the serious business of skin-diving in 25 fathoms. The Mediterranean looked extremely black and deep. I even wondered whether National Health Insurance covered this alien hazard, and when it came to spitting in my mask to clear it I found it difficult to summon the necessary saliva.

I put on 30 lb. of equipment and went over the side and looked down into limitless grey depths and tried to remember to breathe quietly through the aqualung. I swam slowly down and drifted with my arms round the broad tubes of the suction pump. It rattled and shook against me with the upward jet of stones and broken pottery. I looked up at the distant hull of the ship and at the idle screw. The surface of the sea was a sheet of mercury illuminated in one spot, like a star sapphire, by the sun.

My fellow-diver came down past me in a wake of bubbles, and the yellow compressed-air cylinders on his back and his blue webbed feet disappeared beneath me. As I let go of the tube and went slowly after him I wished I had done something like this before.

About halfway down to the wreck my ears began to hurt, and I swam side-ways to the line that reached down to the rope container. They continued to hurt. Cousteau had said they would and that I must wait until the pain stopped. I waited and watched a swarm of sardine-size fish pass by on some common errand.

I went down a few more yards until I could see the distant figure of my fellow-diver flickering round a black area on the bottom – the deep excavation in the after-part of the galley. The pain would not relax and I made my way reluctantly up the cold grey corridor to the surface.

'You would have burst your eardrums if you had gone deeper,' said

Cousteau cheerfully as my equipment was stripped off me. 'I knew the pain would stop you making a fool of yourself. It needs several dives to train the Eustachian tubes. Anyway, now you know what these men have been doing all through the winter. The sun doesn't often shine for us like this.'

He went back to the post by the rail that he never left when one of his men was below.

On that day we brought home 64 three-foot amphoras, 20 of them in pristine condition, many black-finished saucers and plates, a fine wine jar for the table, much timber from the hull – pinewood planks, 18 inches broad by 1½ inches thick, pierced transversely with thin staves to mortise them into their neighbours – a three-foot heavy length of oak judged to have been part of the rudder-oar, a heavy lead running-ring thought to have been attached to the sail, and a handful of square-cut bronze and copper nails up to a foot in length.

'A medium day,' said Cousteau, as he brought the *Calypso* quietly in among the life of the Vieux Port at ten o'clock that night. We dispersed exhausted to our beds, leaving this tireless man and his devoted crew to their final labours.

When I got back to my room I looked up a quotation which I had taken from *The Aquarium*, by Philip Gosse, the great naturalist who a hundred years ago was the first to teach our great-grandfathers and great-grandmothers to poke about the rock pools and discover the secrets of the sea. This is what he wrote in 1854.

A paragraph went the rounds of the papers a month ago to the effect that an eminent French zoologist, in order to prosecute his studies on the marine animals of the Mediterranean had provided himself with a watertight dress, suitable spectacles and a breathing tube, so that he might walk on the bottom in a considerable depth of water. Whether a scheme so elaborate was really attempted I know not, but I should anticipate feeble results from it.

I poured some peroxide into my aching ears and took the lid off my typewriter.

ELDOLLARADO

A TRANSIENT'S IMPRESSIONS OF NEW YORK

A column on New York, published in the Sunday Times *in June 1953 with the heading 'A Transient's Scrapbook from New York'. This is taken from the original typescript. 'Reflections in Stressed Concrete' and 'PS from Bermuda' were not included in the printed version.*

KEEPING UP WITH THE ROCKEFELLERS

Tipping is a pestiferous business and it would be a wonderful thing if UNESCO or the UN Commission on Human Rights would establish a World Tipping Code. On my last night in the *Ocean Belle* my advice on the subject was sought by a group of three American couples bearing names which you would know. My eyes started from my head as each couple showed its hand. 'I always give my cabin steward £20.' 'We've done a lot of entertaining in the Veranda Grill and we're dividing £40 between the head waiter and the two others.' 'Would £5 be enough for the Turkish Bath man?' 'And what about you?' I was torn between various emotions. My feelings for the working-man triumphed. 'I think you're being very generous,' I said. 'You'll certainly all get an extra couple of teeth in the farewell smile.' Under cover of their rather thin laughter I escaped with my pair of Jacks unseen. For the four nights, I tipped my cabin steward £2. He seemed perfectly happy and I am not ashamed to offer the figure as a target for praise or blame.

REFLECTIONS IN STRESSED CONCRETE

There is always a lift of the heart as one drives up from the river into the heart of New York. The line of the streets and the skyscrapers is so clean, the air so clear and blue, the girls on the sidewalks so pretty. Even the howl of the pneumatic drills, the resounding efflatus from the vacuum brakes of the green and silver buses, the tinny clangour of the taxicabs are on that first drive a stimulating part of the harsh but poignant idiom of this majestic city. But already at that first exciting moment one knows that two weeks will be enough of it and one sighs at the thought of all the tasteless frozen food one will eat, all the harsh unnecessary liquor one will drink, all the unsurprising, unspiced, unpersonal conversations one will have and one wonders what is happening in one's own combative little village in that congeries of little warm independent-minded villages that is London. And then one arrives at one's destination and ten minutes later the purring telephone has swept one into the arms of the American welcome and thoughts of home are banished as one's ego takes wing.

THESE NAMES MAKE BAD NEWS

For a time the Coronation ('It's going to mean a great religious revival round the world' is a comment I have heard several times) ousted McCarthy as topic 'A' in New York and I believe throughout America, but now he is top-billing again, and you simply can't stop talking about him or reading about him. There are various reasons for this: he has a really expert publicity machine, he is always springing or cooking-up a new surprise, people are terrified and fascinated by him, and 'he may be a sonofabitch but, darn it, he's always right'. Homosexuals in the State Department, British ships trading with China, un-American books in American embassies abroad. Each scandalous broadside has missed with ninety-nine calumnies and hit with one. And that one is enough in a country where every man is born with a chance to be President and where, in consequence, every man aches to prove the Administration wrong. McCarthy is just pressing the trigger of a gun which is loaded and aimed by a huge cross-section of the public. Walter Winchell has been doing much the same thing for thirty years, and he goes on doing it to a guaranteed public of around ten million every week. Is there a connection between them? And what role does Edgar Hoover of the F.B.I. play in all this, the Washington Fouché who has controlled the American secret police for the amazing span of twenty-seven years? These three men are the recipients of all the private grudges of America. They are the overt and covert crusaders against un-Americanism. The sun would indeed be darkened if history were to bring them together, or any closer together, before this giant country has found itself.

TALES OF KINSEYLAND

But August 20 is K-Day and on that day the topic that transcends all others will sweep away even the sombre thoughts I have touched on above. For on that day will be published Dr. Kinsey's *Sexual Report on the Human Female*, and on that day every newspaper, every dinner table, will go hog-wild. Already the excitement is terrific. The Report is completed and scarifying tales and rumours are leaking out of the peaceful, beautiful campus of Indiana University where what might be described as semesters are being held to allow newspaper and magazine men (and women) to digest the huge tome and squeeze out the meatiest 3000 word thesis for release in each paper on K-Day. Not a word more than 3000 or someone will reach for a lawyer. So far two semesters have been held. One in May and one in June. And there is another to come.

JOTTINGS ON A NYLON CUFF

Canasta has become the favourite card game of America, leading Contract Bridge by ten per cent – a wide margin. Bolivia is the name of a new variation I don't intend to learn. Bolivia is really a standardisation of Samba, which I have also eschewed. Three packs. Going-out requires a sequence canasta and a regular canasta. Wild card canastas score 2500 points. Black threes left in your hand cost a hundred points each against you. Game is 15,000 points.

Who do you think is touring America promoting it? Who but that Queen of the Green Baize, our old friend Ottilie H. Reilly.

The latest and most deadly way of making a dry Martini is to pour a little dry vermouth into a jug, swirl it round and throw it down the sink. Fill jug with gin and place in ice-box until tomorrow. Then serve (or drink from jug). Note that there is no wasteful dilution with ice-cubes.

Despite these two lethal American inventions, canasta and cocktails, expectancy of life in New York City is: White male 66 years. White female 72 years! Corresponding figures for the United Kingdom are 61.4 and 65.8 years. We must be brave about these figures and forget them.

The germ-consciousness of America is rapidly becoming a phobia, battened on by doctors, druggists and advertisers. People actually prefer foods that are frozen or tinned or preserved. They are more hygienic. And what about this? Brown eggs are virtually unobtainable in New York. 'Customers won't touch 'em,' my Super-Market told me. 'They're dirty.'

PS FROM BERMUDA

When Sir Winston Churchill has a whim it is a whim of iron. A detachment of Welch Fusiliers is coming from Jamaica to act as guards for the Bermuda conference. The Prime Minister has personally insisted that their famous regimental goat shall accompany them. Bermuda quarantine laws forbid the importation of any livestock from the Caribbean because of tick fever. Anyway, they said, there was no ship to carry the goat. Delouse the goat, said the Prime Minister. And the goat must fly. I think we can confidently expect the goat to be at the conference.

FIFTY-CENT ANGELS

Broadway Angels Inc. has made a Common Stock issue of 570,000 shares at fifty cents a share to allow 'the small investor an opportunity to employ funds in diversified enterprises connected with the Broadway Theatre'. The stock will be traded on the 'Over-the-Counter-Market'. The issue was made on March 1 and the President of the company, a Mr. Wallace Garland, tells me it is already three-quarters subscribed by some 2000 investors. 'Of course, you *can* lose 100 per cent of the capital invested in one show,' said Mr. Garland. 'But look at *Voice of the Turtle*. 3000 per cent profit. *Mister Roberts*, 500 per cent profit. *Harvey*, 4000 per cent profit. Do you think the British would be interested?' 'I'm sure they would be,' I said. 'I'll tell them about it.'

(P.S. 'Show Business' tells me that normally the angel has a thirty-seventy chance of making his money back. And, of course, there's Treasury permission to get. But it would be fine to own a piece of Ethel Merman.)

TREASURE HUNT AT CREAKE ABBEY

An account for the Sunday Times, *written in July 1953, of Ian Fleming's visit to Creake Abbey in the county of Norfolk, where he used some of the earliest metal detecting technology.*

The needle on the micro-ammeter was steady on zero. There were some rain-clouds in the sky, and through the fringes of them the July sun blazed down with extra heat. From somewhere came the drowsy swish of a scythe. Under the eaves of the neighbouring house the martins twittered softly round a broken nest. Twenty feet away, at the end of the black snake of cable, Corporal Hogg, R.E., slowly swung his locator in a wide arc over the disused herb-garden beneath which, four feet down, lay the tiled floor, untrodden for 400 years, of the Chapter House of the ancient Abbey of Creake.

Suddenly there was a flicker on the control instrument which I was operating. Then a sharp dip, which went on through forty to sixty, then to a hundred, the end of the scale. The Corporal would be seeing the same figures on the dial in front of him, on the frame of his locator. I turned the sensitivity-switch down to nine, then to eight, then to seven. Still the needle clung to the end of the scale.

'Six, Corporal,' I called. 'Sixty on six.' The Corporal inched the long nose of his locator through a clump of rosemary. The needle swung back towards zero. He moved the locator back and at once the needle returned to sixty. He stopped. 'Here,' he said.

'There comes a time in every rightly constructed boy's life when he has a raging desire to go somewhere and dig for hidden treasure,' wrote Mark Twain in the *Adventures of Tom Sawyer.* In me that particular boy has never died.

Ever since, on May 3 last, the *Sunday Times* offered to investigate likely tales of buried treasure, I had been examining the letters that came in to the

171

Editor. I had had helpful talks with the Royal School of Mines on methods of detecting different metals under the ground; Messrs. Siebe Gorman had advised on problems of underwater search and hazards of foul air (in wells, for instance); and the Special Branch of Scotland Yard had told me where people usually hide things.

But it was the Sappers whose perennially adventurous spirit was immediately stirred. Certainly they would help. They would be glad to test out some of their latest mine-detecting equipment on unknown metals in enclosed areas. So long as no cost fell on the public funds and in exchange for a detailed report on the technical results, they would produce two expert men, with equipment, for a maximum of three days. 'UBIQUE' is more than a motto for the Sappers.

The sites that had been suggested were narrowed down to three. Because of its spectral name we finally chose Creake Abbey, the ruins of a twelfth-century Augustine foundation a few fields away from Nelson's birthplace at Burnham Thorpe, and adjoining the great Norfolk estate of Holkham. Rumours of buried treasure have hung round these ruins ever since the sixteenth century, but no attempt has been made to find the treasure since a rascally unfrocked priest named William Stapleton tried to raise the spirits of the monks and make them divulge their secret in 1528, about twenty years after the Abbey had been dissolved. It is recorded that after six weeks he 'returned to London disconsolate'.

The present owners, Rear-Admiral H. G. Thursfield and Mrs. Thursfield, who live in the beautiful house that merges into the ruins, were extremely sceptical but extremely kind, and in due course we assembled on the lawn that now covers the Cloister Garth of the Abbey – myself, my assistant, Mr. Peter Kirk, who provided all the documentation on the site, Captain Hough, R.E., who had come to see that his men were in good hands, Corporal Hogg of the bomb-disposal force of the Royal Engineers, and Emil Schneider, one of the German ex-P.O.W.s who are volunteers in the same dangerous trade. (He at once became 'Emil the Detector'.)

During the whole of that day we worked with the locator (ERA No.1, Mark 2), and with the more familiar Polish mine-detector Mark IV A, the machine that looks rather like a vacuum-cleaner and screams in your ear when it detects any metal down to a depth of about two-feet-six. The ERA locates only ferrous metals, but it is effective to a depth of about six feet. Thus the detector is good for walls and floors and the locator for tumuli and for deep earth over original foundations.

Our hopes were high but inchoate. We didn't know if there was a treasure. We didn't know what metal we were looking for and we didn't know whereabouts in the Abbey ruins and their surroundings to look for it. We covered the supposed site of the Chapter House, of the Abbot's Lodgings, of the Cloisters and the Cloister Garth, and we quartered the grass-grown floor of the Abbey itself. Every time we got a good fix we marked the spot with a bit of paper. And then we started to dig.

In two days we dug up about thirty nails of different sizes, one frying-pan, one mole trap, one oil-drum and about a hundredweight of miscellaneous scrap-iron – all judged to be artefacts of the early twentieth or, at best, late nineteenth century. The sweat poured from our brows and our muscles ached. Our jokes about twelfth-century sardine-tins ceased at an early stage and when we even failed to find the Admiral's lost signet-ring in the chicken run (I mean Abbot's Lodgings) we decided to call it a day.

But somehow we weren't as cast down as might be imagined. We comforted ourselves with the knowledge that this had been in the nature of a 'dummy run'. The machines had exceeded our expectations; we had documented ourselves most carefully on the site and the history of the period; we had conscientiously investigated every possible clue. We really had *hunted* the treasure.

And as for the treasure itself, we felt inclined to agree with Mark Twain that 'It's hid in mighty particular places, Huck – sometimes on islands, sometimes in rotten chests under the end of a limb of an old dead tree, just where the shadow falls at midnight; but mostly under the floor in haunted houses'. But certainly not, we decided, or probably not, or at any rate possibly not, at the Abbey of Creake in Norfolk.

THE CAVES OF ADVENTURE

Two reports on a record-breaking exploration of the cave of
Pierre St Martin in France. Sunday Times, *August 1953.*

I

The Pyrenees are riddled with caves. So are all those counties of France, Corrèze, Vienne, Dordogne and the rest, that lie between the Atlantic and the Mediterranean. Caves that first animals lived in, then men. Caves, like those of Lascaux, that were the private cathedrals or art galleries of man 20,000 years ago. In them, deep underground by the light of bonfires, they painted like Picasso, and then repainted and engraved in the rocks, still through the centuries like Picasso.

And other caves, like some that Norbert Casteret has found, where the animals went to die. Prehistoric cemeteries for bisons and stags and bears. And still other caves, in which today the shepherds of the Pyrenees preserve their meat through the summer. Caves used by bandits and by British soldiers and airmen escaping during the war. Caves like the great Cave of Pierre Saint Martin, which was first explored last year and which contains nothing of interest but millions of gallons of water, running at a speed of a metre a second, that may soon give electricity to an area of France as big as Kent.

I am writing this at the opening of this gigantic cave, 6000 feet up among the lower peaks of the Pyrenees. The shaft goes down into the side of a mile-wide stony amphitheatre that might have been blasted by an atom bomb. It is a desolate place, grey and harsh, with only a few stunted pines to give shade. At the side of the shaft there is the winch covered by a tent and the telephone line to men who are down there now. Two members of the expedition are on watch.

For hours and even days nothing happens, and then the winch starts to whine and more than one hour later a man in a miner's white steel helmet is helped out of the top of the shaft, taken out of his harness and stripped of his dripping overalls.

The people who explore caves are called speleologists, but, in fact, they are adventurers pure and simple. They like going deep into the earth in the same way that Hillary likes climbing a mountain, or Thor Heyerdahl likes drifting across the Pacific on a raft.

This cave at Pierre Saint Martin was discovered in 1950 by a speleologist named Lépineux who saw a jackdaw fly out of a jagged hole in the rock. He knew that jackdaws nest only where there is a long drop below. Lépineux climbed down the hole and enlarged it. He threw a stone down it and could not hear the fall.

In 1952 a team consisting of the greatest speleologists in France made the first exploration. One of them, Marcel Loubens, was killed when his harness broke on that great vertical shaft 1000 feet deep, down which he was being lowered on a quarter-inch steel cable. This morning I attended a Requiem Mass held at the opening of the cave on the anniversary of his death.

Before Loubens was killed the team had mapped the series of caverns and this year most of the same team is present. If there is a leader it is Norbert Casteret, who I suppose is the greatest speleologist in the world. He was born and still lives about 20 miles from here, and has spent his whole life exploring the caves of the Pyrenees.

He has discovered the oldest statuary in the world. He has been down the deepest abyss in France and has also altered the map of south-west Europe by discovering the true source of the River Garonne. His wonderful book *Ten Years Under the Earth* was 'crowned' by the French Academy.

This year the French Government has taken a hand. The French Army carried out a parachute drop last week of all the provisions for the expedition. They dropped ten tons of heavy equipment against the side of the mountain. Nothing was damaged and everything is working perfectly.

So far the team has penetrated nearly two miles along the slowly descending tunnel towards the Kakouetta Gorge. There are about 1¼ miles still to go before the hydro-electric engineers attached to the expedition learn where they can sink a shaft to bring the huge reservoir of hydro-electric power down into the valley with a sufficient drop behind it. Twelve hundred feet below me as I write, in a temperature of three degrees centigrade, there is the base camp with tents, heating devices and special food.

Down there at this moment are five men, including Lépineux, who first discovered the cave and has now been down for three days. They have just broken contact with the telephone and will not be heard again for 24 hours, during which time they may have learned the final course of the underground river, and, incidentally, may have broken the world record for the lowest descent into a natural cave. The record now stands at 2000 feet. They are esti-mated to be 100 feet above this at the moment.

And I sit here, watching the black mouth of the cave – and vaguely mis-trusting it and the validity of the whole enterprise – and the thin life-line that winds on the winch; and one hopes that the living men will come out safely and leave their dead comrade, Marcel Loubens, where he is and would wish to be with the epitaph of Charles Cotton, the friend of Izaak Walton, who wrote:

> O my beloved caves!
> From dogstar's heat
> And all anxieties my safe retreat!
> What safety, privacy, what true delight!
> In the artificial night
> Your gloomy entrails make,
> Have I taken, do I take.

As I came down the mountain this evening a speleologist of a rival group was carried past me on a stretcher. His skull was broken. I hope I shall be able to summon more enthusiasm for this sport before the expedition closes down next Thursday.

II

The 1953 expedition into the great caves of Pierre Saint Martin is over, without accident and with results which, in the realm of speleology, are sensational.

Now that everyone is back in the valley and the mule trains are coming down the mountain with the heavy gear, there is not an individual connected with the expedition who is not profoundly relieved. Since I reported last week there has been a series of alarms.

A majestic thunderstorm hit the central Pyrenees, washed away a small village and killed six of the inhabitants. Lightning is attracted by caves, particularly a cave into which two thousand feet of cable descends. But it never struck.

Communications broke down several times. A member of one of the relief teams (not a Frenchman) had a mild attack of claustrophobia, and had to be brought to the surface. Finally, there was difficulty in bringing out the last man. The unweighted cable would not go down the shaft. Three men had to be lashed at intervals down the face of the shaft to help the end of the cable round the corners.

But now all is well, and here are the results given to me in an exclusive interview by the leaders of the expedition: Robert Levi, the organiser, Norbert Casteret, the chief explorer, and Lépineux, the great speleologist who discovered the cave.

The record for the deepest descent into a natural cave has been handsomely beaten at 728 metres. It was previously held by the Italian Capabranca with a 632 metres' descent into the Preta cave – the 658 metres' descent of Chevalier into the Chartreuse massif is held not to qualify, since several intermediate lateral exits were available (of course there is the old Everest trouble about which member of the expedition actually broke the record. 'It was the team,' is the official and acceptable verdict).

Four more huge chambers were discovered, the last of them far greater even than the Marcel Loubens Cave. This colossal cave is judged by Casteret to be the greatest enclosed cavern so far discovered in the world. It is certainly the deepest. It has been christened the Verna Cave, after the Verna group of speleologists from Lyons (wrongly described as scouts) who have played a great part in the whole saga.

In Casteret's opinion, which will be widely respected, the Verna Cave is undoubtedly one of the wonders of the world. It is domed. The walls and floor are straight and smooth, but the floor is encumbered here and there by uneasily balanced towers of stone blocks, each as big as a cottage, which soar up into the darkness. Through the floor runs the great black river, swift and deep and silent. The air is pure and damp, with a temperature of four degrees centigrade. The water temperature is three degrees centigrade and it runs at half a cubic metre per second.

One or two tiny coleoptra, described to me as 'aphenops' were found, and a centipede, dead white and almost transparent. These were the only living organisms found in the course of the expedition.

Details, distances and dimensions are not yet available. Last year, apparently many errors were made in the estimates, and these will have to be corrected before the official figures of the expedition to date can be made known, but it seems that about a mile and a half of fresh ground was covered, as the result of which much of the underground picture as portrayed in last Sunday's map is changed. This map was adapted from the sketch – now out of date – in Tazieff's *Caves of Adventure* (published by Hamish Hamilton).

In particular what was thought to be a long tunnel extending in an easy slope from the Loubens Cave, turns out to be the new series of four chambers mentioned above, so that the whole underground picture looks like a string of seven different sized sausages joined together by varying lengths of tunnel which is about four times the circumference of the London Tube.

All the chambers and tunnels are encumbered by fallen rock that rendered progress most difficult and exhausting. 'The whole affair was very dangerous,' Casteret told me. Before the last great cave there was a beautiful waterfall with a drop of 20 metres which had to be descended, and then the river ran on over pebbles and stones until at the end of the last cave, it disappeared through broken rock in the floor.

Thus hydro-electrically the expedition seems to have been a failure, and although this is denied by the explorers, I believe it to be the opinion of the experts. But a local group of speleologists from Pau are dynamiting a blow-hole further down the mountain, known as the 'Trou du Vent', which, it is thought, may lead towards a resurgence of the underground river. The wind comes howling up from the earth out of this hole, and there is a distant roar of great waters.

For the rest, the equipment worked perfectly and the health of the explorers was excellent, thanks to the heating of the tents at night by a new system described to me as 'petrol-catalysis' which allows the men to breathe dry air. Sleep, appetite and digestion were normal. No stimulant drugs were used, and the food consumed was unusual only in its high sugar and fat content. The winch worked perfectly.

A full length 35 millimetre film with some sound was made by Hertot, the photographer of Commandant Cousteau, using acetylene torches and magnesium flares for lighting.

The painful arguments about the disposal of the body of Marcel Loubens ended with the agreement of the family to allow his body to remain inside the mountain. It may not be buried or cremated. It must remain under its pile of boulders, perfectly preserved in this frigid air, surmounted by the disintegrating cross of phosphorescent paper that had long since ceased to shine and the epitaph cut into the rock face, 'Ici Marcel Loubens a vécu les derniers jours de sa vie courageuse' – a perpetual warning to the explorers who go down the jagged shaft that rock is stronger than man.

It was the oppression of this knowledge, the awareness of the puny bodies enclosed in the mammoth viscera of this mountain that awoke in most of us, as we sat comfortably above on the surface of the world in the bright light among the Alpine flowers, a deep loathing for this great cave. And it is only now, when all have been spared and when so much has been achieved, that we can grudgingly admit that this most hazardous expedition was justified. But while these men were down in the cruel belly of the mountain – some of them not more than holiday pot-holers – there were desperate misgivings which spread throughout France, and I for one can testify that I had not witnessed such a nightmarish piece of human endeavour since the string-and-stickfast days at the beginning of the war.

But now it is over and these valiant and foolhardy men have been preserved. Casteret tells me he will certainly come back next year, and so, I expect, will many of the others. Meanwhile the rocks will grind and shift in the mountains, and the winter snows will swell the great river underground. And in the awesome Verna Cavern there will be no one to care, least of all the questing sightless centipedes, that this gloomy antechamber of Hell has just been included among the natural wonders of the world.

FULL FATHOM FIVE

A review of Captain Cousteau's Underwater Treasury *by Jacques-Yves Cousteau and James Dugan for the* Sunday Times, *April 1960.*

Swimming is really an extremely dull activity unless you are showing off to the spectators or competing at it. Swimming in the sea is just as dull as going for a walk in the middle of a snowfield or desert. There is nothing to look at or occupy your mind, and you go on, automatically moving your limbs, until you are tired and it is time to go back.

Around 1942 Jacques Cousteau and his happy band of comrades altered all this. It was he who taught the common man to look under the sea as he swam, and, suddenly, swimming became interesting. Interest and curiosity, the act of focusing one's eyes and mind, have results you do not expect. I suppose I can swim for pleasure about half a mile before I get bored and therefore tired, but, with a mask on, and if the underwater territory is a new one, it is almost impossible for me to stop swimming. A mile or two is nothing, and I have a feeling that if I were to visit the Great Barrier Reef, I wouldn't stop until a mud fish or a giant clam got me.

Cousteau, unhonoured and scantily sung, has put man back under the sea where he came from, and, from what the scientists say, he has done this by chance just at the moment in history when anyway we are being driven back into the oceans in search of more food and raw materials. I am sure he never meant to cause this world-wide revolution, though, being the extraordinary man he is, he would certainly have been a pioneer in something. What first inspired him might be expressed in the words of Thomas Fuller: 'He goes a great voyage that goes to the bottom of the sea.'

Unfortunately, Cousteau writes far too little about his experiences. I doubt if *The Silent World* would ever have got written but for James Dugan, who

Ian Fleming at his typewriter, thought to have been taken at the Old Palace, Bekesbourne, Kent

Credit: Ian Fleming Images / © Fionn Morgan

Ian and Mab sitting by the Worthersee lake in Austria, 1937

Credit: Ian Fleming Images / © Fionn Morgan

Ian Fleming in naval uniform from the photograph album of
Maud Russell, c. 1940

Credit: Ian Fleming Images / © Maud Russell Estate Collection

Ian Fleming showing the .25 Browning he acquired during
the war, 1962

Credit: Ian Fleming Images / Loomis Dean / © Ian Fleming Estate

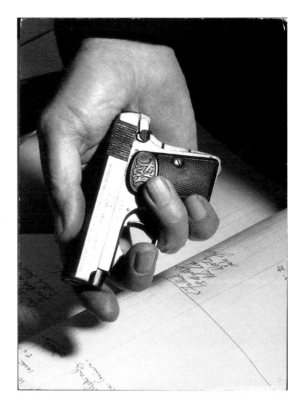

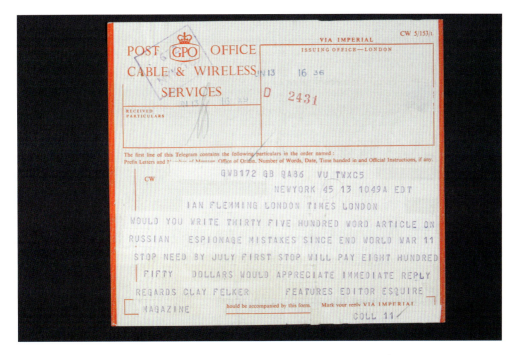

Telegram from Clay Felker, Features Editor at Esquire Magazine, commissioning an article on Russian espionage mistakes since WW2 and offering $850 for the piece.

Credit: Ian Fleming Images / © Ian Fleming Publications

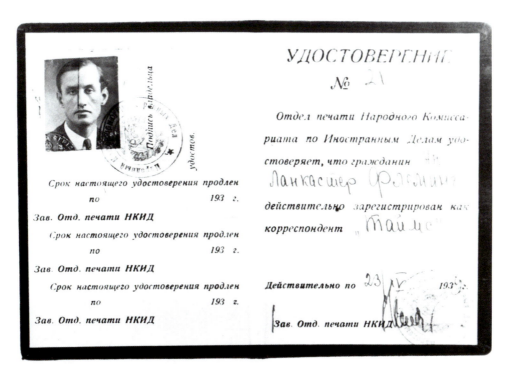

The Russian passport belonging to Ian Fleming

Credit: Ian Fleming Images / © Fleming Family

Soon after buying the paper in 1959 Roy Thomson takes the *Sunday Times* conference with to his right the Editor, H V Hodson, followed by A P T Murphy (Man Ed), Leonard Russell (Lit Ed) and his deputy J W Lambert, Godfrey Smith (News Ed), Ian Lang (Foreign Ed and Jazz critic) and Ian Fleming (Foreign Manager). On Thomson's left is C D Hamilton, later to become Sir Denis Hamilton, Editor-in-Chief of the *Times* and the *Sunday Times*.

Credit: The Times / News Licensing

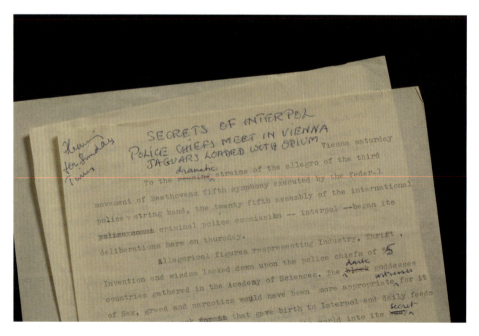

Piece filed for the *Sunday Times* titled 'Secrets of Interpol, Police Chiefs Meet in Vienna, Jaguars Loaded with Opium', 1955

Credit: Ian Fleming Images / © Ian Fleming Publications

THE SHAMEFUL DREAM.

The fat leatherc cushions hissed their resentment at the
contact with the shiny seat of his trousers and hissed again as he leant
back while the chauffeur tucked mutation mink round his knees. The door of
the Rolls closed with a rich double click and with a sigh from the
engine and a pubhtm well-mannered efflatus from the bulb horn the car
nosed with battleship grace away from the station approaches.

Caffery Bone, literary editor of Wnnhn Xour World, eased himself
forward and reached for the cigarette case in his hip pocket and took out
a ciggrette --'selected with care an ivory tube' he reflected andf for
a moment pulled down Elinor Glyn, Ouida and Amanda Ros from the boxroom
and sniffed at their dust. Where were the euphemisms of today ? Perhaps
only in America: 'Comfort Station', 'Powder Room , but then we talked
of Public Conveniences and 'Lous'. Perhaps they had just been stripped
from all languages down to the lingering taboo words, down to sex amd
the lavatory. Yes, there they were : petting,charlies, go somewhere,
pansies, a veritable mine of them. 'The Last Shy Words' would make a
good title. But not for Xour World. Good God no. He could hear the
telephone ringing already :'Mr Bone ?', Yes. 'Linklater speaking. The Chief
says would you slip up a moment'. He could feel the soft pile carpet
and see the drooping walrus moustache saying 'Sit down Mr Bone'. Then the
shiny leather of the single chair, known throughout the building as
'the Hot Squat' hhen the redoubtable 'Icy Pause' then 'Mr Bome, my
attention has been drawn.....'

Bome found that his body had tensed and that the ash had
grown long on his cigarette as he stared wide-eyed at the ghostly
television screen which was the chauffeurs back. He fiddled with the
gadgets in the fat leather arm of his seat in search of an ashtray.
Silently the glass panhn drivers partition slid down and a voice issuing
from nhn nmmnhmnt the walnut pannelling near his right ear said 'Yes Sir?
Bone started and the ash fell onto the mink rug. 'Oh, er , nothing' he
said. He fiddled some more and the partition quietly closed, but in
a moment there came a soft crackling of static and the Nutcracker
Suite sounded down from the ceiling. Bloody box of tricks thought
Bone as he ground out his cigarette on the sole of his shoe
and pushed the stub down between the leather cushions. Different kettle
of fish to the conventionalxexecutives salmon modest Sheerline saloon
which carried Lord Ower to and from his offices in Fleet Street. Must
be Lady Ower's car. Everyone said that she was the one who spent the
money.

Bone stared moodily mnt ahead at the rain and the dripping
hedgerows and at the shaft of the headlights probing the wet tarmac
of thexx secondary road which would bring hham him in due course to The
Towers.

Local driving licence for the Seychelles issued to
Ian Fleming in 1958

Credit: Ian Fleming Images / © Ian Fleming Publications

Ephemera collected from Ian Fleming's trip to the Seychelles
including a postcard and the Seychelles Government Bulletin

Credit: Ian Fleming Images / © Ian Fleming Publications

BOAC route map and flight information booklet decorated with illustrations of sites from all over their routes, c. 1960

Credit: Ian Fleming Images / © Ian Fleming Publications

Ian Fleming at Yugawara, Japan, after enjoying the resort's hot springs, 1960

Credit: Ian Fleming Images / © Ian Fleming Estate

Ian and Ann Fleming with Ivar
Bryce and Robert Harling. Fleming
took Ivar Bryce's middle name and
his friend Tommy Leiter's surname
for his CIA character Felix Leiter

Credit: Ian Fleming Images /
© Private Collection

Photograph sent to Ian Fleming with a letter from Mr Ross Napier with correct information on the location of Smersh headquarters in Moscow which had been wrongly described in *From Russia With Love*, 30 September 1961

Credit: Ian Fleming Images / © Ian Fleming Publications

Ian Fleming and Geoffrey Boothroyd

Series of illustrations of guns with annotations sent by Mr Graham Woodward to Ian Fleming to aid his research. This one shows a Centennial .38" Special Smith and Wesson and a Cobra .38" Special Colt

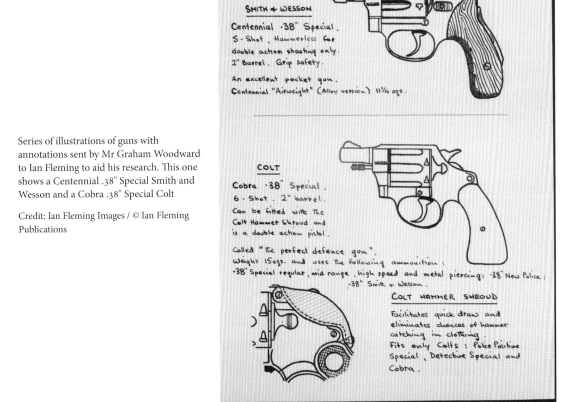

Ian Fleming getting into his
Studebaker Avanti

Credit: Ian Fleming
Images / © Private Collection

Ian Fleming playing bridge, 1962

Credit: Ian Fleming Images /
Loomis Dean / © Ian Fleming Estate

Ian Fleming inspecting old Brazilian pirate coins through a magnifying glass, 1962

Credit: Ian Fleming Images / Loomis Dean / © Ian Fleming Estate

(& I would love to *be able to* ~~be~~ on Cadbury's *milk* chocolate ~~a~~ flakes)   1

'PIRATE GOLD

I have always been interested in buried treasure ~~and~~ I think most men are. Women ~~I think~~ are less interested either because they have a more realistic turn of mind or because they were brought up on differnet childrens books. ~~Am~~ Early reading of 'Coral Island', the Blue Lagoon, Treasure Island and other Stephensonia, Jules Verne and Rider Haggard gives a boy that golden treasure bug which he rarely gets out of his blood stream even in much later years.

I found my first treasure at the age of nine. We were staying in the summer holidays at the Tregenna Castle Hotel at St Ives and I spent much of my time looking for amethyst quartz in the caves along the beaches. One day, far from the town, I penetrated deep into a little cave and found ~~right~~ at the back a lump of ambergris as big as a childs football. I knew all about ambergris from Stackpool. It should have the consistency of thick paste, be greyish in colour and have no smell. There simply wasn't any doubt about it, ~~and~~ I was thrilled ~~to the marrow~~. Now I would be rich *I would* ~~and~~ not have to go back to my private school or indeed do any more work at all. I had found the short cut out of all my childish woes. But how to get it back to the hotel ? Carefully I extracted the heavy lump, picked out some of the pebbles that had stuck to it, and hoisted it into the lap of the grey jersey, which, with grey shorts, I was wearing. The long walk back was exhausting and the hot sun and my hot body melted a fraction of my treasure (I could easily afford the small wastage at £1000 an ounce) so that soon my jersey and shorts were a dreadful sight. What did I care. There would be no scolding or punishments ever again. People looked curiously at me as I climbed the narrow street and went through the big gates and ~~down~~ the drive. I stared haughtily back. My mother was having tea in the palm court (as I remember it) of the hotel with a handsome ~~and titled~~ admirer. I *hurried* ~~walked~~ through the crowded tables and stopped in front of her. She looked startled at my expression and my filthy appearance. Quite casually I released the lap of my jersey and let the lump of Ambergris fall with a soft squelch (it was rather more melted than I had thought) at her feet. I said 'There' and stood waiting for her, or for someone else to say 'Ambergris , by Jove !' My mother looked astonished. 'What is it darling' she asked 'What a mess youve got your clothes into.' 'Its ambergris' I said 'Its worth £1000 an ounce and there must be two pounds of it. How much does that make ? I'm not going back to school.' A horrified head waiter bustled up and looked down at the dreadful grey mess on his parquet floor. 'Dont touch it' I said imperiously' Its Ambergris.' Kindly or unkindly, I ~~cant~~ *cannot* remember which, he asked where I had found it. I *told him* ~~explained~~ and then, I hope kindly, he explained. It was butter I had found. A lump of butter from a supply ship that had been torpedoed several months before. ~~It~~ had been carrying a cargo of butter *from New Zealand* and lumps of the stuff had been washing up on the coast from time to time. No doubt I burst into tears.

Memories of this bitter experience came to me two years ago when i first got a sight

Original typescript of 'Pirate Gold,' 1958

Credit: Ian Fleming Images / © Ian Fleming Estate

Ian Fleming standing by his desk, Goldeneye, Jamaica

Credit: Ian Fleming Images / © Ian Fleming Estate

View from the interior of Goldeneye, Jamaica with Ian Fleming in the doorway

Credit: Ian Fleming Images / © Ian Fleming Estate

Ian Fleming at Goldeneye, Jamaica

Credit: Ian Fleming Images /
© Ian Fleming Estate

Ian Fleming on the beach at
Goldeneye, Jamaica

Credit: Ian Fleming Images /
© Ian Fleming Estate

Ian Fleming cooking scrambled eggs at home, 1962

Credit: Ian Fleming Images / Loomis Dean / © Ian Fleming Estate

Ian Fleming playing golf, 1962

Credit: Ian Fleming Images / Loomis Dean / © Ian Fleming Estate

Ian Fleming at his desk in London, 1962

Credit: Ian Fleming Images / Loomis Dean / © Ian Fleming Estate

Ian Fleming at Cogswell & Harrison, gun maker, holding a .22 Ruger Mark I target pistol, 1962

Credit: Ian Fleming Images / Loomis Dean / © Ian Fleming Estate

THE ART, OR CRAFT, OF WRITING THRILLERS.

by Ian Fleming.

When I was ~~your age~~ *being educated,* I was occasionally

forced, for I never went willingly, to "go to a

lecture". — *a lecture, that is, by some eminent booby who enjoyed showing off to the younger generation.* Today I don't remember a single word

of anything any *such* lecturer lectured me about.

I would watch the man's face, rather as one does

when one stops the car to ask someone the way.

You watch the man's face without listening to

his instructions and you then say thank you and

drive on.

Apart from watching the lecturer's face,

I used to keep a sharp eye on the pile of

typescript in front of him and gratefully note

the turning of each sheet.   Having come to my

private conclusions about his face and his clothes

and the probable length of his lecture, I would

drift off into a pleasant day-dream until the

wonderful moment when the doors were opened and

one could dash out into real life again.

So/...

somehow squeezed the book out of him. Cousteau just has not got patience for writing, and he is totally uninterested in the paraphernalia of fame. Fortunately, James Dugan keeps on at him, and one day we shall get his second volume of biography, the fantastic tale of his last ten years in the Indian Ocean, the Seychelles, prospecting for oil for the Anglo-Persian Oil Company (most successfully, I understand), plumbing the great ocean deeps, and other thrilling exploits of which we read only scraps in the newspapers.

But now James Dugan, who I am sure again did most of the work, has made him put together in this thick and beautifully illustrated volume more than sixty of his favourite underwater adventure stories from all literature. Everything is here – sharks, octopuses, treasure, submarine battles, exploration, archaeology, the glorious beauty of the coral reefs. Everyone who has ever put on an underwater mask will enjoy this fat, rich anthology, and if any teacher is looking for a wonderful source for reading aloud to boys – and girls, for that matter – of from ten to over twenty, then this, and especially now, on the threshold of the Ocean Age, is the book for him.

ADVENTURE IN THE SUN

In April 1956, Ian Fleming wrote these three articles for the Sunday Times *following his annual stay in Jamaica.*

I
THE REMORA'S KISS

Before the morning breeze came to ruffle the mirror of the bay, I walked through the palm trees and down the slope of pale gold sand and slipped into the sea. The water was even warmer than the nine o'clock air and I swam slowly out towards the dark shadow that marked the deep shoal where there might be something more to see than the sting-rays or flounders that inhabit the open plains of sand.

I was naked except for a Pirelli mask and I was equipped with a simple underwater spear-gun. After ten years of underwater fishing round Jamaica I have long since given up shooting fish except for the pot, but this was an expedition to a remote beach and we would be glad of a langouste or a jack or snapper for dinner. And this was unknown terrain, with the protecting reef at least five miles out, and while I pretend not to mind barracuda or shark, even the underwater equivalent of a catapult allows one to forget about them.

The bay in which I was swimming is the most beautiful I have seen in the world. It is the classic back-drop of Stevenson and Stacpoole – a five-mile crescent of unbroken, soft, white-gold sand, fringed for all its dazzling length with leaning palm trees in whose shade an occasional canoe is drawn up between a thatched hut and a pile of discarded conch shells as tall as the hut itself. The great sweep of water is milky blue during the day and in the evening, when the sun – with its famous green flash – sets in your face, it runs through all the blues and greens in the spectrum.

The huge anchorage, sheltered even from the trades, was used by the pirates, and Nelson and Rodney used to anchor here and send parties ashore to hunt wild hogs. Walt Disney filmed part of *Twenty Thousand Leagues Under The Sea* here paying the 'cannibals' 25s. a day.

It is still the occasional haunt of the manatee or sea cow, those large and friendly mammals which are becoming rapidly extinct. They are supposed to be the origin of the mermaid. The female has two rudimentary breasts and occasionally rises out of the waves holding her young in her flippers, perhaps to teach it to breathe. (There are at present two in the London Zoo and the contemporary print entitled 'Real and Ideal' was inspired by the first manatee shown in England in 1889.) One was caught in a fisherman's nets in the bay in February and the inhabitants feasted on him for days, for as one of them said to me: 'Them have all meat – beef an' mutton an' pork.'

Only the most adventurous tourists know of this great secret beach and perhaps no more than five per cent of Jamaicans have ever paid it a visit. For the time being it is one of the most beautiful hidden places in the world. One dreadful day this remote corner of Jamaica will be as famous a sunshine holiday resort as any in the world.

For the last ten years I have held a key to this paradise and the only white man I have ever met there is a bearded character straight out of Somerset Maugham called Dr. Drew. Dr. Drew threw up his practice in Oxford forty years ago and somehow came half across the world to this secret place. He built himself a modest stone-and-plaster dwelling and beside it (believe me!) a fives court, which now has wild orchids growing out of the cracks in the cement. He is ninety-three and healthy and happy and if someone wants the bare bones of a mystery, there it is.

On this particular morning, not many days ago, the great crescent bay was empty except for one sailing dinghy belonging to an employee of a sugar company. The dinghy, moored in about three fathoms, cast its wavering shadow on the edge of the long shoal to which I was swimming.

The fishing canoes had left at first light and were now specks on the horizon round the distant reef and behind me along the five miles of sand there were only a few children playing and an occasional lonely figure taking the morning walk to the little rum-shop and store that, with Dr. Drew's bungalow, is the centre of the bay's life. Below me the endless plain of marcelled sand was quite empty and it was a relief to the eyes to come to the first half-buried rocks and grassy seaweed of the acre or so of shoal.

I swam slowly over the shoal looking down for signs of life or even for those symmetrical patterns in the sand that betray the camouflage of Atlantic flounders or buried conch and helmet shells. There was nothing.

I 'felt' a barracuda (one really does 'feel' them) and looked behind me to see a big one, perhaps ten pounds, lying motionless near the surface, watching me out of one golden tiger's eye. Its stripes were not showing (there is a theory that when the stripes are vivid the barracuda is hungry or angry) and I swam towards it. As barracudas do, it kept ahead of me exactly to its ten yards, but, as I finally put my gun off safe and took him, it opened its mouth with what might have been a yawn and swanned off into the grey mist.

The barracuda had led me towards the moored dinghy, and I was suddenly surprised to see, swimming fast towards me in the great empty hall of the sea, a small grey and black fish with a diamond shaped head. The fish swam very busily, with a motion rather like an eel or a snake, and almost before I could take it in it had come up and bumped softly into me. This was as extraordinary as if walking across a field, a flying pigeon had bumped into one.

Even more surprising, the fish then proceeded to flutter round me, prodding me with its blunt nose and easily dodging my free arm as I tried to shoo it away. Under my arms, between my legs, down my back, I felt the slithery exploration while I trod water and tried to parry these familiarities. And then suddenly the fish clamped itself firmly to my stomach and I knew with a touch of queasy dismay that this was a remora, the parasite fish of the sharks.

Off my own reef in Jamaica I once saw a shark quite close with two remoras attached to it, and I had watched the host and its parasite guests for some time. The remora has a suction area in the back of its flattish head and it attaches itself to the shark's stomach rather like a small fighter plane beneath a bomber. It travels with the shark and feeds on the scraps that fall from the shark's jaws, as do the little yellow and black pilot fish that are the companions of many big fish.

The remoras I had seen off my reef did not stay in the same position on the shark, but again and again detached themselves and executed a graceful game of tag with each other round the huge fish, flattening themselves against him at different points, then flitting to another spot as he cruised majestically through my reef. It had been a beautiful and fascinating sight, but there was something rather different in the idea of this eighteen-inch-long hard, snaky fish clamping itself to my own pale, defenceless, and it seemed to me at that moment, diaphanous skin. I banged hard on the remora's head and it let go, and after a few more attempts to get a hold, snaked away.

I felt relieved but rather churlish, and I had the *esprit de l'escalier* reflection that it would have been extremely smart to carry for ever the marks of a remora's sucker on one's stomach – so much more chic than the claw scars of a tiger or even the fang-marks of a *fer-de-lance* (which I was to see a few days later on the leg of a distinguished American naturalist). So hoping that my remora had not gone home to a shark, I swam hurriedly after him and soon there was a long shadow on the sand and the chains of the two anchors and I came up with the sailing dinghy and all was clear to me.

There, under the hull of the boat, were two remoras, flitting from spot to spot as I had once seen them do on the shark, waiting in vain for scraps to fall out of the wooden jaws of the boat. I have no idea how long they had been attached to this dummy host, but there is no doubt that, when one of them caught a distant glimpse or sound of me, he hurried off to inspect the alternative 'shark'.

I am sorry now that I shot one and took it ashore to examine. They are harmless and extraordinary fish and afterwards it was easy to sentimentalise the encounter so that the remora became some charming bird that had flown into one's pocket to live with one and eat the crumbs from one's meals. But later the fishermen told me that I was lucky he had not taken a firm hold. The sucker is extremely powerful (as mysterious a mechanism as the charge in an electric eel that is strong enough to kill a horse, and as the phosphorus lures carried by some fish), draws blood immediately, and can be detached only by pressing the remora hard behind the eyes.

Even so, now that I am back in London and the sunburn is fading, how dashing to be able to display in suitable company, that dreadful stigma of the tropic seas – the bloody kiss of the remora on one's stomach!

II
BLUE MOUNTAIN SOLITAIRE

'I received,' wrote Philip Gosse, the great naturalist, in 1847, 'the following note from Mr. Hill in reference to an intention I then had of ascending that magnificent ridge called the Blue Mountains, whose summits are 8000 feet high.

'There are two living attractions in these mountains, a crested snake [since killed off by the mongoose – I.F.], and a sweetly mysterious singing bird called the Solitaire. This bird is a thrush and it is worth a journey to hear his wonderful song . . . As soon as the first indications of daylight are perceived, even while the mists hang over the forests, these minstrels are heard pouring forth their wild notes in a concert of many voices, sweet and lengthened like those of the harmonica or musical glasses. It is the sweetest, the most solemn, and most unearthly of all the woodland singing I have ever heard.'

Philip Gosse, who taught our great-grandparents all about birds and fish, was immortalised by his son Sir Edmund Gosse in that most *bitter* of all family memoirs *Father and Son*. Although his *Birds of Jamaica* is one of my handbooks, I abhor this bearded, mealy-mouthed old Victorian pedagogue. The sight of a beautiful bird sends him at once to the Scriptures and thence to reflections on 'God's handiwork' which positively drip with hypocrisy. Having thus squared himself with the Almighty and with the Victorian reader, he forthwith despatches his Negro killer, Sam, after the bird with a gun. God's handiwork is promptly slaughtered and Gosse then treats us to a list of what he found in its entrails.

So it is in his chapter on the Solitaire from which I have quoted. Inevitably, 'I sent in Sam with a gun with orders to follow the sound. He crept silently to a spot whence he heard it proceed and saw two birds of this species which neither he nor I had seen before, chasing each other among the boughs. He shot one of them.' Later the other bird, no doubt the mate, flew out after Sam. 'He fired at this also and it fell, but emitted the remarkable note at the moment of falling.'

The intestine, notes Gosse, was seven inches long.

I am neither an ornithologist, nor any other kind of naturalist, but ever since I came to Jamaica I have been intrigued by the Solitaire, this rare and secretive bird with the unearthly song and beautiful name (which I stole for the heroine of one of my books), and I have always wanted to climb the Blue Mountain, the highest peak in the whole Caribbean and inhabited by the aristocracy of Jamaican 'duppies', or ghosts. But it seems a wearisome business to leave the soft enchantments of the tropic reef and the sunbaked sand of my pirates' cove on the north shore, motor over to Kingston and then make the long, hard climb up into the wintry forests of the great mountain.

But, in the first week of last month, four friends dragged me out of the *luxe, calme et volupté* of my beachcombing existence and, at three o'clock on a blazing afternoon, we had abandoned our car at the little hamlet of Mavis Bank in the foothills of the Blue Mountains and had taken to the mules.

It is a long trek to the little guest-house of Torregarda, 5000 feet up at the base of the final peak, but the beauty of the ride is fabulous. This part of Jamaica is completely remote and as unspoilt as the whole island must have been in the days of Tom Cringle's Log and Lady Nugent's Diary. It is enchanting to be greeted with 'Good evening, young master' by the occasional Negress carrying her sack of coffee berries down the mountain to market (it is from this wild area that comes Blue Mountain coffee, considered by many to be the finest in the world, and every 'wattle-an'-daub' hut has its acre of the pretty bush) and to be met everywhere along the path with those warm, wide smiles that 'progress' is so rapidly wiping off the face of modern Jamaica.

To the right the Yallers Valley stretches away in great soft undulating sweeps towards the distant haze of the sea, and this March the mangoes everywhere were flaming in purple and gold, their early flowering meaning in Jamaica a rainy year. All the way there was the chirrup of the Vervaine hummingbird, the second smallest in the world, and the only one, I believe, with a true song, and as the tropical vegetation gave way to almost Swiss meadows strewn with small mountain flowers there was a steady, continuous drone of bees.

We reached Torregarda at five to be greeted by the unusual sight of hydrangeas and azaleas. Torregarda is a sensationally situated chalet in a setting of incomparable beauty and peace. The bedrooms are extremely comfortable, but the food is of the boiled mutton and lemon curd variety and water shortage reduces the viability of the bathroom and lavatory. Poets or lovers would give it five stars.

We went to bed early and were awakened at the grisly hour of 2 a.m., drank some coffee, climbed on to our mules in pitch darkness and started off again in single file behind a man with a lantern.

To begin with this was all very romantic and beautiful – the wavering light of the lantern on ahead, the occasional clink of hooves on rock and the vast concourse of stars above our heads – but soon the path grew narrower and more precipitous, it became colder, and a chill mist came down and hid everything but the rump of the mule in front and the occasional branch that whipped at one out of the darkness. And, like all mountain climbs, mile stretched upon mile and the summit walked slowly away from us as we advanced.

It began to rain, and then to pour, and all the gloomy prognostications of our sea-level friends were suddenly true. We were fools, they had said – the precipices, the discomfort, the rain, the cold, the aching behinds, 'and even when you get to the top you'll see nothing because it's always in the clouds'. We had pooh-poohed these counsels. This was the lily-livered talk of thin-blooded plantocrats without an ounce of romance or adventure in their souls, who only knew the stinking Turkish bath of Kingston. But now, thinking of them lying comfortably sleeping under their single sheets down on the coast, or perhaps sitting sipping their last drink in the delicious (as it then seemed) tropic tug of a night-club, we had second thoughts.

At last, after a three-hour climb, there was a small stone hut in the fog and driving rain, and we got down bow-legged off our mules and staggered inside and started a fire whose smoke soon drove us out again into the bitter cold.

Coffee and whisky and a mess of bacon and fried bread did nothing to revive our spirits and when, at six o'clock, the mist paled and we knew it was dawn, we set off down the valley rather than catch pneumonia waiting for the fabulous view that we had promised ourselves – that view that, on May 3, 1494, had included the flagship of Columbus and his straggling fleet of caravels.

My companions disappeared into the mist with a barrage of oaths and bitter jokes. At least, I thought, as I started down after them on foot, I will save something from the wreck by seeing, or at least hearing, the Solitaire.

With the exercise, my spirits revived, and soon the rain stopped and the light improved sufficiently for me to take an interest in my ghostly surroundings. It was deadly quiet, except for the water dripping from the Spanish moss which everywhere festooned the skeleton soapwoods, and the thick damp mist deadened the footfall.

At first it was like walking through the landscape of a Gothic fairy tale, and then there were banks of beautiful and exotic treeferns which transferred one into the pages of W. H. Hudson, somewhere deep in an Amazonian jungle. The mountainside along which the narrow path ran, with a smoking precipice on the left, was solid with orchids and parasite plants, alas not yet blooming, and with the tortured leaves of wild pineapples. And there were occasional bramble roses and wild strawberries and blackberries which were bitter to the taste. It seemed extraordinary to find this dank and exotic profusion only a few hours away from the mangrove swamps and the great, dry, sugar-cane, banana and coconut lands in the plains and on the coast. I regretted that my ignorance of botany would not allow me an orgy of Latin namedropping when I got back to sea level, which at that moment seemed a thousand miles away.

The silence was complete and only occasionally broken by the chirrup of a tree-frog that didn't know it was day, and I passed the time trying to invent a limerick beginning with the line 'A sapient bird is the Solitaire', but had got no further when I suddenly came through the clouds and out into the sunshine and saw the great panorama of a quarter of Jamaica below me and, across the mountains, the distant arm of Port Royal reaching into the sea beyond Kingston Harbour.

After a rest I moved on and came into a place of great beauty – a long glade over which the moss-hung trees joined to form a glistening tunnel through which the sun penetrated in solid bars of misty gold. The path ran between moss borders of brilliant dew-sparkling green, and on either side there was a dense mysterious tangle of tall tree-ferns and ghostly grey tree skeletons weighed down with orchids and Spanish moss and other parasites. It was like some fabulous setting for *Les Sylphides* – the most intoxicating landscape I have ever seen.

And it was while standing in the middle of this hundred yards of silent dripping grove that I suddenly heard the sound of a breath-taking melodious, long-drawn, melancholy and slowly dying policeman's whistle. I can think of no other way of describing the song of the Solitaire, and since I learn that in Dominica the bird is known as the *Siffle Montagne* perhaps the simile will pass. It was calling to its mate, which answered from somewhere far away in the dripping woods, and I stood and listened to the pair for a quarter of an hour as they exchanged their poignant 'Bonjour Tristesse'.

Then I went on my way down to Torregarda.

For those who are interested in a more expert description of the song, here is a further extract from Gosse's chapter on the Solitaire in his *Birds of Jamaica*:

Mr. Hill, having made some inquiries of a gentleman residing among the Blue Mountains, Andrew G. Johnston, Esq., received the following reply: 'I have no copy of my musical score of the Solitaire's song. The bird now (July 27th) uses only its long breve notes and its octave, often out of tune, more often so than perfect. In the spring they are very numerous in the deep forests, and warble very prettily, somewhat like this:

sometimes thus:

The pointed crotchets are very sweet sounds, and seem to sound 'E–vil evil.' I tried in vain to get one this spring, but I find the Negroes know nothing about them. I may add that the most common notes that I have heard are these:

I never caught sight of the Solitaire and even the muleteers said they had rarely seen one. They described it, as does Gosse, as being more or less the size of a mocking-bird, but with upper parts of blue-grey, wings black with grey edges, tail black, with a touch of copper beneath, breast grey and hazel eyes.

But at least I heard the song of the Solitaire, and it is a song I dare say I will never forget.

III
TO FLAMINGO LAND

After the age of forty, time begins to be important, and one is inclined to say, 'Yes' to every experience. One should, of course, be taught to say 'Yes' from childhood, but Wet Feet, Catching Cold, Getting a Temperature and Breaking Something add up to a traumatic 'No' that is apt to become a permanent ball-and-chain.

ESSENTIAL YOU ACCOMPANY FIRST SCIENTIFIC VISIT SINCE 1916
TO FLAMINGO COLONY INAGUA MARCH FIFTEEN STOP PARTY
CONSISTS ARTHUR VERNAY PRESIDENT BAHAMAS FLAMINGO
PROTECTION SOCIETY COMMA ROBERT MURPHY OF AMERICAN
NATURAL HISTORY MUSEUM AND SELF STOP FAIL NOT BRYCE

I had only one week of my Jamaica holiday left to me and I am not particularly interested in flamingoes. I looked up Inagua on a map. It looked remote and exciting.

I cabled back 'Yes' and flew up to Nassau on March 13 and spent two nights in a remarkable tropic folly and bird sanctuary called Xanadu which my friend Ivar Bryce has built in a remote corner of the island. There, in between the feverish life of Nassau and exploring the off-shore waters of Xanadu, I learnt about the Society for the Protection of the Flamingo in the Bahamas.

The flamingo, like so many other rare and beautiful species of birds, is disappearing from the Bahamas, its traditional habitat, as from other parts of the world. For example, in 1940 there were 10,000 on the island of Andros in the Bahamas. Today there are ten.

People are beginning to worry about animal and bird species being wiped off the face of the globe, and Mr. Arthur Vernay, who lives in Nassau and is an explorer and naturalist of distinction, decided three years ago to do something about it. He founded the society, enlisted world-wide support, and set to work to save the flamingoes.

At dawn on March 15, crushed together in a tiny CESNA plane, we flew the 400 miles down the beautiful necklace of the Bahama Group to Inagua where there is the largest flamingo colony in the world. The object of the expedition was to make an approximate count of the colony and to see that the society's protective measures were working well on the eve of the mating season.

Inagua is the most southerly of the Bahama Islands and it lies about 100 miles north of the famous Windward Passage between Cuba and Haiti. It is a hideous island and nobody in his senses ever goes near the place. It is known only for its flamingoes and its salt industry and, apart from its bird-life, its only redeeming feature is the charming Ericson family, originally from Boston, who work the salt and are the royalty of the island. Inagua is a British possession, but if the Ericsons don't want you there the island will give you no welcome. They employ the entire population of 1000 souls and the last thing they want is the coming of tourists or of any other 'civilising' influence. I don't think they need worry.

We stayed the night with this admirable and splendidly feudal family in Matthew Town, a scatter of more-or-less solid shacks with a fine lighthouse, a hard hot wind that makes any form of garden impossible (the few plants are protected by great ugly sheets of tin), one communal store and a mound of salt awaiting shipment. We learned a great deal about salt. We were also told that it was lucky we hadn't arrived a few weeks later in the mosquito season.

The mosquitoes on the salt pans are so thick that they literally choke you. The wild donkeys that infest the island are killed by them. Their bites are nothing. They smother by their numbers. As our hosts talked, I could sense the millions of larvae stirring hungrily in the mangrove swamps and on the salt pans. Even in the comfortable house, there was the whiff of tropical marsh gas brought by the hot maddening wind. Islands in the Sun? There are many kinds of them.

We left before dawn on a lorry with the two Bahamian bird wardens. Bryce and I sat with Dr. Robert Murphy in garden chairs placed on the platform of the truck – a fine way to ride and see the country. We drove through the acres of salt pans, great ghastly expanses of brine, white and crusty at the edges, drying in the hot wind that is vital to the industry, to the edge of Lake Windsor, the hundred square miles of brackish water that covers the centre of the island.

Only the light and the sky redeem this dreadful lake. Dreadful? Well, its base is marl mud, very fine in texture and the colour of a corpse. The lake is only two to three feet deep for the whole of its area and the bottom is pock-marked every few feet with sharp limestone coral excrescences. The shores and cays are thick with mangroves, scraggly and leggy, from which came the rotten-egg smell of the marsh gas in which we lived for two days. And yet it was also wonderful. The great mirrored expanse of water through which we were pushed for ten miles in flat-bottomed boats, the mirages, the silence, the sense of being on Mars. And then the birds.

Flamingoes? Every horizon was shocking pink with them, hundreds of them, thousands of them, reflected double in the blue-green glass of the lake, talking away and going about their business in huge congregations that literally owned this world across which we were moving like water-boatmen across a pond.

As we got closer to a group, the necks would start craning, and the chuck-ling, honking talk would redouble as if gangsters were spied approaching a great fashionable garden party. At first there would be a slow and stately walk-ing away, an aloof withdrawal, and then one nerve would break and with great hurrying strides a single bird would scamper a dozen leggy steps to gain momentum and the great red wings would open and suddenly he was up with the long red legs tucked under his tail. And then, one by one, the others would follow, until at last all were in the air and making, with stately wing-beat, for the lea of a mangrove cay farther up the lake.

Fabulous birds, seven feet across the wings, perhaps six from orange beak to claw tip, and, under the wings, a great dash of black primary feathers. Not handsome, except in their flame-red colour and the grace of their flight, and their heads remind one of bottle-openers, but bizarre in their strange beauty, like great red and black bombers, purposeful and awe-inspiring.

New horizons opened up, all quivering with pink. The excitement of my expert companions was great. It was clear that the protective measures carried out by the society – the appointment of the wardens, the strict policing of the lake against pilferers of eggs and young (flamingo tongues are considered a great delicacy) and the regulations against low-flying aircraft had, within little more than two years, been dramatically successful, and in this time one of the major spectacles in the world of birds had been created. Dr. Robert Murphy, who had been alternately gazing through binoculars and writing busily in his notebook ever since we had sighted our first Banana Quit in Matthew Town, organised an industrious 'count' which rapidly climbed into the thousands, and there was much informed talk about mating dances and the colour-cycle, which is from pure white, through grey to pink and then red flame.

I felt left out and racked my brains for an ornithological gambit, however modest. I could only think to ask if this flamingo, which is the American flamingo, or *Phoenicopterus Ruber*, was the largest red bird in the world. I spent some time clothing this juvenile question in the appropriate mumbo-jumbology. Finally: 'Would you say, Doctor, that the overall dimensions of the *Phoenicopterus* are the largest of any rubrous bird?' 'Yes,' said Dr. Murphy briefly, and I felt like the triangle player in an orchestra who has managed to hit his triangle at the right place in the score.

In fact, Dr. Murphy, who has just retired as chairman of the Department of Birds in the American Museum of Natural History, although he is one of the greatest ornithologists who has ever lived, is entirely human, a splendid and most entertaining companion and the only man I have met who could make scrambled eggs with a basis of Nestlés condensed milk (sweetened). He also has the supreme distinction (which I mentioned in an earlier article) of bearing the fang-marks of a *fer-de-lance* on his ankle.

It took us three hours to reach Long Cay, where our tent was pitched and where we had breakfast. Then we went on again, now under a blazing sun, towards the ever-retreating horizon, behind which we hoped to find the first nesting-colony of the flamingoes. But we were a week or so early. The birds had not yet started to build those extraordinary townships of foot-high mud volcanoes in whose crater they lay one large amateurish white egg. So the boats were pushed on again, deep into the mangrove swamps, where a myriad other sea birds were already nesting and where the tumult and the stench were at times almost overwhelming.

Here were great colonies of the Louisiana Heron, the Black-necked Stilt, flocks of which skimmed round us with astonishing beauty and precision, American and Reddish Egrets and other exotic birds, and here, on wading through a marsh that bubbled with gas, we came upon a combination of bird colours that outdid even the spectacular flamingoes.

First, there was an unexpected swarm of our familiar Double-crested Cormorants, perching in ranks of black witness among the low trees, then, above and around them, the noise of our arrival had exploded hundreds of Roseate Spoon-bills and white Egrets into the sky. The combination of black and white and pale pink against the vivid green of the mangroves and the deep blue sky gave an impression of some extraordinary daylight firework display in which the rockets always went on bursting.

As I stood up to my knees in the mud and gazed with awe on the great wheeling galaxies of black and white and pink, my companions were more scientifically engaged photographing the nests full of eggs and young with which each mangrove bush was laden, and I am glad to say that not only this extraordinary place but also the whole expedition has been recorded by Dr. Murphy upon countless rolls of colour film.

Towards evening, and after many other bird species had been identified, we trekked back to our tent on the Cay and at once stripped off our clothes and lay down in the lake to relieve our sunburn and get rid of some of the mud. It was then clear why Lake Windsor on Inagua will always be one of the great bird preserves of the world, for the shallow waters are almost solid with food. No sooner had we lain down than countless tiny fish no longer than a thumbnail came to nibble us and we found that the silt beneath our bodies was largely composed of minute shells and fingernail clams – ideal fare for the curiously shaped beak of the flamingo with its reversed scooping motion.

The rest of our expedition was more or less an extension of what I have already described. The final estimate of the flamingo colony of Inagua was 15,000, and, if this year's hurricanes miss the island, the nesting season, which will now be under way, will perhaps add another 5000.

A film of the colony will shortly be made by Mr. Robert P. Allen (the Audubon Society associate who, more or less single-handed, saved the Whooping Crane from extinction) and the public will then be able to see for themselves that the labours of Mr. Arthur Vernay and his society have added considerably to the beauty of the world.

As a postscript to these notes in Inagua I should mention that an exceptionally interesting man died on the island last year. He was a very aged fisherman and, two or three times each year, for many years past, he would slip quietly into the Commissioner's office, which also serves as a rudimentary bank for the Inaguans. Without saying anything, he would place upon the Commissioner's table a neat pile of Spanish doubloons of the sixteenth century. After receiving pound notes in exchange for his gold, he would leave as discreetly as he had come.

Now the old fisherman has died, and his secret has died with him, but it seems clear that, in or around Inagua, there is something else beside salt and flamingoes.

MORE ADVENTURES IN THE SUN

Three further tales of Ian Fleming's life in the Caribbean.
Sunday Times *March/April 1957.*

I
MY FRIEND THE OCTOPUS

Probably no living creature inspires such universal loathing and terror as the octopus. The reputation of this sea shell (for the octopus belongs to the same family of molluscs as the clam) stems from the fact that the octopus remains one of the few unexploded myths.

It is still a credible villain in children's stories and its relative, the giant squid, is probably the most fearsome creature in the world.

But the octopus and the squid should not be confused. The giant squid lives thousands of fathoms deep and engages in titanic battles with sounding whales who are often found marked with its suckers. (Not long ago the eye of a squid was found in the stomach of a whale. It was two feet in diameter!) So, even in fiction, it is difficult to invent circumstances in which giant squids could be a threat to man.

An authentic case was the squid engaged by the French battleship *Alecton* in mid-Atlantic in 1869. The squid was 50 feet long, exclusive of the arms. The *Alecton* engaged the monster in battle but her cannon-balls traversed the glutinous mass without causing any vital injury. The Frenchmen at last got a harpoon to bite and passed a bowling hitch round the rear end of the squid and attempted to haul it on board. But the line cut through the flesh of the beast and the *Alecton* only salvaged a chunk weighing about 40 lb. From this morsel the total weight of the squid was estimated at two tons. But this is a very different creature from *octopus vulgaris*.

When I first started spending my holidays in Jamaica and skin-diving I was infected by the octopus myth and waged war upon the tribe. This year an octopus came to live at the bottom of my garden and I have quite changed my mind.

There are certain disagreeable features about octopuses. Their appearance is, to say the least, unusual and they have tentacles which seem to us supernatural. They can change colour from off-white to dark brown. They can turn luminous in the dark. They travel very fast by jet propulsion and the suckers on their eight arms exert terrific and unrelenting pressure. They are also slimy and creepy-crawly and are very difficult to kill unless, as is the custom with Jamaican fishermen, you bite off their heads.

In Jamaican waters they are not feared. They are not called 'devil fish', as they are in many parts of the world, nor yet 'pusfellers', in the tough lingo of deep-sea divers, but 'sea cats' – a much more friendly name.

In fact, *octopus vulgaris* is an extremely shy creature which, although it has few enemies apart from man, has little confidence in its natural weapons and spends a disproportionate amount of its time trying to hide. It hides very effectively, squeezing itself like thick paste into rock crannies or choosing the nearest place of coral and flattening itself against this after changing its colour to an almost exact camouflage.

As I say, I first regarded these creatures as enemies and had many, in retrospect, cruel and untidy battles with them. Then one day, standing on a rock at the side of my beach, I saw through the clear water a few inches down an octopus asleep just below me.

It had turned itself into a kind of clumsy saucer with its tentacles wrapped round its body. Now and then the tip of a tentacle moved delicately, like the tail of a sleeping kitten. It did not seem to have attached itself to the shelf of coral and rocked slightly in the small currents. There were one or two leaves on the water. When the shadow of a leaf floated over the octopus it blushed a dark brown. Occasionally it opened a sleepy eye and then closed it again.

I defy anyone to watch a sleeping octopus for some time and not be captivated by its defencelessness and astounded by the bizarre mechanisms of its camouflage.

Finally I moved so that my shadow fell across it. At once the creature was fully awake. It turned exactly the colour of its coral bed and, with incredible stealth, its tentacles unfurled on the rock and took hold. The eyes watched me. I moved again and the octopus took a deep breath to prime the tanks of its jet mechanism and started slowly crawling sideways. I lifted a hand and it gathered itself up like the sheet in M. R. James's ghost story, *Whistle and I'll Come to You*, and launched itself sideways with streamlined compactness and shot into the deeps.

It was from that day that I decided to befriend the octopus and when, this year, one took up residence a few yards out from the beach it was given a warm welcome and christened 'Pussy'.

If you happen to collect shells, an octopus can be a very valuable pet. Each morning when we visited 'Pussy' in her comfortable burrow in the coral, we would find a new tribute of shells on the doorstep. They were not very rare shells – clams, tulip shells and small helmets – but they were in pristine condition. Octopuses have an easy way with shells. They simply attach their suckers to each side, or to the operculum, or door, to a shell, and pull, and go on pulling, until the muscles of the animal in the shell are exhausted. Then they eat the animal.

'Pussy' became a valued feature of the property and privileged visitors were taken to inspect her. She would playfully tug at the blunt end of a spear and occasionally display a shy tentacle or a watchful, stealthily retreating eye. I had hopes of developing the relationship by giving her crushed sea urchins to eat. Then I had to be away from the house for a couple of days.

On my return, I was greeted with disquieting news. My small son, never quite clear who 'Pussy' was, but merely accepting her daily tribute of shells, informed me that fishermen had caught a fine sea cat and presented it to Beryl, the housemaid.

I hastily swam out and placed a fat meal of sea urchin at the door of 'Pussy's' burrow. Nothing happened. Perhaps she was out hunting. I let a day go by and still she did not reappear.

I asked the housekeeper. Yes, indeed. Beryl had been given a fine sea cat by the fishermen.

Where was it? What had happened to it?

'Beryl mash her and cut her up and cook her in holive hoil and eat her out of a coconut.'

That is the worst of pets. Something always happens to them.

II
TREASURES OF THE SEA

The Cayman Islands have always sounded to me extremely romantic. Columbus discovered them and named them 'Las Tortugas', after the turtles which swarmed on them. Lying to the north-west of Jamaica and to the south of Cuba, well away from the shipping lanes, they were the principal hide-out of the buccaneers and have been the haunt of treasure-seekers for 200 years.

The Caymanians also sounded a most attractive people. Descendants of the pirates or of Cromwellian soldiers, they have somehow managed to keep their bloodstream free of negroid strains and they have built up a tradition as some of the finest sailors in the world. Until last year it was very difficult to get to the Caymans, but now there are almost daily flights from Jamaica and Miami, and last month, with two girl Fridays, I went to Grand Cayman to collect sea-shells in the imagined paradise.

Grand Cayman is some 20 miles long, and, at its broadest, eight miles wide. The island is more or less in the shape of a giant bottle-opener and the North Sound where the pirates used to careen their ships, almost cuts the island in two. It is very flat and marshy, and only occasional palm trees stand up above the covering of mangroves, sea grape and sea almond. A hot, dry, ugly wind blows almost continuously, but not hard enough to disperse the mosquitoes which render the place almost uninhabitable in the summer.

The population is about 7000 and the capital, Georgetown, is a pretty clap-boarded little village with a vaguely Cornish air. Beside the natural harbour crouches an exquisite Presbyterian chapel. The Caymans are a Scottish Presbyterian stronghold, and no doubt, this accounts for their staunch, sober character and for the fact that the four-cell gaol is rarely occupied. On the principal beach a new and luxurious hotel was opened last year, but its rates, £8 15s. for a single room and bath, were not for us, and we put up at the excellent Pageant Beach Hotel, a single-storey motel-like affair, entirely on the American style. There are three other simple, small hotels, and the total number of hotel rooms on the island is about 300.

The Roneoed information bulletin on the Caymans was written by the last Commissioner, Mr. Gerrard, and is a model of what such things should be: modest, humorous, and realistic. (It can be obtained from the Tourist Board in Kingston, Jamaica, or from the Commissioner's Office, Grand Cayman.) One paragraph which had attracted me was 'The coasts and beaches of the Cayman Islands abound in shells of an astonishing variety'. I happen to collect tropical shells in an amateurish fashion and was looking forward to much treasure. I am ashamed to say that I am uninterested in rare dull shells and only collect those which are huge or beautiful or strange. I do not even ticket or catalogue my collection, but leave it piled on shelves for other amateurs to admire and the sun to spoil. But the collection amuses me, and, now that I will not shoot fish, adds purpose to the exploration of tropical beaches, underwater landscapes and reefs.

I could not begin to give details of my collection but Hyatt Verrill's excellent *Shell Collector's Handbook*, published by Putnams, New York, shows Caribbean treasures I do not possess and which I hoped against hope might turn up in the Caymans.

Our taxi driver from the airport, Conrad Hilton, was helpful, 'I often takes folks huntin' for shells. Only las' week I takes Mr. German huntin' shells. Him comes from New York. Mebbe you knows him.' (Residents of small remote places assume that all visitors know each other, just as they know every single one of the local inhabitants.) 'Him was mos' satisfied. Ah takes him to Bodden.'

Who was this rival shell-collector who had forestalled us and doubtless skimmed the cream from Conrad Hilton's private treasure beach? However, perhaps since we have underwater masks we shall do better than this serious-minded, though no doubt expert, conchologist with his topee, sneakers, sun glasses, khaki shorts down to the knee and blistering nose (as we imagined him).

'There's a man at Bodden collects shells. Mr. Willywaw. Sells them. Mebbe you like to buy some?'

We had a vision of the cunning Mr. Willywaw sitting in his treasure house waiting for boobies from overseas and lovingly caressing a Precious Wentle Trap as he talked of the requests he had had from American museums.

'We'd like to see his collection but we don't want to buy shells. We like to find them.'

'You find plenty shells at Bodden.' Conrad Hilton was definite.

There was a great stretch of sandy beach between our hotel and the jagged dead coral against which the waves crashed. (It crossed my mind, and still crosses it, to wonder where the sand came from since the rocks were between it and the sea.) As soon as we arrived we put on our masks and took spears and went into the sea to explore. No doubt, even opposite the hotel, there would be pickings from this paradise of sea-shells.

It was the most ghastly sea bottom I have ever explored. An endless vista of dead grey coral, interspersed with sharp and angry niggerheads, and positively infested with huge black sea eggs – a type of sea urchin with four-inch, needle-sharp spines which break off and fester in your flesh. There were few fish about and no crabs or lobsters – just an endless, dead landscape bristling with black spines. Worse, the American way of life, which has Grand Cayman in its grip, had penetrated the surrounding sea. Everywhere there was refuse – the permanent unbreakable refuse of a people that has given up eating fish and fruit and now lives out of American bottles and cans.

The bottom of the sea was littered with rusty (and rustless) cans, disintegrating cartons and the particularly vivid green of broken Pepsi-Cola bottles. (The company must have a monopoly on the island. Other soft drinks were poorly represented.) And the place was a sort of bottletopia. Everywhere were bottle tops; the sad, rusty coinage of our civilisation.

We swam for an hour along the rocks and round into the yacht harbour where grey silt and slime covered everything. We came ashore disgusted. Thank heavens tomorrow would be different!

At 9 o'clock Conrad Hilton came to fetch us and we rattled off along the appalling roads on our way to Bodden. The roads on Grand Cayman had once been metalled – perhaps during the war when there were a few defences on the island against its use as a possible refuge for U-boats – but the surface has melted and eroded into ridges and waves and potholes. Fine sand, which makes even bicycling very difficult, has covered them. A few motor-cars ply for hire during the 'season' and then, over the next nine months, get wired and soldered together again.

Bodden turned out to be no 'secret' place, but Grand Cayman's other 'town' – a handful of houses and bungalows at one end of a six-mile sandy beach. Conrad Hilton drove us to the Presbyterian minister's bungalow and this charming padre allowed us to leave our picnic lunch and bits and pieces on his wooden verandah. Strung with empty knapsacks for our shell burdens, we hurried down to the beach and started tramping into the wind and sun to where, six miles away, the beach ended at Betty Bay Point.

There were, practically speaking, no shells at all. Surely there would be more when we got away from the houses! There were none, or at any rate none worth picking up. For mile after mile we trudged towards the distant shimmering rocks that never came nearer. From time to time we stopped and put on our masks and went into the sea. At once the sand ended and it was another dead landscape scattered, but more sparsely than on Georgetown, with tins and bottle tops. A bright flash of colour caught my eye in deep water and I dived. It was a disintegrating Quaker Oats carton.

Deep depression filled us. Where was this paradise of sea-shells? Surely Mr. Willywaw could not have scoured the place clean that morning in the four hours since dawn. He and his minions could not possibly have covered the whole six miles of beach. There were a few fishermen about and occasional heaps of conchs that had been broken to remove their animals, but there were miles of shelving sand without a single footstep below the high tide mark. My companions gave up and stopped. Obstinately I covered another two miles, my face gradually stiffening and smarting in the sun and wind. I came to the point and turned. Now there were six miles of baking sand without the spur of treasure hunting. I set off on the return journey.

III
HE SELLS SEA-SHELLS

Philosophically we had our lunch and curled up to sleep in the shade to wait for 3 o'clock. When Conrad Hilton arrived I was sharp with him. What did he mean by saying that this was just the place for us? There weren't any shells. Wasn't there somewhere else he knew of? Anyway, let's go and see Mr. Willywaw.

Mr. and Mrs. Willy Wood (for that was their name) lived in a neat concrete bungalow. They were quite charming. Willy Wood was a handsome, middle-aged Caymanian with the sort of face you would find on the quay at Brixham. His living-room contained much inappropriate and overstuffed furniture. There was a battered wireless set, and faded photographs round the walls. Chickens and dogs scratched about in the bushes between the house and beach. There was no sign of sea-shells.

I summoned my scant expertise and questioned him. 'Tiger cowries?' No, he did not know them. 'Cone shells. Did he find many like this?' I produced a broken Marbled Cone I had found that morning. No, he could not say he did. They found small ones which they used as spinning tops for the children. 'Well, do you find any giant Queen Helmets?'

'No, just small ones.'

'Olives?'

'Sometimes, not often.' (These pretty, highly polished shells are common on my Jamaican beach.)

Well, what were his most valuable shells? Willy Wood smiled secretively. He reached under the sofa and pulled out a large grocery box untidily heaped with brown paper bags. He peered into several of these and threw them carelessly back. I thought that he was even more careless of his collection than I was. Finally he found the right one.

'These are my best ones,' he said. 'Ever seen these?' He tipped the bag on to the floor. A pile of small slivers of brown cuticle fell out. They looked rather like morsels of tortoise shell. The small bag must have contained thousands of them. They were ugly, dirty little scraps and extremely dull. We gazed in astonishment.

Willy Wood said, 'You know the Bleeding Tooth shell?' (Despite its interesting name, this hermite is one of the commonest shells in the whole of the Caribbean. Members of the same family, but without the bloody looking teeth, can be found in their billions round the coasts of England.) 'Those are the "doors" of the shell.'

Willy Wood was referring to the opercula – the tough membrane with which the animal shuts itself inside its shell.

Astonished, I said, 'But why are they so valuable?'

'Don't know,' said Willy Wood. 'But I get 18 dollars for these.'

'Eighteen dollars! Each?'

Willy Wood smiled pityingly. 'No, 18 dollars a gallon. A gallon of these scraps of stuff would number, I suppose, about 10,000.'

'Who do you sell them to? What do they use them for?'

'Dealers in the States – St. Petersburg, Miami, New York. They use them in artificial jewellery. Make necklaces and so forth.'

Willy Wood picked up another brown bag and poured a pile of tiny white volutes on to the floor. 'We call these Rice Shells. They fetch 12 dollars. When I need some of these I just bring up a sack of sand and pour it out on the porch and put on my spectacles and spend an afternoon picking out the shells.'

More bags were opened. More piles of incredibly dull little shells were poured out. 'Ten dollars, nine dollars a gallon. They say they use these for sewing on materials.' Willy Wood laughed indulgently at the notion. He said that he was not doing so well now. There were too many people round the world in the business. He used to ship gallons and gallons of shells every week. Now the prices were going down and he only made a shipment once every two or three months.

Now it was all clear to us. The 'paradise of sea-shells' myth had grown out of this strange, but rewarding, activity of Willy Wood paying pennies to the children of Bodden to pick up thousands upon thousands of the commonest sea-shells in the world to go off to the sham jewellery factories in the States. Of course, to a Caymanian the place was a 'paradise', where you could just pick up the ground you were standing on and sell it at 18 dollars a gallon. But as for rare or beautiful sea-shells, maybe there would be some specimens in the Cayman seas but no one was in the least interested. They were not what Mr. Bloomfeld in Miami wanted.

It is true that I also was not very clear what I wanted, except that it should be something handsome and something new to me. I do not collect shells seriously. I was not looking, for instance, for a Left-Handed Cone shell, or a Double-Spined Fighting Conch or for some of the Treasures of the Sea that can be found in the Caribbean and that might be worth £20 or £30 each.

As Mr. Verrill points out in his *Shell Collector's Handbook*, no shell is really rare. There are species that live in remote places or very deep or those that are fragile. One such is the Slot Shell, or *Pieurotomeria*, found off Japan – dull shells with rusty and brown markings, but still selling for £20–£40 a specimen, because they usually live at 100 fathoms or more and are fragile. An example of this tricky market is the Glory-of-the-Seas Cone which, for 200 years, was considered the rarest of shells. By 1944, 25 specimens were known and the value of a fine specimen was around £500. Since then many more examples have been found and, in 1945, the price had dived to about £20.

Today Mr. Verrill says that two of the rarest shells are the Prince of Wales Cowrie, of which only four specimens are known, and the White-Toothed Cowrie, the only specimen of which is in the British Museum.

Before the war one of the prizes was the Precious Wentle Trap found off China and Japan. The ingenious Chinese counterfeited them in rice paste and sold them for hundreds of pounds to collectors. Then came the war and the G.I.s started looking for shells and buying them in the Pacific Islands, and the bottom fell out of the market in Wentle Traps and in such rarities as the Great Golden Cowrie. This shell was a symbol of aboriginal royalty and all specimens found had to be delivered to the island chieftains. 'Civilisation' came with the war and now Great Golden Cowries are a drug on the market.

But there are still prizes to be found in Caribbean waters – such as the *Murex Argo* of which one of the few specimens is in the Liverpool Museum of Natural History – and our minds had been inflamed with the hope of legendary treasures such as these when we came to the Caymans. Faced with Willy Wood's famous 'shell collection', we realised that our quest had been fruitless. We edged the conversation away from shells to pirate gold.

Willy Wood said, Yes, indeed. People were always hunting for it. After the war he had bought a mine-detector in Florida and spent months searching round the beaches and caves. 'And I dug. I dug for days and weeks and I kept on finding it again and again. And do you know what it always was?' Willy Wood roared with laughter. 'Bottle tops and suchlike. And do you know, some folks from here even went over the cemetery with a mine-detector? They heard that the Spaniards were buried with their swords. They dug up plenty of graves before the Minister and the police got after them.'

Conrad Hilton, who had been observing the whole scene from the doorway, felt that this was a slur on the island. He broke in 'But, Willywaw, don' you member that man who came an' when he gone away his suitcase was heavy as lead. He wouldn't allow no one carry it out to the plane. Took him quarter of an hour to get out to the plane moving his suitcase a few feet at a time. And he got into the plane and no one never saw him again.'

Willy Wood shrugged indifferently. 'If that had been gold,' he said practically, 'it would have bust through the floor of the plane. Maybe the man was sick or something.'

We parted, the two shell-collectors, despite their common bond, misunited and crashed and banged our way back to Georgetown, the day saved by the charm of Willy Wood and the strangeness of his trade.

On the way, I questioned Conrad Hilton about the turtles for which Grand Cayman has always been famous. Apparently these were also a myth. There are no turtles in the Cayman Islands. The Caymanians catch them off the coasts of Nicaragua, 500 miles away. We have a treaty with Nicaragua which allows them to do so but even in this tiny remote trade we have just been slapped in the face. A month ago the Nicaraguans arrested two Caymanian ships and threw their crews into gaol. Nicaragua had done a 'Suez' and torn up the turtle treaty without warning.

But what about this business of the turtle soup for the Lord Mayor of London? Was that a fable too?

Conrad Hilton said no, that was about all that was left of the turtle trade. The Caymanians caught enough turtles to feed them and their families. They kept them in a lagoon with each fisherman's initials carved in the tortoiseshell. Two or three times a year they shipped a few to Kingston to be flown to London.

There is no industry in the Cayman Islands, except banking the money which the Caymanian seamen send back to the island from all round the world. It is time the encyclopaedias and guide books got these things right.

We left Grand Cayman with only mild regret and were glad to get back to the lush green beauty of Jamaica. Grand Cayman, like the other small Caribbean and Bahamian Islands I have visited, is, when you have taken away the sun and the colours of the sea, an ugly, lonely little island once brushed excitingly by history but now a refuge for the two-week American tourist who cannot afford, or who is disgusted by, Florida. Tourism will certainly be developed for these people, the roads will be metalled again and there will be attempts to spray the mosquitoes and sand flies. The staunch cheerful Caymanians, the nicest feature of the island, will not be more than superficially spoilt by this traffic until the modern pirates discover the place.

Then the Island will be given over to the pirates again – to the modern pirates who discover that the only direct tax in the Cayman Islands is a head tax on adult males, between 16 and 60, amounting to eight shillings a year.

TREASURE HUNT IN EDEN

In April 1958 Ian Fleming travelled to the Seychelles to follow a story about buried treasure. Five articles were edited into three in the Sunday Times. *This version is taken from the original five typescripts, but with the long prospectus of Mr R. H. Wilkins edited.*

I
PIRATE GOLD

I have always been interested in buried treasure. I think most men are. Women are less interested either because they have a more realistic turn of mind or because they were brought up on different children's books. Early reading of *Coral Island, The Blue Lagoon, Treasure Island* and other Stephensonia, Jules Verne and Rider Haggard gives a boy that golden treasure bug which he rarely gets out of his bloodstream even in much later years.

I found my first treasure at the age of nine. We were staying in the summer holidays at the Tregenna Castle Hotel at St. Ives and I spent much of my time looking for amethyst quartz in the caves along the beaches. One day, far from the town, I penetrated deep into a little cave and found at the back a lump of ambergris as big as a child's football. I knew all about ambergris from Stacpoole. It should have the consistency of thick paste, be greyish in colour and have no smell. There simply wasn't any doubt about it. I was thrilled. Now I would be rich and I would be able to live on Cadbury's milk chocolate flakes and I would not have to go back to my private school or indeed do any more work at all. I had found the short cut out of all my childish woes.

But how to get it back to the hotel? Carefully I extracted the heavy lump, picked out some of the pebbles that had stuck to it, and hoisted it into the lap of the grey jersey, which, with grey shorts, I was wearing. The long walk back was exhausting and the hot sun and my hot body melted a fraction of my treasure (at £1000 an ounce I could easily afford the small wastage) so that soon my jersey and shorts were a dreadful sight. What did I care? There would be no scolding or punishments ever again. People looked curiously at me as I climbed the narrow street and went through the big gates and up the drive. I stared haughtily back. My mother was having tea in the palm court (as I remember it) of the hotel with a handsome admirer. I stumped through the crowded tables and stopped in front of her. She looked startled at my expression and my filthy appearance. Quite casually I released the lap of my jersey and let the lump of ambergris fall with a soft squelch (it was rather more melted than I had thought) at her feet. I said 'There', and stood waiting for her, or for someone else, to say 'Ambergris, by Jove!' My mother looked astonished. 'What is it darling?' she asked. 'What a mess you've got your clothes into.' 'It's ambergris,' I said. 'It's worth £1000 an ounce and there must be two pounds of it. How much does that make? I'm not going back to school.'

A horrified waiter bustled up and looked down at the dreadful grey mess on his parquet floor. 'Don't touch it,' I said imperiously. 'It's ambergris.' Kindly or unkindly, I cannot remember which, he asked where I had found it. I told him and then, I hope kindly, he explained. It was butter I had found. A lump of butter from a supply ship that had been torpedoed several months before. She had been carrying a cargo of New Zealand butter and lumps of the stuff had been washing up on the coast from time to time. No doubt I burst into tears.

Memories of this bitter experience came to me when I first got a sight of the Wilkins Treasure Prospectus, and without wasting space on my own picayune treasure tales, here is the gist of it – cut, but with the wording unaltered:

A short précis of the story of the treasure and details in brief of the work done by Mr. R.H. Wilkins up to the 31st December 1955.

Olivier Le Vasseur commenced his piracy in 1716 in the Caribbean where he stayed for some time, at the end of which he refused to return to France but turned pirate and came into the Indian Ocean in 1721 in his vessel *Le Victorieux*. He was joined by an English pirate named Taylor in his ship *Defence*, and together they took over control of the shipping lanes from John Avery, the English pirate, who had become ruler of Madagascar in former years and whose greatest prize had been the capture of the daughter of the Grand Mogul with her marriage dowry while she was on her way to Persia to marry its ruler, the Shah. Avery was driven from Madagascar and returned to England to die penniless in Bideford, Devon.

Le Vasseur and Taylor took two French treasure ships belonging to the Compagnie de France, namely *La Duchesse de Neuilly* and *La Ville d'Ostende*. Up to this time Le Vasseur had been offered a free pardon if he would bring his treasure in but he sealed his fate by taking the Royal Portuguese Papal vessel *Le Cap de Ver* which was returning to Europe with the Bishop of Goa and his treasure – church plate, diamond cross and staff, etc. – on board. The treasure in the first two ships is believed to be ninety million gold francs and estimated to be some one hundred and twenty million pounds' worth at present-day values. The value of the treasure in the ship *Le Cap de Ver* is not known, nor is there anywhere any record of the amount of treasure taken from Avery or brought by Le Vasseur from the Caribbean.

As a consequence of taking the Bishop of Goa's treasure ship, Le Vasseur realised he could expect a pardon no longer. It is believed that he then set about burying the treasure and the French archives indicate that this took Le Vasseur some four to five years to bury.

The taking of the Bishop of Goa's ship caused the wrath of the Pope and representations were, it is believed, made to the French Government through papal channels which resulted in renewed efforts on the part of the French. Le Vasseur was eventually captured by a naval vessel, *La Méduse*, under Captain d'Hermitte, in 1730, and was taken to the Isle of Bourbon (now Reunion). After various attempts to make him disclose the whereabouts of his treasure were made without avail he was hanged on July 17, 1730. On the scaffold he threw to the crowd a number of papers crying 'Find it who can'. These papers were held by various families and some came into the hands of the Paris archives.

When I was in the Seychelles in January, 1949, I came across some documents in the form of a cryptogram, a cryptic map and other papers which interested me . . . I started to try to interpret the documents and papers. I did not get very far at this stage but I did discover that the documents had some relation of Greek mythological figures pertaining to their astronomical values. I also found certain carvings on rocks at a particular place on the coast of Mahé, the island of the Seychelles on which I was at the time. I particularly observed the mythological figure of 'Musca' or 'Asp' carved on a rock.

I took the documents and papers I then had back to Kenya with me and spent several months working on them. I managed to translate them and the translation I got indicated to me that I should look for an area where there would be indications of the northern and southern hemispheres containing the mythological figures of Greek mythology relating to the heavenly bodies or stars and probably indications which had something to do with the story of Jason and the search for the Golden Fleece.

I returned to the Seychelles and . . . found other carvings in the area, some above ground and some underground. They all related to the mythological figures I have mentioned above. I soon discovered a complete hemisphere with these figures set out correctly in the right position one from the other. I then found indications of other hemispheres in the same area and I found carvings and other indications which clearly referred to the Jason and the Golden Fleece story. I found buried the bones of an ox many feet below ground. I also found a complete skeleton of a horse buried without doubt to indicate Pegasus the Horse. I found Andromeda both carved and in statuette form. Indeed in my five- to six-year search I have found many things to prove that my interpretations of the documents and papers is correct and to prove, which is even more important, that no one has been on this site before me.

In all I have found eight hemispheres. All have been complete in themselves and each has led me in turn to the next. In each except the last hemisphere the Golden Fleece – the treasure – has been stolen by the fox and there are indications to this effect left there by the pirates. In the last hemisphere these indications are absent and the fox itself is shown within the hemisphere. I therefore believe the treasure to be intact from this evidence.

I am now on the last hemisphere. I know this to be so because I am led no further by the documents and papers and I have found the triangle, the angles of which are given on the translation of the cryptogram. This triangle indicates in my view the size and whereabouts of the cavern in which the treasure is buried. It is within a mighty rock and to get to it is my remaining task. The rock I believe to contain a cavern. The whole of the base of this rock has been under the sand and the soil – it is very close to the sea and is washed by the sea at high tide – built up with man-laid stones and rock and set in place by a form of cement made from coral.

It is impossible to get under this rock except in maybe three places and the flow of water from the mountain and underground streams makes digging without pumping this water out impossible. There are many streams flowing into the cavern under this rock as well and if the build-up below it is rashly removed away a great rush of water would result and might well wash away everything buried therein.

Extreme caution is now needed and suitable pumping equipment has to be available to keep the water under control to enable digging operations to proceed but I have complete confidence in getting into the cavern – given the equipment if not this year then next.

Le Vasseur gives at least two indications of where the entrances are. In his cryptogram he says of the ultimate destination of the treasure, 'Island marbles are to be looked for well on entering.' These I have found at a possible entrance.

He says, 'Find the third circle and it – the treasure will be opened unto you.' I have found the third circle . . .

The French archives reveal that this treasure took almost four years to bury. I am not now surprised. I have seen all the pirate's work and it is phenomenal. No one could have laid out this work unless there was a real purpose behind it. I am certain the treasure is there and is untouched. I intend with the help of those who support me to continue this search to the very end as I myself have no doubt that I have found the actual and untouched spot where it is buried.

The prospector for whom I act has the full co-operation of the Seychelles Government in this search for treasure and there is an agreement in writing properly stamped and registered under which this Government gets a certain share of the treasure in consideration of the Government providing many useful and free facilities to me as the prospector's Attorney to help me in this search.

In the Seychelles there is no law of Treasure Trove and in the event of the treasure being found and no agreement to the contrary being made one half of that which is found belongs to the owner of the land upon which the treasure is found and the other half to the person or persons finding the treasure . . .

Those persons advancing money for the purchase of any one share or portion of a share are asked to sign a formal application . . . It is pointed out for avoidance of doubt, that should the treasure not be found then any balance of money paid by persons for the purchase of shares or portions of shares will belong to the Prospector absolutely.

Well, that's the prospectus (more or less), roneoed and without signature or address. I later made the acquaintance of a shareholder and I have a complete set of the subsequent progress reports that reached shareholders from Nairobi. My particular shareholder is an interesting man by the way. In 1938 an elephant knelt on his left leg while a tigress chewed off his right. But that is how it is in this story. Even the smallest walk-on parts have a touch of the bizarre.

II
THE TREASURE ISLANDS

A treasure hunt for £120 million, with shareholders scattered all over the world, is an interesting business and I was surprised to find that only snippets of news about its progress had leaked out during the nine years' dig. The whole thing made up the sort of adventure story that intrigues me and, having made sure through the Colonial Office that the hunt was still on, I shook the Easter snows of England off my boots and twenty-four hours later the sweat was pouring off me in Bombay. The next day I sailed in the excellent S.S. *Karanja* of the British India Line and just over four days later I came on deck at five o'clock in the morning and watched the Seychelles materialise out of the darkness.

As we crept in towards the islands, I was somehow unsurprised when instead of the usual seagulls a single large bat flew out to inspect the ship and, no doubt, report back. The night before I had filled in my customs declaration form and had sniffed the wind of a treasure island in its old-fashioned print. Instead of the usual warning about importing alcohol, tobacco, agricultural machinery and parrots, I was cautioned that 'Passengers must specifically state if they have in their possession OPIATES, ARMS AND AMMUNITION,

BASE OR COUNTERFEIT COINS.' After this I was only surprised at not being required to sign the form in my blood.

With an almost audible blare of trumpets and crash of cymbals the sun hurled its javelins into the heavens over the Garden of Eden a few miles away on the port side. The dull geographers call it Praslin Island, the second largest of the Seychelles, but General Gordon wrote a book proving conclusively that these islands were originally joined to the northern bulge of East Africa and he pin-pointed the famous 'Vallais de Mai', home of the bizarre Coco de Mer, as the original Garden of Eden. I am sure he is right.

We slowly engraved our wake across the mirror of the doldrums and at breakfast time the roar of our anchor chain echoed back to us from the emerald flanks of Mahé, biggest island of the group and home of Port Victoria, the capital. (Again appropriately as it seemed to me we were flying the yellow flag with a central black square to signify that we were an object of suspicion to quarantine. In fact there was a case of smallpox among the 700 Indians in the third class, but the few Seychelles passengers were mercifully allowed ashore.)

The captain bade me farewell with a final warning: 'First thing you do, you get your return passage fixed up. Left a chap here last year and the next thing I heard he'd hanged himself with his braces in the Pirates Arms. Couldn't get a passage out. Claustrophobia.' I thanked the captain, told him I didn't wear braces, and went down the ladder to the launch and the twenty-minute trip in through the reef.

Of Mahé, Ommaney wrote: 'As we passed slowly along the coast, I thought I had never seen a lovelier place in my life. Many people, seeing it thus for the first time, have said to themselves: "This is where I will spend the rest of my life and here, with God's help, I will die".' But when Ommaney landed he changed his mind and found much to criticise in the island and its inhabitants. So did Alec Waugh in his gossipy *Where the Clocks Chime Twice*. For my part, having known tropical island life in the Caribbean and having seen something of it in the Pacific, I found nothing either surprising or unpleasant, except one or two of the inhabitants, in this authentic though in parts ramshackle tropical paradise. It is true that the Seychelles are fifty years behind the times in almost everything unconnected with the Government – a Government incidentally which under the light but firm reign of Mr. John Thorp, lately Governor of the Leeward Islands, is quite astonishingly efficient and forward-looking in all departments – but most of us would count that a blessing. Apart from the humidity, which is exasperating to the new arrival, poor communications and the standard of living, the Seychelles are remarkably blessed.

The temperature varies between 75 and 85 degrees through the year and the sea temperature is much the same. Scenically the islands are some of the most beautiful in the world, the waters that surround them are almost paved with game and other fish (while I wrote this a young woman was catching a 200lb grey marlin on a 34lb line), the bird life includes ten species unique to the Seychelles (including the famous black parrot, *coracopsis barklyi,* of Praslin) and botanically there is almost every tropical species of tree and shrub including the majestic Coco de Mer which grows naturally nowhere else in the world. On a drabber note, the tax rates are not attractive but servants are around ten shillings a week. Incomparable beach sites can be bought for about two to five hundred pounds an acre and a substantial bungalow would cost around £3000 to build and furnish. On the reverse of the medal is lack of refrigeration, shortage of electricity, telephones, meat, vegetables, except tropical varieties, poor roads and, from March to May and in October and November the aforesaid humidity. To make up for lack of snakes and malarial mosquitoes there are centipedes and scorpions, though in a month I never saw either, and occasional Stone Fish, one of the Scorpionidae. If you have the misfortune to step on any of these there is an excellent medical service. Some knowledge of French is important since the man in the street speaks Creole, an incomprehensible language consisting almost entirely of bastard French nouns stitched together with grunts and facial expressions.

Anyone who is attracted by the sound of this patchwork paradise would do well to write to the Tourist Officer, Port Victoria, Seychelles, Indian Ocean, and enclose a postal order for 3/-. By return, i.e. in about a month, he will receive a workmanlike tourist handbook.

The only reason why these beautiful British possessions are not overrun with tourists and settlers from Africa and England and why there are still only about 150 rather tatterdemalion hotel and guest rooms on Mahé is poor communications. In theory you can fly from London in a day to Bombay or in a little longer to Mombasa via Nairobi and have a pleasant three to four days' voyage to Port Victoria. But in fact there are only about two sailings per month by British India and the Eastern Shipping Company. At one time or another the Union Castle, Royal Interocean, Bank and Messageries Maritimes lines have called at the Seychelles, but copra is the only large outward cargo and the rest of the traffic and mails are not economic. It is the chicken and the egg. If the British India line will take a view and increase calls on the Seychelles to twice a month, then the tourist marionettes will start to revolve. The hotels will get built, the roads will improve, the electricity company will operate for twenty-four hours instead of twelve, the cargoes will materialise for the returning ships and the British India Company will benefit. But however much Government is willing to help with guarantees and tax reliefs, private industry must make the first move. In this part of the world there are two spectres that commemorate the failure of two majestic treasure hunts carried out by the last Socialist Government – the ground nut scheme in Tanganyika that cost you and me 36 million pounds and the quarter of a million pound Seychelles fisheries scheme which, thanks to the fact that there is a great difference between spending your money and someone else's, became so weighed down with overheads that it never got off the ground. It became what the Americans call a 'Lead Balloon'. No. The tourist future of this small paradise lies in the first place in the hands of the British India line, perhaps using their excellent S.S. *Mombasa* which was originally built for the aforesaid ground nuts fairyland and which is now paying half of its way on the African coastal trade. However, tourism is the mundane side of the Seychelles treasure story and this is not a travel series. All I can say is that, having spent a month in the islands, the true treasure of the Seychelles, as the Roman Catholic Bishop was tartly to remind me at a Government House reception, lies in the natural resources of the islands – their sunshine, their beauty and their simple, kindly people. If I were a British millionaire, I would invest in them before the American millionaires get there first as they have in the Caribbean.

But I was in pursuit of more earthly objectives and, after ascertaining that Wilkins, the treasure-hunter, had abandoned operations during the high tides of the South East monsoon, and had retired to the neighbouring island of Praslin, I jumped a schooner trip to the outer islands with the object of looking into the treasure myth that pervades the whole group. We set sail in the MV *De Quincy*, an elderly ex-minesweeper of 100 tons with a single 100 hp Parsons diesel, eight berths, a splendid captain named Houareau and a solid crew of Seychellois wearing the black-ribboned flat straw hats of Nelson's time.

As we chugged round North Point on our thirty-hour voyage to the Amirantes we were passed by the most beautiful ship in the Indian Ocean coming home from the islands. She is a 50-ton schooner called *Le Revenant*, with a pale blue hull and grey sails and woodwork silvered by the sun. This is how she came by her name. As the *Juanetta* she was caught by the cyclone of 1951 when lying at anchor off Farquahar Island in the Aldabras. By the time the cyclone had blown itself out the remains of her were lying 300 yards inland, among the palm trees. Lloyds' surveyor from Mauritius agreed that she was 100 per cent loss and her owner was paid £10,000. He at once began digging a channel to the sea, refloated and rebuilt her, and after years of work she set sail again among the islands as *Le Revenant*. That day, as The Ghost Ship hissed quietly by with all sails set, coming into harbour with the dawn, I felt a pang of the heart such as the sight of no other ship has given me.

We carried three suckling pigs and twelve chickens to eat on the way, a super-cargo of a beautiful Negress with baby, one temperamental dog and several tribes of ants, cockroaches and spiders. The other seven passengers were Mr. Frank Cook, Editor of 'World Crops' (immediately dubbed 'koko') who had been sent out by the Colonial Office to advise on coconuts on which he said, and we all ultimately agreed, he is the world's leading expert, Mr. Jefferiss, Director of Agriculture, a sardonic, wafer-thin, pipe-smoking character whose photography embellishes this series, his assistant, Mr. Guy Lyonnet, who remained silently immersed in *La Loi*, the Prix Goncourt winner, throughout the voyage, and three representatives of the Seychelles plantocracy – Mr. Douglas Baillie who, beside planting coconuts, is an administrator of note and a formidable, though tight-lipped, conchologist and stamp collector, Mr. Jimmy Oliaji, a leading Hindu merchant, heir to the Temoolgees, the 'Sassoons' of the Seychelles, and a compulsive talker, and Mr. André Delhomme, a witty and very Parisian member of the 'Grand blancs' who are alleged, with the help of the Roman Catholic Church, to rule the Seychelles from behind the scenes.

In this good company I wallowed, at six knots, 150 miles across the ocean to Alphonse, just south of the Amirante group, and thence to Poivre and Desroches and so back to Mahé and the blessings of iced drinks and water closets. It was a wonderful, romantic voyage through the squalls and doldrums to lost coral islands – the endless chunkachunka-chunk of the diesel, the skimming following sooty terns, boobies and shearwaters, the death-flap of the bonitoes, king fish and tuna on deck and the subsequent stench of the salted flesh drying in the sun, the varying but always sad cloudscapes that strung along our horizons and had always so strung, through the ages of pterodactyls, pirates and U-boats, and then, from time to time, the smudge on the horizon that grew into a coral atoll, the pirogue out through the reef and the ride back through the surf, the clear sea bottom aflash with life and colour, the jump to land on the wet sand and the huddle of palm-thatched houses with the central boat-house with the tall white cross which also acts as a guide through the reef on its roof. There would be brief public relations with the local manager and his family, the rude discomfort of the earth closet and the brief ease of the blood-heat water in the bath house, and then, while the others went seriously about their work, I would talk to the fishermen about their local treasure myth and then put on my mask and get my face under the sea and away from the roasting sun and escape to the sergeant majors and the bat fish, the globe fish and the morays and compare, greatly to its disadvantage, the underbelly of the Indian Ocean with the underbelly of the Caribbean.

It was a wonderful, simple voyage which scraped off the civilised scales and parasites and hurled you back fifty, a hundred years. Wallowing through the doldrums with a queasy stomach and suckling pig and 60 degree beer for dinner and with only the blazing Southern Cross and the symmetrical jewels of Orion's Belt to think about is a good therapy for Strontium 90, and the future of England and the world – let alone one's own private puzzles. The talk in the tiny wardroom was splendidly remote from these things – Melitomma, Rhinoceros beetle and other coconut pests, the future of Vanilla, what can we do about Nutmeg and the turtle industry? Isn't it a shame about Patchouli! Secondary crops. Praedial larceny. 'All right. We start a pilot scheme to kill the beetle but how can you assess it. I mean scientifically. If people steal the nuts and you can't count the crop. You've got to raise the cost of living so that they don't need to steal.' Tourism. Communications. The British India Line. But the hotels are hopeless. The fishing's all right but you can't charter boats. Well, you've got to start somewhere. Don't be so defeatist. Oh we've tried everything in the Seychelles. It's the fault of the Roman Catholics, of the climate, of high taxation, of the last governor, of the one before, of the French influence, of the British, of the Indian merchants. Oh well. Prosper! More beer. Encore de la biere. And Prosper would nod and dig more bottles out of the tepid zinc bath.

I spent much time with the captain, a huge man with a feminine voice and feet that hurt him so much that he bathed them for half an hour every morning in the deck pump. Captain Houareau is a brilliant navigator and he and the *De Quincy* are just what you need if you are after doubloons. He knows all the stories, has his own ideas and has not lost faith in Treasure as a real thing.

How real is treasure in the Seychelles? To my great surprise it is more real than you might think. First of all you have to differentiate between what the locals call 'Le Grand Trésor' and 'Le Petit Trésor'. It is a logical definition. The captain of the ship, *Le Grand Corsair,* had of course the Big Treasure in chests in his cabin. He slept on them. Traditionally his leather-bound chests contained pieces of eight, Maria Theresa thalers, doubloons and Louis d'or. There were also ropes of pearls and, as inevitably as the hundred grand in American thrillers, a richly jewelled cross. (This features prominently in the Wilkins Treasure in search of which we are bound.) In due course, when the going got hard or he got old, the captain would work out his hiding-place on a remote island, pick out an identifiable hiding-place, mark it by physical features and the stars and then get his treasure ashore, bury it and murder the witnesses. This must have been difficult. My ship is lying off a coral atoll surmounted by two humps probably called 'Les Tetons'. I take bearings and make my plan, perhaps obscured by clues and traps – childish ones, for I am not very well educated – and then I get fifty of my sixty crew dead drunk. (But how do I keep my boat's crew sober? How do I lull their suspicions? These things are difficult among criminals, each with his own secrets and suspicions, in a 500-ton ship.) And then my heavy chests are borne over the side into the whaler and we pull for the shore, our oars muffled with sacking, and I leave my ship without a watch. (Who is my second in command? How do I explain my actions to him?) We come to the spot. We carry these heavy chests up above the tide-line to the cave, or the big rocks, or the single palm tree (so soon to be blown down) and under my directions we dig. How do I keep them at it while I anxiously examine my turnip-watch, the stars, the lifeless ship lying offshore, on which one among the rum-soaked crew may soon revive and watch the swaying lanterns ashore? Then the hole is dug and the chests lowered in. By how many men? I have single-shot pistols, perhaps four of them, though that in itself would have aroused suspicions. There were no revolvers in those days and the labour force, for the rowing and the digging, could not have been less than six. And when the work is done and the hole covered in, I shoot the men and we set sail. But the next morning? Where is La Barbe, the second mate? What has happened to Le Cossu, Simon le Grand, L'Espagnol, L'Homme-singe, Petit Phillipe? Did not someone hear the sound of oars last night, see lights ashore? Can I silence these murmurings with a torrent of oaths, with a threatening plank run out over the heaving stern.

I don't know the answers to any of these questions. The security problem of burying heavy treasure is to me the greatest argument against the 'Grand Trésor'. But I can more easily comprehend the hiding of the Petit Trésor which every man on the ship had round his waist or hidden in the wooden walls of his ship. These little treasures were bags full of gold coins which were every man's portion. To get them ashore and bury them in a water jar would not have been too difficult. There was always fear of one's shipmates and of defeat in battle to spur one on. But even then one can see the shifty, ever-watchful eyes of one's 'best friends' and one can feel the treasure-guilt and guile that must have sailed in these small, desperate ships.

Houareau, captain of the *De Quincy*, told me the story of one such Petit Trésor. He told me how it had been hidden and found and of the way the finder had got it away from the treasure island and through the customs at Port Victoria. Houareau had carried it for this man, not long ago, in 1936. And the man had got the treasure away to France and had lived on it. I was to hear of other such treasures before I came back to the Wilkins Grand Trésor. I am told by a solid enough witness, for instance, that there is one on the Island of Praslin at this moment and that the finder has baked the gold, which is in bars, into loaves of bread which sit innocently on the shelves of his larder. And, if you want Captain Houareau's own best bet, it is the island of Astove, in the Aldabra group, and a headland called 'Pointe aux Canons' where you can see the sunken cannon of a Portuguese ship below the sea. However, these are unproven. The treasure trove of 1936 is fact.

III
BUTTERFLIES AND BEACHCOMBERS

The island of Desroches, where the treasure was found in 1936, is a dot in the Indian Ocean just East of the Amirante group and about 120 miles from Mahé, the chief island of the Seychelles. It was a great rendezvous of the Black-birders, and, long after the abolition of slavery, the remnants of the 'Ebony Trade' continued to flourish in the outlying islands, using Desroches as an *entrepôt*. Even today you can see the ruins of a great underground cellar into which a nineteenth-century owner of the island used to herd his slaves whenever a sail was sighted. On a day at the end of April I stood on the bridge of the fairly good ship *De Quincy* and watched Desroches grow from a smudge on the horizon to a Robinson Crusoe paradise of brilliant green palm trees and dazzling sand while Captain Houareau kept a sharp eye on the back of the lookout man in the bows and told me the story.

Captain Houareau had been a young sailor in one of the inter-island schooners at the time, and the overseer of Desroches, which was owned by one of the 'grands blancs' of Mahé, had been a man called Lemière. One day in 1936 the schooner had visited Desroches to take off Lemière who had suddenly and inexplicably thrown up his job. The reason he had done so, as was subsequently discovered, was a good one. He had found a rich treasure of gold coins (small gold coins, his abandoned Desroches mistress was later to say) and he was escaping with them to France. The discovery had come about like this.

One day a labourer working on the pier at which I was soon to land had come upon the first links of a rusty chain. He had followed the chain a little way through the sand in which it lay deeply buried, but gave up when he had got out of his depth towards the reef. He had then reported his find to Lemière, the overseer. Everyone in these islands is highly treasure-conscious and Lemière waited until dawn when all his small labour force was busy inland husking the day's quota (today, 400 nuts – wage 3/-) of coconuts and he had then followed the chain out towards the reef in a pirogue. At the end of the chain he found an ancient metal cauldron which he had somehow managed to heave into his boat. When he got this home and forced off the sealed lid he found a small fortune in gold coin.

Lemière was a good carpenter and he spent the next few weeks building three stout wooden trunks with false bottoms. Then he packed his clothes, and, having sent his resignation into Mahé by a passing fishing boat, he set sail in the schooner of which Houareau was one of the crew.

'I helped carry those trunks into the customs shed,' said Captain Houareau dolefully, 'and each one weighed a ton. The customs men were suspicious but short of smashing the trunks they could do nothing. Although I remember they even searched his accordion. The very next day this Lemière sailed for France in a Norwegian ship.'

'What happened to him?'

'Ah, he was a sly one, that Lemière. When the true story leaked out through the *ménagère* he had forsaken on Desroches a certain Seychellois called Michel got together all his money and his family's money and sailed for France to beard this Lemière and find out where the treasure was. He thought there might be some gold left. Lemière sold him a plan, a true plan of the treasure place, and Michel came back to the Seychelles and went as soon as he could to Desroches. He found the chain where the plan said he would, and he followed it out to the reef and pulled up the end. But of course there was no treasure. Jules had taken it all.'

The Captain laughed hugely at Michel's stupidity.

When we landed on Desroches and were drinking coconut milk with gin added, I asked the present owner of Desroches, Monsieur André Delhomme, who had sailed with us, if the story was true. He said it was and he added these details. Lemière had lived comfortably off his treasure and had married a French woman who had worked for Nobel Industries in Paris. Through her he came to know the famous – or, as it was stated at the collaborationalist trials – infamous Louis Renault, head of the Renault companies. Renault was impressed with Lemière and allowed him to purchase some of the privately owned Renault stock with his gold pieces. After the war, Lemière was tarred with the same brush as Renault, was imprisoned and is believed to have died two years ago in Brittany.

While the coconut experts strode round the tiny island I got down under the milk-warm sea and hunted for cowries of which every round rock yielded two or three. Collecting shells is one of the minor treasure industries of the Seychelles, for the islands are astonishingly rich, particularly in cowries of whose 164 species no fewer than 64 are found in these waters. Everybody, from the Chief of Police downwards, has his hoard, and everyone has his secret beach. Later I was to hear scraps of conversation like the following: 'Found an odd-looking Valkyrie the other day. Must find time to give her a tooth-count. Might be a subspecies.' 'There he was sitting by his pirogue with a pile, an absolute pile of Talparia Argus in front of him – you know, the pheasant cowrie. Ten dollars at least in the catalogues. And you won't believe it, but he'd smashed the whole blooming lot to pieces for bait!' Or 'You want to look out for her. She knows more than she says. Came along to see my collection the other day and I saw her fingers straying among the Mappas. So I said "Mrs Trumper, I'm watching you." Just like that. "I'm watching you." Blushed like a spathodea.' But it's a peaceful, harmless occupation and that afternoon I made a modest start with two of the beautiful Tiger cowries that are twice as big as golf balls and that shine out from the rock crevices like great jewels.

Then at dusk we were rowed on board again to a beautiful, lilting rowing-song with the refrain 'Oh Marie, qui a des jolies tetons' and sailed through the night and the next day home to Mahé.

We had previously visited Alphonse, south of the Amirantes, and Poivre, a member of that group, and at each one there had been tales of adventure and treasure. On Alphonse, for example, there still lay in the palm-thatched boat-house a tiny coracle of boards in which a Canadian had sailed 1500 miles with nothing but seagulls and flying fish to eat. He had been sailing alone round the world and had been wrecked on the Chagos group. From the remains of his boat he had built this little six foot tub and had sailed vaguely in the direction of Africa to land, by God's grace, when he was hardly a day away from death, on Alphonse. If he is alive today he may care to know that his little coracle is still preserved and his courage venerated by the fifty inhabitants of Alphonse.

At Poivre, Mr. Baillie, one of the leading English planters on Mahé told me of the lost treasure of the German raider *Koenigsberg* of the 1914–18 war. The *Koenigsberg* used the vast landlocked lagoon of Aldabra as her hiding-place, her engines being just powerful enough to get her up the main hundred foot wide tidal channel that connects the lagoon with the sea. She was sunk there by the Royal Navy, but when her wreck was searched for the gold coin she had been forced to use as currency for supplies, there was no trace of the treasure.

Three years ago, the Seychelles Government put the leases of Aldabra and the not-far-distant island of Cosmoledo out to tender and they were surprised to get many offers from Germany. It transpired that the *Koenigsberg* treasure is a favourite myth with the Germans and there are many secret maps giving its location. None of the German offers was accepted, but two years ago a party of Germans in an Italian schooner landed on Cosmoledo, carried out a quick dig and hurried away. Perhaps they were as lucky as Lemière.

I was later to find that treasure is as much the topic of everyday conversation in the Seychelles as are the football pools in England, and that secret digs are the order of the day. Just before I arrived, a citizen had written feverishly to the Governor asking that, on the next visit of one of H.M. ships, she should be instructed to fire a salvo from her main armament at a particular rock-face the writer would designate. If she would do this and lay bare the riches beneath, he would go halves with the Government. This dashing request inspired the Governor to draw a most appropriate cartoon for the *Sunday Times*.

On our long voyage home to Mahé through the doldrums, Captain Houareau told me of his own private treasure hunt – a grisly tale. Five years or so ago he had been sailing north of the Amirantes when, off the African Banks, which rise just above the surface of the sea, he was hailed by some excited fishermen. The night before, a big cargo ship, wearing so far as they could see no flag, had hove to off the banks and a boat had come ashore carrying two officers and four Chinamen. The Chinamen had carried a heavy chest ashore and this they had buried under the supervision of the officers. Then the boat had been hoist inboard again and the ship had departed. Hardly had he heard the end of the story than Captain Houareau was ashore with a spade and a machete. Sure enough, the edge of a box soon appeared and when he cut through the wood, his machete rang on metal. It was lead. He cut a hole in it and a dreadful odour emerged. It was a coffin. When Houareau despondently told the story to his owner in Mahé the man said, 'Houareau. You are a bigger fool than I thought. Of course it is a treasure and they have thrown some meat on top of it to put people off the scent (so to speak). Go back, dig up the treasure and we will go halves.' Excited anew, Houareau ploughed back across the ocean to the African banks and this time he took the whole lid off the coffin. Captain Houareau looked at me delightedly. 'And there was gold, gold, gold.'

He held up three fingers. 'Three times gold. Three gold teeth in the mouth of a poor old Chinaman *endormi*.' He roared with laughter at the memory of his disappointment. 'No I did not take that gold. I covered up the old man again and left him to sleep.'

Back in Mahé I ascertained that it was still the closed season for my own, the Wilkins treasure hunt, because the site is tidal until the beginning of the South East monsoon, and that Wilkins had himself retired to the neighbouring island of Praslin but would be back in a few days to begin operations. To pass the time I visited Silhouette, three hours' sail away, and the remarkable man, Monsieur Henri Dauban, who is its 'king'. Over a dish of jugged bat (yes, *Pteropus celaeno*, the flying fox. Not recommended. Despite the jugging it tastes exactly like bat) Henri Dauban told me a series of vertiginously tall tales.

He had been a card-carrying Communist, he had mounted and ridden on a forty foot Chagrin shark and helped it to scratch the parasites off its 'shagreen', he had the only real treasure in the Seychelles, a butterfly that lived on the summit of his thousand foot peak and was worth £2000 per specimen, he had represented England in the Olympic Games. This seemed a verifiable tale. I stopped the flow and asked for details. This is the story Henri Dauban told me.

In 1924 he had left the Seychelles and gone to England to learn about world commodities and he had worked on essential oils for a famous Mincing Lane firm. He lived in a boarding house in the suburbs adjacent to a sports ground owned by one of the big five banks. One day, looking out of his window, he observed to his great surprise a group of young men 'throwing the harpoon' in a distant corner of the ground. They were doing it very badly, getting no distance, and 'the harpoon' was flying crooked. Dauban had fished with the harpoon since he was a child and he couldn't understand why these men were practising so badly and yet so seriously, so he went down and across the sports ground and asked them what they were trying to do.

'We are practising throwing the javelin for the Olympic Games in Paris,' explained one of the young men. 'Then England will not win,' said Dauban. 'I also can throw the harpoon. May I try?' They allowed him to and he threw the harpoon straight and true forty metres, double as far as any of them had achieved. He did this as if standing in a pirogue and without taking any run.

The young men were very excited and told Dauban that he must come with them to Twickenham on the following Saturday for the semi-finals of the eliminating trials. Dauban laughed and said he would if he got a proper invitation. The young men arranged this. Dauban won easily at Twickenham and again, on the following Saturday, at Wembley. On these occasions instead of throwing his harpoon as if he was standing in a boat he copied the standard run. Everyone was delighted and in due course he received the official invitation to represent England at Paris. His event was to be on a Saturday and he didn't think his boss would let him have the extra half day off. He decided to consult the other clerks in his office. Apparently he was always playing jokes on them and they refused to believe his extraordinary story until he produced the official invitation. Then they were thrilled and told him to go and tell his story to the boss who not only gave him the half day off but paid his passage over by aeroplane. No he hadn't won. The Finns and the Norwegians were far too good for him, but he hadn't disgraced England. He had come in fairly near the top.

I took this delightful story, as I had taken the others, with a cubic metre of salt. When I got back to England I consulted the Olympic records. It was quite true, Henri Dauban had represented England in the javelin in Paris in 1924. And now what about the Communism and the shark and the butterfly? The Communism I cannot check, but Chagrin shark is in fact a docile creature and not carnivorous. It occasionally capsizes boats by rubbing against them to remove its parasites. As for the butterfly, was this perhaps the unique *Cirrhochrista mulleralis* Legrand captured by the eminent French entomologist Legrand on the haunch of his attractive secretary Yvonne Muller? His visit to the Seychelles in 1956 on behalf of the Museum de Paris was the most recent of a long list of scientific expeditions, starting with Charles Darwin who said that the islands should be made a natural history preserve. Each scientist has added some new species to the rich variety of flora and fauna that are endemic to the Seychelles – birds, butterflies, insects (including the bizarre leaf insect whose camouflage is so perfect that other members of the family alight upon it and try to eat it), sea-shells, fish, the coco de mer palm – everywhere in these islands you come across paragraphs in natural history you will read nowhere else in the world.

And let me here mention that the occasional Latin name I have used to describe this or that species is not showing off. My own scientific knowledge is minimal. I have diligently obtained the correct nomenclature so that my more knowledgeable readers will not be frustrated by my description of priceless species as 'big brown butterflies' or 'a sort of cowrie covered with spots'.

Cousteau filmed most of *The Silent World* here and Professor J. L. B. 'Coelacanth' Smith left his mark with an incident worthy of Dr Strabismus of Utrecht. Professor Smith was collecting specimens on Aldabra and he wanted to discover what fish lived in the deep water tidal channel I have mentioned in connection with the German raider *Koenigsberg*. At slack tide he proceeded to mid-channel in a dinghy rowed by Mrs Smith, a most useful type of wife who, in addition to rowing him about his business, illustrates his fish books. There he took a charge of forty pounds of gelignite, attached a short fuse, threw it overboard and instructed Mrs Smith to row like blazes. Mrs Smith did so, but unfortunately the tide was just on the turn and the dinghy remained motionless in mid-channel until the gelignite exploded under its hull and blew it and the family Smith high into the air. Professor Smith landed in the shallows and, oblivious to the struggles of the shell-shocked Mrs Smith, loudly called for his sun-helmet. The little scene gave much pleasure to the native witnesses who thoroughly disapproved of the Professor and the death-dealing explosives and poisons he was scattering around their seas.

Having said a reluctant goodbye to Silhouette and its local Baron Munchausen I returned to Mahé and spent a few days meeting local notabilities and eccentrics while waiting for a boat to take me over to Praslin to beard Wilkins the treasure hunter in his den. There are not as many true eccentrics in the Seychelles as some writers would have us believe. There are innumerable wafer-thin 'Colonels' living on five hundred a year with their *ménagères* and they are the subject of much gossip, but in fact they are uninteresting people, the flotsam and jetsam of our receding Empire, and poor citizens of Mahé who put nothing, not even a touch of the authentic beachcomber, back into the haven they have chosen to whine out their lives in. But there is a crusty and excellent Knight of the British Empire who acts as a public scribe to the local malcontents and unsplits their infinitives when they wish to have a bash at Government – the national sport among the plantocracy and small middle class. There is the ninety-year-old 'father' of the Seychelles who claims, and can name, 167 illegitimate children. And then there is, of course, Sharkey.

Sharkey Clark, purveyor to the beast in man, is a most valuable citizen of Port Victoria and is held, except by the Roman Catholic Bishop, in general esteem. He came to the Seychelles, with a 100 per cent disability pension from the Canadian Navy, as engineer of the *Cumulus*, Ommaney's C.D.C. fishery research vessel. Today, with the help of an iron-muscled bouncer named Bob, he runs 'Sharkey's Club', where the visiting seaman pays a shilling entrance fee and can then carouse till dawn with a dusky Seychelloise on each knee and be certain that Sharkey's machine will get him back on board his ship in time. It is the good old London 'club' system with a straw skirt on and successive Governors have been grateful for this well-oiled safety valve in the town.

Only once did Sharkey Clark nearly come to grief. There had been a reception at Government House under the last régime, and Sharkey, who is invited to such functions as a matter of course, consumed, under the strain of polite conversation, fourteen glasses of champagne (the exact details of this imbroglio have been lovingly preserved). In due course he and several other guests proceeded to the Seychelles Club, the social Mecca of Port Victoria and an agreeable place. Sharkey, needing to 'freshen up', retired into the shower room opposite the long bar. There was no towel and all Sharkey could find to dry himself with was a red, white and blue cloth lying on the floor. Draped in this, Sharkey, a short man with steely blue eyes, a limp and a huge paunch, found he made a fetching picture. Certain that others would agree, he threw open the door and proceeded to do the dance of the seven veils before the applauding company. But one man, prominent in the French community, did not applaud but ran tight-lipped to the telephone and rang up the French Consul. The flag of La Belle France was being insulted! The French Consul hurried to the scene – high words, uproar, scandal! Passions, always rather near the surface in local Anglo-French differences, boiled through the days. Sharkey must resign. The Committee must resign. All of French blood would certainly resign.

Sir Michael Nethersole, leader of the British community, who is usually appealed to for a settlement to every contretemps, mildly inquired why, if the French set so much store by their flag, they left it lying around the floor of the washroom. Anyway, where was this flag? Let it be produced. The flag was produced. Consternation, relief, apologies given and accepted! It was not the

French flag. It was square and not oblong. It was the signal letter T belonging to the yacht club. Sharkey was saved, so was La Belle France, and the Colony sat back, exhilarated and refreshed by the little williwaw that had come, as it periodically does in this Anglo-French, Anglican-Catholic community, to ruffle the calm surface of the doldrums which is the normal social weather in the Seychelles.

Also, so to speak, on the dexter side of Seychelles life is the local gangster. This young crook, black sheep of a 'grand blanc' family, has something of the Arsene Lupin touch. He has a dummy telephone in his abode and, when cornered by his victims, he has often got himself out of a tight spot by having impressive telephone conversations with 'The Governor', 'The Chief Justice' or the 'Chief of Police'. Another example of his flair. Not long ago he took against a Chinese storekeeper. When the next ship, a unit of the Royal Navy, put in, he stationed himself outside the Chinaman's shop and accosted the first sizeable batch of sailors. 'You're lucky, boys,' he said winningly. 'I've got a fine shop here, full of everything you want, liquor, souvenirs, wristwatches, cameras. But I'm selling up. Going off to Africa. Tell you what I'll do. Each of you give me a quid and you can help yourself to as much as you can carry away.' Eagerly the sailors paid up and poured into the shop. The gangster melted away and left the Chinaman with his problems.

But all this is beachcomber history, the backstairs stuff of any tropical colony, and I chronicle it only as an appendix to the local lore handed down by Ommaney, Mockford, Waugh and others. And yet I could convey no picture of these treasure islands without explaining that the bizarre is the norm of a visitor's life and the vivid highlights of the Seychelles are in extraordinary contrast to the creeping drabness, the lowest-common-denominator atmosphere that is rapidly engulfing us in Britain.

For example: here the cathedral clock strikes twice, the second time, two minutes after the first, for those who didn't hear it the first time. It is a criminal offence to carry more than one coconut. With two, you will be stopped on suspicion of praedial larceny. You may not own a whip made out of a sting-ray's tail. If you own one of these deadly things, it must not be longer than three feet and it must be bound or tipped at each end and used as a walking stick. A single lash with the five foot tail can maim for life. One night, at dinner with the Governor and Mrs. Thorp, a horde of Spanish Fly, *Cantharides*, whose powdered wings make the notorious aphrodisiac, swarmed on a picture in the elegant drawing room. 'Flying ants,' we all agreed and talked with animation about the vanilla crop while the evil lepidoptera radioed their lascivious messages to the company. There is talk of trouble in the leper colony on Curieuse Island. One of the staff hates the Superintendent and also hates Leper Annie, an inmate who rejects his advances. He has written a gris-gris (black magic) letter to the head gris-gris man on the neighbouring Praslin, detailing exactly how he wants these two to die. Foolishly he has signed the letter. The gris-gris man will have none of it and takes the letter to the local schoolmaster. Who is to handle the case? The Chief of Police, or the Director of Medical Services who administers the leper colony? Better hurry! The chap may blow his top.

That's what I mean. It's an odd sort of place. That was what they were talking about at dinner parties when I left the island. That and the latest case up before the Chief Justice. This is how it appeared in the Seychelles Bulletin, 'REGINA V ARCHANGE MICHEL. Indecent Assault.' What do you make of that? Abroad's a funny place.

IV
THE STUFF OF DREAMS

Let it not be thought that all these minor escapades round the islands and on Mahé had been a waste of time. My researches among the archives and among the soldier citizens of the Seychelles had been most fruitful in helping to penetrate the secrecy and false witness that have always surrounded this modern tale of treasure. But now, armed with the basic facts, it was time to beard the great treasure hunter himself, and I took passage in the schooner Janetta for Praslin where Wilkins was said to be girding his loins for the coming open season on Mahé. It was a false trail. Wilkins had left the day before for Mahé. We had almost passed each other at sea.

Faced with an exasperating three days on Praslin, there was only one thing to do – visit the famous 'Vallais de Mai,' home of the notorious Coco de Mer palm and the unique black parrot and the authentic, or almost, site of the Garden of Eden. After that I would sit down in one of the excellent but primitive beach bungalows of the 'hotel' and get the history of the treasure hunt as far as I knew it, down on paper.

Praslin is a mountainous island about half as big as the Isle of Wight. At the southern end there is a saddle between peaks and this is the Vallais de Mai. It is a slow, very hot two hours' walk to traverse the Garden of Eden, or half an hour if you run through it as the natives often do two or three times a day. The walk has often been described in poetic flights of varying emotional temperature and I will commend to you once again Ommaney's 'Shoals of Capricorn' and myself be brief. It is a strange and beautiful walk into pre-history through a dark silent forest of giant palms. The only sounds are the trees' softly chattered comment on your passage and the occasional distant whistle of the parrots. I was later to see several of these in the distance. They are sooty grey, very wild and have never been domesticated.

Nothing lives under the trees except one of the world's largest snails – *Helix studeriana* – but the golden-barred gloom is full of the imagined shapes and shadows of those monsters one knows from museums. The great trunks of the trees rise straight as gun-barrels to the green shell-bursts a hundred feet above your head and above them again the broken patches of blue sky seem to belong to quite a different, a more modern world of familiar people and familiar shapes. Here, down below, you have seen none of it before and you gaze with curiosity at these elephantine vegetables, many of them over 600 years old, and think how odd it must have been then.

Everyone who has visited the Vallais de Mai has been struck by the strange sense of original sin that hangs in this secret place. It comes partly from the grotesque impudicity of the huge fruit of the female tree – the largest fruit in the world – and from the phallic shape of the inflorescence of the male, but also from the strong aroma of animal sweat the trees exude. The natives will not go there at night-time. When it is dark, they say that the trees march down to the sea and bathe and then march back up the valley and make massive love under the moon. I can well believe it.

It is small wonder that the fruit of the coco de mer, found occasionally washed up on the shores of Africa or India, should have gained its extravagant reputation as an aphrodisiac. It looks like one. Specimens changed hands for small fortunes and Rudoph I of Habsburg in fact paid 4000 gold florins, the equivalent of some £16,000, for one nut. I consulted the Director of Medical

Services on the subject. He averred that not only had it no stimulant properties whatsoever but equally no nutritive value. My own researches, carried out on behalf of the *Sunday Times,* confirmed the prognosis of the D.M.S. Well iced and cut into cubes, the firm jellied fruit of the double nut has a milky transparency, is glutinous to the palate like the cubes of turtle fat in turtle soup, and tastes of nothing at all. All the same, in appropriately shaped bottles, inscribed Elixir de Mai above a great deal of small type telling its story, the coco de mer represents the quickest way to make a million I have yet come across.

In due course, after indulging in a riot of strange thoughts, I found my way out on to the well-beaten mud path. Where I came out there was a piece of paper on the ground. It was a page from a child's exercise book – clearly a message to me from Eve. Repeated ten times down the page in a clear, young hand, were the words '*Le chagrin la menait et elle versait des torrents de larmes amères.*' Puzzling over the significance of these melancholy words I walked thoughtfully down the mountain and back into the world.

With a couple of days to waste before I finally met Wilkins, the treasure hunter, on the main island of Mahé, I sat down in one of the excellent but primitive beach bungalows of the 'hotel' on Praslin Island and put down on paper what I had been able to piece together of the ten-year history of the treasure hunt. My sources are such documents as are available and the evidence of reliable witnesses. I subsequently checked these with Wilkins himself.

The treasure prospectus of 1955 was issued under the impeccable auspices of Messrs. Hamilton, Harrison and Mathews, Nairobi solicitors, and Messrs. Gill and Johnson, a leading firm of Kenya accountants. The result was an immediate subscription of some £24,000 by some 400 shareholders. Since then, single shares have been bought for £4000 when the market was good – that is when it leaked out that Wilkins had found Pegasus in the tenth hemisphere or whatever – but today I dare say the market is not so firm. But this as they say on Wall Street 'should not be construed as an attempt to induce the public to subscribe for shares' and I personally have no holding.

I do not in any way condemn this splendid document. Even if no treasure is found, nobody can complain at being cheated by the prospectus which can be read, like many other more sober prospectuses, as wishful drivel or as the stuff of solider dreams. Four hundred romantics have had a bet on Pegasus for the Treasure Stakes and after nine years he is still running. They have had great fun and occasional heart attacks and if in the end no one draws a winning ticket they've at least been given a splendid serial story to follow through the years.

This is how it all came about. My sources are Wilkins himself, such documents as are available and the evidence of reliable witnesses.

Reginald Herbert Cruise Wilkins was born forty-five years ago near Bideford, in Devon, of good yeoman stock. He decided to join the Army and went into the Coldstream Guards. He rose no higher than guardsman. His only military claim to fame is having been a sentry outside Buckingham Palace. In the middle of 1940 he was discharged from the Coldstream Guards as unfit and somehow found his way to East Africa where he became a white hunter. (He has often been described as Captain, Major and even Colonel but, I suspect, more often than not by jobbers in the shares of his venture.) Later, in court in the Seychelles, he described himself as having been responsible for finding food for 300,000 people in Africa, but which people and why and where in Africa I have not been able to discover. He then branched out into a trucking business called The Yellow Hood Co. which did well until, in 1949, his doctor told him he was on the edge of a nervous breakdown and must have a rest. He went to the Seychelles and dabbled with the idea of starting a shark-fishery and meanwhile settled down in a bungalow adjacent to the present treasure site. The whole area was the property of a Miss Berthe Morel, subsequently to become the wife of a famous Seychellois, Mr. Arthur Savy, who can proudly boast more than 100 illegitimate children.

Mrs. Arthur Savy was then about 75 and she died two years ago aged 84, having, for the last ten years of her life, kept her coffin slung from the roof of her sitting-room. She is very important in the treasure story. She owned the famous cryptogram and documents which Wilkins is using today and she herself had hunted the treasure on and off for over forty years. Labour is cheap in the Seychelles and to keep a labour force digging and wall-making all that time would not have been too expensive a business. She also owned the land on which the treasure 'is'. Wilkins quite naturally met this elderly lady and was several times asked up to her house for tea. On each occasion, he tells me, as he came into the room, Mrs. Savy, as I will now call her, appeared to shove some papers hastily under the tea-tray. This would have seemed to my suspicious mind as something like a 'come-on', but not to Wilkins, and in due course he 'came-on' and asked what Mrs. Savy was hiding. Then reluctantly and bit by bit the story of the Le Vasseur treasure came out and papers were revealed. I have little to add to what is set out in the prospectus except that Wilkins believes that the secret papers were originally stolen from Government archives in Mauritius where Le Vasseur was held prisoner before going to the gallows in France.

I asked if this story had been checked in Mauritius. The answer was no and it seems as if it was always no whenever I queried some, to me, vital link in the treasure chain. Wilkins, fired with the story, cabled for his mother to come with the idea that he would invest a hundred or two in a hunt for the treasure. (In all he and his mother spent £6700 between 1949 and 1955 when they went to the public for more funds.)

Wilkins then sat down and 'deciphered' the cryptogram. Having done this to his satisfaction he was convinced that the treasure lay almost under his feet and he went back to Kenya, his head, as mine would have been, stuffed with dreams. As soon as he landed, and as if the Fates had paid for the insertion, he saw in a local paper an advertisement offering to divine copper, gold and diamond mines. Colonel Dudley Michael Leslie Hennessy, a name that will ring a bell with many of my readers, comes on the stage. Colonel Hennessy, a member of the British Society of Water Diviners was, and perhaps still is, a curious bird. He was a Eurasian, born in Bangalore (and not as some have thought on an Irish estate) and had just ceased being Embarcation Intelligence Officer in Bombay (and not, as went the rounds, Head of the British Secret Service in India). Colonel Hennessy's writing paper of that date describes him as 'General Consultant, Water and Mineral Diviner, Lands, Estates and Insurances, air travel and General Agencies. Nawasha, Kenya.' He listened to Wilkins, sent for his lawyer, Mervyn James Eversfield Morgan, barrister-at-law, of Nairobi and the three of them drew up a partnership deed dated July 18, 1949. There is nothing particularly interesting in the deed except that they all agree to use their particular powers to find the treasure, and very soon they went off to the Seychelles to do so. Sure enough, Colonel Hennessy's pendulum swung like mad over the treasure site, whirled clockwise here and twirled anti-clockwise there, and the Big Dig was on.

I have seen a copy of Colonel Hennessy's official report on his divinations and this is a typical extract: 'Plot V.: Cavity plus, Gas plus, Fresh water, Salt water, Diamonds and Sapphires, Emerald, Ruby, Brass, Lead, Gold coins, Silk, Steel plus, Copper plus, semi-precious stones, Whale oil, Pearl, Parchment.' – forgetting the 'gas plus', a pretty attractive inventory.

The partnership lasted for something over a year and what a year it was! They had found it. They hadn't. Now they were on the threshold and a nurse must be in constant attendance at the site in case Wilkins had heart failure when he saw the gold. The treasure hunters solemnly went to the Government and asked that a cruiser should stand by off the Bauvallon Hotel and be prepared to repel the gold-crazy populace and transport the treasure away to the vaults of the Bank of England. But the tempo, the emotional pressure on the partnership, was too great and at the end of this time the treasure hunters fell out. Wilkins brought a case for 'Rescission and Nullity of Deed' against Hennessy and a certain J. P. G. Harris, a Kenya lawyer who seems somehow to have replaced Morgan as Hennessy's attorney.

It was a complicated case which centred round a spirit control, known as SOQ, over Mrs. Harris, wife of the attorney, the hiring of a certain Moustache, Wilkins' foreman, to spy upon Wilkins, and alleged 'dolosive manoeuvres' employed by Hennessy and Harris to sabotage Wilkins. I have read the court records and listened to Wilkins on the case, but I cannot quite understand what it is really all about except that Mrs. Harris, under the guidance of SOQ, was told in séance that she should visit the treasure area and walk over it. When she was exactly over the treasure SOQ would 'give her a pinch and a sharp pain in the neck'. This apparently impressed Hennessy and he, with Mr. and Mrs. Harris, took ship for the Seychelles and, without explaining the situation to Wilkins, walked over the site. At a given moment Mrs. Harris gave a shrill scream and clutched with one hand her neck and with the other her behind. Then apparently, Harris engaged a labour force and began to dig on the vital spot. Though this was not where Wilkins was digging, he regarded the rival dig as a breach of faith by Hennessy and brought the suit. There followed a short hearing and the months during which affidavits, injunctions and adjournments made fortunes for the cream of the Seychelles Bar until, in April, 1951, Chief Justice Lyon declared the case to have lapsed and it faded out. Hennessy, Morgan and Harris then left the stage and their connection with the treasure hunt seems to have ended.

This law suit is remembered all over the Seychelles for one happy exchange between defending counsel and the aged Mrs. Savy on whose land the alleged torts had taken place. She was being questioned about Colonel Hennessy and his divining activities. The counsel asked, *'Madame Savy, avez vous vu la pendule du Colonel Hennessy?'* to which the good lady, blushing furiously, bridled, *'Monsieur, je suis une honnête femme!'*

From 1951 to 1955 Wilkins dug furiously in, under and around the giant rock to which he grandly refers as 'the glacis'. The only event of note was his success in involving Government in the affair. The Government investment was a small one. In exchange for two full shares they provided some £750-worth of labour and other services by the Public Works Department, but the agreement, dated July 19, 1954, did allow Wilkins and subsequently less respectable people to say quite truthfully that the British Government had come in as a junior partner. I certainly do not blame the local government of the day for having bought a sweepstake ticket for a price that would solve the Colony's economic problems for years to come but I think they should have somehow contrived to seal Wilkins' lips. As it was the then Governor, Sir William Addis, was most unkindly dubbed 'Addis in Wonderland' by the harder headed section of the community and the tin can the Government had contrived to tie to their tail rattled embarrassingly ever since. So much so that the present Government, while I was on the island, wrote Wilkins a firm note, copy to Secretariat, Nairobi, forbidding any further use of its good name in connection with the treasure hunt.

However, the small subsidy of 1954 was only a temporary stop-gap. Pumps became necessary and Wilkins had exhausted every penny of his own and much of his mother's money. There was nothing for it but to give up some shares in the giant treasure in exchange for a modest amount of ready cash. Wilkins went to Kenya, the prospectus was issued and in due course he was back on the site with the necessary equipment.

Now the hunt was again on in earnest and the impatient shareholders in Kenya, thirsting for news, despatched as their representative a certain Colonel J. Kent whose reports on progress caused the market in the treasure shares to veer wildly over the next two years. This was not Colonel Kent's fault, but Wilkins became more and more unhappy at the jobbery going on in the shares and he fell out with Colonel Kent at the end of 1957.

I have read all the reports to shareholders and to me they make fascinating reading as this or that 'clue' is discovered, is run excitedly to earth and in the end turns out to have been a false trail, or as Wilkins insists, a deliberate trap set by Le Vasseur. Alas, there is no space for them here.

V
GOLD OR NO GOLD

Before leaving Praslin to return to Mahé and hunt down the treasure hunter I paid a quick visit to the neighbouring Aride island, one of the several bird sanctuaries in the Seychelles. Here is a vast colony of sooty terns, tropic birds, shearwaters and white terns. The latter is a beautiful bird which will certainly be part of the indelible memories of any visitor to the Seychelles. It is pure white with a beak that is royal blue merging to black and soft, rather dramatic, black eyes. They seem uninterested in the sea and spend their time flying, always in couples, among the giant sang-dragon trees – which bleed red when cut – playing and fluttering and tumbling while uttering a melodious rasping coo. From time to time they interrupt their play to hurl themselves out to sea, locked, as it seems, in each other's arms, in a breathtaking swoop of flight like perfect skaters on a giant rink of blue ice. Then they soar round and back, still locked together, until they are hovering and fluttering again under the heavy trees. These birds have a purity of colouring and flight such as I have seen in no other species and I am surprised they are not more renowned.

Aride is also notable for its lizards, emerald green with blood-red toenails, that are so fat at this time of the year they can hardly walk. For it is the nesting season and these sapient pachyderms have discovered a way of getting at the birds eggs. With their noses, they roll the eggs off the nests and push them along the ground until there is a drop. They push the egg over this so that it smashes and they then devour the yolk. Another 'believe it or not' predator on the birds is the sinister 'liane sans fin', a creeper that creeps into the nests and strangles the chicks.

Miffed at your disbelief I will now cut the nature notes and get back to Mahé, by way of the MV *Jeanette*, and back to treasure-hunting.

East of Longitude 10 and South of Latitude 35, that is, approximately East and South of Switzerland, is I reckon, the septic zone as opposed to the antiseptic in which Britons are fortunate enough to live. Go farther East or farther South of these lifelines and a scratched midge bite may mean an amputation. Beyond this cordon sanitaire live the lice, the mosquitoes, the flies, the poisonous fish and corals. This is the stinging, biting, infecting world and here are the monster diseases – smallpox, cholera, malaria, amoebic dysentery, elephantiasis, tetanus, leprosy. I know this is a wild generalisation, but that is my own ready reckoner which I am glad to hand over to the World Health Organisation and Miss Elizabeth Nicholas. Anyway, by the time I had explored the Seychelles and talked treasure with everyone that mattered, a small coral cut on the left shin, which I had foolishly not dabbed with Merthiolate, had become a deep festering wound and I was stuffed with medicaments, unsuspected glands were aching and I had a mild fever. So I was already slightly airborne when I landed on Mahé and motored along the bumpy coast road towards the treasure site across the wide bay from Fairhaven, the admirable guest house in which I had the most luxurious bedroom in the Indian Ocean.

Most unusually for the Seychelles there was an occasional growl of thunder. Rain began to fall heavily and at four in the afternoon it grew dark. To my right it was low tide and, in the shallows out to the reef, the octopus fishermen were bent over the livid pools. An occasional flash of Satan's Fire, which is more like a huge magnesium flare than our lightning, lit up the scene from time to time as if some celestial recorder wanted a photograph of my first meeting with Wilkins and, due to the gloom, was having to use flash.

I bumped and clattered round the bay, past the romantic Crusoe cottages of the Hôtel des Seychelles and the Beauvallon, where most of the keen fishermen seem to stay, and came to an unusually unkempt fishermen's village in which all the inhabitants seemed to be suffering from pigmentation troubles. I asked the way of a piebald face and was directed onwards a hundred yards. As I pulled up at the side of the road, a skeletal white hound with elemental eyes dashed at the car with a snarl. I knew that the son of the proprietor of the land was in hospital with lockjaw. Rabies raised its dreadful head in my fevered mind. But the hound, after paying an unwelcome attention to my off front wheel, slunk away.

The treasure site, as a treasure site, has much to recommend it. It is well and solidly landmarked, being exactly at the western horn of the longest stretch of sand on Mahé – the mile long North West, or Beauvallon Bay. More or less directly above this point is the 2000-foot high Mount Simpson. The site itself, at the point and below the mountain, is a giant 100-foot square elephant's flank of granite that plunges almost vertically down to the edge of the road and into a small tidal bay. Le Vasseur would have said to himself that this cliff of granite would never be obscured by vegetation and it never has been. Somewhere beneath this 1000-ton rock, according to Wilkins, lies the great treasure and, for all I know, he is right.

I got out of my car and walked towards a lean-to engine shed at the foot of the 'glacis' (the Wilkins treasure lingo creeps up on one). Around me for about two acres, the ground between the coconut palms looked as if it had been used for a film of the battle of the Somme. Everywhere there were craters full of greenish water, half shored-up walls, rough bits of masonry, little fortifications erected to try to keep back the sea, and the stumps of broken hoists. It was rather pathetic, as if some huge child had been playing with his spade and bucket. The engine shed, containing a well-kept Lister Diesel and a Holman Compressor, stood on the brink of a large and deep-looking crater full of water that extended round the base of the 'glacis'. A dozen coloured workers were tinkering, digging, wrestling with chunks of rock. On the edge of the crater sat a middle-aged man, dressed in a clean white shirt, blue trousers and sandals, gazing moodily at an oil slick on the surface of the pea-soup water. I introduced myself and, after dissipating sundry suspicions, we were off into Treasure Land.

Wilkins is a pleasant man. He engenders sympathy. He has steady, truthful but rather blank blue eyes in a totally unlined round face. His thin fair hair, neatly brushed back, and his modest, well-tended moustache are up to guardsman standards. He has a pleasant voice, and if he never smiled in my company, and certainly never laughed, it is perhaps because nothing he or I said amused him. More probably he has absolutely no sense of humour.

For the next hour it was all Andromedas and the Collarbones of Solomon (a hoary treasure puzzle I have not bothered to explore), The Golden Fleece, Pegasus and, of course, these infernal hemispheres (for which I had the good manners not to suggest there was a very much shorter word). Finally I interrupted. I pointed down into the scummy water. 'Well, at least you've found oil,' I said encouragingly.

Wilkins's calm eyes looked down at the rainbow slick. 'It's ambergris,' he said reverently.

Thinking 'Oh Lord, this is where I came in,' I said sympathetically, 'What makes you think that?'

'They buried whale oil with the treasure. Must have been a lump of ambergris mixed up with it.'

'Why did they bury whale oil with the treasure?'

'To make poison gas. We've had to be jolly careful. They were full of tricks those chaps – always trying to lead us up the garden path into some booby trap. Here, Joe, bring the crowbar.'

A large Negro brought the crowbar and prodded not the murky depths. More oil came to the surface. I said, 'Have you had the stuff tested or tried tasting it?'

'No.'

It was always so when I asked Wilkins if he had made the obvious tests. They had never been made. They might have destroyed the dream. I knelt down and dipped my finger in the stuff and tasted it. It was oil, petrol probably. I said so. I also pointed out that the gusher was about six feet away from the engines. Could someone have thrown a half empty can of oil or petrol into the pool at the end of the last dig?

'No, old man,' said Wilkins pleasantly. 'Now just come and have a look at the Andromeda in the fourth hemisphere.'

We scrambled up and over the road to the sand. The tide was coming in and we had to jump for it once or twice. We walked and skipped from granite lump to granite lump. 'Now you see over there, old man,' there was a vague pock-mark in the rock, 'that circle with the dot in the middle, that represents the sun. And there,' there was an irregular scab on the granite, 'Taurus, the bull. See the horns? Now just look down.' I was standing on a ton of rock, more or less, I admit, cruciform. 'That's just one of the Andromedas. The best one, with her left leg bent, is in Kenya. Now just come over here . . .'

Newspapers and Government departments occasionally get letters of many pages in which this sort of stuff is mixed up with the future of Palestine, or a demand for a higher pension, or an attack on Kitchener. Very often every word is written in a different coloured ink and sometimes, when additional emphasis is required, each letter in an important word is in a different colour. In my rather feverish state, under the dark livery sky, Wilkins's richly studded, evenly spoken chronicle of his discoveries began to work upon me like one of these letters and I became desperate to escape. Fortunately rain stopped play. It came down in heavy straight rods out of the doom-fraught sky. With a babble of thanks and a promise to come again I made a dash for my car, whirled it round and was off back through the looking glass.

Looking back at our first of many meetings, I am sure I am doing Wilkins an injustice, or at the very least abusing his hospitable reception of me, in writing this highly charged stuff. My fever did not abate and the next day I was in hospital having a mega-shot of penicillin and giant snacks of aureomycin, and I have a scar on my shin as big as a doubloon to show for it. So it was not until a week later that, more soberly, I had my further talks with Wilkins, and I will try to keep the purple out of my prose in recounting the gist of them.

Wilkins is certainly no slouch. When I saw him again he had already pumped out the site ('2000 gallons a minute, old man') and a solid looking four foot high wall was marching out into the shallows. 'I'm going to curve it round like this,' explained Wilkins drawing with his finger in the sand. 'That'll keep the sea back while I dig under the road.'

'Why under the road?'

'Just have a look over here. We're in the tenth (I think it was) hemisphere and I've found the star and the circle. And dead on the bearing at that.'

I followed him reluctantly and waited with some impatience while a workman dug round the base of a large granite boulder and fetched sea water to clean the exhibit. But then I must admit I was impressed and you can judge for yourself from the photograph whether or not I was right. There indeed were two clearly outlined circles or wheels in the rock and these could not possibly, I think, have been cut into granite by anything but human agency. Now suddenly I began to doubt my own scepticism. Certainly a great number of Wilkins's 'clues' were wishful, but now it seemed to me that at any rate some of the rock markings I had been shown, and perhaps many more I had not bothered to look at, could have been made by man.

'How are you going to get under the road?'

'Have to get Public Works to agree and then build them a bridge, sixty foot, steel and concrete.'

'That's going to cost a lot of money.'

Wilkins shrugged. 'I've cabled for Jabby Trent (the latest liaison man with the shareholders) and he's coming by the next boat. Perhaps we can make do with a trestle bridge. Come along to the house and I'll show you the plot of all the clues and you can have a look at the original papers if you like.'

When he is working on the site, Wilkins lives in a neat little two-roomed bungalow some fifty yards from the engine shed. We sat down and Wilkins spread out a yard square 'map'. It was the sort of map I draw – starting on generous lines and then gradually getting more and more cramped towards the bottom of the paper. There were a lot of crabby hemispheres and childish shapes joined by very thin lines. I couldn't be bothered with it and tactfully moved on to the documents which we extracted from a bulging briefcase. These all looked very much like what such documents might look like. The basic cryptogram is written in ink on a piece of cloth (not vellum, as Wilkins thinks) without any margins. The whole of it is said to be reproduced in a rare book *Le Trésor Caché* by La Roncière which I have not been able to trace.

I asked Wilkins if he had submitted the cryptogram to any expert cryptographer. No – because after four months' hard work he had been able to decipher the puzzle himself. He showed me his translation. It was full of compass bearings and Greek mythology. The last line read: 'Make diagonal at 62 degrees – here is the gold.' The translation had been in French. Wilkins had known no French. He had had to teach himself the language. I picked up the photostat of a kind of chessboard with the German words 'Gut', 'Böse' and 'Mittel' (good, evil, middling) neatly scattered among the squares opposite the signs of the Zodiac written down the right-hand margin. Wilkins said indulgently, 'They suddenly broke into Prussian.' Had he unravelled this one? 'No. That one got me stumped.' There were various cryptic letters in spidery French and some aged correspondence with the Bibliothèque Nationale in Paris.

There was no particular coherence about the papers and no history of their origin or details of previous work on the treasure. I asked Wilkins if he had been able to find out anything about Le Vasseur himself. Had he been a man of education? Was there any reason to suppose he had been acquainted with Greek mythology? According to Wilkins, he had taken four years to bury the treasure. Why had he taken so long and made such an incredible rigmarole out of it when a few true bearings mixed up with some false ones would have served as well? Wilkins had no satisfactory answers to these questions and there is no reason he should have. He was quite certain the treasure was there. He had believed it for nearly ten years and he still believed it. He intends to go on looking for it until the money (£9000 remains) runs out or until his lease of the property expires in 1962. His untroubled blue eyes gazed calmly into mine. We called it a day.

I called on Wilkins twice more to try to sort out the jumble of facts and phantasy that jostled each other round and round in my head. I heard the story of the numerous betrayals and attempts at sabotage he had suffered, his persecution by gris-gris (he had suffered mysterious poisoning, showers of stones had descended on his bungalow), the accusations of jobbery in his shares and, at no time throughout this catalogue of slings and arrows, did his even, good-humoured tone of voice become disturbed. It was as if his faith in the treasure had armoured him against all misfortune or as if he disregarded every adversary except the great pirate who had set his puzzle and laid his traps 200 years before expressly for a man called Reginald Herbert Cruise Wilkins, ex-sentry at Buckingham Palace.

On each occasion I managed to see more clues. There was the copy of the original treasure 'map' which, alas, I was not permitted to transcribe. This was a simple affair – a few curved lines, a few straight ones, and some groups of numerals. It looked very haphazard to me but Wilkins explained it with a few airy phrases involving the compass and the heavens. I dare say that if anything among the papers is in fact a guide to a treasure, this map might be the most significant. It looked to me more like the sort of thing a pirate of 1720 might have drawn – no frills and certainly no Andromeda. I was also shown some interesting fragments of glazed earthenware jars or phials. One of them bore on its base the following inscription in what seemed to me appropriately antique black lettering:

Pommade de Sain Bois

de

Ls DUBOUAIS Me LECHAUX Phen

Succr

BORDEAUX

Bearing in mind that the Seychelles were French until 1814, these fragments could have been left by a previous inhabitant or even by a previous treasure hunter, but Wilkins found them ten feet under the earth and he is sure they were left by Le Vasseur or his men. I suggested that submission of the fragments to the Muséum de Paris would resolve the problem, but here again – and I repeat, it was always so when a common-sense piece of research seemed desirable – Wilkins was satisfied with his own conclusions and with certain inquiries that had been made for him in London.

And so in due course our conversations came to an end and I thanked Wilkins and wished him luck and drove away down the dusty treasure road under the palm trees and left the dreamer dreaming in his dreamland. The next day I said goodbye to this beautiful, romantic, rather haunted paradise and started the long trudge back across the Indian Ocean and to Bombay and thence, in a flick of time, over the roof of the world to London – where the clocks strike only once and where the only treasure trove is an unexpected repayment of income tax under Schedule D.

Out of paradise and back in realty, what is one to make of The Great Wilkins Treasure? First of all, I am of the opinion that Wilkins is an honest, though possibly a deluded man. The best evidence of his honesty is that, in accordance with the terms of the prospectus, at any time during the past four years, Wilkins could have downed tools and pocketed the remaining cash. He could do so today and be the richer by £9000. No, Wilkins honestly believes in the treasure and he is spending his shareholders' money in honest and unremitting efforts to find it.

I cross-questioned him closely about his own finances and personal expenditure and I am satisfied that the shareholders' money is being correctly disbursed under the supervision of the thoroughly respectable Kenya firms of lawyers and accountants. The lawyers originally paid Wilkins a personal allowance of £100 per month and they agreed when he reduced this to £30 and bought himself a small vanilla property on Praslins out of what he thus saved. In my opinion the shareholders should be glad that he spent his allowance on vanilla rather than whiskey. I am also satisfied that Wilkins is quite innocent of any jobbery in the shares, though I guess a judicious leak of the occasional sensational 'clue' has been used by others to rig the stock in Nairobi.

And what to make of these 'clues' he has found? Some, as I have suggested, may be genuine, but a vast number such as the skeleton of a horse (Pegasus), 'island marbles' made of clay, fragments of bottles, a sea boot, a doll's head (the best of the 'Andromedas') and suchlike are surely the remains of former human habitation on and around the site. As for the 'door' which Wilkins found, fragments of wall and cement and other signs of human activity in and around the site, I feel sure that these are the remains of the forty-year search by the landowner, Mrs Savy. Wilkins is simply uncovering 'clues' left by Mrs Savy and not by Le Vasseur and he would have done well, ten years ago, to get some idea of her diggings before he began digging himself. As usual, when it comes to some basic bit of commonsense like this, we find that Wilkins preferred the solitary, passionate quest. But, when all is said and done and one has cleared away all the mumbo-jumbo, one is left, I think, with the following conclusion: If Le Vasseur buried a treasure, and if some of his shipmates didn't come and dig it up after he had been hanged, this would have been an excellent site on which to bury it.

And, of course, there is that circle and that star on the rock and, even as you read this, the pumps will be chugging and the twelve men will be digging and blasting while Wilkins sits in the shade with his back against a rock. And, who knows, perhaps at this very moment, a great shout has gone up and Wilkins has struggled to his feet and is running forward – 'Gold, Master! Gold! Gold!'

One hundred and twenty million pounds isn't a figure – it's a fever!

INTRODUCING JAMAICA

The introduction for Ian Fleming Introduces Jamaica *edited by*
Morris Cargill, 1965. Fleming wished to compile a book about Jamaica
by Jamaicans but died before it was completed.

Jamaica has now been my second home for eighteen years. Since 1946 I have been coming here, as regularly as clockwork, from January 15 to March 15 and, each year when the time comes to leave, I say my goodbyes with a lump in the throat. In this long span of time everything has changed and yet nothing. Jamaica has grown from a child into a man, she has flirted with Federation and then broken off the engagement, she has gained her Independence and Membership of the United Nations, Bauxite and tourism have changed her economy, emigration to the United Kingdom, with all its problems, brings around £7,000,000 back into the island every year, the West Indian cricketers have become the darlings of the Commonwealth and a Jamaican girl has been chosen Miss World. But the Doctor's Wind continues to blow in from the sea during the day and the Undertaker's Wind blows the stale air out again at night, and the news in *The Daily Gleaner*, the 'Country Newsbits', is just the same. A family at Maggotty has been wiped out by 'vomiting sickness' (the paper still will not add the medical diagnosis of 'eating unripe ackee'), there has been a pirate treasure trove at . . . . and Cornelius Brown has 'mashed' Agatha Brown with his cutlass and has been sentenced to prison and twelve strokes of the tamarind switch. And the people are just the same, always laughing and bawling each other out, singing the old banana songs as they load the fruit into the ships, getting drunk on cheap rum when the ship has sailed, sneaking an illicit whiff of ganja, or an equally illicit visit to the obeah-man when they are ill or in trouble, driving motor cars like lunatics, behaving like zanies at the cricket matches and the races, making the night hideous with the 'Sound System' on pay night, and all the while moving gracefully and lazily through the day and fearing the 'rolling calf' at night.

And yet, against this background of 'plus ça change, plus c'est la même chose' my own life has been turned upside down at, or perhaps even by, the small house named 'Goldeneye' I built 18 years ago on the North shore, and by my life in Jamaica. In 1952, I got married here, in the Registry Office in the neighbouring Port Maria. Noël Coward and his secretary Cole Leslie were the witnesses and Noël tied the shoe on to the back of his own car by mistake. Encouraged by, or as an antidote to this dangerous transmogrification after 43 years of bachelorhood, I sat down at the Red Bullet-wood desk where I am now typing this, and, for better or for worse, wrote the first of twelve best selling thrillers that have sold around twenty million copies and been translated into 23 languages. I wrote every one of them at this desk with the jalousies closed around me so that I would not be distracted by the birds and the flowers and the sunshine outside until I had completed my daily stint. (I have interrupted my sticky thirteenth to write these words). The books feature a man called James Bond. Here is another Jamaican link. I was looking for a name for my hero – nothing like Peregrine Carruthers or 'Steadfast' Maltravers – and I found it on the cover of one of my Jamaican bibles, *Birds of the West Indies* by James Bond, an ornithological classic. (Only a couple of weeks ago, I met him, the real James Bond, and Mrs. Bond, for the first time. They arrived out of the blue and couldn't have been nicer about my theft of the family name. It helped at the customs, they said!) Would these books have been born if I had not been living in the gorgeous vacuum of a Jamaican holiday? I doubt it. Noël Coward has written much of his later music and prose here and you will find other still more famous writers, let alone painters, who have been stimulated by Jamaica, in the bibliographical appendix to this book. I suppose it is the peace and silence and cut-offness from the madding world that urges people to create here. There is certainly enough native talent to support the theory. And my life has been changed in other ways. I first learned about the bottom of the sea from the reefs around my property and that has added a new dimension to my view of the world and, a vital postgraduate study, I learned about living amongst, and appreciating, coloured people – two very different lessons I would never have absorbed if my life

246

had continued in its pre-Jamaican metropolitan rut. But, above all, Jamaica has provided a wonderful annual escape from the cold and grime of winters in England, into blazing sunshine, natural beauty and the most healthy life I could wish to live.

My house, Goldeneye, has also lived through many changes. The 30 or so acres in which it stands were a barren donkey's racecourse when I built it. Now the land is a jungle of tall trees and tropical shrubs and we could live on the citrus and coconuts and the fish from the sea. Couples have spent their honeymoons here, stricken friends have regained their health, painters and writers – Cecil Beaton, Truman Capote, Lucian Freud, Graham Greene, Robert Harling, Patrick Leigh-Fermor, Rosamund Lehmann, Peter Quennell, Alan Ross, Stephen Spender, Evelyn Waugh – have stayed here and worked here, and a British Prime Minister and his wife, Sir Anthony and Lady Eden, were here for three weeks during his convalescence in the winter of 1956, after Suez. (The Jamaican government turned my little gazebo on the Western corner of the property into a direct teleprinter link with No. 10 Downing Street. The police guards cut 'God Bless Sir Anthony and Lady Eden' into the bark of my cedar trees. The detective, sleeping in the back room, shot at the bush rats, beloved by my wife, with his revolver, but the two trees, of a species still wrapped in mystery, which they planted, have flourished mightily.) But this is name-dropping. Why should this modest house, with wooden jalousies and no glass in the windows, with three bedrooms with shower baths and lavatories that often hiss like vipers or ululate like stricken blood hounds, with its modest staff of local help, headed by Violet, my incomparable housekeeper for all these years, have attracted all these famous people to its meagre bosom come rain (which can often fall, as it does on all corners of the world) or shine which it always will in my memory? Noël Coward provides a comment. He is given to hyperbole. In 1948, from March 22 to May 31, he stayed at Goldeneye, at, he claims, an exorbitant rent. He wrote in the visitors' book, and foolishly signed them, the following words 'The happiest two months I have ever spent'. He then went off and, as close to me as he could get, built a house (What am I saying? Four houses) and – to hell with the charms of Bermuda and Switzerland! – comes here every year. But, before he left Goldeneye, he wrote the ode which I now reprint, not for its merit, which is small, but purely to fill up space.

Noël Coward Memorial Ode

Alas! I cannot adequately praise
The dignity, the virtue and the grace
Of this most virile and imposing place
Wherein I passed so many airless days.

Alas! Were I to write 'till crack of doom
No typewriter, no pencil, nib, nor quill
Could ever recapitulate the chill
And arid vastness of the living-room.

Alas! I cannot accurately find
Words to express the hardness of the seat
Which, when I cheerfully sat down to eat
Seared with such cunning into my behind.

Alas! However much I raved and roared
No rhetoric, no witty diatribe
Could ever, even partially, describe
The impact of the spare-room bed – and board.

Alas! I am not someone who exclaims
With rapture over ancient equine prints.
Ah no dear Ian I can only wince
At *all* those horses framed in *all* those frames.

Alas! My sensitivity rebels,
Not at loose shutters; not at plagues of ants,
Nor other 'sub-let' bludgeoning of chance,
But, at those hordes of ageing faded shells.

Alas! If only common-sense could teach
The stubborn heart to heed the crafty brain
You would, before you let your house again
Remove the barracudas from the beach.

But still my dear Commander, I admit,
No matter how I criticise and grouse,
That I was strangely happy in your house
In fact I'm very fond of it.

Signed 'Noël'. February 1949

(Note that it took the man nine months to dream up this insulting doggerel!)

Well, I am still devoted to the monster (misprint for 'Master') and the rivalry between our houses (he refers to mine as 'Goldeneye, Nose and Throat') has continued all these fifteen years. (He wanted to build a swimming bath (his beach is lousy) and asked his 'attorney' what strength of pump he would need to keep the water clean. The attorney replied 'Hit depend, Mister Cowhard, how much soap you use'.) But the point is clear. It is not the rude comforts of my house that appeal nor, I think, entirely my wife, who is as honey to a humming bird. It is the friendly embrace of Jamaica and of the Jamaican way of life, and the fact, as the advertisements put it, that Jamaica is no place like home!

THE PERPLEXING DATE LINE

Originally published in Holiday, *1960. This article was cut and re-named 'Honolulu' when published as the fourth chapter of* Thrilling Cities *in November, 1963.*

'Have a good fright.' The pretty hostess bowed demurely as I left the unfortunately named "Final Departure Lounge" of the Tokyo airport to board a Japan Air Lines DC-6 for Honolulu. It was 10:30 in the evening of Friday the 13th and we were due to arrive in Hawaii before we had started – at 4:20 in the afternoon of Friday the 13th. The reason for this phenomenon was the International Date Line, which wends its mysterious way down the middle of the Pacific. To fly on Friday the 13th seemed foolhardy enough, but to leave on an air journey on Friday the 13th that continues into the next day – also Friday the 13th – seemed downright reckless. A tight round-the-world schedule and a somewhat shaky disdain for superstition emboldened me to board the plane.

Japan Air Lines had, to an exquisite degree, the desire to please – almost too much of it.

From the outset I was cosseted and begged to drink champagne. A mite of mistrust began to build as gift after gift was heaped upon me – a sandalwood scented fan, a black silk box containing masculine cosmetics and finally a sleeveless garment called a "happi" coat.

A suspicion springing from my Scottish ancestry warned me to beware of all this generosity. Perhaps those in charge of the flight were no more relaxed about toying with the mysteries of the International Date Line than I, and sought to distract the passengers with presents. Drinks were brought and a midnight snack, and then it was time to climb into a comfortable bunk, say my thanks and farewells to the Orient and prepare my mind for the impact of the West.

Four hours later we were almost at the point of no return between Tokyo and Honolulu, about two thousand miles out over the Pacific and perilously close to the International Date Line. At this fateful moment I was awakened by an authoritative voice. 'Ladies and gentlemen, this is your captain speaking. There has been an explosion in number three engine and a fire, which has been got under control. I have no hydraulic pressure. We have altered course for Wake Island where I shall carry out a no-flap landing, coming in faster and from a higher altitude than is the usual custom. I have made many three-engine landings and also many without hydraulic pressure, so see you on the ground!' How many, I wondered, had he made as the stuffing between two Fridays the 13th?

I dressed and climbed out of my bunk. People were sitting very still and looking straight in front of them. The passengers from the front had been moved to the back while the fire-fighting went on. I gazed out of the window at the dead, blackened engine that now drooped somewhat from the horizontal. A beautiful dawn was beginning to fill a cloudless sky. We went down to 10,000 feet, and the flat calm of the Pacific looked positively inviting. I remembered the standard instructions about surviving in the sea. You must not struggle, but remain calm and conserve your energies, floating as much as possible. The salinity of the Pacific, I guessed, would be a help.

We hummed sturdily on, the aircraft vibrating slightly because of the unco-operative number three engine.

Half an hour later there was suddenly a big, four-engine air-sea rescue plane only fifty yards away to starboard. It had a yellow nose and a yellow tail and belonged to the U.S. Air Force at Wake Island. She stayed at our side, dead steady, ready to throw out life rafts. A quarter of an hour later, far below us, just above the surface of the sea, two PBY amphibians of the American Navy were shadowing us, ready to come down on the surface and pick up the bits.

The calm voice of authority again. 'This is your captain speaking. To lighten the plane I am about to dump fuel, so there will be no smoking, please.' (As if she had heard the announcement, the air-sea rescue plane edged away from us.) 'This aircraft will be unserviceable for many days. I have been in touch with our Tokyo headquarters and a relief plane is on its way. Not much farther to go!'

We all continued to stare in front of us.

In due course there was the speck of Wake, a tiny coral island fringed with surf and with a big, pale-green lagoon in its center. We circled gently several times, losing height, and then, only just above sea level, came in at a good 200 miles an hour.

We hit the runway smoothly, the captain juggling the engines to keep us going straight; a few mild zig-zags and we came to rest with a screech of tires. The fire engines and ambulances swept down on us. Then the hatch opened and we were back on terra firma.

For the remainder of that day we were a little dazed and shaky and passed the time nodding enthusiastically as successive ground and crew personnel came up and assured us how lucky we had been, Bud.

The next evening the relief aircraft arrived from Tokyo with a director of the airlines; he was extremely polite and thanked us all for our "co-operation." More unguents and scented fans, fresh "happi" coats; then we were out of the second Friday the 13th and drowsily bound for Honolulu

I had had my "good fright." My disdain for superstition had evaporated. In addition, the experience had intensified the uneasiness I had always felt about the International Date Line. As a world traveller in good standing I had dutifully learned the rule about losing a day when crossing the Pacific from east to west and gaining one when coming the other way. But there is an enormous gulf between memorizing this rule and understanding the subject.

I did not look forward to a future bedecked with talismans, to closeting myself on Friday the 13th and going into trembles at the mention of the International Date Line.

I told myself to do some scientific research about the date line, unlock its mysteries and declare an enlightened peace with the cosmos that I had taunted.

Back in London, the first thing I learned about the date line is that it does not exist – that is officially. Then I learned that it is not really a line but a highly irregular boundary. The term "line," however, is a justifiable euphemism, as no one could be expected to take seriously something called the International Date Zigzag. The matter of its legitimacy was more disturbing.

I first suspected something was amiss when I started my inquiries at Her

Majesty's Stationery Office in London, where official publications can be obtained by the British public. There surely, I felt, I would find some record. Every conceivable catalogue of publications was checked and mysterious characters in charge of ancient archives were consulted by telephone. But it was all to no avail. None could offer any information.

The United Nations Office of Public Information was also unable to help. A leading map specialist had nothing to offer. The Admiralty preserved a characteristic naval reticence. Even the ever-obliging United States Information Service shrugged its shoulders helplessly.

It was the Meteorological Office that gave me my first clue. Unable to be useful themselves, they suggested I consult the Astronomer Royal, Mr. Richard van der Riet Woolley, at the Royal Greenwich Observatory, now removed from Greenwich to the 15th Century Herstmonceux Castle in Sussex.

I sent off my inquiry and by return post received a reply advising me that the International Date Line was the natural result of the adoption of a universal standard time. For information on this I should consult the proceedings of an international conference held in Washington in 1884 for the purpose of fixing a prime meridian. From then on my way was easier, but only to the extent that the more I investigated, the clearer it became that I was in search of something that had no official existence.

Prior to the 1884 conference, I learned, timekeeping was a random game with no rules. Maritime fleets usually kept the time of their home ports. The situation on land was every bit as chaotic. In the United States, for instance, as the country opened up, each community established its own private time. At one stage in the early 19th Century someone hazarded that there were seventy-five different standards of time in North America.

The first move toward achieving a world standard time was made by a New Yorker, David Dudley Field, at a meeting of the British Association for the Promotion of Social Science held in Manchester in 1866. On his motion a committee was appointed to report on the possibilities of establishing a standard time. Subsequent scientific conferences in Venice and Rome urged its establishment. Pressure in the United States reached such a pitch that a petition bearing several thousand signatures was sent to Congress. The result was an Act authorizing President Arthur to invite governments of all nations to fix one prime meridian from which universal standard time could be reckoned.

The conference, held in Washington in 1884, quickly agreed to adopt a single world-wide meridian passing through Greenwich, and to count longitude 180 degrees east and 180 degrees west of this line.

But what of the International Date Line? The extraordinary thing was, that, although Greenwich time had now achieved world status, no international agreement seems to have been reached, either then or later, firmly defining the date line. Nor has it, in its present form, ever been formally approved by the countries of the world.

The conference had made the need for a date line even clearer. The world was now officially divided into twenty-four time zones, with a different hour of the day in each zone. There would always be one complete day – one A.M. through midnight – moving around the globe. Accordingly, midnight in any one place would be followed in due course by one A.M., but of the same day. Without a date line the same day would renew itself perpetually. I began to look upon the date with enthusiasm.

Long before the Washington conference navigators had realized the necessity of adjusting the date somewhere. The convenience of doing this in a largely uninhabited area made the Pacific the logical place.

Exactly where in the Pacific was a different matter. After Magellan discovered the Philippines in 1521, the Spanish colonizers who followed observed the American date because they had approached the islands from the Pacific coast of America.

This eventually became so absurd that in 1884 the Archbishop of Manila decreed that December 30 of that year should be immediately followed by January 1, 1885, thus bringing the islands under the Asiatic date instead of the American. Alaska moved the other way. Until it was bought from Russia by the United States in 1867 it used the Asiatic date. In other words, when it was Wednesday in Fairbanks it was Tuesday in San Francisco. With the American purchase, Alaska was brought into line with the United States.

Almost everyone knows the great climax to Jules Verne's *Around the World in Eighty Days*. Phileas Fogg arrived back in London on what he thought was a Sunday – one day too late to win his bet of £20,000 with members of the Reform Club. Imperturbable as ever, he sent his valet

Passepartout out to arrange his immediate marriage with the seductive Aouda, the Parsee widow he had saved from death in the heart of India. Passepartout returned to say that the marriage was impossible "for tomorrow," as it was Sunday.

'Monday,' replied Mr. Fogg.

'No; today is Saturday.'

'Saturday? Impossible!'

'Yes, yes, yes, yes,' cried Passepartout. 'You have made the mistake of a day. We have arrived twenty-four hours ahead of time.'

Thus, with ten minutes to go, Phileas Fogg rushes to the Reform Club and wins his bet.

Verne wrote his classic in 1872, and the story was set in the same year. I have always been surprised that the very meticulous Mr. Fogg could make such a mistake. After all, he must have been one day wrong throughout his adventurous crossing of the United States, not to mention his Atlantic passage and his journey from Liverpool to London.

I have a little more sympathy with him now. Doubtless the master of the paddle steamer which carried him across the Pacific did not worry overmuch about the date, and although there was a uniform date in the United States, the variety of local times and his pressing problems of transport may well have bemused the redoubtable Mr. Fogg. Certainly he had the excuse that there was as yet no universally accepted standard of time based on Greenwich, much less any International Date Line.

The acceptance in 1884 of Greenwich as the prime meridian gave at least shadowy status to its anti-meridian, the 180th, in the Pacific as the logical date line. But as late as 1895 cartographers were still trying to discover which countries in the Pacific kept Asiatic and which American dates. In other words, no one knew how the date line worked in practice, however admirable the theory might be that it was superimposed on the 180th meridian.

The great increase in swift sea and air travel in the last fifty years has at last formalized the line by constant usage. Starting from the North Pole, it takes a twisting course through the Bering Strait, with Russia on the Asiatic date and Alaska on the American. Thence it runs southwest to the tip of the Aleutian Islands, so that they are on the American date and not the Asiatic, as they would be otherwise. The line then rejoins the 180th meridian but goes off again farther south, swinging eastward so that various Pacific islands, including Fiji and the Tongas, have Asiatic dating similar to that of New Zealand and Australia, with which they have close connections. Only after a diversion of some 3000 miles does the line rejoin the 180th meridian well south of New Zealand and continue regularly to the South Pole.

Thanks to my research, I now felt I was master of the subject of the International Date Line. I could cross it without a care on Friday the 13th or any other day. I was also ready to tackle problems concerning Pacific timetables and dates. For example, one airline schedules a jet flight that leaves San Francisco at 6:30 in the evening on Monday and arrives in Tokyo at 6:00 in the morning on Wednesday. What happened to Tuesday? What indeed; my foundation of historical research crumbled beneath me and I felt myself returning to zero. People in Chicago and Liverpool have a Tuesday; why doesn't the traveller who flies from San Francisco to Tokyo? I refused to accept the fact that he crossed the date line as an adequate answer.

I closeted myself with a globe and vowed not to stir until I had solved the mystery of the missing Tuesday. In order to make it clear to myself, I had to take a few liberties with the popular rules of the solar system. I thought of the earth as stationary; twelve midnight then becomes a line moving around the globe from east to west. Every twenty-four hours this line hits the International Date Line and changes from midnight of one day to midnight of the next. At the instant the midnight line is right on the date line, there exists in the world only one complete day. The instant the midnight line passes the date line, a new day is born, which is like a thin crescent. As the midnight line passes on around the globe it pulls the new day along behind it.

When you leave San Francisco at 6:30 P.M. Monday, the midnight line is five and a half hours east of you, somewhere off the Atlantic coast, dutifully pulling Tuesday along behind it. The trick lies in that, although you are moving rapidly westward, the midnight line is too, but much faster than you. If it passes you before you reach the International Date Line, you will be in Tuesday for a while. But as the midnight line, now ahead of you, crosses the International Date Line, it changes from midnight Monday to midnight Tuesday and begins pulling a crescent Wednesday. By the time you arrive in Tokyo the midnight line is well ahead of you – speeding over China – and the area between this point in China and the International Date Line is Wednesday. This includes Tokyo, of course, where you arrive at 6:00 A.M.

The crisis had now, like midnight, passed, and I was once again master of the subject. Fearlessly, I now viewed the Pacific as an area where man has drawn a logical line to avoid a future of endlessly repeating Mondays or for that matter, of Fridays the 13th.

ON OTHER MATTERS

THE ORGANISATION OF
A FOREIGN NEWS SERVICE

*An unpublished speech given December 16, 1948 at The Royal
Institute of International Affairs [RIIA]*

I am going to speak about the nuts and bolts of running a world-wide foreign service, and not about foreign news as such. I ask you to remember that the type of foreign service which I have to run for the group of Kemsley newspapers is very different from a foreign service run for one newspaper only. The group consists of a very different and variegated collection of publications, ranging from the *Sunday Times*, many solid provincial newspapers – from Aberdeen down to Cardiff – the *Daily Graphic*, the leading sports newspaper, the *Sporting Chronicle*, to a modest but sturdy and prosperous organ, the *Green 'Un*, of Sheffield, the foreign interests of which do not extend further than the activities of the Dynamo Football Team. Those names show what a very large group it is and how wide are its interests.

In some respects the needs of this group in the foreign news field are rather similar to those met by Reuter's for all English newspapers, and they differ in many respects from the needs of a single newspaper, such as the *Daily Mail*.

One of the main aspects of running a foreign news service is, of course, the economies of it. The average staff correspondent abroad costs approximately four thousand pounds a year; this includes his salary, his transport – which is a very important item – his living expenses, a certain amount of entertainment expenses, and his office space. The cables and telephone tolls and costs for a service such as we run amount to approximately five hundred pounds a week. String correspondents – i.e., correspondents who are paid on the space rates only, with possibly a small retainer, will probably cost about five hundred pounds a year on an average. Therefore, if one takes a foreign service consisting of only ten staff correspondents and twenty string correspondents, plus their communications, one finds that it is already a matter of costs amounting to about seventy-five thousand pounds a year. This gives you some indication of the basic costs of running even a reasonably modest foreign service such as the sample one I have described.

The next point that has to be decided is where to dispose the correspondents, and in that regard the particular interests of the newspaper or newspaper group have to be taken into account. Kemsley newspapers are particularly interested in the Empire, and therefore we are heavily represented in the main Dominions. This is a very expensive item in the foreign service. We have staff correspondents in South Africa, Canada and Australia, a very nice coverage of India and representation in many areas and territories of the African Continent, as well as Malta, Gibraltar, Colombo, and so on. Naturally, it is also necessary to cover the main centres of the world – Paris, New York and Washington, and at the present time Berlin. It is also necessary to have representation in as many of the Iron Curtain countries as will give visas. I will return to that point later on. On the large centres I have mentioned there are offices manned by several men: in Paris, for instance, there is a staff of four, in New York four, and in Washington two. It will be seen, therefore, that there is a pretty heavy backbone of staff representation before one comes to the other important points of the world.

The interests of our readers being very considerably in the provincial field, the Kemsley foreign service has to cope with the requirements of editors in, for instance, Manchester for textiles, Sheffield for steel, Cardiff and Glasgow for shipping and shipbuilding, and Aberdeen for the fishing industry. These may seem to be rather secondary interests, but they are certainly not so to the editors of those newspapers or to the public who read them.

Consequently, the next point to consider is where to have correspondents who will serve those particular industrial and economic interests of the provincial centres. It is important to have strong representatives in Tokyo, not only because of the importance of Japan itself, but because of the importance of the Japanese textile industry; in China, not necessarily because of the political situation there, but for the purpose of watching our trade interests; and in such secondary centres as Milan and Turin because of the Italian textile industry; Copenhagen because of the agricultural interests of many of our newspapers. It is essential for us to have capable correspondents in these secondary centres.

To revert to the Iron Curtain countries, it is naturally the ambition of every foreign service of any newspaper group to have a strong representation in these states.

To take Moscow first, I think I am right in saying that it is really quite impossible to have a correspondent in Moscow at the present time. For over two years we have been trying to get a visa for a correspondent. We have sent personal letters to the Ambassador in Moscow, to the Soviet Foreign Ministry, and have employed every kind of channel; but the result has not even been a negative reply – it has just been silence. I believe I am right in saying that *The Times* has been trying for over a year to get a visa for an excellent correspondent in Moscow, with the same results as we have had. Whether it is worth having a correspondent in Moscow is much debated, but personally I think it is. I think that if you have the right man in Moscow, he can continue to exist and not be turned out, by reporting what he can discover from the technical and provincial press of Russia and what he observes, with certain exceptions, around him in the streets of Moscow. I believe that if one had such a correspondent, he could give a very reasonable picture – slightly rosy but quite reasonable – of the atmosphere and interests of the capital. I do not pretend for a moment that this would represent complete coverage of Russia, but it would certainly be a start.

We have representatives in Prague and Warsaw who have survived reasonably happily. One of our Warsaw correspondents during the past three years fell by the wayside, but that was largely because he chose to report what were, I think, slightly unwise criticisms of local Polish politics, which might have been avoided.

In Prague, despite the departure of various other correspondents, we have managed to keep our man there, and he is doing very well.

We have tried to get a staff representative into Belgrade on various occasions, but only this last week I had to divert the man who was to go to Belgrade because, after two months, no reply has been received regarding his visa.

About the value of having correspondents in the Iron Curtain countries, I do not think there can be any question. They can be restricted in many respects in regard to their 'copy' and they may have many difficulties put in their way, but despite the restrictions and difficulties, the news which they can send out is better than nothing. I find that so far as Warsaw is concerned, there is practically no censorship and that correspondents are reasonably free to travel where they like in the country.

The situation in Prague is slightly different from that in Poland. There is in Prague no censorship as such, but there is considerable delay in messages, both in and out. Recently we endeavoured to send two of our editors to Czechoslovakia on a tour of ten days, as part of a scheme to send our editors to various centres in Europe, but we had no success; the unofficial reply from the Czech Foreign Minister was that one Kemsley correspondent was quite enough, and that they did not want to see any more representatives of Kemsley newspapers.

There is then the question of listening posts, which arises if there is a strong censorship in a particular area. Foreign editors are rather inclined to post correspondents in neighbouring centres in the hope that some diluted news can be extracted. In that respect, of course, Stockholm is the old favourite. Personally, I am not interested in the system. We have a correspondent in Stockholm, but we do not use Stockholm in any way as a source of Soviet news. Stockholm is full of individuals who are prepared to sell the secrets of the Kremlin at any time of the day or night, but my experience is that the secrets generally turn out to be pretty stale and dusty news by the time they arrive. The same thing applies to Helsinki, which is a far more valuable listening post than Stockholm; but it is very expensive to have a correspondent there, and if you have one he generally gets filled up with rumours and second-class information. As a result, the obtaining of Soviet news is an extremely difficult affair, and Kemsley newspapers regard it as practically a lost cause.

During the war in Lisbon was a listening post where all the countries were very heavily represented by Intelligence services, but I think that the net useful results to either the Allied cause or to the German cause were very small. It was, however, regarded as a most important centre by the Intelligence peoples.

There are one or two centres which appear on the surface to be important towns in which to have representatives and correspondents, but which on further examination turn out not to be so. Rome is a case in point. There are in Rome at the present time several staff correspondents of various newspapers whose excellent despatches constantly go on the spike, largely because at the moment Italian news, with the exception of one or two side issues, is not of very great interest to the British public. Therefore, we have no staff correspondent in Rome and concentrate more on the northern area of Milan and Turin.

The same applied to Istanbul, which one would think would be an excellent centre for news both from the Balkans and from the Black Sea area, as well as news about Turkey itself; but in fact I have had a good correspondent there for about eighteen months and the result has been extremely meagre – and the correspondent has just been moved.

Much the same applies to Tehran. Most of us would agree that it would be unwise not to be represented in Persia and that anything might happen in Persia in the near or distant future; we have a string correspondent in Tehran, but the net result is extremely meagre. The same holds good of the South American states, with the exception of Buenos Aires. The other centres in South America are very unrewarding, except very occasionally. It is a very expensive continent to cover in any reasonable way, and apart from representation through our New York office, we are represented only by one full-time correspondent in Buenos Aires.

Those points will explain in some way why most of our correspondents are where they are and why I have thought it necessary to have them there, and also why certain areas of the world are less well covered than they might be.

Of course, one has to take into account the fact that it is no good having correspondents if the newspapers cannot publish their despatches. The current shortage of newsprint makes that a grievous problem. There is much waste in cable tolls and much wasted enthusiasm and effort among the correspondents themselves.

At the present time – or rather before the Tribunal took up all the space in our newspapers – we were publishing throughout the Kemsley newspapers about sixty per cent of the total intake of cables, which is a fairly reasonable percentage. I think that the average for a single national newspaper is probably more in the nature of forty per cent. Owing to the wide diversity of our editor's interests, we can achieve a higher percentage than that.

I am not in favour of roaming correspondents – men who suddenly fly off from London and report on the situation in China, for instance, within about three or four days. I think that very often they are apt to be mistaken in their appreciation after such a short stay, and I also think it is rather bad luck on the local correspondent whose eye is wiped by some big bug from London, who is given a great deal of space in the paper and very large headlines, whereas the hardworking local correspondent has probably slogged away for months and had no results. There is, however, something to be said for having a man who can travel at a moment's notice to any trouble spot. The fresh eye and fresh perspective of the well-equipped correspondent arriving at the present moment, in Pekin, would be of inestimable value. I dare say many of you read the excellent despatch from Patrick Donovan in the *Observer* on Sunday last – a rival newspaper, I may say! He had moved up from Singapore and was able to communicate to the ordinary reader a very vivid and excellent picture of the China war, due to his fresh eye and to his not being too close to the subject. But it is an expensive business flying people around the world, and for the various reasons which I have mentioned we have no roaming correspondent.

The perfect type of correspondent, I should imagine, is clear enough. He has to be well educated and to have a good historical grounding in the country to which he is accredited. He has to like being abroad. He has to be a good journalist and to report what he sees and hears in an attractive way. He has to be pretty resourceful. For instance, the man in Prague has to cover a large area, he has to have contacts with the police, with the British Embassy and with as many Ministers as he can arrange; and he has to be prepared to cover an air crash, or any item of spot news of that sort. He has to be a good representative of his country and has to accept the position accorded to British foreign correspondents in foreign capitals of being something slightly lower than the Embassy concierge!

There is no denying that the English foreign correspondent does not enjoy the same prestige abroad as his American colleague. The American foreign correspondent is the hero in his own country and in a foreign capital he is regarded as being almost as important as the Ambassador. Whether that should be so or not depends very largely on the correspondent and on the Ambassador! There is no denying that it is a great start for a correspondent to be able to have some prestige in the capital to which he is accredited and to have that prestige supported by the Ambassador or the diplomatic representative.

The correspondent who is, broadly speaking, useless is the man who has probably served throughout the last war, possibly having been a prisoner of war in Italy or Germany, who likes being abroad, and has a smattering of one or two languages – and thinks that this is enough to qualify him to be a good foreign correspondent. I get an average of probably two letters a week from such individuals wishing to go abroad. On one or two occasions I have been beguiled into appointing individuals with those sort of qualifications to string correspondent appointments somewhere or other.

They are excellent men but unfortunately they invariably write their despatches for an imaginary newspaper which is somewhere between the Royal Geographical Society's Journal and the *New York Times*. Each story generally runs to several thousand words – not typed, because the correspondent is learning to type – and these vast documents report the entire situation in, say, Leopoldville, and contain a great deal of semi-humorous descriptive material which these correspondents seem to think is popular in journalism. That is merely an example of the sort of person who is really no good as a correspondent, however keen he may be.

I have mentioned that communications are a very heavy item in running a foreign service. On the whole, you can take it that the further a cable comes, the more expensive it is – which is reasonable enough – but an exception is the Empire rate, which is 1d. a word all round the world and which is a most valuable invention from the point of view of communications between the Commonwealth countries. You will see that the cost of reporting the China war is a very considerable item. For instance, today we received something over 2,000 words, which works out at 7d. a word to something like sixty pounds.

It is extremely difficult to report a war in an area as vast as China. Our Pekin representative is now somewhere between Tientsin and Shanghai. We have a representative in Shanghai, and we have a representative in Hong Kong. We have a man somewhere between Shanghai and Pekin going back in the opposite direction to the staff correspondent who is coming down to Shanghai. Those four people are all trying hard – and duplicating each other – to describe what they think the British public wish to know about what is going on in China. The result is very confused, because the local rumours and counter-rumours are very thick at the moment. Either Pekin is being shelled or it is not – I really do not know which. At the present moment I think the noise of gun-fire can be heard, but yesterday there was definitely shelling in Pekin. One has to try to keep up with an extremely fluctuating situation which does not follow any definite front line, and most newspapers are endeavouring to cover the China war from Washington. I do not think our readers will be any wiser than theirs.

To describe briefly the sort of day-to-day activities of the foreign department, I will read one or two cables which have gone off during the last two or three days in an endeavour to get a good report on what the China war means, and which show what is in fact happening, for the *Sunday Times* in preparation for next Sunday's edition.

[*The lecturer then read a cablegram sent to Mr. Leslie Smith in Pekin asking for one thousand words by noon of 16 December*]

That cable was sent to Mr. Smith on 14 December, and this morning a cable was sent to our correspondent in Tokyo asking for the reaction of the Japanese man-in-the-street to the war; and another cable was sent to our staff correspondent in Australia asking for the reaction of Australia to this new threat to her safety. The idea was thus to produce on Sunday for the readers of the *Sunday Times* a pretty representative picture not only of what is going on in China, but what the consequences may possibly be.

Unfortunately, it was discovered this morning that the Pekin representative, Mr. Smith, had left for Tientsin and therefore was unlikely to have received the cable; so a further cable was hastily sent to Tientsin. That cable was sent at almost the same moment as we received a cable from Mr. Smith saying that he had left Tientsin and gone to Shanghai. We therefore assumed that he had not received the cable to Pekin and the cable to Tientsin, so that the whole of the original cable had to be repeated to him care of the Foreign Correspondent's Club in Shanghai.

It will be interesting to see on Sunday whether this complicated piece of machinery has worked. All this may sound rather light-hearted, but it is the ordinary day-to-day business of trying to get out of correspondents many thousands of miles away what the editor thinks that he wants.

That is an effort to meet a straight news requirement. A more light-hearted effort was made for the *Sunday Empire News*, which is a large and important member of the Kemsley group; a cable was sent to a string correspondent in Rome saying that the Florence correspondent reported that dress designer Christian Dior was rumoured to be in Rome and instructing the Rome correspondent to find out what modifications Dior contemplated in spring styles. The result of that will appear in the *Sunday Empire News* next Sunday. This cable shows that in a group the size of the Kemsley group the requirements for so-called foreign news are extremely varied.

The difficulty of keeping in touch with correspondents and preventing them from becoming de-nationalised cannot be too much emphasised. After these men have been away from home perhaps for a matter of years, they forget what English newspapers look like and what English writers want to read. We write to all our staff correspondents once a month, and of course we send them all the cuttings of their despatches that have appeared in the newspapers, and any news from home that appears to be relevant to them. They also receive every week a record sheet showing how the news is running in the newspapers, how much foreign news is published, and how their particular stories have fared.

Finally, I should like to mention syndication. We syndicate throughout the world the results of our foreign services, both features and news, and that syndication is a very great success. Our despatches are being reprinted in a very large number of foreign and Commonwealth newspapers. Having given this rather light-hearted account of how a foreign service is organised and run, I should now be pleased to try to answer any questions that may be asked.

PARTNER! YOU HAVE TRIUMPHED MY ACE

A review of The Complete Card Player *by Albert Ostrow for the* Daily Graphic, *September 1949. Ian Fleming was a keen bridge player.*

Did you know that 'trump' was originally 'triumph'? Did you know that spades, hearts, diamonds, clubs were originally swords, cups, coins and staves, representing the nobility, the clergy, tradesmen and peasants – the main social classes in the Middle Ages?

Had you reflected that not even the French Revolution or the Communists succeeded in replacing the kings and queens in the pack with other symbols, and were you aware that Wild Bill Hickock shot all the pips out of a ten of spades at twelve paces?

Nor me, and I still don't know the rules of 'Canasta', the new card game which is sweeping America on the heels of gin rummy, after reading *The Complete Card Player*. Nor do I know the latest contract bridge rules and I don't know the odds for drawing a card at 'chemin de fer'. These are serious lapses in an American card encyclopaedia 'which should challenge Hoyle as the general reference book'.

But if you want to play Bimbo high-low at poker, Blind Hookey, Cedarhurst, Gin, Clobberyash, Double-dummy with a widow, Idiot's delight, Oh Pshaw, Seven-toed Pete or Stealing the Old Man's Bundle – this is the book for you.

DANGEROUS KNOW-HOW

A *review of* Scarne on Cards *by*
John Scarne for the Sunday Times, *April 1956.*

Although cheating at cards is not numbered among the cardinal sins, I suppose it is the only anti-social act that remains as heinous and as severely punished today as it was during the last century. Card cheats still have to resign from their clubs and suffer social ostracism, and there is not a woman who reads this who would not tremble at the idea of a husband or brother being caught in the act.

Yet the polite card cheat sits at every humdrum bridge or whist table, peering slant-eyed into his neighbours' hands, signalling to his partner with voice or expression or gesture, and, in games where this is possible, fudging the score.

It is not with these humble practitioners that John Scarne deals in his cheats' encyclopedia, but with the card hustler who knows just that bit more about the game than you and I, the professional gambler who makes his living by operating games of chance, and the straight card sharp, known in the profession as a 'mechanic'.

Scarne can do anything with cards and Nate Leipzig and Harry Houdini, now both in the Valhalla of magicians once put their signature to the statement: 'John Scarne is the most expert exponent of wonderful card effects and table work that I have ever seen in my life', and yet Scarne uses no apparatus except ten steel spring fingers and fifty-two playing cards. He moves up close to you. You tear the wrapper off a new pack of cards and shuffle it as much as you like. You give it to Scarne and he cuts it four times at the aces. He counts that his greatest trick. Trick? It is a work of art on which he practised six hours a day for several years before the war.

During the war Scarne worked for the American War Department, writing a weekly article for *Yank* to educate the G.I. into not losing his pay to card sharps, and this book is a distillation of his knowledge not only of cheating but of strategy and other aspects of popular American card games except alas bridge.

This is not perhaps a book for the general public. It is expensive and, although pleasantly written, highly professional. Moreover it concentrates largely on American games such as the poker and rummy families, and – a grave fault – bridge is not mentioned; but every club and library should have a copy to be issued to the accredited card lover with the proviso 'for your eyes only'.

Why? Because this is a dangerous book to leave lying about.

PREFACE TO *THE EDUCATION OF A POKER PLAYER*

The Education of a Poker Player by Herbert Yardley was first published by Simon and Schuster in the USA in 1957. Ian Fleming was responsible for it being published in the UK by Jonathan Cape (1959) and wrote the preface.

If it were possible to have worse laws than our sex laws they would be the laws that regulate our gambling. Prostitution is illegal in this country yet our streets are congested with the rejects from Continental bagnios who are fit only for the knackers yard. In exchange for what amounts to a weekly rental of £2 to the courts, these rump-sprung beldames give sexual short-weight to bug-eyed provincial business men after brief trading in a square mile of open air market place. Every whore has her pitch in this market place and the police look the other way if there is a fight to protect it. Similar and even more blatant hypocrisy operates in our gambling laws. To deal only with what is relevant to this brief note, while twenty million adults gamble on the football pools each week, ten million on horse-racing and five million on premium bonds, playing poker for money, a legal game over half the world including most of the British Commonwealth, is illegal. And really illegal. The Hamilton, a respectable and leading private London card club, found this out in a police action which effectively warned the whole of England off the game. In 1945, at Bow Street, it cost them £500. The grounds for this action? That poker is not a game of skill! Of course an old woman who marks her football pool and wins £70,000 for her shilling bet has done nothing but study football form for 50 years. No luck in that little gamble! Moreover she and the other 20 million experts bring in £22 million a year to the Exchequer while the poker player brings in nothing. So the pools are legal and poker isn't. Balderdash and lying, hypocritical balderdash at that, to the power of n.

Which brings me, after the smoke has cleared, to this book. It is a book whose publication in London I am proud to have fathered. The circumstances were these. Knowing that I love cards, a friend sent me a cutting from an American magazine that handsomely 'trailed' *The Education of a Poker Player* with some of Mr. Yardley's most intriguing hands. I at once sent to America for the book, was delighted with it and gave some copies away for Christmas. The next time I talked with my publishers, Messrs. Jonathan Cape, I urged them to publish the book here. They demurred. No one in the British Isles played poker. It would not do well. I said that the book contained only a dozen pages of instruction – brilliant instruction – and that the rest was a hatful of some of the finest gambling stories I had ever read. It didn't matter that the game was poker. These were wonderful, thrilling stories about cards. The book would certainly become a gambling classic. English card players would read it and love it. The book had zest, blood, sex, and a tough, wry humour reminiscent of Raymond Chandler. It was sharply, tautly written. It would be a best seller – well, anyway, it would look very well on the back-list. The mention of this holy word in publishing was, I think, the clincher. Cape's readers, that sapient, humorous, receptive duet, read the book. Yes, it was certainly all that I had said. Perhaps, if I would write a preface . . . I said I would and here it is and here is the book that Mr. Yardley wrote.

Myself, as fine writers phrase it, I am not a good poker player. I drink and smoke and enjoy the game too much. You shouldn't do any of these things if you want to win at poker. Poker is a cold-hearted, deadly game that breaks and bankrupts men today just as, in the seventeenth and eighteenth centuries, écarté, backgammon, ombre and faro bankrupted our rakehelly ancestors. The last time I played poker I lost more than I could afford in rich brassy company in a house at Sunningdale, in what is now known as 'The Canasta Belt'. These people *would* introduce variations which I was mocked for not understanding. In the end, numb with martinis and false bonhomie, I pretended I understood the intricacies of 'Minnie Everley'. I remember the name but not the variation. It was named in memory of one of the Everley sisters who, in Chicago at the turn of the century, kept the finest brothel America has ever known. The chamber pots were of solid gold and the sisters paraded their girls through the town, be-feathered and be-flounced, in open landaus, every Sunday morning when the bells were ringing and the quality of Chicago were on the streets and making for the churches. I learned all this afterwards. At the time, and in the name of Minnie, I played a ragged, brash game that cost me dear. I was fleeced and deserved to be. I would not have been fleeced if I had read Mr. Yardley's book and if I had, above all, digested the card-playing philosophy which lies behind his stories and his instruction. Every fine card player I have ever known has this philosophy, but I will caution you that very few fine card players are the sort of people you and I would like to play with. It's not fun playing against cold hearted butchers, however soft their words, and as you read about them in these gay, smoke-filled pages I think you will often feel a chill of apprehension. But it will be an authentic chill. That is why, not as a poker player but as a writer of thrillers, I can recommend this book to every adult consenting card-player in Great Britain.

NIGHTMARE AMONG THE MIGHTY

An account by Ian Fleming for the Sunday Times *of his
participation in a pro-am golf tournament. June 1957.*

Every sport has its own nightmare – the dropped baton, the goal scored against your own side, running out your captain when he has scored ninety-nine; and, in your dreams, they all have the same ghastly background – the packed stands, the serried ranks of spectators, the incredulous hush and then the deep condemnatory groan.

In golf the two-foot putt missed on the eighteenth green is quickly over, and you are at once awake, sweating and whimpering. This terror must be common to even the greatest in the game, but for the week-end golfer, there is a far longer, more horrible nightmare – partnership with a world champion over a course black with crowds.

Last week-end I endured this nightmare, thirty-six holes of it, and I live, but only just, to tell the tale.

It came about like this. Three weeks ago a friend said he wanted me to play in the Bowmaker Amateur/Professional Tournament at the Berkshire. 'It's great fun,' he said. 'All the best professionals take two amateurs each, and you play a threesome against bogey. Each team puts in three cards – the professional's for the best scratch score and the professional plus each amateur for the lowest better ball score. The amateur plays off full handicap, and if he makes good use of his strokes he and his pro can get a better ball score around 60. You can pick up when you've played too many. They have film stars and such like to amuse the crowds. Come on.'

It sounded fun. I said, 'Yes', and forgot about it.

I forgot about it until I got the draw. I was to play with Peter Thomson, three times Open champion, and Alec Shepperson, handicap plus 1, a Walker Cup probable. I was to be on the first tee of the Red Course at 2.15 last Sunday.

That was Tuesday the eighteenth. On the Wednesday, Peter Thomson, fresh from a fine performance in the American Open, equalled the course record of Sand Moor with a 65 in the Yorkshire Evening News tournament. He followed this with a 67, 64 and 68. He won the tournament by fifteen strokes and broke a handful of records. The golfing world gasped.

Apart from praying that the biggest thunderstorm in living memory would deluge the home counties on the following Sunday and Monday (it was a two-day contest), there was really nothing I could do about it. I am a nine handicap week-end golfer with a short, flat swing that has been likened to a housemaid sweeping under a bed. It's a fast swing with reserves of fantastic acceleration in moments of stress.

The only reason I am a nine is that I absolutely try to play down to it rather than take life more easily off twelve, which I should be.

I have never had a golf lesson, except from my grandmother at the age of about fifteen, and my only equipment for the game is a natural 'eye' and strong forearms. Against these virtues it should be said that I remember to keep my head down only on one shot in three and that, on occasional shots, 'everything moves except the ball'.

The greatest weakness of my essentially immaculate game is that I am unable to 'repeat' my swing. Even on the putting green, my stance and stroke are at the mercy of the moment's whim. The fact that I have played golf for some thirty years with occasional success and great pleasure is due to enjoying the company, the exercise and the zest of competition. In short I am the quintessential amateur.

The virtues of amateurishness are all right in a friendly game, perhaps sharpened by a gamble, in the privacy of one's home course. There the quick, sharp dunch into a bunker is a matter for hilarity only mildly tinged with bitterness. But how, I wondered feverishly as the dreadful day approached, would my insouciance stand up to playing before vast crowds with the greatest, or at any rate the second greatest, golfer in the world?

But why worry? It's only a game. The ball won't move. Just walk up and hit it. These and other specious exhortations were mouthed at me through wolfish grins by my friends. The worst you can do is maim a few spectators, perhaps even kill one. But the club will be insured. Have a double kummel before you start. Take an Oblivion.

Steeled by the relish of my friends, I assumed a nonchalant mask. I looked to my equipment. The head of my driver (*circa* 1930, one of the earliest, surely, of the steel shafts and known around Sandwich as 'Excalibur') was loose. I had it fixed. My double-faced chipper (Tom Morris, 1935), a beloved but temperamental club, was rebound. I bought two pairs of expensive socks in pale blue. I re-read the red ink passages in Armour's *How To Play Your Best Golf All The Time,* watched Peter Thomson's unearthly progress through the Yorkshire Evening News Tournament and waited queasily for H- (for Horror) Day.

H-Day dawned bright and clear. No earthquakes. No tornadoes. No thunderstorms. I drove at an even pace to the Berkshire, parked my car among the hundreds, proceeded to the seventh fairway of the Blue Course, which a number of young gods were bisecting with arrow-straight drives and iron shots using mounds of practice balls.

I retired to an inconspicuous corner with my caddie, six balls and a No.3 iron. It took me about twenty minutes, in my usual ratio of one good shot in three, to lose four of the balls in the woods.

Then came lunch and the unwelcome news that the matches were running over an hour late. I wandered out among the dreadful trappings of my nightmare – the marquees, the huge scoreboard ablaze with the most famous names in professional and amateur golf, and already showing the results of the early starters and in the background the loudspeaker giving the position on the nearby 17th tee.

Henry Cotton passed me, his face a mask of concentration, and Locke, majestic, indomitable. Henry Longhurst tossed me a few phrases of gleeful commiseration. And then there were Peter Thomson and Alec Shepperson, and I was explaining who I was and apologising in advance for the dreadful things that they would shortly be witnessing.

For the first time I felt a ray of comfort. All golfers have their problems. Shepperson was a candidate for the Walker Cup team and he knew the names would be announced the next day and that the selectors were on the course. Thomson knew that every spectator would expect him to go round in level threes. We commiserated with one another over the swelling crowds and in due course there we were standing on the first tee.

The starter's voice rang out – unnecessarily loudly. Thomson drove 250 yards down the centre of the fairway.

'Mr. Iarn Fleming.'

I wiped my hand on the seat of my trousers and stepped forward. Half-conscious, I teed up and gave a practice swing, listening with half my mind for the hiss of astonishment. The crowd was too well bred. I addressed the ball and promptly knocked it off its peg. I put it on again.

Then there was a moment when the world stood still, a brief glimpse of the ball through a mist of tears, a more or less articulated swirl of motion and the blessed ball was well airborne and on its way with a slight draw to come to rest in the rough fifty yards behind Thomson's.

Shepperson hit a beauty and we were off and away, with the crowd streaming after us. One of my chief tortures, easily foreseen, was that I should always be playing first of the trio. I hacked the ball out of the shallow heather and got it 100 yards on its way down the fairway. Thomson pushed his to the right of the green. Shepperson fluffed with a 4 wood, and there I was having to hit mine again.

I had a stroke at all the odd holes. Now it was vital that I should hit the simplest of simple shots 150 yards on to the green. I took out my blaster, with which I thought I would be safest. There was a respectful hush. Head down, you fool! Slow back! BOING!!! The ball, hit off the sole, whizzed along the ground, bumbled up the green, and stopped within three yards of the pin.

Muttering something about 'Dundee run-up' I strode after it, and to cut a long story short, both Thomson and Shepperson got fives and all I had to do was to get down in two putts to win a net 4 for Thomson and our better ball. I putted, or rather twitched, the ball a yard past, missing the hole by three inches. Then, with a thumping heart, stroked, or more accurately topped, the ball into the hole amid heartfelt applause from the agonised crowd.

I will pass over the second hole where I hit a No.7 over the green and picked up and where Thomson got an immaculate 3.

Another stroke at the 3rd. An adequate drive. A fluffed spoon and a smothered 4 iron which again rattled up on the green. Again, I somehow got my net 4 to Thomson's 5. I had 'improved' twice for Thomson, but by the foulest means, and there was no question of my golf having settled down.

I forget what happened at the 4th, but at the par three 5th, having been advised by Thomson to take a 7 instead of an 8, I at last hit the ball in the middle of the bat and got a net two, which I followed up with another net two, also well played, at the 7th. Again at the 9th, but this time again by foul means, I scrambled a net four. I had helped Peter Thomson five times in nine holes!

Those treacherous crocodiles, my friends, who had come to gloat at my discomfiture, changed their tune. Now they edged up and whispered that my handicap would have to be reduced at Sandwich. I brushed them aside. The sun was shining, the course was beautiful. What fun it was playing with the Open Champion!

Alas, while by dunch, scuffle and fluff I somehow played the next nine holes I was no further help to Peter Thomson and all I can remember of the inward half is the most glorious three I have ever seen, by Shepperson, at the bogey five 15th, and an appalling shank by myself at the 17th. It was with a No.8, off a downhill under a lie and the air positively quivered with the horrible clang as the ball sped at right angles through the spectators' legs into the deep rough.

And then the round was over, with a 72 for Peter Thomson and net 66s for Alec Shepperson and myself. No earthly good, but at least I hadn't played Thomson's ball by mistake, or done an air shot or killed a spectator. It was in a mood of euphoria that I returned to London.

Monday was not so good, and I did many terrible things that even now make me shudder, but it had rained very heavily and there were fewer witnesses. Thomson did a 69 and Shepperson, who by this time had been nominated for the Walker Cup, and I repeated our 66s, which meant that at least I had been able to help Thomson on three holes.

And now the dreadful glory of the occasion is fading and this weekend I shall be playing either a new kind of golf, tempered to the finest steel by its visit to the blast furnace or, more probably, wilted by the fierce flame.

Alas, when my friends or my grandchildren ask me how Peter Thomson played this shot or Alec Shepperson that, I shall be unable to tell them. I shall have many memories of the two men – of Peter Thomson, justly renowned for a bearing as fine as his golf, and of the modest, charming Shepperson – but of the champion's golf I shall recall nothing but the immortal words of Leonard Crawley in last Monday's *Daily Telegraph*.

'Though Peter Thomson was assisted five times by Ian Fleming, the champion had evidently spent much of his force at Leeds last week.'

WHEN DID YOU STOP EATING YOUR WIFE?

'London's Best Dining' was published in Holiday *in America in April 1956.*
This is taken from the original typescript of which the title used here was
the working title. The manuscript resides in the Michael L. VanBlaricum
Collection of Ian Fleming and Bondiana in The Rare Book and
Manuscript Library at the University of Illinois Urbana-Champaign.

My friends may raise their eyebrows at finding me masquerading as an authority on what are coyly known as the 'pleasures of the table', but in fact my credentials are exceptional.

To begin with, I am not a card-carrying gourmet. The words Chevalier du Tastevin have never passed my lips and although I own a first edition of Brillat-Savarin's 'Physiologie du Gout', I opened it only once to read the curious passage relating to aphrodisiacs.

Secondly, I have no allergies and I will eat or drink almost anything so long as it tastes good.

Finally, and most important of all, I have never received a free mouthful of food or drink from any restaurant in the world and I therefore don't care what I say, short of libel, of any place where you consume food and drink. I don't even know the name of any restaurateur or head waiter in London, and I regard name-dropping in restaurants as a vulgar affectation.

To be absolutely accurate, I do know the name of the head waiter on the first floor at Scott's. It is Baker, and I know it because he did his best to have me arrested as a German spy at the beginning of the war. I was in Naval Intelligence, and a fellow officer from the Submarine Service and I were trying to get the first Captain and Navigator we had captured from a U-boat drunk at Scott's so as to worm out of them how they avoided our mine fields in the Skagerrak. They had been 'allowed out' of their prison camp for a day's 'sightseeing' in London, and we were playing the rather clumsy role of brother officers talking chummily about the sea with other brother officers whom we were only fighting because of the politicians.

Baker, then a waiter in the downstairs Grill Room, became suspicious of our extraordinary conduct and extremely loose talk and by about half past three we were encircled by harmless looking couples picking at bits of fish.

It was only when we got back to the Admiralty, befuddled and no wiser about the Skagerrak, that a furious Director of Naval Intelligence told us that the only result of our secret mission had been to mobilise half the narks of the Special Branch of Scotland Yard.

But that is the only reason I happen to know Baker's name.

I think good English food is the best in the world. French food gives me a permanent headache and spots before the eyes. My quarrel with American food is that there is always too much of it and that it is insipid; and anyway, I don't like food that has lain so long in the morgue. I don't care what the experts say, but I am convinced that frozen food neither tastes so good nor is so nourishing as fresh food.

The food I like eating in London and which I regard as unsurpassed is: Colchester and Whitstable oysters, all English fish, particularly Dover sole; Scottish smoked salmon, potted shrimps, lamb cutlets, roast beef, York ham, nearly all the English vegetables, particularly asparagus and peas, English savouries and most English fruits. I don't think much of the famous English cheeses and, just to show how much of a gourmet I am, my favourite cheese in the world is American domestic Camembert.

The problem in England is how to eat good English food without bad English cooking. Just as in America I think the only things Americans cook well are fried eggs and bacon, so in England I think the best lowest common denominator dish is fish and chips, and I strongly recommend the adventurous-minded American tourist travelling round Britain to eat his lunch in a fish and chip shop rather than in a hotel or a restaurant. If he is dismayed by the slatternly interiors of these places, he can always take his meal out in a paper bag and eat it in the woods or the fields. (I'm afraid that will finish me with 'The Wine and Food Society'.)

One other practical hint for the tourist: it is extremely difficult to get a good Martini anywhere in England. In London restaurants and hotels the way to get one is to ask for a double dry Martini made with Vodka. The way to get one in any pub is to walk calmly and confidently up to the counter and, speaking very distinctly, ask the man or girl behind it to put plenty of ice in the shaker (they nearly all have a shaker), pour in six gins and one dry vermouth (enunciate 'dry' carefully) and shake until I tell them to stop.

You then point to a suitably large glass and ask them to pour the mixture in. Your behaviour will create a certain amount of astonishment, not unmixed with fear, but you will have achieved a very large and fairly good Martini, equal in size to about three New York Martinis, and it will cost you about $1.25.

To return to food. I see that Congressman James Tumulty, of New Jersey, on his return home this week described England as 'the only country where it takes ten men in formal clothes to serve you melted mud'.

To this I will only quote that even more famous American citizen, Miss Gypsy Rose Lee: 'In Europe you have a different taste sensation every ten miles. In America you can travel six thousand miles and you get the same taste every mile. If it isn't the same, it's ketchup. Eat in those roadside joints and die on the highway.'

But I know what Mr. Tumulty means. He probably tried having luncheon in railway hotels at 12:30. I cannot identify the melted mud. It may have been chocolate mousse or cottage pie. I would have substituted boiled boots.

In fact, I repeat that English food is the best in the world and that you can eat a good meal of it, including a glass of lager or wine, coffee and tip (10 to 15 per cent, according to your mood), for something under $3.00.

But it does mean departing from the 'Admass' meal of shrimp or grapefruit cocktail, steak with french fries, and ice cream. In London, you should start with smoked salmon, potted shrimps, or *pâté maison*, and then have English sole, turbot, plaice, lobster or crab, with fresh vegetables, followed by cheese or a savoury. (Savouries seem to be unknown in America. You should try 'Angels on Horseback' which are oysters wrapped in bacon on toast; soft herring roes on toast; or a 'Scotch Woodcock' which is a small amount of scrambled eggs crisscrossed with anchovies.) Instead of the fish, double lamb cutlets, roast beef or saddle of lamb are nearly always on the menu, and, except in the case of lamb, are rarely frozen in the best restaurants.

Steaks can be had, of course, but in England they are not a usual cut of meat and seldom come up to American expectations. As for ice cream, I personally wouldn't think of eating it, and anyway I rarely eat sweets, but you can get it in various forms if you want it.

Drinking coffee or tea *with* your meal is unheard of in English restaurants, and anyway the coffee is disgusting except in the espresso bars. You probably won't very much care for the beer either, but the lagers (English, German and Dutch) are quite like American beer and are frequently served iced (!). Most restaurants have good wines *en carafe*. Wines in bottles and champagnes are first class but often farcically expensive. If restaurateurs would reduce their profit margins from 150% to 50% they would sell so much more that it would make the reduction worthwhile. Stout, notably Guinness, is an excellent drink with oysters and fish. Even better is Black Velvet, which is half-and-half stout and champagne in a tankard.

Prices are lower than in most of the world's capitals and considerably lower than in New York where charges in the best restaurants have been murderously inflated by expense account aristocracy. (I have it on good authority that over 80 per cent of M. Soulié's customers at the Pavilion belong to this category.)

If you hope to see 'interesting people' during mealtime, you may not be in luck. There are no 'cotèrie' restaurants in London any more, in the sense that the old Café Royal in Regent Street used to be the haunt of artists and writers; after-the-theatre supper at the Savoy Grill is probably your best bet.

Here are my favourite London restaurants – those where I go to eat the meals I have talked about, well served and in pleasant surroundings – in alphabetical order:

> L'Etoile
> The Ivy
> Overton's (opposite Victoria Station)
> Overton's (St. James's Street)
> Pimm's (several of them in the City)
> Quo Vadis
> Ritz Grill
> Savoy Grill
> Scott's
> Wheeler's (Old Compton Street)

Wheeler's (Duke of York Street)
Wilton's

Addresses are in the telephone book. Better book a table.

There are countless other restaurants and hotels where you can eat first class English, French, Italian or Hungarian cooking. A reliable selection is in *The Good Food Guide* by Raymond Postgate, which you can buy at any London bookstore. Though the book is heavily becluttered with gourmetship, his choices are sound. He even knows places hidden away in the English countryside where *l'homme moyen sensuel* in a motorcar can eat superbly. I have not tried any of them, but I have sufficient confidence in Mr. Postgate to pass on his nominations for best British inns:

> Aston Clinton (Bucks): The Bell,
> Eastbourne: Chez Maurice,
> Colerne (Wilts): The Vineyard,
> Bath (Somerset): The Hole in the Wall,
> Exmouth (Devon): Seagull Hotel,
> Nottingham (Notts): L'Aperitif,
> Newbridge-on-Wye (Radnor): New Inn,
> Llanarmon Dyffryn Ceiriog (Denbigh): West Arms,
> Foel Ferry (Anglesey): The Mermaid,
> Scarborough (Yorks): Pavilion Hotel,
> Eskdale (Cumberland): Bower House Inn,
> Fortingall, by Aberfeldy (Perth): Fortingall Hotel.

That is about all I have to say about English food. If one eats badly in England – or in any other country, for the matter of that – it is generally one's own fault. But I am glad Congressman Tumulty didn't see a misprint in one of our papers the other day. It was a court case and the magistrate was reported as saying to the accused: 'A term of imprisonment may encourage you to stop eating your wife.'

English cooking hasn't driven us quite that far.

DEATH IS SO PERMANENT

An open letter on road safety published in
the Daily Graphic, *September 1952.*

An open letter to the Transport Minister
Copy to the Royal Society for the Prevention of Accidents and all borough and
county councils

Dear Mr. Lennox Boyd,

With road casualties mounting towards the quarter of a million a year mark, there is genteel heart-searching in the public prints and a new coat of paint for the Zebras. The cosy fiction that 'SLOUGH WELCOMES CAREFUL DRIVERS' no more stems the tide of death and shattered limbs and lives than do the other polite admonitions and mild scolds which greet the hasting family saloon on its merry way to that last rendezvous.

It seems that so long as 'MAJOR ROAD AHEAD' remains our most strident warning alike of a dangerous crossroad with a notorious death-roll and of a fairly innocent intersection, the price of myosis and well-bred understatement will continue to be about 4000 casualties every week. (500 casualties a day on our railways or air services would cause a bit of a stir!) Even the compelling Black Widow poster, a most notable attempt by the authorities to make us think about keeping death off the roads, was the subject of so much squeamish clamour from our sensitive citizens that it was replaced by those folksy exhortations, seen but not perceived, to do something about sudden death, civil defence, the Lord Mayor's fund, or making fish-cakes out of barracuda – one never reads far enough to find out which.

Are good manners more valuable than all these lives and all this misery? Is it not time to borrow a little emphasis from abroad and let our road safety signs raise their voices a trifle? In America, at black spots which have caused many deaths, there are skull and crossbones signs with the previous year's casualty total inscribed below. Different towns and districts and even private concerns have their own campaigns and slogans, the latter often on two or three hoardings some twenty yards apart, building up to a punch-line. Here are some of them: 'DON'T LEARN SAFETY … BY ACCIDENT', 'WANT TO DIE? … DRIVE CAREFULLY', 'LOSE A MINUTE … SAVE A LIFE', 'DRIVE CAREFULLY … THE LIFE YOU SAVE … MAY BE YOUR OWN', and the poignant 'DEATH IS SO PERMANENT'.

Wrecks of cars are left at dangerous corners with 'HE DIDN'T MEAN TO' inscribed above them, and garages put out signs like this: 'DANGEROUS CORNER … SLOW DOWN … WE'LL FIX YOUR WRECK … IF YOU DON'T'. An undertaker had this: 'STEEP HILL … BAD CURVE HALFWAY DOWN … WANT AN APPOINTMENT? … ZOKOWSKIS' FUNERALS … WE'RE WATCHING YOU'.

At holiday times you will see the following: 'DON'T LET DEATH TAKE YOUR HOLIDAY', 'DON'T GIVE YOUR LIFE FOR CHRISTMAS', 'DON'T GO OUT WITH THE OLD YEAR'. At pedestrian crossings: 'DON'T KILL A PEDESTRIAN … BECAUSE HE IS WRONG', and 'LOOK FIRST … LIVE LONGER', 'DON'T TAKE A SHORT CUT … TO DEATH', 'THE SMALLER THE CHILD … THE BIGGER THE ACCIDENT', 'KIDS DON'T KNOW … HELP THEM … DRIVE CAREFULLY', and so forth.

I admit these signs are strident, vulgar and ugly. But I really believe they'll make the road-hog in his Juggernaut and the motor-cyclist trying to break through the sound barrier remember that he is aiming a loaded gun from the moment he leaves the garage – and that goes for the havering, crown-of-the-road, pride-of-the-family saloon too.

Incidentally, 'SLOUGH WELCOMES CAREFUL DRIVERS' was the fragrant thought (and the waste of paint) of another government.

I hope you'll agree, Mr Lennox-Boyd, that something more Winstonian should now be tried.

P.S. An afterthought – please declare illegal all stickers, celluloid canaries, pendant dollies and notices saying 'KEEP OFF MY TAIL' on the windows of motor-cars. They obscure the vision. They are cheaply ostentatious and they diminish one's love of one's neighbour.

AUTOMOBILIA

Ian Fleming wrote about his love for his cars in The Spectator, *April 1958.*

'Dig that T-bird!' I had cut it a bit fine round Queen Victoria's skirts and my wing mirror had almost dashed the Leica from the G.I.'s hand. If the tourists don't snap the Queen, at about 10 a.m. on most mornings they can at least get a picture of me and my Ford Thunderbird with Buckingham Palace in the background.

I suspect that all motorists are vain about their cars. I certainly am, and have been ever since the khaki Standard with the enamelled Union Jack on its nose which founded my écurie in the '20s. Today the chorus of 'Smashing!', 'Cor!' and 'Rraauu!' which greets my passage is the perfume of Araby.

One man who is even more childishly vain than myself is Noël Coward. Last year, in Jamaica, he took delivery of a sky-blue Chevrolet Belair Convertible which he immediately drove round to show off to me. We went for a long ride to *épater la bourgeoisie.* Our passage along the coast road was as triumphal as, a year before, Princess Margaret's had been. As we swept through a tiny village, a Negro lounger, galvanised by the glorious vision, threw his hands up to heaven and cried, 'Cheesus-Kerist!'

'How did he know?' said Coward.

Our pride was to have a fall. We stopped for petrol.

'Fill her up,' said Coward.

There was a prolonged pause, followed by some quiet tinkering and jabbering from behind the car.

'What's going on, Coley?'

'They can't find the hole,' said Leslie Cole from the rear seat.

'We've all had that trouble at one time or another,' said Coward. 'Help them.'

Coley got out. There was more and louder argumentation. A crowd gathered. I got out and, while Coward stared loftily, patiently at the sky, went over the car front and back with a tooth-comb. There was no hole. I told Coward so.

'Don't be silly, dear boy. The Americans are very clever at making motorcars. They wouldn't forget a thing like that. In fact, they probably started with the hole and then built the car round it.'

'Come and look for yourself.'

'I wouldn't think of demeaning myself before the natives.'

'Well, have you got an instruction book?'

'How should I know? Don't ask silly questions.'

The crowd gazed earnestly at us, trying to fathom whether we were ignorant or playing some white man's game. I found the trick catch of the glove compartment and took out the instruction book. The secret was on the last page. You had to unscrew the stop-light. The filler cap was behind it.

'Anyone could have told you that,' commented Coward airily.

I looked at him coldly. 'It's interesting,' I said. 'When you sweat with embarrassment the sweat runs down your face and drops off your first chin on to your second.'

'Don't be childish.'

I am not only vain about my Thunderbird, but proud of it. It is by far the best car I have ever possessed, although, on looking back through my motley stud book, I admit that there is no string of Bentleys and Jaguars and Aston Martins with which to compare it.

After the khaki Standard, I went to a khaki Morris Oxford which was demolished between Munich and Kufstein. I had passed a notice saying 'Achtung Rollbahn!' and was keeping my eyes peeled for a steamroller when, just before I crossed a small bridge over a stream, I heard a yell in my ear and had time to see a terrified peasant leap off a gravity-propelled trolley laden with cement blocks when it hit broadside and hurled the car, with me in it, upside down into the stream.

I then had an excellent second-hand black Buick sports saloon in which I had the only serious accident to date. A child ran out from behind a stationary baker's van. This taught me the most important lesson of motoring – that it isn't the things *you* do, but what the other person does.

I changed to the worst car I have ever had, a 16/80 open Lagonda. I fell in love with the whine of its gears and its outside brake. But it would barely do seventy, which made me ashamed of its sporty appearance.

I transferred to a supercharged Graham Paige Convertible Coupe, an excellent car which I stupidly gave to the ambulance service when war broke out.

Half-way through the war I had, for a time, a battered but handy little Opel. One night at the height of the Blitz I was dining with Sefton Delmer in his top floor flat in Lincoln's Inn. A direct hit blew out the lower three floors and left us swilling champagne and waiting for the top floor to fall into the chasm. The fireman who finally hauled us out and down his ladder was so indignant at our tipsy insouciance that I made him a present of the crumpled remains of the Opel.

After the war I had an umpteenth-hand beetle-shaped Renault and a pre-war Hillman Minx before buying my first expensive car – a 2½ litre Riley, which ran well for a year before developing really expensive troubles for which I only obtained some compensation through a personal appeal to Lord Nuffield.

I transferred to one of the first of the Sapphires, a fast, comfortable car, but one which made me feel too elderly when it was going slowly and too nervous when it was going fast. I decided to revert to an open car and, on the advice of a friend, bought a Daimler Convertible. Very soon I couldn't stand the ugliness of its rump and, when the winter came and I found the engine ran so coolly that the heater wouldn't heat, I got fed up with post-war English cars.

It was then that a fairly handsome ship came home and I decided to buy myself a luxurious present. I first toyed with the idea of a Lancia Gran Turismo, a really beautiful piece of machinery, but it was small and rather too busy – like driving an angry washing machine – and it cost over £3000 which seemed ridiculous. I happened to see a Thunderbird in the street and fell head over heels in love. I rang up Lincoln's. Apparently there was no difficulty in buying any make of American car out of the small import quota which we accept in part exchange for our big motor car exports to the States. The sales-man brought along a fire-engine red model with white upholstery which I drove nervously round Battersea Park.

I dickered and wavered. Why not a Mercedes? But they are still more expensive and selfish and the highly desirable S.S. has only room beside the driver for a diminutive blonde with a sponge bag. Moreover, when you open those bat-like doors in the rain, the rain pours straight into the car.

I ordered a Thunderbird. Black, with conventional gear change plus overdrive, and as few power assists as possible. In due course it appeared. My wife was indignant. The car was hideous. There was no room for taking people to the station (a point I found greatly in its favour) and, anyway, why hadn't I bought her a mink coat? To this day she hasn't relented. She has invented a new disease called 'Thunderbird neck' which she complains she gets in the passenger seat. The truth is that she has a prejudice against all American artefacts and, indeed, against artefacts of any kind.

She herself drives like Evelyn Waugh's Lady Metroland, using the pavement as if it were part of the road. Like many women, she prides herself on her 'quick reactions' and is constantly twitting me with my sluggish consideration for others in traffic. She is unmoved when I remind her that in her previous car, a grey and heavily scarred Sunbeam Talbot whose interior always looked as if it had just been used as dustcart for the circus at Olympia, she had been guilty of misdemeanours which would have landed any man in gaol. She once hit an old man in a motorised bathchair so hard in the rear that he was propelled right across Oxford Street against the traffic lights. Turning into Dover Street, she had cut a milk cart so fine that she had left her onside door-handle embedded in the rump of the horse. Unfortunately, she is unmoved by these memories, having that most valuable of all feminine attributes – the ability to see her vices as virtues.

I have now had my Thunderbird for over two years. It has done 27,000 miles without a single mechanical failure, without developing a squeak or a rattle. Its paintwork is immaculate and there is not a spot of discoloration anywhere on its rather over-lavish chrome, despite the fact that it is never garaged at night and gets a wash only twice a week. I have it serviced every quarter, but this is only a matter of the usual oil-changing, etc. The only time it ever stopped in traffic was carefully planned to give me a short, sharp reminder that, like fine pieces of machine, it has a temperament.

The occasion was, for the car's purposes, well chosen – exactly half-way under the Thames in the Blackwall Tunnel, with lorries howling by nose to tail a few inches away in the ill-lit gloom, and with a giant petrol tanker snoring impatiently down my neck. The din was so terrific that I hadn't even noticed that the engine had stopped when the traffic in front moved on after a halt. It was only then that I noticed the rev counter at zero. I ground feverishly at the starter without result. The perspiration poured down my face at the thought of the ghastly walk I would have to take through the tunnel to get the breakdown van and pay the £5 fine. Then, having reminded me never again to take its services for granted, the engine stuttered and fired and we got going.

The reason why I particularly like the Thunderbird, apart from the beauty of its line and the drama of its snarling mouth and the giant, flaring nostril of its air-intake, is that everything works. Absolutely nothing goes wrong. True, it isn't a precision instrument like English sports cars, but that I count a virtue. The mechanical margin of error on its construction is wider. Everything has a solid feel. The engine – a huge adapted low-revving Mercury V-8 of 5 litre capacity – never gives the impression of stress or strain. When, on occasion, you can do a hundred without danger of going over the edge of this small island, you have not only the knowledge that you have an extra twenty m.p.h. in reserve, but the feel of it. As for acceleration, when the two extra barrels of the 4-barrel carburretor come in, at around 3000 revs, it is a real thump in the back. The brakes are good enough for fast driving, but would have to be better if you wanted to drive dangerously. The same applies to the suspension, where rigidity has been sacrificed slightly to give a comfortable ride. Petrol consumption, using overdrive for long runs, averages 17 m.p.g. Water and oil, practically nil.

There is a hard top for the winter which you take off and store during the summer when the soft top is resurrected from its completely disappeared position behind the seat. The soft top can be put up or down without effort and both tops have remained absolutely weatherproof, which after two years, is miraculous.

One outstanding virtue is that all accessories seem to be infallible, though the speedometer, as with most American cars, is a maddening 10 per cent optimistic. The heater really heats; the wipers, though unfortunately suction-operated, really wipe; and not a fuse has blown nor a lamp bulb died. The engine never overheats and has never failed to start immediately from cold, even after all night outside in a frost. The solidity of the manufacture is, of course, the result of designing cars for a seller's market and for a country with great extremes of heat and cold.

Cyril Connolly once said to me that, if men were honest, they would admit that their motor cars came next after their women and children in their list of loves. I won't go all the way with him on that, but I do enjoy well-designed and attractively wrapped bits of machinery that really work – and that's what the Thunderbird is, a first-class express carriage.

IF I WERE PRIME MINISTER

From The Spectator, *October 1959.*

I am a totally non-political animal. I prefer the *name* of the Liberal Party to the *name* of any other and I vote Conservative rather than Labour, mainly because the Conservatives have bigger bottoms and I believe that big bottoms make for better government than scrawny ones. I only once attended a debate in the House of Commons. It was, I think, towards the end of 1938 when we were unattractively trying to cajole Mussolini away from Hitler. I found the hollowness and futility of the speeches degrading and infantile and the well-fed, deep-throated, 'Hear hears' for each mendacious platitude verging on the obscene. If this is politics, I reflected, I would much rather not see it happening and I swore never to re-enter the Chamber. I never have.

My own particular hero is Sir Alan Herbert, an independent-minded though admittedly thin-shanked man, who, swimming alone, stayed out of the muddy red and blue stream and more or less single-handed changed a section of our law for the benefit of the common man. And of course I have the affectionate reverence for Sir Winston Churchill that most of us share. But in general I regard politicians as a 'rasse à part' and if the Bottle Imp were to offer me high office I would accept, and that with reluctance, nothing less than the Premiership.

On taking office, I would concentrate on small things.

The big things – the H-bomb, the conquest of outer space, the colour problem – these are time-wasting matters, too vast and confused for one man's brain; I would leave them to my Ministers and to the wave of common sense, which, it seems to me, by a process of osmosis between peoples rather than between politicians, is taking rapid and healthy control of the world.

My first 'Action This Day', through my Minister of Transport, would be simple but significant: on the road signs displaying a diamond-studded black banana with the word 'CURVE' underneath, I would have the word 'CURVE' removed. By this and other small tokens, I would proclaim that the English people are no longer babies and that, after all these years of universal education, I propose to deal with the citizens as if they were in fact universally educated. All my legislation would start with this assumption.

Next, I would try and stop people being ashamed of themselves. In the United Kingdom we have a basically nonconformist conscience and the fact that taxation, controls and certain features of the Welfare State have turned the majority of us into petty criminals, liars and work-dodgers is, I am sure, having a very bad effect on the psyche of the kingdom. Tax-dodging in all its forms would have my attention and I would proceed to reduce income tax, surtax and death duties by the maximum amount possible in exchange for abolishing all expense accounts and other forms of fiscal chicanery. Motor cars, whether Rolls-Royces or Fords, owned by a company, would have the name of that company displayed in half-inch letters in a prominent position so that if a company's car was seen disgorging a load of mink and cigar smoke in theatreland in the evening, any of the company's shareholders who happened to be a witness could, if he wanted, ask the company to justify this use of a company vehicle. But the real deterrent would be snobbery. I think everyone would gain morally by this legislation and no real harm would be done to anyone. To begin with, of course, the restaurants would suffer from the absence of the expense-account aristocracy who have ridiculously inflated the price of meals all over the world, while at the same time deflating the quality of the food. I would hope that the really good restaurants would survive, but that the host of bogus eating places with Algerian 'Infuriator' (otherwise known as 'Instant' Burgundy) described as Beaujolais selling at 15s, for half a carafe, would disappear.

Having looked after the moral fibre of the 'Haves', I would next direct my attention to the work-shy 'Have-nots', being convinced that the man who is not returning good work for good money is basically ashamed of himself. In consultation with the Trades Unions, I would devise a scheme of benevolent Stakhanovism. There would be a minimum wage in every industry, but rapidly mounting merit bonuses for real work in either quantity or quality. This would not abolish tea breaks or the games of whist but make them unpopular with the wives. I would also request the trades unions to re-examine the whole question of overtime. Having obtained an eight-hour day and a five-day week, it seems to me wrong that workers should use the two extra days and many extra hours earning overtime double money when they should be enjoying the leisure and repose they have fought to obtain.

And, while on the subject of leisure, I would certainly consider appointing a Minister of Leisure, with a small staff, to make every effort to enhance the pleasure people get from their increasing spare time.

Having observed at close quarters the great waste of money on paint and canvases in one of our art schools, I am not convinced that the Welfare 'artist', copying, as he usually does, one or another, or very often several, of the modern theories of painting, is worth encouraging any further. Instead, therefore, of spending larger sums on the arts, I would spend them on the crafts. I would encourage the fine metal workers, enamellers, binders, print-ers, woodworkers, etc., in a most lavish fashion and attempt to arrest at once the decline of the craftsman, even down to the lowly thatcher.

To give the craftsman, the designer and, of course, the artist an outlet for his capabilities, I would take the Rolls-Royce motor-car as an example and persuade all manufacturers that, let us say, 5 per cent of output should con-sist of an absolutely top-grade, luxury product in which price is an entirely secondary consideration. Every firm would then be producing, perhaps only in small quantities, the Rolls-Royce of its particular line of manufacture – real grain whisky and gin, quintessentially distilled, ice-cream made with real strawberries and real cream, lavatory paper as luxurious as a peach skin, scis-sors that actually cut your nails, and so on through the list of all our products. By this means I would make quality goods available to those here and abroad who like these things and can afford them and I would hope to educate the admass to eschew the shoddy. Coincidentally, in the world's markets, 'British made' would go back to the place where it used to belong.

Next I should proceed to a complete reform of our sex and gambling laws and endeavour to cleanse the country of the hypocrisy with which we so unat-tractively clothe our vices. To deal only with my most far-reaching proposal, I would consult with my Minister of Leisure about the possibility of turning the Isle of Wight into one vast pleasuredrome (cf. fr. Baisodrome) which would be a mixture of Monte Carlo, Las Vegas, pre-war Paris and Macao.

Here there would be casinos (they are building one on Gibraltar and they have one in Nassau; why not one on the Isle of Wight?) and the most luxurious *maisons de tolérance* in the world. Bingo, poker, faro, fantan, craps – even whist drives with money prizes! This would be a world where the frustrated citizen of every class could give full rein to those basic instincts for sex and gambling which have been crushed through the ages. At last our cliff-girt libido would have an outlet and the sleazy strip-tease joints, rump-sprung street walkers and back-room card games would be out of business for ever. Since it is impossible to suppress the weaknesses of mankind, I would at least put an honest face on the problem and do something to release the *homme moyen sensuel*, or *femme* for the matter of that, from some of their burden of shame and sin.

After dealing with the spiritual comfort of the electorate, I would proceed to his physical state, and my first step would be the abatement of noise, carbon monoxide gas and exasperation caused by the traffic problem in our big towns. I would solve these with the help of Mr. Francis Bacon's recently invented, much-publicised battery. Our present internal combustion engine is a ridiculous steam-age contraption which turns only a modest proportion of fuel into energy and spews the rest out in the form of petrol vapour of a more or less solid consistency. When there is no wind, this lies in a dense layer in our streets and we breathe it in day and night. It then rises into the upper atmosphere, where, I am told, it forms a kind of envelope round the world which has the effect of interfering with the beneficial rays of the sun. Whether that is so or not, the petrol engine is obviously a noxious and noisy machine, and I would gradually abolish it and replace it by some form of electric motor. This would take some time, but I would hope that, within three years of assuming office, I could have converted the whole of central London to electric transport. Very cheap, State-owned garages would be built at the point of entry into London of our main roads and drivers would there transfer into electric buses or the Underground and later into cheap, State-run electric taxis. There would be quiet, no smell and no parking problems. Gradually I would extend this system to our other great towns and in due course the problem would be solved for the whole country.

In an attempt to make government more honest, I would face up to the fact that my Exchequer battens fatly on the vices and follies of the electorate and

I would have H.M. Stationery Office publish quarterly a periodical entitled 'Hazard'. 'Hazard' would give, without comment, the very latest information obtainable anywhere in the world on the ill-effects of smoking too much, drinking too much and consuming white bread, TT tested milk, refined sugar, foods too long frozen, etc. 'Hazard' would also give the correct odds for football pools and Premium Bonds and, from time to time, publish the annual accounts of the bookmaking firms throughout the country. Road accident figures would be given in detail, and in cases where mechanical failure (those shattering windscreens, for instance) attributable to faulty manufacture was involved, the name of the manufacturer would be published. There would, as I say, be no editorial comment in the magazine, but I should be able to face with a clear conscience the fact that, from the Exchequer's point of view, the most valuable citizen is the man who drinks or smokes himself to death.

There are various other small matters I would attend to, such as men's clothing, which I regard as out-of-date, unhygienic and rather ridiculous; Press reform – we have the grimiest press in the world; the matter of titles – I would greatly reinforce the Orders of Chivalry and, if a Lord or a Baron or an Earl did not behave as a lord or a baron or an earl should, he would lose his title after the third offence (as is more or less the case with Service rank); rich State prizes for all inventions or innovations that were even of remote benefit to the Commonwealth; enthusiastic encouragement of emigration, but more particularly of a constant flow of peoples within the Commonwealth; a Commonwealth super-Parliament; and less fried food for the constipated masses.

All these, as I have said, are small, workaday things – too small, alas, for the attention of either Mr. Harold Macmillan or Mr. Gaitskell. So I look forward, with squared shoulders and glazed resignation, to five years of Summitry, pensions and the 11-plus.

SIX QUESTIONS

Questions posed by Elizabeth Jane Howard to Ian Fleming and several other writers about the new decade of the 1960s for the centenary issue of Queen. *1961.*

What do you expect to achieve in the sixties? Are you aiming at any particular quality or quantity of work?

One can never expect to achieve anything – even less if one is in the fifties and living in the sixties.

Since I am a writer of thrillers I would like to leave behind me one classic in this genre – a mixture of Tolstoy, Simenon, Ambler and Koestler, with a pinch of ground Fleming. Unfortunately I have become the slave of a serial character and I suppose, in fact, since it amuses me to write about James Bond, I shall go on doing so for the fun of it.

I would also like to write a really stimulating travel guide to the Commonwealth and the remainder of the Colonies, regarding this as a public duty. But this would require too much time and energy from me and, in fact, would better be done by a central editor using a different writer, but good ones, for each territory.

I would also like to write the biography of a contemporary woman, once a professional prostitute and spy, who has changed the face of a country. But the source material would be difficult to get, the story would be bristling with libel, and I expect the idea will be stillborn.

What do you feel is different about the sixties? (Better, or worse, or simply different?)

During my lifetime life in general has accelerated fantastically – communications, inventions and the pace of people's lives. This process will continue in the Sixties together with the further destruction of gods and images and heroes which the age of Realism is achieving. Orwell's *1984* and Huxley's *Brave New World* will come closer and closer, life will become more comfortable and much duller and basically uglier, though people will be healthier and live longer. Boredom with and distaste for this kind of broiler existence may attract an atomic disaster of one sort or another, and then some of us will start again in caves, and life on this planet will become an adventure again.

Do you want to make any particular public impact in this time? (Political, moral, spiritual, intellectual or any combination of these?)

Certainly not. Personal privacy is becoming worth diamonds. But I would like to continue in the thin literary seam that is mine, to provide occasional slices of excitement and fantasy which will briefly hoist people out of their broilerdom.

Do you expect, or hope for, any change in your way of life as a writer, and if so, what kind of change?

No. All I ask for is more zest and inventiveness – and time.

What medium, first in all the arts, secondly in writing, do you think is the most influential today?

If television could develop from a craft to an art it would be more influential than any of the individual painters, writers, actors, etc. who would be presented through its medium to the public.

What three living writers do you think have, or will have (in this decade) the most impact a) on you, b) on society?

a) William Plomer, for his quietude and irony in the midst of chaos. Simenon, because he is the master of my particular craft. Graham Greene, because each sentence he writes interests me, both as an individual and as a writer.

b) At a wild guess – Muriel Spark, Bernard Levin, and the partnership of author and draftsman known as Trog.

[*Fleming also wrote, presumably before reading the last question correctly,* Homer, Shakespeare, Beatrix Potter.]

ENVOI

From an interview with René MacColl in Jamaica, February 1964.

One can only be grateful to the talent that came out of the air, and to one's capacity for hard, concentrated effort. I am perhaps the smallest and most profitable one-man factory in the world.

I don't want yachts, race-horses or a Rolls-Royce. I want my family and my friends and good health and to have a small treadmill with a temperature of 80 degrees in the shade and in the sea to come to every year for two months.

And to be able to work there and look at the flowers and fish, and somehow to give pleasure, whether innocent or illicit, to people in their millions. Well you can't ask for more.

IAN FLEMING PUBLICATIONS

Ian Lancaster Fleming was born in London on 28 May 1908 and was educated at Eton College before spending a formative period studying languages in Europe. His first job was with Reuters news agency, followed by a brief spell as a stockbroker. On the outbreak of the Second World War he was appointed assistant to the Director of Naval Intelligence, Admiral Godfrey, where he played a key part in British and Allied espionage operations.

After the war he joined Kemsley Newspapers as Foreign Manager of *The Sunday Times,* running a network of correspondents who were intimately involved in the Cold War. His first novel, *Casino Royale,* was published in 1953 and introduced James Bond, Special Agent 007, to the world. The first print run sold out within a month. Following this initial success, he published a Bond title every year until his death. His own travels, interests and wartime experience gave authority to everything he wrote. Raymond Chandler hailed him as 'the most forceful and driving writer of thrillers in England.' The fifth title, *From Russia With Love,* was particularly well received and sales soared when President Kennedy named it as one of his favourite books. The Bond novels have sold more than 100 million copies and inspired a hugely successful film franchise which began in 1962 with the release of *Dr No,* starring Sean Connery as 007.

The Bond books were written in Jamaica, a country Fleming fell in love with during the war and where he built a house, 'Goldeneye'. He married Ann Rothermere in 1952. His story about a magical car, written in 1961 for their only child, Caspar, went on to become the well-loved novel and film, *Chitty Chitty Bang Bang.*

Fleming died of heart failure on 12 August 1964.

www.ianfleming.com

𝕏 TheIanFleming

◎ Ianflemings007

f IanFlemingBooks

Also by Ian Fleming

Fiction

Casino Royale
Live and Let Die
Moonraker
Diamonds are Forever
From Russia with Love
Dr No
Goldfinger
For Your Eyes Only
Thunderball
The Spy Who Loved Me
On Her Majesty's Secret Service
You Only Live Twice
The Man with the Golden Gun
Octopussy and The Living Daylights

Chitty Chitty Bang Bang

Non-fiction

The Diamond Smugglers
Thrilling Cities